# UNLUCKY SEVEN

## A Novel

### By

# J. P. Bidula

*Keep fighting the good fight.*

This novel is a work of fiction.

The resemblance of characters to any persons, living or dead, was more than likely intentional and should be taken in stride because, in the end, you've been immortalized in fiction. Granted, it wasn't like you were some Dickensian Hero who will live forever in the hearts of a million readers or something, but it's also not like you had Mark Twain eviscerating you across the printed page. If you think you're in this book remember that it's just a story and at least I didn't give the world your full name that they could develop some fandom-based hate-cult against your non-fictional persona and burn your real-life house down.

So, yeah, if these characters bear a resemblance to you, just be cool about the fact that your potential and, legally speaking, largely unidentifiable likeness has been entered into the annals of middling sci-fi/fantasy which, you have to admit, is at least kinda neat. And, now you've got that going for you. Which is nice.

This story is dedicated to everyone who ever put on a cape or a mask and decided to pretend.

This story is also dedicated to my first and, quite possibly, only fan. Thanks for getting my back all these years. This is as much yours as it is mine.

On with the show.

I

Nothing was special about the group of friends now lying on the street covered in black ooze. At least, they didn't think anything was special about them beyond the fact that they continued to remain friends despite their obvious social differences. That was sort of a taboo subject, though. They all ran in different circles but, in the end, they were all part of their own separate circle. Sounds shallow, right? Let's move on.

Justin was the first to sit up after the pressurized explosion of this black substance knocked them down. Taking off his glasses, he saw a blurry representation of the accident scene. A minute ago, a white late-80s hatchback slammed into the side of a turning tanker truck causing it to blow all its seals and erupt into a wave of the black sludge which now covered him from head to toe.

His girlfriend Char was still on the ground. Glasses or no, he knew that it was her. She was standing directly behind him when the blast hit and was perfectly positioned to take the least of the blast. Most of her was clean. She was covered from her knees down with a few splotches on her face.

Their other friends were represented by raised lumps in the black sludge layer now covering the outside of their favorite bar. It appeared that Char was the only one coming out of this without the need to throw away all of her clothes.

Justin had seen everything happen in that slow motion sort of way that seems to happen when something very bad is about to happen. He knew what was going to happen and, while he could have screamed "Run!" or "Get down!" or any number of action movie-sounding clichés which sound like they should be screamed in Arnold Schwarzenegger's voice, he instead stood still, closed his eyes, and braced for the impact.

Now the air was still and the scene held an eerie silence. Either that, or Justin's ears were just clogged with black sludge.

To his right, one of the black blobs began to stir and cough.

"Mike," Justin said, "Mike, are you ok?"

Mike had fallen forward, but had the clarity of reflex to put his arms in front of his face before it hit the pavement. He rolled onto his back, his front half clear of any goo.

"That just happened, didn't it?" Mike asked.

"Yeah," Justin answered.

Both of them sat dumbfounded, staring at the accident scene.

Other sludge-coated lumps started to stir. Justin counted. It appeared that all seven of his friends, plus a few more, were now stirring and slowly getting to their feet in various states of disrepair.

He reached inside his leather jacket, grabbing a swatch of t-shirt which had not been soiled, and cleaned his glasses. It took some effort.

He wondered what this would mean for his hair and his goatee. For the moment, it didn't seem that any store-bought solution would help to get this muck off of his body.

When his glasses were usable but still horribly smeared, he took a clear-eyed look at the accident. He could see what was left of the hatchback, its roof jammed like a knife in the side of the large tanker which, he noticed, had a placard on the back proclaiming its contents "Hazardous Materials" along with two skull symbols inside triangles. His heart nearly stopped. He looked back at Mike who was now getting to his feet, then looked back for Char, who was also beginning to stand.

"Are you ok?" Justin asked her.

"Fine," she said, "What happened? What the hell is this stuff?"

"I don't know," Justin said, "But it can't be good."

He peeled the scarf, thoroughly saturated with the black mess, from around his neck with the tips of his fingers. He didn't know why he handled it so briskly, considering his hands were already completely covered in the same substance. He pulled the t-shirt on his chest forward to unstick it from himself, glanced down his collar, and found that whatever this was had soaked through his clothing and left a black residue on his skin.

Sirens, presumably from a rescue crew, echoed in the distance. They were on the sidewalk of a busy main drag in an urban area, so it was just as likely that those sirens were for some other emergency. Justin figured this would rate pretty high considering the placard on the back of the truck.

"I love you," he whispered.

"I love you, too," Char whispered back.

"I'm so glad you're safe," he said, moving in to embrace her.

"Um, no," she said, taking a step back, "You're dirty, I'm relatively clean. Don't touch me."

"I'll hug you, buddy," said Mike, "It's not like I don't have this crap all over me already anyway."

"Thanks, man," Justin said, embracing his friend.

"It's ok," Mike said, "It's not like we're dying or... aw, crap, this stuff got in my beard when I hugged you!"

Justin sighed. He presumed Mike didn't see the placard and didn't think they were in danger. Really, Mike was scared to death but putting up a pretty good front to make it seem like he wasn't freaked out by being completely covered in hazardous materials.

Others were standing up: a woman whose face and hair were mostly shielded though the rest of her had been covered and a man who looked like he had been painted half-black.

The tips of her auburn hair now dipped into the mess coating her once pink winter coat.

"Well, these clothes are ruined," she said.

"You have other clothes, Jess," the man countered.

"This was my favorite pair of jeans," she argued, grabbing at her low-cut, now black, designer pants, "There is no way this crap is going to wash out."

"These are my favorite pants, too," he said, clutching at his worn jeans with holes in the knees, "You think I'm not going to try to wash them?"

"Are you both crazy?" shouted another man, thin and covered head to toe, looking as if he sought out the best splash zone for this incident, "Kurt, tell me you don't see the placard on the back of that truck. Tell me you didn't read where it says 'Hazardous Materials'. Tell me that and keep arguing about your stupid clothes and about how we're not all going to die in like five seconds."

Five seconds passed before anyone spoke. They did not die.

"Budda," said Jess, "Calm down."

"I will not calm down," Budda shouted, "I'm probably getting cancer as we speak!"

Further down the sidewalk, as his vocal friends argued, Justin counted and realized that they were missing their seventh member, Josh. Frantic, he looked around and saw one unmoving pile of slop near the window of the bar they had exited only moments before the accident.

Josh was lying face up on the ground, more coated in the substance than any of the others. Justin rolled him on his side and slapped his back hard. Josh coughed and spat out a long stream of black. Justin saw blood on the bare pavement where Josh's head had been. He must have hit the window ledge when the explosion occurred.

Justin shook him and tried to wake him up before Mike told him it probably wasn't a good idea to shake someone with a concussion. They sat him up against the wall. Mike did his best to put pressure on the back of Josh's head.

Justin swiped at the window of the bar with his sleeve, trying in vain to clear the glass. Two of their group, Emma - Josh's girlfriend - and Steph – Budda's girlfriend and Char's sister, were still inside and no doubt freaking out about the explosion and the black goo and their friends and significant others out here. He wanted to let them know they were all, for the moment, alive and well.

When he realized that clearing the window was less effective than cleaning his glasses, he wrote in the muck with his finger: ALL OK. He realized later that he wrote the letters backwards, as he should, but he did not spell it backwards. Emma, Steph, and the remainder of the patrons in the bar were left to ponder the significance of KO LLA.

By the time he made this realization, he was otherwise occupied.

The group of them outside had now circled up, surrounding the unconscious Josh near the window.

"Is he ok?" Kurt asked.

"Bumped his head pretty bad," Mike said, still applying pressure with a clean portion of his shirt, "Probably concussed. He's out cold at the moment."

"Not like it makes a difference," Budda said, "We're probably all dead anyway."

Justin clenched his eyes shut. He wanted to agree with Budda, but he didn't want to be so quick to admit defeat and bring down morale.

"Come on man," Kurt said, "It's not like we're melting or anything."

"Yet," said Budda.

"Hey," Jess interjected, "Maybe they left that sign on the truck by accident. Maybe it was there from the last load and they just forgot to take it off."

"Not likely," Budda said.

"Would you stop being so negative?" Justin shouted.

"You guys ok over there?" called a stranger, another accident victim noticeable by his coating in black sludge.

"We're all good," called Justin, noticing that others covered in the black stuff now stood on the sidewalk, speaking with each other, looking equally confused.

Police and ambulances arrived one after the other. Medics began to separate people for treatment, cops questioned everyone individually about what they'd seen of the accident. It would be a few hours before everyone was together again.

Inside the bar, Emma and Steph were doing their best not to panic as the other patrons continued to stare into an opaque mess of black dripping down the front window interrupted only by Justin's vain attempt to clear a spot with his sleeve and his cryptic message, KO LLA.

Emma took to pacing and twirling a lock of her curly, bottle-red hair around her finger. Steph sat in an empty booth and stared at the floor. The place was quiet except for the occasional slurring bark from one of the other patrons regarding the nature of the sludge. Some speculated that it was toxic, some claimed it was waste oil, one guy said that he'd seen it before but another person countered by telling them they were thinking of a movie.

They could see the red and blue lights glowing through the upper part of the window where the black stuff was slowly running off, leaving smears behind. They were now being joined by yellow lights. Emma assumed it was either the HAZMAT team or a tow truck.

"Attention bar patrons," said a voice over a loudspeaker outside, "Please proceed to the rear of the building and exit into the alley. Repeat: please proceed to the rear of the building and exit into the alley. If you require access to the front of the building for any reason, please speak to the police representative who will meet you at the perimeter. Thank you for your cooperation."

The bartender took this as a sign that she was closing for the night and chased all of her patrons including pacing Emma and catatonic Steph out the back door and into the cold winter night.

"We've got to go now that we're out," said Emma, "We've got to find out what happened to them."

Steph nodded and remained silent, putting the hood of her bright green sweatshirt over her short brown hair. She followed Emma down the alleyway. They were the last patrons out of the building. The others all drifted away to their cars and then home, chalking this up as another You'll-Never-Guess-What-Happened-At-The-Bar story. Steph and Emma approached the policeman instead.

"Our friends," Steph blurted as they got near him.

The officer turned, spotting them. Steph was now pointing emphatically toward the front of the bar. Emma remained silent which she knew was her right. She wasn't a huge fan of cops.

"You knew people out there?" the cop asked, motioning to the area which suddenly began to glow with the spotlights of the HAZMAT team.

"My sister," Steph said nodding, "Our boyfriends, a few others… they were waiting for us. We ran back to go to the bathroom and missed everything. We should have been out there with them. We could have been."

"Ok, calm down," the cop said, "Don't worry, we'll help you reconnect. Latest I heard everyone was relatively fine. One person has a concussion from hitting his head on the windowsill, but other than that, it's just some scrapes and bruises."

"What about that toxic waste crap?" Emma asked in an angry shout, "How can you say they're fine when they're covered in that stuff?"

"Look, Miss," said the cop, "I don't know anything about the chemicals or whatever was involved. All I know is that if you have someone up front, they're taking them to the hospital."

"I walked here," said Steph, "I can't get to the hospital."

"I don't have a car," Emma added, "There's no way we're going to be able to follow the ambulances."

The cop sighed.

"If you need some help, I guess you can hop in the back of my cruiser," he said, "I can get you out there, but you'll have to find your own ride home."

"Deal," said Emma, speaking for both of them.

The nervous pair of ladies sat in the back of the police cruiser until the ambulances blared away from the scene. They sped off after them. There was no communication between them other than Steph grabbing Emma's hand for support as they neared the hospital doors.

The cop walked them in and told them to stay put in the waiting room. He promised them he'd be back quickly with some information on their friends.

As he walked away, Emma noticed something out of the corner of her eye and brought it to Steph's attention as she turned to look. Emma told her not to stare, just in case.

The something Emma noticed was a man, older and pale with perfectly placed white hair. He wore a black suit with black necktie. The pair of sunglasses covering his eyes seemed odd considering they were inside and it was the middle of the night. A pin on his lapel gleamed catching the reflection of the overhead fluorescent lights.

The man turned his head in their direction. He was staring at them. Emma could feel it even though his eyes were hidden. He began walking toward them; all business, no expression. She felt the same bubble of hot fear in her stomach as she did when the accident first happened.

They both averted their eyes quickly, thinking that he might go away if they weren't looking anymore.

"You were at the accident scene?" he asked, his voice as emotionless as his face.

"Yes," Steph managed, stammering, "We... we're looking for our friends. They came in from the chemical..."

"I know who your friends are," he interrupted, "We are taking care of them. They are not currently in any danger. Please follow me."

He turned on his heels and walked at his brisk, business-like pace. The girls looked at each other for approval before deciding to take his suggestion. They both felt there was no other choice. If they were going to see their friends, they would have to do as this man said.

The pale man lead them through a series of white hallways and back corridors not usually seen by the public. They reached a maintenance elevator and stepped on. He pushed a button, neither of them paid attention to which one.

They tried to ask him questions as the elevator rose. He silenced them with a quick gesture of his hand. Emma got the feeling that this man was an authority figure of some magnitude and did not enjoy answering to anyone.

They exited the elevator onto one of the upper floors. It appeared to be a typical ward but the hallway, usually frantic with activity between the nurses' station and the orderlies, was silent and abandoned. Computers sat dark, chairs were empty, and the desktops were completely clean.

At the end of the hall, he ushered them into a dark, empty room.

"So," Emma said, "Where are our friends?"

"They are being seen to, Emma," he said.

"How do you know my name?" she asked, "What the hell is going on here? Where is everyone? Who the hell are you?"

He sighed. He didn't attempt to silence her. Emma got the feeling that it was time for answers.

"My name is Agent Williams," he said, removing his sunglasses to reveal his cold, blue eyes, "I am with the government agency responsible for the substance involved in the accident. Your friends are currently being taken care of by our team of experts. You will be given liberty to see them as soon as they are detoxified and tested."

"When will that be?" Steph asked.

"Soon, Ms. Gentile," he said, "Until then, we must ask that you remain quarantined to this room and this ward."

"Quarantined?" Emma said, "We didn't touch that stuff. Why do we need to be quarantined?"

"For your own safety," he said in a manner which didn't make Emma feel safe, "As well as the safety and comfort of your friends and significant others. I understand both of your boyfriends were touched by this incident. It is likely that your attachment to this group of people would warrant your constant attention. Am I correct?"

"Yes," said Emma.

"Then you will remain on this ward, in this room until such time as you may visit your friends. We are offering you this as a courtesy. I understand this may not be the most hospitable of surroundings but I assure you that we will take you to your friends and loved ones as soon as they have been cleared by our physicians. Is this agreeable?"

"Uh," Emma said, looking at Steph who simply shrugged, "Fine." He nodded.

"There will be an agent posted on your door. Should you need anything which this room does not already provide, ask them and it will be provided within reason. Thank you for your... patience with us."

He put his sunglasses on and turned to leave.

"Agent Williams," Emma asked, causing him to stop, "What agency did you say you were with again?"

The corner of his mouth perked up into a strained smirk. It scared Emma more than anything else which had happened that night.

He closed the door as he left.

"What the hell is going on?" Steph asked.

"I don't know," Emma said, "But it's not good."

Emma took her cell phone from her purse only to find it had no signal. Steph's was the same. When they lifted the receiver on the room's archaic corded phone, there was no dial tone.

Emma ran to the door and opened it. At the corner of the hall was another agent – dressed in the same suit as Williams – except this one was disproportionately huge. His shoulders were so broad they could take up most of the hallway. He was around seven feet tall, bald, with a pair of eyebrow piercings glinting from behind the same style of dark shades Williams wore.

Just his turning to look at Emma gave her the creeps and she slammed the door.

"What's out there?" said Steph, going to the window of the room and holding her phone to the glass, praying for signal.

"I don't know what you would call it but it's gigantic and scary," she said.

"What do we do now?" Steph asked, "It's not like any of us has done anything wrong, have we?"

"It doesn't look like any of them have really done anything wrong, sir" said a younger female as Agent Williams walked into a small makeshift situation room, "The worst they've got between them is a couple of speeding tickets and parking violations. These guys are totally clean. Too clean."

"What about the personality profiles, Agent Briggs," Williams asked her, "I do not care what they have done, I am more concerned with who they are."

She tapped at a thick piece of glass with the image of a keyboard on the surface. A set of pictures appeared showing all of the people involved in the accident.

"None of them seem to be a threat, sir," she said, "Offer them the package and it's likely they'll keep their mouths shut without any issue."

"Have any of them been exhibiting the side effects?" he asked.

"Three, sir," she said, nodding. She tapped at the glass screen and highlighted three of the pictures.

He sighed.

"Three will be... difficult to handle," he said, "Are any related to the large group?"

"One," she said, "Subject began exhibiting symptoms almost as soon as she arrived at the hospital."

"Details on the group," he said.

"Not much to tell, sir," she said, "Seven effected, nine total in the group counting the two you just brought up. They're mostly college students with retail jobs. Again, none are classified as a threat. From the intel I could gather they're just a bunch of nerds. Spend most of their nights playing video games or watching movies."

"I will have to know how to spin this," he said, "I want a full report in an hour."

"Yes, sir," she said, "You'll have it in half-an-hour."

"Very good," he said, "Three."

"I know, sir," she said, "It could be a bigger problem than we anticipated."

"If the rest have not yet shown signs, it is likely we should experience no further issue," he said, "Leave them their memories, Agent Briggs. Soon it will be all they have of her. There is no need to continue complicating this matter."

"Sir?" she began.

"Yes," he interrupted, "I am sure."

II

His eyes opened to complete darkness.

Josh panicked and sat straight up. His eyes were wide open but he could still see nothing but black. His hand reached out for his bedside lamp and struck something which fell to the floor with a clatter and a splash.

He groped around eventually finding a plastic bedrail. Moving his hand down the side, he pressed a button in a recessed panel causing his feet to elevate. He felt a sharp tug in his arm as he reached and used his other hand to find a thin tube leading away from him. He realized where he was.

As he blinked, he felt his eyelashes scrape against something. He felt at his face and found gauze covering his eyes like a blindfold. His heart pumped with anxiety as he wondered what happened. The last thing he remembered was going drinking with his friends. He hoped this wasn't some kind of urban legend scenario where someone slipped him a ruffie and removed his eyeballs to be sold on the black market.

The back of his head throbbed with pain. He reached to console it and found another piece of gauze covering what felt like a hell of a lump. He winced as his hand ran over it.

"The impact knocked you back," said a serious and unfamiliar voice, "You hit your head on the windowsill of the bar."

"Who is that?" he asked, his voice strained and scratchy, "Where am I?"

"Relax," said the serious man, "You have nothing to fear."

Josh tried to shout out an objection and began coughing. His mouth was overly dry. He felt like he had been gargling beach sand.

A strong hand grasped his wrist and placed a plastic cup in his hand.

"Drink," he said, "You will need to rehydrate. You have been through an intense series of detoxification treatments. Of all those caught in the accident, you were the most saturated by the chemical material."

It came rushing back to him as he chugged water from the plastic cup. The little white car, the big tanker truck, the crash, the black stuff...

"Oh, God," he said, dropping the cup, "I'm blind. It got in my eyes, didn't it? That's why I'm bandaged. You had to cut out my eyes or something, didn't you? I'm never going to see again."

"Calm down," said the man, "You are safe to remove the gauze from your eyes."

Josh felt for the tape on the back of his head and ripped at the bandages. When he reached the end of the six overlapping layers, he could feel cotton balls taped to his eyes. He quickly ripped them off.

His eyes were dry and it hurt to blink. He reached out for another cup of water and poured it over his face with his eyes wide open granting him much relief.

The room was a wash out of bright white light whose only interruption was a blurred figure of black sitting next to him. His head now throbbed in the front as well as the back as he struggled to focus.

The black blur reached out to him with something that glinted in the light. Josh jumped back, hoping he wasn't about to be stabbed with a scalpel by some crazy guy who broke into his hospital room.

"Your glasses," said the man.

Josh reached out tentatively, snatched them from his hand and quickly put them on.

"Guess you're not the doctor," Josh said, looking at his visitor.

"Decidedly not," he said.

"Am I in some kind of trouble?" Josh asked, concerned why a man in a black suit with black sunglasses would be sitting at his bedside.

"You are in the hospital," the man said, "I believe that would constitute being in a particular degree of trouble."

"Who are you?" Josh asked.

"My name is Agent Williams," he replied, his face expressionless, "The substance in the tanker was property of our organization and was on its way to be destroyed before it was violently released in the accident."

"Great," Josh said, retreating again to panic, "So this is some kind of crazy government-level toxic waste. Are you here to tell me I'm melting? Am I being liquefied from the inside out? Am I radioactive?"

"I assure you," said Agent Williams in a non-assuring manner, "The substance in which you were covered will have no adverse effects on your health."

"Then what was with the eye wraps?" Josh asked, "What was with this 'intense series of detox treatments' you mentioned?"

"We had to be sure that none of the chemical remained in your system," he said, "We don't want to be responsible for any as-yet-unknown issue resulting from long-term exposure to the substance. Our physicians tell us that it is better to expel it now. You may be pleased to know that aside from the bump on your head our doctors have found you to be perfectly healthy."

"Fantastic," Josh said, "Except for the fact that I have no idea where I am or if any of my friends survived."

"Again, you are in the hospital," said Williams, his expression unchanging and his bedside manner leaving Josh wanting now that he could see this, "Your friends are doing well. They are waiting for you in another room. You and Ms. Gentile were the only two from your small group who had extensive problems following the incident. We had to hold you both separately."

"You mean Char," Josh said, "What happened to her?"

14

"There were fifteen people involved in the accident, including the drivers of the vehicles," said Williams, "As of now there have been no fatalities."

Josh felt only slightly relieved. "No fatalities" was rather ambiguous. He was sure this was a common tactic for someone claiming to be a government agent. The look was right, but he wasn't sure he bought it yet. One thing stood out to him and it was a pin worn on the lapel of the Agent's suit – a black circle around a Roman numeral XIII over a red background. Agent Williams caught him staring and stood to leave.

"There are scrubs in the dresser," he said, "I suggest you put them on. We have destroyed your clothes and personal effects due to their potential saturation with the substance. You will be provided with exact duplicates of your belongings at the end of your quarantine."

"Quarantine?" Josh asked, swinging his legs off the bed and catching a cold draft up the back of his hospital gown.

"We are doing what is necessary for your safety," he said, "Trust us. Everything will be fine. When you are through dressing, please knock on the door. I will wait for you outside."

The Agent left the room.

Josh didn't trust him. Josh didn't believe that everything would be fine.

He dropped his hospital gown and changed into the blue scrubs he'd been provided.

Looking himself over in the mirror, he saw that his skin was pale, his lips were cracked and chapped, and his eyes were bloodshot. He looked like hell.

He also caught sight of a piece of white tape attached to his elbow. Ripping it off quickly, he realized it was the cotton balls which were originally taped to his eyes. He stepped on the pedal of the biohazard bin in his room and noticed something just before throwing them away which made him stop dead.

It was the ooze – the black stuff in which they'd all been covered – two small dots of it clinging to the cotton. Obviously the detox wasn't as intense as the Agent had hoped. He knew he had to keep it. He had a friend at his college with a lab. He could get it analyzed and find out the exact flavor of danger they'd stumbled into. He was very confident that things would not turn out well after this, but he wanted to be sure of his fear.

He pulled a latex glove from a box mounted to the wall, stuffed the cotton balls inside, tied it shut and stuffed it into the pocket of the scrubs. He was fairly certain he wouldn't be subject to a pat down when he left the room, but the thought had crossed his mind.

He tapped twice on the door.

"Ready to go back to Gen-Pop, Warden," he said.

The door opened. Though he couldn't see the eyes of Agent Williams, he was sure he was being given quite a stern look before being lead down the hallway.

In the corner of the large operating room which had been converted into a temporary ward sat Justin. He sat on the bleached white tile floor, his back against a steel instrument cabinet, staring at the wall. He scratched idly at his back, his mind racing with thoughts of Char and Josh, neither of whom had rejoined their small collective.

The operating room was a creepy and overly quiet place. The more Justin thought about that, the creepier it became.

At some point, he postulated, blood had likely spattered across almost every inch of this floor. Hundreds of people had probably died in this room from complications due to who knows what. How many – ectomies and –otomies and amputations had taken place here? How much gore and guts had been exposed to the open air before someone called for the time of death? He stopped thinking about Char and Josh because he couldn't get the gruesome thoughts of this room out of his head. These Agents had taken them out of a horrifying situation, promising safety, and shoved them in a room Justin saw as a place people go to die.

To top this all off, the place smelled heavily of burning hair.

"You ok?" asked Jess, standing over him in identical blue scrubs.

Justin just shook his head.

"Come on," she said, "Get up. Talk to everyone. Don't sulk, it's not good for you right now."

Justin sighed and stood up.

The room had been furnished with a few sub-divided couches with individual seats separated by wooden armrests and a large coffee table currently occupied by a game of Solitaire being played by Mike. The furniture had been dragged in from the lobby earlier by a few of the custodial staff. It had been, he assumed, commandeered by whoever was in charge of this operation to make their extended stay seem more comfortable. It would have made him more comfortable if it didn't look like furniture from a hospital lobby.

A TV had been wheeled in on a cart and connected to the Hospital's cable. Budda knelt in front of it like a six-year old as he watched cartoons. His tall, lanky frame made this look especially immature.

Kurt was lying in one of the hospital beds on which they slept. He was using a lighted ear probe to read a three-month old magazine, also commandeered from the lobby.

Jess sat down in one of the couch sections and resumed coloring a picture in a book with crayons that had been stripped of all paper, worn down to nubs, and broken on one end.

"I'm supposed to be at work right now," Justin said.

16

"Most of us are," Mike answered, "I own a business. You know how much money it's costing me to be closed today? Cookies don't bake themselves."

"I'm missing class," Jess said, "Typically you're not supposed to ditch when you're in grad school."

"We're missing from the world," Kurt said, "We all are. No one out there knows what happened to us. No one knows about the accident except the people who were at the bar last night and none of them are close friends of ours, so no one would have said anything about it outside our circle."

"I'm not missing," said Budda, his eyes still glued to the TV.

Kurt narrowed his eyes and returned to his magazine.

"What about Char and Josh?" Justin asked, "Why aren't they here?"

"Josh smacked his head pretty hard," Budda said, zoned out, "Probably had to get treated for a concussion or something."

"What is with you and that TV?" Jess asked, "Is it really that interesting?"

"It's the only thing keeping me calm right now," Budda answered through clenched teeth.

"I understand Josh hit his head," said Justin, his volume escalating, "But, Char was perfectly fine when we left the scene. What happened and why are they keeping her from us?"

"I'm sure everything's fine," said Kurt.

"It's obviously not fine," shouted Justin, "If it were fine, she'd be here right now."

"Relax," said Jess, "Stay calm. I think we're all letting the captivity get to us."

"Not getting to me. I'm fine," said Mike, sniffing the air, "What smells like burning hair?"

"You're right," said Justin, sniffing the air and acknowledging Mike's observation rather than Jess's request to calm down, "Wasn't there a second ago."

The opaque automatic doors of the operating room swished open revealing Josh dressed in the same blue scrubs as the rest of them. The five of them rushed the door to greet their friend. Amidst handshakes and hugs and questions of well-being from both sides, the Agent entered the room behind him.

The room went dead silent at his appearance. No one in the room but Josh had seen him or any other authority figure beyond the hospital staff who kindly encouraged them to stay in this temporary ward during their detox treatments. They all watched as his head swiveled to survey the room through his dark sunglasses.

"I have not yet been properly introduced to most of you," he started, "That is acceptable. After your stay, you are to forget you ever met me.  If you feel that you will have difficulty with this task, we are fully equipped to assist you."

The room remained silent.  No one offered an objection.

"My name is Agent Williams," he continued, "I represent the agency responsible for the substance in which you were covered during the unfortunate accident last night.  It was fortunate we were able to get you to the hospital quickly enough to flush the chemical from you and ensure that the foreign substance was completely removed from your bodies.

"This particular chemical exhibits no abreaction to a majority of subjects, however, we have discovered that a small percentage..."

"Char," Justin interrupted causing the rest of the group to gasp, as if he had just pulled the pin on a grenade, "You're talking about Char, right?"

The Agent's gaze turned to Justin.

"Please understand that..." the Agent started.

"What did you do to her?" Justin shouted, cutting the Agent off.  The rest of the group notably cringed at his second interruption as if they expected him to be dragged away and never heard from again, "Where is she?  Is she dying?  Is she dead?"

The Agent waited a moment before answering, causing a palpable tension in the room.  Even Justin now thought that this guy was a half-second away from punching him in the face.  He didn't seem like the type of person who was used to insubordination.

"We respect that you have a relationship with her," the Agent continued, now clearly staring at Justin, his calm and emotionless demeanor never breaking which caused the lot of them to be completely unnerved, "At the moment, there is nothing to report.  We recognized the preliminary symptoms of the abreaction and her condition has, for the moment, been stabilized.  As I was previously stating before the interruption, this only occurs in a small percentage of persons affected."

"So," Josh said, making sure to wait until the Agent paused, "You lied to me when you said this stuff would have 'no adverse effects on my health."

"No," he said, "I stated that you would experience no adverse effects from the chemical, which is true.  You do not possess the same genetic marker which causes the noted abreaction.  None of you do.  However, due to the amount of the chemical present on you as a result of the rather unfortunate circumstances, you must remain here under observation for another twenty-four hours before you will be able to depart."

"Twenty-four hours?" shouted Kurt, "Seriously?  Some of us have jobs.  I can't just blow off work."

"Some of us run businesses," Mike said, "I can't keep my doors closed this long."

"Absence from your jobs has been discussed with your respective employers," said the Agent, "Your misfortune has been relayed to them along with the fact that you are currently in government custody for your own safety. They have all agreed to our terms and you will receive no reprimand of any kind due to your brief absence. As for the business owner, your losses will be compensated."

"What's happening to her," Justin said, clenching his fists and his teeth, "Tell me."

"I have told you," said the Agent, "She is part of a small percentage of..."

"No," Justin said, trying to get into the Agent's face before realizing that the guy was a good five inches taller than he was, "What's happening to her?"

That last phrase came out as more of a growl. Justin was now face-to-chin with the agent, looking up at him in a rather threatening manner. The rest of the group would later converse about how this was probably a horrible idea. Justin would scoff at them because it got results.

The Agent removed his sunglasses and stared down at Justin with piercing blue eyes.

"Currently," he said, his voice not wavering from its past tone, "She is undergoing treatment to attempt to stop the damage being done to her body. The abreaction noted previously causes severe and extremely painful chemical burns. We are doing everything we can to help her and your patience will be appreciated as the situation develops. She is under the care of government physicians and is receiving the most expert care available. Please relax in the knowledge that we are looking after her and have only her best interests in mind."

Justin kept his eyes locked with the Agent for a moment causing absolutely no visible intimidation and then turned away. The Agent replaced his sunglasses.

"What about our families?" Budda asked, "If you called our jobs, did you call them too? Can we do it ourselves? People are going to be nervous and looking for us."

"Anyone searching for you by means of a cellular phone call has been informed of your predicament," the Agent said, "This includes some of your family members. They have been instructed to be present if they feel it necessary when you are released from the hospital. It is preferable that you do not attempt to contact them at this time."

"What's that supposed to mean?" Jess asked, "Is this, like, a cover-up or something?"

"We would prefer to disseminate only information which includes the proper and complete details," the Agent answered, "You have not yet been informed of these details in their entirety. This would allow for speculation on the part of those with whom you speak. You will be fully informed during a small debriefing before your departure tomorrow.

"If you will excuse me, I must tend to other things.  You are not the only ones who were involved in this incident.  There are eight others who require my consolation before the end of the day.  An agent will be posted on your door.  You may request anything within reason for your entertainment or nourishment."

Justin opened his mouth to say something.

"You will be informed of any changes in her condition," said the Agent as he turned to leave.

The automatic doors swished open and closed followed by the loud click of the lock.

"You ok?" Jess asked, approaching Justin.

He grunted and walked back to his instrument cabinet near the corner to sulk.

"Dude," Josh said, pulling his shirt over his nose, "This place stinks."

"We know," Mike said, "Like burning hair.  You'll get used to it over the next hour or so.  Come on, let's play some cards or something. We've got a whole day to kill."

Kurt returned to his magazine, Jess lay next to him to take a nap, Budda resumed his spot in front of the television, and Josh and Mike began a game which had not yet been decided.

Justin stared at the wall, lost in his anger and emotion.  He didn't want to think about the worst happening to Char, but, at the same time, he couldn't avoid it.  He sat with his hands on his knees and closed his eyes.  Tears streamed down his cheeks, feeling cool against his hot angry skin.

It was not yet detectable, but the smell in the room was slowly growing stronger.

## III

Emma and Steph awoke to sore backs and the blare of a ringing phone.

A bell in a phone was an unfamiliar sound to both of them. The only time they heard that sort of thing anymore was either in a period movie or when someone thought it was a clever cell phone ringtone.

The phone, from what they had established as fact over the past two days, was non-functional. They had tried to use it about once an hour and it never produced a dial tone. This added to the element of surprise even more than the suddenly shattered silence or the thought of the bell.

Emma picked up the receiver slowly as if it were a trap. Steph watched from the safety of her bed, hoping that this wasn't something awful.

"Hello?" she muttered, her voice tinged with surprise.

"This is Agent Williams," said the voice on the other end, "You will be escorted to the lobby in ten minutes. Make whatever preparations are required."

Emma could hear the click of the hang-up, then the click of the phone once again going dead. She slapped at the cradle, hoping still yet for a dial tone, and getting nothing in return. She gently placed the receiver back where it belonged.

"Ten minutes," Emma said, "I think they're letting us out."

Steph nodded and started her preparations for departure.

This was the first time they were instructed to leave. They had been brought meals and afforded the luxury of cable during their stay. The beds were uncomfortable and the lack of communication and social media was enough to put both of them on edge. Emma imagined that this must be what minimum-security prison was like and suddenly thought that anyone who called it Camp Cupcake or the like only did so because they didn't understand how difficult isolation would be, even with some luxuries.

They did not understand why they had to be kept in the hospital, presumably far away from their group of friends. Both of them wanted very badly to just go home until this whole thing was complete.

Emma pulled her wild mane of curly red hair back into a pony tail and dressed herself. Steph sorted her short brown hair out with a barrette or two she'd had in her purse. Neither of them thought they would look good in any way considering their last forty-eight or so hours.

Earlier, the idea had crossed Emma's mind that they might be able to overcome the agent posted across the hall from them and escape from their temporary prison. Aside from the fact that his head nearly exceeded the maximum height of the hallway and his shoulders its maximum width, not to mention the obvious bulge of a firearm inside his coat, she thought she could probably take him. Steph wound up talking her down, citing only that it might get their friends in a greater degree of trouble. She never mentioned anything about Emma being out of her league as far as taking the big guy down.

In precisely ten minutes, there was a knock at the door.

The gigantic agent stood waiting for them, the top of the door jamb obscuring most of his bald head. The pin on his lapel glinted in the light. It was the same one Emma had seen on Agent Williams – a black roman numeral XIII inside a black circle over a red background. Obviously all the agents Williams had referred to were playing on his team.

"Ladies, please follow me," he said.

His voice was deep and carried a heavy southern accent. He offered a smile to them as he turned to lead. Both of them would later agree that he was probably a charmer in addition to being akin to the Incredible Hulk.

"You sure don't look like any kind of government agent," Emma said as they walked, "Bald head, no eyebrows, body piercings... I thought you couldn't have any identifying features?"

He stopped. Both of them flinched as if he was going to turn around swinging. He leaned down to her and lowered his sunglasses along his nose. They stared each other in the eye, Emma trying her best to show no intimidation.

"You watch too many movies, darlin'," he said before continuing on.

"This is amazing," Josh said, "How did you do that? I mean, someone hand-made that shirt for me, like, a million years ago. Where did you find this fabric?"

Agent Williams didn't answer. His expression was deadpan as he supervised the return of the group's goods. Each of them had a sealed plastic bag full of every item on their person on the night of the incident down to the smallest detail, from the duct tape around Kurt's shoes to the flour sticking to Mike's fleece shirt from the bakery.

Justin stared at the pile in front of him. He looked at Agent Williams with disdain.

"Is something not to your satisfaction?" asked the Agent.

"Yeah," Justin said, "This scarf isn't the same."

"I assure you, it is," he responded, "The utmost care was taken in the reproduction of these items down to the thread count. We accounted for inconsistencies in the knitting stroke as we knew it was hand-made. We have matched the colors exactly."

"Did you get my grandmother to knit it?" Justin asked.

The Agent stared silently at him from behind his sunglasses.

"Then it's not the same thing," Justin said, "My grandmother knitted that scarf for me. This is just a reproduction. I want my real scarf back."

"Dude," Jess said, putting her hand on his shoulder, "Let it go."

"I'm not going to let it go," Justin said, shrugging her hand away and fixing his stare on the Agent, "It was my scarf and I want it back. The real one."

"Your previous possessions have been incinerated," Williams said, his tone unchanging, "They were contaminated and, as such, were considered a risk. I believe I have explained this to you twice already. We have extended you the courtesy of duplicate items. Please do not take our hospitality for granted. What you have could just as easily be taken away from you."

"I'm just trying to make a point," Justin said.

"Your point has been noted," said Williams.

The two stared each other down for a moment longer before Justin began redressing himself along with the rest of his friends.

While the agent wasn't looking, Josh was busy stuffing something into his jacket pocket.

"Playing cards?" Mike asked in a whisper, "You're taking the cards with you?"

"What?" Josh asked, giving Mike an over-obvious look to silence him, "I don't know what you're talking about."

"You are stealing a pack of playing cards from the hospital," Mike whispered, recognizing but ignoring Josh's signs.

"So what if I am?" Josh said, continuing his look.

"You're a kleptomaniac, that's what," Mike said, "Dude, that's like taking candy from a baby."

"I guess it is," said Josh, "I'll explain later, just shut the hell up."

When they were dressed and ready, Agent Williams led them beyond the automatic doors and into the hallway. They were all excited to leave the place due to the continuous smell of burning hair. Though not as bad, it seemed to follow them as they were lead away from the ward.

As they walked, Agent Williams was met by a younger woman with a suit and sunglasses identical to his down to the lapel pin. Black hair was pulled into a bun at the back of her head, held in place by two red chopsticks.

"Sir," she mumbled (everyone could hear), "I'd like to suggest the alternate method we discussed earlier. I still believe that this is a bad idea and that you should leave the situation to me."

"Your objection is noted, Agent Briggs," he said in a normal tone.

"Sir, we can fix this permanently," she said, still trying to whisper, "I can fix this."

"Your report was enlightening, Agent Briggs, however I believe that this is the proper course of action," he continued, "'No perceivable threat' were your exact words. I intend to abide by that. We must leave this as untouched as possible considering what has already been done."

"Yes, sir," she said, sighing before she disappeared down another hallway.

The group reached the door of the hospital's chapel. Inside, they found Emma and Steph as well as some of their parents and family who had come after being given the phone messages Williams had described. There were a few strangers, presumably the loved ones of the others they'd seen covered in the black goo.

The next hour or so was a blur for all of them. Tearful reunions, Agent Williams recounting the accident blow for blow, explaining the nature of the "abreaction" which, they found, had happened to Char and two others. None of them really paid attention to anything until Williams started talking money.

"Due to the intense emotional stress visited upon victims of this extreme situation," said Williams, "Both at the scene and during their quarantine here, our agency will compensate those affected to help ease your burden.

"We realize that we can neither replace the time you have lost, nor can we reverse any permanent side effects which may carry over should the afflicted survive. What we can offer is a substantial monetary allotment to aid you in this hour of need. You will leave here today with cash in hand. Each settlement will be discussed with the appropriate parties. This money is given freely under one condition: you must never reveal anything regarding this incident to any media source."

"Hush money," Budda said, nodding in understanding.

The rest of the room turned their attention to him, then began talking amongst themselves.

Agent Williams turned to Budda with what Justin was sure was the same look he'd been given behind those sunglasses.

"Understand that this is compensation for services rendered," Williams said, "The service you provide will be your discretion. For this, your compensation will be remarkable. In order to guarantee this exchange, all those present will be required to sign a non-disclosure agreement. I have been told that, if you remain living within your budgets, you will never have to work another day in your life."

This quieted any objections spurred by Budda's comment. The kind of money Williams was talking about was nothing to shirk at and everyone in the room knew it.

"If there are no further objections, I will now adjourn our meeting," Williams said, "My subordinate, Agent Moorsblade, will be waiting at the door for your signature upon which you will receive your settlement. Thank you again for your patience and your discretion."

Agent Williams disappeared through a back door. The crowd mulled around before Agent Moorsblade called everyone's attention and told them to line up for their money. His accent and general demeanor would have helped to make him more approachable if he were not the size of a large truck.

They could now see everyone involved who had not exhibited the mysterious abreaction mentioned multiple times over the course of their stay.

A goth girl, probably college age, fought with her father near the front of the line. Her purple-streaked bottle-black hair together with her leather jacket and exaggerated eye makeup gave her scene affiliation away. They were beginning to draw attention, but what they were saying was made largely unintelligible by their sheer volume let alone the fact that the man was very drunk. Agent Moorsblade had to stand up to get their attention. This was all he had to do to let them know he meant business. They signed their document, received a brief case, and continued fighting outside.

A tall, dark-skinned man, also college age, stared after her. He was easy to pick out in the crowd not just because of his height but due to the fact that he was dressed in red athletic gear from head to toe. His head was neatly shaved bald. He, unlike the girl his eyes followed out of the room, was unaccompanied as were most of those present. He was the next to sign and leave.

Behind him was another accompanied girl, a teenager with long blonde hair, standing with a slightly older but still attractive woman who could probably pass for an older sister rather than her mother if she were so complimented. The girl was the only one in the room who still wore the blue scrubs. Draped over her shoulder was a clear garment bag containing an elaborate, sequined, purple gown. She carried a pair of matching high-heeled shoes in her other hand. Their posture indicated they were currently not speaking to each other.

The group was next. Agent Moorsblade would say to each of them in his calming southern drawl:

"What you are about to sign is a legal document stating that you will neither pursue the matter of this incident any further nor will you discuss said incident with anyone aside from those who already know of it, including, but not limited to, the media – print, broadcast or otherwise. If any details of this incident reaching a public source are traced back to you, you will forfeit the right to all titles, properties, goods, and assets granted to you by both your previous merit and this monetary settlement you agree to receive forthwith following the placement of your good ol' Johnny Hancock right here on this little black line.

"In short; you sign, we give you money. You screw us, we screw you harder. Get it?"

"I get it," Justin said, rolling his eyes when he received the speech.

They all scribbled their names on the bottom of the thick document and received a black briefcase in turn.

Agent Moorsblade stopped Steph at the end of the group's line. He whispered a few things to her before Budda rushed to catch her as she almost fainted.

25

"Y'all have a good day, now," said Moorsblade through a fake and dangerous smile, returning to his desk to deal with the rest of those in line.

When they were all safely outside, Justin grabbed Steph's arm and asked:

"What did he tell you? Was it something about Char?"

"Sort of," Steph managed, "He told me… He told me because of the severity of her issue, they were going to give our family a little more than everyone else."

"How much more?" Justin asked.

Steph stepped up and whispered a few things to him before Mike rushed to catch him as he almost feinted. Justin was a deal heavier than Steph, however, and both of them ended up on the ground.

"That's not good," Justin said, looking up at her.

"I know," she said, sighing and helping him up, "But, there isn't really anything we can do."

Justin's blood boiled with the thought. That much money given to Char's family could only mean one thing.

He decided against rushing back into the hospital and fighting his way to her, mostly because the tiny bit of his brain which was still rational told him that he'd probably get himself killed or arrested. There was also nothing he could do for her. He wasn't a doctor. Most of his medical knowledge derived from primetime dramas. The rest of it came from WebMD. While these qualifications made him feel as though he could help, he realized that his Dr. House impression would not help professionals break the case.

The government had sent black cars staffed by chauffeurs wearing the same lapel pin they'd seen on Agents Williams and Moorsblade. The group agreed to go to lunch together and left their five government drivers idling in the parking lot of the restaurant as they did.

Justin remained pensive and angry even while everyone cracked jokes about their situation. Typically, he would be leading the charge, however, with Char in dire straits his mind would not let itself wander. He remained silent, continuing to think about whatever horrors she was going through. He could feel the rage building inside him, even after lunch when he had arrived back at their apartment.

He felt warm. His fingers and toes were tingling. He figured he should lie down but, when he did, he found himself staring at the empty side of their queen-sized bed where Char would normally have been. Sniffing the air, trying to find some solace in the familiar scent of their bedroom, he could smell nothing but the same burning hair stench as he had back in the makeshift ward.

He got up, frustrated, stripped his clothes, tossed them into the hamper and changed. He sprayed at the hamper with an air freshener just to be safe.

He wandered into the living room and sat down in his armchair. He thought he might be able to distract himself by watching a little TV only to find that the cable was having technical difficulties, as dictated by his cable box.

He was fed up, quite literally. He felt as if the rage had filled him to his brim. His head felt like it was going to explode right before it actually did.

His hair, with a loud whoosh as if throwing a match on a puddle of lighter fluid, exploded into a pillar of flames.

IV

The next morning, on the other side of town, Emma sat at her computer.

She felt restored from sleeping on her own bed and, as she had crawled into it shortly after returning home, had no time to check her social media. She felt disconnected and unplugged from the world after two days trapped in the dead zone of the hospital room.

She searched local news sites but there was no mention of the accident. She assumed that this was the work of Agent Williams and his mystery organization. He mentioned wanting to keep it out of the media. She didn't realize they'd instituted the full government blackout until just now.

The sun crept into the small apartment as it rose over the adjacent building and through her fourth floor window just as Josh crept out of the bedroom.

He mumbled a good morning and kissed her on the cheek. She jumped back as the kiss delivered a heavy static shock.

"What?" Josh asked.

"You shocked me," she said.

"What's so shocking about your boyfriend wanting to kiss you?" he asked, offended.

"No, moron," she said, "Static electricity. You literally shocked me."

"Oh," he said, "Sorry, I must have been dragging my feet."

He closed in for another kiss and Emma jumped again.

"That's enough for now, loverboy," she said, putting her arms up.

"Did I do it again?" Josh asked.

"Yes, now give it a rest," she said, "Go watch TV or something."

"Sorry," Josh said, slumping off to the couch.

As he turned around, she saw a sock, a pair of her panties, and a crumpled up black t-shirt stuck to his back.

"Hang on," she said

She stood and peeled the clothes from his back. It felt like taking a heavy magnet off of a refrigerator.

"What the hell did you do," she asked, "Sleep on balloons covered in wool? You're like a damned science experiment or something."

He offered no answer as she sat back down.

The TV blared as Josh turned it on and began cycling through channels.

"Turn it down," she shouted, "Some of us are trying to catch up on our lives here."

The volume decreased.

"Thank you," she said, frustrated, before looking down at her desk and seeing their cluster of remote controls sitting next to her keyboard.

She turned around and watched as Josh sluggishly touched his thumb to his finger, miming the action of using a remote, and making things happen to the TV.

She stopped what she was doing and sat next to him on the couch, staring at his hand. It responded to his every whim. She could see a small arc of electricity as his fingers touched together. She reached up to his hand and, as her finger made contact...

"Ow! Son of a bitch!" she screamed, shaking her hand off, feeling like she just stuck her finger into an outlet.

Josh turned to look at her.

"What now?" he asked.

"Do you even see what you're doing?" she asked in return.

"I'm watching TV," he said, "Look, I'm sorry if I shocked you a couple of times. It's winter, it's dry, this happens. I've got no control over it."

"No," she said, "You've got control of something else."

She pointed to his hand, still clicking away through the channels. They watched his hand in amazement as he continued clicking. They couldn't believe that something like this was happening until they put all the pieces together.

"Superpowers," Justin said, "We're all going to get superpowers." Mike laughed.

"You've finally lost it, man," Mike said, "One too many comic books."

Mike's bakery was extraordinarily busy. His place was popular among many of the locals and he had been closed for two days. The orders on his answering machine had stacked up. He'd only let Justin into the bakery proper because Justin made it seem urgent. That feeling was quickly disappearing along with his patience.

Justin took his theory to Mike first, not just because they were practically brothers, but because the apartment he and Char rented was located three floors above the bakery. This put Mike in the strange position of being Justin's best friend as well as his landlord. This was the first time Mike felt that having his friend in his building may have been a bad idea. He went on preparing cookies as Justin continued talking.

"I'm serious, dude," Justin said.

"Look," Mike said, "I get it. We play tabletop games together. I understand the desire for fantasy but, really, we should be more excited we don't have seven kinds of cancer from that black stuff rather than waiting for superpowers to happen."

29

"It's the trope, though," Justin said, "This is how tons of superhero origin stories start. Think about it: shady government agency, unknown chemical, extended observation in the hospital…"

"I have thought about it," Mike said, "My thoughts were that I'm excited to be alive and not immediately reduced to a puddle or riddled with tumors."

Justin glared at him. He was still worried about Char and her fate in the hospital. She didn't make it out as lucky as Mike had described. He thought Mike was being flippant and dismissive of her condition. She got whatever this was the worst of anyone.

"I want you to believe me before-" Justin started.

"Before what?" Mike interrupted, "Before I call dibs on being Wolverine because your pop-culture stuffed brain is short-circuiting with PTSD?"

"That's mean, man," Justin said, clenching his fists, "Why would you say something like that?"

"Because you need to be real," Mike said, "Do you think those government guys would have ever let us out of the hospital if super powers were on the table? Hell no. They'd be on you like white on rice. You'd be shadowed 24/7. They wouldn't want to push a liability like that out into the open world."

"I don't think they knew this would happen," Justin said.

"They had to know," Mike replied, "They kept us under observation for a reason."

"Yeah, to make sure what's happening to Char right now didn't happen to us," Justin shouted, "But I don't think they took this kind of thing into consideration."

"Prove it, then," Mike said, "Prove to me that something other than what's going on is… do you smell smoke?"

"Took you long enough," Justin said.

"Something's burning," Mike said, running to the ovens, checking every tray.

"Mike," Justin said, trying to get his attention.

"I know that smell," Mike said, "It's familiar. Like what we smelled in the hospital. Burning hair."

"Mike," Justin said again.

"Where would that be coming from," Mike pondered, checking himself over, patting at his head.

"Mike," Justin shouted, finally gaining his attention.

Justin took off his stocking cap to reveal his hair, which had now become a floating stream of smoke over his bald head. It looked as if he were a match which had just been blown out. The smoke rose a few inches from his scalp, shifting and smoldering,

Mike was stunned. He stood silent, his jaw agape, for a few moments. He stepped closer and slowly put his hand into the smoke,

30

watching it move around his fingers. It didn't leave a billowing cloud; it either dissipated or stopped at a fair height without leaving any trace.

"This is a trick, right?" Mike asked.

Justin rolled his eyes.

"Dude, your head is smoking," Mike said.

"Yeah," Justin replied, "It kinda exploded yesterday after we got home from the hospital."

"Exploded?" Mike asked, pausing, then adding, "You didn't set the apartment on fire did you?"

"Dude, more important things are happening," Justin said, "I know you're my land lord and all, but we're talking about real-deal super human abilities here. This is crazy mutant power stuff!"

"The top of your head exploded," Mike said, deadpan.

"Yes," Justin explained, "In a giant pillar of flame which may or may not have scorched the living room ceiling."

"Really?" Mike pleaded, "Dammit, man."

"Oh, come on," Justin said, "I'll pay for the damages, if there are any. We all got briefcases full of cash. Shouldn't be much of a problem. Now, let's not worry about the damn ceiling. Super powers!"

Justin shouted the last part while pointing at his head.

Mike turned around.

"You're serious," he said.

"As a heart attack," Justin said, "I don't think there's any way I could make my head constantly smolder. It's either super powers or real-life CGI. Either way, it's amazing."

"Ok," Mike said, turning back to face Justin, "Can you do anything other than smoke hair?"

"Well, I was messing around a bit while trying to light a cigarette," Justin said, "I found out I can do this."

Justin flicked his thumb at his index finger. His thumb was now on fire.

Mike jumped back. He was suddenly a caveman seeing the miracle of flames for the first time. He reached out to touch it and pulled his hand away as it burned.

"Yes," Justin said, "Fire hot."

"Have you talked to anyone else yet?" Mike asked.

"You're the first," Justin said, "I probably would have sounded crazy to anyone over the phone. I had to show you. I knew you would believe me."

"Do you think the rest of us will get superpowers?" Mike asked.

"I assume so," Justin said, "We're all part of the same origin story. It wouldn't go along with the trope if we didn't all get something out of it. We were covered in that same chemical, most of us with no horrifying side-effects."

"I would consider super abilities a pretty damn horrifying side-effect," Mike said.

"Horrifying?  Nah," Justin said, "Awesome more like."

"Horrifying until you learn to really control that," Mike said, "What if you fly off the handle and incinerate someone?"

"Doubtful," Justin said, "I've read all the comics.  I've played the RPGs.  I'm in full control."

As he said this, he dropped his still flaming thumb and hand to his side and caught his sleeve on fire.  Mike quickly grabbed a fire-extinguisher and put him out.  Both of them started laughing when the situation was over.

"What's my super power, then?" Mike asked.

"I think I picked up on it while we've been talking," Justin said.

"Ok, what is it?" Mike asked, "Danger sense?  Ability to predict when people's words will bite them in the ass?  Cookie making?"

"Your feet haven't touched the ground since we started talking," Justin said, pointing, "Take a look."

As Justin said, Mike had been floating a full six inches from the ground the entire time.

"Well," Mike said, taking off his apron, "That's a start.  Let's make some phone calls."

The phone was ringing.

Budda rolled over and looked at the clock.  It was a few minutes after noon.

He called in to work earlier to tell them that he quit and slept comfortably knowing that the money given to him by the government would be enough to sustain him for a very long time.

He was attempting to sleep in but was having a very difficult time of it.  He didn't feel like he needed to sleep and took to lying in bed either staring at the ceiling or the back of his eyelids.  While neither seemed like a very rewarding pastime, he had no desire to get up and greet the day just yet.

The phone was still ringing.  Likely someone trying to end his lazy streak was on the other end.  He sighed as he rolled over, his bed creaking hideously, and grabbed the phone.

"Hello," he muttered.

"Dude," said Josh's voice, "Dude, get up.  It's like Christmas."

"Christmas isn't for like a month and a half," he said, "What the hell are you talking about?"

There was pause on the other end of the line.

"Nothing weird has been going on with you today?" Josh asked.

"I've been lying in bed all day staring at nothing," Budda answered, "The only weird thing is that some d-bag named Josh called me and interrupted my little bit of silent meditation time.  I'm going to go now."

"Budda, wait!" Josh called right before Budda slammed the phone down, shattering it to pieces with his gigantic slate-blue stone hand.

He sprang up, looking at his arms in front of him. He threw the blankets from his legs and observed them as well. Looking down at himself, he could see that every visible part of him was now made of blue-gray rock.

He quickly swung his legs out of bed, his feet hitting the floor with a loud thunk. He stood up and his entire head blew through the drywall and wood of the low ceiling of his bedroom. He quickly figured he must now be somewhere around eight or nine feet tall.

He ducked his head back down and moved for the door of his bedroom, blowing out the doorway with his now four-foot wide shoulders and his underestimated head height. None of this hurt him, so it would take a while for him to realize what he'd done and attempt to clean it up.

He ran to the bathroom, exploding that doorway as well. He hunched down to look at himself in the mirror. He yelped in surprise.

His face was, as the rest of his body, slate-blue stone. All hair on his body was now gone. His eyes weren't eyes but black orbs which, when he touched them, made a light tink, like a pebble hitting glass. He assumed they were some sort of obsidian. He didn't feel anything as he did this, but his lack of a sense of touch or an active tactile nervous system was as yet unapparent to him.

His hands, both at the edge of the sink as he leaned over, now crushed the porcelain into powder. Curious, he crushed the rest of the sink with ease and pinched the pipes of the faucet closed once they started leaking. He looked down at his hands, noting that they were undamaged by the amazing thing he'd just done. He ran back into his living room, further demolishing his bathroom door, and grabbed the phone in that room.

He obliterated the number pad (and the rest of the phone for the most part) as he attempted to call Josh back.

"Dude," Budda said as Josh picked up, "Something weird is definitely going on."

Kurt had also called in to quit that morning. He was the one who put the idea into Budda's head. Working in an office just didn't have the appeal of living off the government's generous settlement for the rest of his life. It would give him a better chance to work on his hobbies, which is why on the way back to Kurt's small house, the car he and Jess had been given made a rather long detour to a music equipment store on the edge of the city.

He figured with all this time and money, he might finally be able to put up a semi-professional recording studio in his basement. He wanted to charge cheap rates so that lesser-known bands, as he had once been a part of, would have an easier time getting their music out there.

He knew just what he wanted and finally had the capital to buy it. It now sat in boxes on his basement floor along with a book about home studio construction. He cracked his knuckles and dove right in.

Without using the book, the studio came together quickly. He attributed the speed of this assembly to the fact that he had experienced hooking up a large sound board before. He didn't think a project this large would be so intuitive and easy to put together. As he touched each component, it seemed as though he knew exactly what to do to get it to perform at its maximum. He even started to get ideas about how to boost output or increase efficiency. He wondered when he had become so handy.

It had been about three hours. He was satisfied with everything and figured he should give it a test run.

As he lifted the cover of the used laptop he'd purchased to tie everything together, a strange sensation pulsed through him. He would later describe it as feeling like a sponge. He was absorbing the knowledge from the computer. Every file, every program was drawn into his brain for instantaneous analysis, copied, and saved. He had just absorbed hundreds of gigabytes worth of data.

He did not yet realize what exactly he had done. It accumulated so suddenly that he could not react. He knew what he possessed and immediately set about doing something with it.

He shook it off and continued with turning the computer on. He found that he had mastered the complex sound-editing program as well as the operating system, programming languages, and technical knowledge. He felt that this was taking too long and had a sudden realization that he could build a much better computer than this piece of junk. He realized that he was calling a computer which had been top-of-the-line for music production a piece of junk and didn't care. He opened the back panel, grabbed his soldering gun, and went straight for the motherboard.

"What are you doing?" asked Jess.

"Well," Kurt said without looking up, "I've been setting up my studio and I got to thinking that this computer needs to be optimized in order for everything to function at peak. Shouldn't take me long to soup this thing up."

"I need your help with something," she said.

"Can it wait like twenty minutes?" Kurt asked.

"This is serious," Jess said, "I need your help now."

"Just give me a min..." Kurt stopped as he looked up. He expected to see her standing at the bottom of the basement stairs, from where her voice seemed to be coming.

He looked around the room, no sign of her.

"Jess?" he called.

"Yes?" she answered, still nowhere to be seen.

"Where are you?" he asked.

"I'm upstairs," she said, "I'm in the bedroom. I'm sort of incapacitated. I need your help."

"How are you doing this?" he asked.

"Telepathy, I think," she said, "It's really hard right now, though. Could you please come up and help me?"

Kurt ran up the stairs and found her lying face up on their bed, blood was trickling from her nose. She was breathing rapidly and shaking as though she were having a seizure.

"Oh my god," he said, "Jess, what's happening?"

"Voices," she muttered, actually speaking to him now, "So many voices."

"I'm going to call for help," Kurt said, grabbing his cell phone from the top of their dresser.

He staggered backwards as suddenly he had knowledge of all the intimate workings of the device. His contact list had been downloaded into his head. He knew how to program for a smart phone. He knew how it was constructed and how it worked in the most detailed way possible. He could build a cell phone from scratch. All this occurred to him instantly.

He knew he had to get help. Without touching anything, the phone began to dial 911. This was interrupted, however, by an incoming call from Justin. Kurt answered, speaking through the device with his mind.

"Now isn't a good time, man," he said, "Jess is in some serious trouble."

"What's happening?" Justin asked, sounding very serious.

"She says she's hearing voices," Kurt said, "She was talking to me with telekinesis or something."

"Telepathy," Justin corrected him, "Quick, put her on the line."

Kurt held the phone to Jess's ear.

"Jess," Justin said while Kurt eavesdropped as the signal channeled through his mind, "If you can hear me, darling, try to take deep breaths and concentrate on me and only on me."

She did as he said. Justin offered more calming words of encouragement until finally she stopped shaking, her nose stopped bleeding, and she was able to sit up in bed. After ten minutes, she seemed almost normal again.

"Ok," Justin said, "I'm assuming you both can hear me right now and I'm also assuming you already know what's going on."

"No," Kurt said.

"Superpowers," Jess said, "I can see inside your mind, Justin. You're calling to ask if we have superpowers."

"No sense in asking at this point, I suppose," Justin said, "Look, I'm trying to get everyone together at my place. We all need to talk."

V

"This makes no sense in reality," Emma shouted, "There's no such thing as superpowers, there's no such thing as some mystery ooze that can grant them, and this is not some kind of comic book origin story."

The entire group of them, including Steph, looked at her in utter disbelief. Justin's hair smoldered and remained smoke. Budda's now gigantic form looked like it was chiseled out of a piece of blue slate. Her tirade to them all meant only one thing:

"What kind of denial are you in, exactly?" Justin said, "You realize this is happening. You've seen it all with your own eyes. This is not a dream. This is not a hallucination. This is real."

He waved his hand through his hair, causing it to stir but not to stray.

"This is real," he said, creating a fireball in his hand, then extinguishing it.

"This," he continued, pounding on Budda's chest, "Is real."

"This," Josh imitated, "Is real."

He touched Emma on the thigh and jolted her into the air with a static shock. She rolled her sleeves over her arms and started slapping at him.

"Seriously, though," Justin said, "I know it's hard to wrap our heads around. It's something that isn't supposed to exist. It's the stuff we read about in comics or see in movies. We just have to get used to the idea that these things are now very real."

"I'm confident that we can make it past that," said Kurt, "The problem is going to be hiding it from the public. If people you like this or realize that any of us are using superpowers, they're going to freak out. Not to mention we were told by some serious government spooks not to draw attention to ourselves."

"They said not to talk about the accident in public," Mike argued, "They didn't say we had to lead sheltered lives from now on."

"Just asking," Justin interjected, "But how many people do we all typically interact with. I mean, we're all sort of cynical antisocial bastards. We don't usually associate with anyone but each other and maybe a few others outside of this room. If we just keep living our lives, I don't think there's going to be much of an issue with us being out in the public eye."

"I'm still in school," said Jess, "But, I still look normal, so it shouldn't be a big deal."

Budda shot her a dirty look. Justin sighed, but gave her the benefit of the doubt. Kurt pointed at Justin and began speaking.

"You're going to have a problem," said Kurt, "So is Budda. You two had physical effects to go along with your abilities. How are either of you ever going to get around?"

"I own many hats," Justin said, "Most of them do an ok job of hiding the smoke."

"What about me?" Budda asked.

"Don't any of you read comics?" Justin said, "I can't possibly be the only one who immediately thought of the reverse-costume costume."

"Meaning?" Kurt asked.

"Ben Grimm, Fantastic Four," Justin said, "Big rock guy who wears a heavy trench coat and a fedora every time he goes out so people don't realize he's different. We do a bit of that, maybe cover up the face some, Budda should be fine."

"We're gonna have to go to the big and tall shop," Budda said, "The only thing I fit into were these button-down track pants and this stocking cap. Nothing else in my closet fits anymore."

"If we're going to do this," Kurt said, "We've got to know each other's capabilities."

"Wait, wait, wait," Mike said, waving his hands, "Do what?"

"Be superheroes," Kurt said.

The room went silent as everyone stared at him.

"We all assembled to talk about powers," Mike said, "You're telling me that none of you thought of this?"

"You're falling into it," Justin said, shaking his head.

"Falling into what?" Kurt asked.

"The trope," Justin said, "We've all been conditioned by pop culture and movies to think that becoming a superhero is the obvious next step to gaining powers. We've been Uncle Ben'd by every comic book, movie, and novel we've ever read about people who suddenly gain power to think that because we have this, we've got some great responsibility to live up to."

"Well," said Budda, "Don't we?"

"No," Justin said, "We don't have to do anything but lay low and continue to live our lives."

"I agree," Mike said, "I've got a business. I can't afford to shut up shop and join the circus."

"We should do something good with this stuff," Kurt continued, "I don't care how many stereotypes or 'tropes' you think we're falling into. It's the right thing to do."

"Except it's not," Justin said, "Vigilantism is illegal and frowned upon in real life."

"I've always wanted to be a hero," said Josh, "I'm with it, I say we give it a try."

"You're going to put your life on the line for strangers?" Justin asked.

"Yes," Josh said.

"You're going to stop violent crime?" Justin asked.

"Yes," Josh said.

"You're willing to take a bullet to defend the innocent?" Justin asked.

"Well," Josh said, trailing off.

"My point exactly," Justin said, "While Budda may be bulletproof – and, I stress, may be – the rest of us are decidedly not. We are not knife-proof or blunt-object-proof or fist-proof. This is not to mention that we live in a relatively calm city. There aren't any serial murderers or supervillains. No one is on the lamb from the cops and, if they are, they're usually caught by simple police detective work. There won't be a need for our level of power in the local crime fighting community. It's just overkill."

"There will be something, someday," Kurt said, "When that day comes don't you want to be able to help? And, until then, why couldn't we patrol and keep the streets clean. Come on, man, you're the comic book nerd. This is supposed to be your life-long fantasy fulfilled!"

Justin sighed and sat down, putting his hands over his face.

"I'm still in agreement with Justin," Mike said, "We're severely overpowered for petty crime. We won't be able to prevent anything like arson or murder because we can't predict the future. We might be able to track people down and bring them to justice or whatever, but we're going to be overlapping the cops – you know, the people who actually get paid to protect the innocent and uphold the law."

"Guys, look," Jess said, standing up and looking very frustrated, "I understand what everyone's thinking, not just because I can actually read your thoughts, but because I am split as to what to do with this stuff. I'm not very experienced. Justin, Mike, Josh, you guys play role-playing games and stuff, I'm going to need a lot of help figuring out how this works and what I can actually do which is why I don't think we should talk about any of this superhero stuff until we know what we're doing.

"What if I make some innocent person's head explode? What if Justin throws a fireball and misses and burns a house down? What if Budda punches someone into oblivion because he doesn't know his own strength?"

"Worst I could do is give someone a welt from a static shock," Josh said.

"Doesn't matter," Jess said, "You just haven't found your full potential yet. None of us have. This is like day one-point-five of us having these abilities and it's too soon to even have this discussion on the table. It took a lot for me to admit that I was psychic to you guys because I knew that you knew about this stuff, even if fictional, and that you'd be afraid of me. I'm here because I now have a super ability and, as strange as it is, you guys are the experts because you've role played characters like this before. I'm here because I need help, not because I want to run off and club purse-snatchers over the head."

"She's right," Budda said, "I don't know my own strength. I've been crushing everything I touch which is why Steph's been doing everything for me. I don't eat anymore, I don't sleep anymore, and I can't feel things anymore. I need support to help me get through this part or I'm going to go insane. I don't need to be fighting crime."

"Thank you for talking sense," said Justin, "We don't need to go looking for trouble when we have so much here."

"But we will someday," Budda says, "I'm with Kurt. I don't think this should be pushed aside and used for nothing. My life is going to be very different now. If my problem can be someone else's solution, so be it."

"Cliché," Justin said with a dismissive wave, "All of this. It's too familiar. We cannot fall into this trap. It's like someone's writing this story and they just want everything to happen in a way that would set us up as a superteam. Next thing you know, there will be a villain out of the other victims who we're going to have to fight."

The room turned to him and stayed silent for a moment.

"That's actually not a bad idea," Kurt said.

"No, it's a horrible idea," Justin said, "It's horrible and stupid and we don't need it. I'm not about to get shoehorned into some corny comic book drama."

"You don't have to," Mike said, "This is real life. Like you said before, we keep our heads down and we stay out of this lifestyle."

"But, what if," Kurt said, "What if someone isn't so complacent? What if one of those other victims decides to use their power for evil?"

"Now you're just antagonizing me," Justin said, "You sound like the to-be-continued page."

"I'm serious, man," said Kurt, "Someone will need to bring them down. Traditional methods would likely be useless."

"Assumption," Justin interjected.

"Assumption or not," Kurt said, "We should be ready for it. And Jess is right, regardless of our individual stances on the hero bit, we should concentrate on learning more about our abilities right now."

"Learned quite a bit, myself," Mike said, "Stayed up all night on the internet looking things up. Determined I have gravity control."

"Wow, that's badass," said Josh.

"Not only can I levitate," Mike said, demonstrating this by standing and floating a few feet from the ground, "But, I can also increase the pull of gravity on objects."

He raised his hand and pointed at a cigarette butt in Justin's ashtray. He levitated it up about an inch before slamming it down. It made a clean hole in the ashtray, the end table, the floor of the room, the apartment below, and one of the industrial mixers in the bakery. Mike, shocked, ran to the hole and peered through it.

"Ok, I guess I could stand to learn a little more about control," he said.

"I hope you know that's not coming out of my deposit," Justin said.

"Keep your mouth shut and it's a deal," Mike muttered.

"If we do go into 'hero training'," Josh said, "Where the hell are we supposed to do it? We don't exactly have a Danger Room or anything."

"I have a pretty big coal cellar below the basement of my house," Kurt said, "Rough stone walls, nothing to write home about. I keep some of my stuff down there. We could clear it out and, with a little work, make it big enough to do whatever we need to do."

"Six of us cooped up with no fresh air and no windows," Justin said, "Coal dust in the air. Sounds like the perfect place to practice pyrokinesis."

"It's not ideal," Kurt said, raising his voice, "But it's something for now."

"Certainly not practical, either," said Justin, "This whole thing is a stupid idea."

"I'm trying to help you here," Kurt shouted, "I'm trying to help all of us."

"You're trying to help all of us run straight out into the streets," Justin shouted back, "Where we'll wind up causing massive collateral damage in order to stop purse-snatchers and car thieves!"

Justin's hair sparked and sputtered. Small flames appeared and snuffed out periodically.

"Let's just calm down here," said Jess, "Clearly, there are some issues which will need hammered out eventually. For right now, you can both agree that we need to work on training and control before we do anything else, right?"

"Yes," said Kurt.

"I guess," said Justin, his hair calming down and returning to its constant smolder, "Really, I don't agree with any of it. It feels like this is some kind of train that we can't get off. We're stuck on the track of this origin story and we have to wait until it plays out. Being a comic book nerd in this situation is both helpful and awful because I can see everything coming."

Justin's cell phone rang.

"Including this call from the hospital, about Char," he said, tears forming in the corners of his eyes, "Which is sure to be some of the worst news I'm ever going to hear."

***

He watched from the rooftop across the street, lined up perfectly with the curtain-free third floor windows of the living room. The fat, goateed, nerdy one with the smoking head fell to his knees and cried. The one with the designer clothes and the auburn hair moved to comfort him first, followed by the rest. Even the guy who was a big blue rock man moved in to hug the group as most of them were now sobbing openly, embracing each other.

He laughed as the sadness kicked in. He almost couldn't contain himself. He was sure anyone out on the street on this cold night would hear him but he didn't care. He wasn't afraid of anything, least of all getting caught laughing on a rooftop. The only thing he cared about was that the eight people in the living room across the street didn't realize he was there. The funniest part was that no matter how hard he laughed and no matter how much attention he would draw to himself, they would never look in his direction because their sadness drew them instantly inward on each other.

His finely tuned sense of hearing caught every sob, every utterance of an apology, every expression of woe and mourning. He thought this made it even more hilarious.

He was a purveyor of schadenfreude. It was part of his job. He was conditioned for it from the moment he started with the program. Never, though, had it been this funny.

After getting his laughter out, he thought better of the situation. He wiped the tears from his eyes, still chuckling, realizing that a very large bald man on a rooftop in a tight black jumpsuit in the middle of the night laughing hysterically, even maniacally, would probably be something about which people would be concerned.

"13-A," said a deep, calm voice in his ear piece, "This is Control. Report."

He still needed a moment to catch his breath. His ears were still picking up the ongoing wails from the living room and he had to stifle another fit of laughter. He coughed a few times before the voice began again.

"13-A," it said, "This is Control. Please respond."

He got a handle on himself and tapped at the large metal bracer on his wrist before responding.

"Control, this is 13-A," he said through a thick southern accent, "Reckon they got the message. Awaiting further instructions."

"13-A, Control," said the voice, "Phase one complete. Return to base at your earliest convenience."

"Copy," he said.

He took another moment to compose himself and took one parting look through the window, smirking as he crouched down before shooting off the roof like a rocket into the night sky and flying himself back to base.

## VI

Zoey sat in her bathtub, curled up with her hands around her legs, as the hot water from the shower rushed over her. The bruises on her face throbbed. The cut above her eye was bleeding less now, but still offered a swirl of red as the water rolled off her body.

The last three days had been the most awful time of her life. She was having difficulty thinking of a response to her most recent actions and the first, and best, conclusion she could arrive at was to run. She decided a few minutes into her catatonic thinking episode in the bathtub that this would be exactly what she would do. She had a briefcase full of government money and a new lease on life. Now, it was a matter of figuring out where to go.

She ran her fingers through her hair and screamed as she came back with a handful of bottle-black strands tipped with purple. She dropped the clump into the tub where it circled the drain as she realized the rest of her hair was falling out.

Three days earlier, Zoey finally heard from her boyfriend.

Chaucer had been notoriously difficult to track down. Her low self-esteem and the nearly three years of long-distance relationship drove her into depression that she hadn't felt since high school.

The two of them together always seemed a strange match to her. The longer things went on, the less she could believe that the most popular kid in her high school – the captain of the basketball team, the class president, the one with the Harvard scholarship – would have ever been interested in her.

In those days, she had a reputation.

Zoey was the token Goth loner of her school. She had no real friends and barely spoke to anyone, even when spoken to. She found that she was extremely anti-social and, though she would never confess it to anyone, attributed this to her intellect. She refused to buy in to the hoi polloi and politics of high school drama and chose to distance herself from any social scene. In her mind, these concerns weren't worth her time.

In reality, it wasn't so much her intellect driving her social tendencies, rather, it was the schism in her family caused by her mother and father splitting when she was fourteen. He was an artist, she ran an art gallery. When her mother got the opportunity to manage a big-ticket gallery in New York, she took it and left her father behind, her parting criticism of his body of work crushing him and only serving to further his feelings of inadequacy. Zoey's feelings of inadequacy were amplified by the fact that her mother never even said goodbye and didn't think twice about leaving her daughter behind to further her career.

The terms of their divorce left her father enough money to help them get by, but barely. His only job after this point was full-time alcoholic. Zoey begged him to take some kind of work but he shouted that he had a job. He was an artist. That was all he wanted to be even though most times he couldn't stand up straight. When he did work on a piece, he usually destroyed it and shouted about how nothing was ever good enough for Zoey's mother.

Zoey took it upon herself to care for her father and the house. At sixteen, as soon as she was able, she got a part time job. The child support money from her mother was enough to keep the bills paid and her father drunk. She worked to take care of herself.

She fell into reading as escapism and spent half her pay on books. The other half she spent buying the accoutrements of the Goth style into which she had fallen.

Her outsider look combined with her nose constantly in a book tended to keep people from engaging her in conversation. She liked that. Between work and taking care of her father, she didn't have time to worry about what boys were hot or who was calling who a slut. She wanted no part of it and worked hard to keep it away.

Her plan backfired.

The air of mystery with which she surrounded herself led to mass speculation. People thought she was dangerous. They thought she was a slut. The rumor spread that she came to their school because she assaulted a teacher at her old one and was forcibly transferred. The vicious politics of high school painted her as some sort of rebel menace. She didn't mind as long as it kept the people away.

On her off-days, she kept a regular table at the main branch of the library; far in the back corner, away from any distractions. She would sit and read anything she could get her hands on, sometimes skipping class to finish a chapter. The books were a way to put herself into a world where she didn't have to worry about her dad puking on the carpet and passing out again. She wished as she read that things could change. She wanted nothing more than a new life, away from her dad and the mess he had made.

Then, one day, Chaucer sat down at her table.

She knew of him, of course. Every kid in her school knew Chaucer Davies. All the girls swooned over him. Handsome, tall, smooth mocha skin… even Zoey couldn't deny him a glance.

When he sat down with her that day, her heart skipped a beat.

"Hey, girl," he said, throwing the obligatory head flick at her. His eyes narrow and his lips pursed in his best attempt to appear alluring.

She laughed.

"Seriously?" she asked, dropping her book to the table, "'Hey, girl,'? That's all you've got? Dude, cheesy."

"Works most of the time," he said.

"Well, I'm not a moron," she said, "And I certainly don't fall for the 'hey, girl,' routine."

"Ok," he said, snapping out of attack mode, "Hi. My name's Chaucer. You're Zoey, right? Would you mind if I sit with you and talk?"

"Now you sound like a dork," she said, laughing, "I think I liked the 'hey, girl' better."

"Whatever," he said, "So, what are you reading?"

"Are you doing this on a bet or something?" she asked, "Where's the camera? Am I going to get pranked and posted to YouTube?"

"Nothing like that, I promise," he said.

"Then what are you doing here?" she asked.

"What I said before," he answered, "I wanted to come over and talk to you."

"You wanted to talk to me," she said, incredulous, "There has to be something wrong here."

"I see you here all the time, reading," he said, "You hide from everyone when you should be front and center. Girl, you are gorgeous."

Zoey's low self-esteem didn't allow her to realize that Chaucer was right. She was gorgeous. She had an inkling of this somewhere in the back of her mind. Even when she was dressed in her baggy work attire, slinging ice cream, guys always seemed to give her extra attention. She blocked most of this out. She didn't want to be flirted with. She didn't want the social interaction. Still, here she was in the library, being chatted up by the most popular kid in school under presumably no ulterior motives.

"I…" she said, her brain not sure how to process a response, "I, um… I… thanks?"

"So, what are you reading?" he asked again.

"Uh," she started, still trying to wrap her mind around the gorgeous comment, "Emerson. Self-Reliance. Not really my thing, usually, I mean. Kind of an egghead book."

She stumbled through that last part. She was in the middle of a love affair with philosophical books, trying to force herself to think better rather than just escape.

"Huh," he said, sounding interested. She expected no follow up.

"Self-Reliance is good, but I've always liked On Walden Pond better," he said, "Emerson was too much of a nerd. Thoreau was out there, you know, living it. Always seemed like Emerson was just talking about it, not actually doing anything."

She stared at him, her face blank.

"What's wrong?" Chaucer said, smiling, "You surprised that a brotha like me reads?"

"Sort of," she said, nodding.

"Yeah, I keep it on the DL," he said, "Not like I'm ashamed, but I can't talk to any of my friends about books or philosophy. It's not really their thing."

"I can imagine," she said, her eyes narrowing.

He sighed, sensing her cynicism.

"Yeah, I know," he said, "I run with the jock crew. It's a dumb old saying, but you can't judge a book by its cover. I know what I look like and I know what I really am. I could judge you by your cover, too, but here I am, talking to you, trying to get to know you."

"What's my cover look like, then?" she asked.

"You think you're above it all," he said, "You make yourself unapproachable. Toxic. You don't dispute any of the rumors about you. You use it like a force field to keep the world out because you don't want to be hurt. Your cover says that you would never have a kind word for someone like me. Your cover says you never wanted me to sit down in the first place. Your cover says you never want anyone to sit with you here."

She was stunned. Her jaw hung agape as she tried to come up with a response.

"I know I'm right," he said, "You ain't gotta tell me. Not to sound like a creeper or anything but I've been watching you for a while. Right here in the library. You never see me because you never look up from your book long enough to show anyone those pretty blue eyes."

He smiled. She blushed.

"For real?" she asked, followed by a nervous chuckle, "Where's the camera? Seriously this time. This isn't happening right now without some kind of prank involved. Is there a bucket of blood over my head right now?"

"It ain't like that," he said.

"Then what is it like?" she asked.

"It's like this," he said, "Every relationship that happens in my clique winds up turning into a soap opera. Nobody has private business and nobody minds their own. If I'm ever gonna have a real relationship with someone, I don't want it to be with one of those chicks. I want someone real, someone smart, and someone outside the box. Someone who can really know me beyond the front. I want someone who doesn't want the public spotlight. Someone beautiful and intelligent and well read. Someone who doesn't care what anyone thinks."

"Hang on," she said, "You keep saying relationship. That's what this is? You're asking me out?"

"I thought it was kind of obvious," he said shrugging, "But, yeah. I want to find out what's inside your shell. I want to know who you really are because, seriously, you seem like someone I could really get along with."

"But, I'm social cancer," she said, "You know a lot better than I do how high school politics works. You tell people you're dating me and you'll be socially dismembered while I get stomped further into the ground."

"Then we don't tell anyone," he said, "We're seniors. I don't care about this place or any of these people after the next three months are over. The clique I run with, sure I got a couple of boys I keep tight because we came up together, but they'll understand. You'll get to know them. I'm tired of the shallow people around me. I don't care if they don't like you."

"Big talk," she said.

"For real," he said.

"Keep your ego intact," she said, closing her book and standing up, "I'd hate to see the damage."

"Come have coffee with me," he said, "I'll prove to you I ain't messing around."

She thought about this for a moment. On one hand, there was the cutest boy in school asking her out for coffee. On the other hand, there was a severe chance that she was going to be lead into some kind of prank trap once they left the library.

"Ok," she said, "At the risk of embarrassment to both of us, I'll go."

They talked all day. No pranks, no unexpected turns, nothing odd. Just two people talking to each other, realizing they had a lot in common. They talked about books, movies, music, history, mythology and philosophy, coming to the conclusion that Chaucer's assumption was right – they were very compatible.

He gave her a ride home. She told him to drop her off at the end of the block. She was afraid her father might see him and freak out. She had a feeling that her father's idea of relationships didn't really include the acceptance of mixed race couples.

Before she could go, he stole a kiss. To her, it was electric. Small and short, but life-changing.

She had convinced Chaucer that it would be better if they avoided each other in school. There were only three more months until graduation but she didn't want to blow up his social scene and certainly didn't want to become a part of it.

They went out almost every night. Eventually he introduced her to his parents, who both immediately fell in love with her. She knew her father would never afford Chaucer the same respect, so she stayed away from home.

Before the school year was out, Chaucer found out that he was accepted to Harvard on a basketball scholarship. His plan was to ride basketball through undergrad and to get into Harvard Law. She was excited to hear about his dreams but realized that she could never go with him. She would likely get caught up in the community college system and be forced to stay local due to her father's lack of motivation and her lack of a significant salary.

They spent the entire summer together with Chaucer practically ditching the rest of his friends in favor of Zoey. When fall came, she went along with his family to help move Chaucer in. After that, they talked on the phone every night. They texted, they Skyped, they did everything possible to stay in very close touch.

For the first semester, that is.

When basketball season picked up, his calls slowed down. By the end of the first year, he called once a week and saw her at the holidays. By the holiday break of his second year, they spoke every once in a while, but still expressed the same love for each other that they always had.

That break, they had plans. He called her, three days before she was screaming in her bathtub, to call those plans off.

She found out that he was meeting some of his friends at a local bar. Later that night, she decided to take her dad's car to confront him about blowing her off.

She ran a red light. She was driving too fast. She looked away from the road because she saw him exit the bar and step onto the sidewalk. She was completely ignorant of the tanker truck slowing down to make a turn.

In that slow-motion instant where something horrible is about to happen, she remembered slamming on the brakes. Loose objects flew around her. She realized there was nothing she could do to stop in time. She closed her eyes and lowered her head, then bang.

When she woke up, she was in the hospital. She was told about the accident, the black fluid, and how many people were affected by a man calling himself Agent Williams. She wanted Chaucer, but, as they didn't know the two of them were together, they kept them in separate rooms.

The first time they saw each other again was in the conference. They couldn't say anything to each other because, as his name was on the car, her father had been summoned to the hospital. There were a few longing looks, but, she got the impression that Chaucer was more upset than he was relieved.

In addition to the briefcase full of government money, they were presented with an exact replica of the car which had been destroyed in the incident. Her father grumbled, took the keys, and drove very silently home.

When they arrived, her father revealed that the hospital had told him about her boyfriend. Her black boyfriend.

What started as a shouting match ended with her father punching her in the face. She screamed, but he didn't stop. Blow after blow landed on her pale skin, bruising it almost immediately. He shouted that his daughter was a dirty whore not knowing that Chaucer was the only boy she'd ever kissed let alone slept with.

She had enough. He stepped back to take a breath and she seized the opportunity.

With quickness she did not know she possessed, she snatched an empty liquor bottle from the living room table and smashed it across the side of his head. He fell to the ground, limp. She checked his pulse, worried for a moment that she might have killed him, and was only slightly thankful that she could feel his heart beating.

She dragged him into his bedroom and tied him up with an extension cord. She trussed his hands and his feet together then gagged him with his pillowcase. She wanted time to think. She knew that he wouldn't give it to her if he woke up without restraint.

She went to her room. The clothes she wore now bore blood stains from a cut over her eye where her father's wedding band had struck. Frantically, she started throwing clothes into a duffel bag. She grabbed the briefcase full of money and threw it on her bed when she was done. She didn't clearly know what she was doing. She needed time to concentrate.

She decided to clean up and jumped into the shower.

When the first clump of hair came out of her scalp, she thought perhaps it was her father's doing. When the second clump pulled loose, she realized that something was very wrong. Maybe it was the black chemicals, she didn't know. This could be a side effect. Panicking, she pulled clump after clump of her perfectly dyed purple and black hair out by the root. It slipped right out and didn't hurt, which is what made her nervous.

She ran her hands over her newly bald head, errant strands of what used to be her pride now clogging the drain to the point that the bathtub began filling itself. She felt something strange. Something cold and smooth accumulated on the top of her head.

A shock of fear ran through her and every bit of water touching her – the slowly filling bathtub, the drops on her skin, and the streams coming from the showerhead – froze instantly. She could hear the pipes behind the wall bursting as the water expanded into solid ice. She tried to leap out of it in fear, but her feet were now trapped in the bottom of the tub.

She screamed and the ice shot away from her feet, creating frozen waves along the walls. She shivered, more from fear than from the cold, and stepped out to look at herself in the mirror.

She frightened herself more when she was confronted with the foot-and-a-half long spikes of ice now jutting out of her head, swept up and at an angle, where her hair used to be. Her heart thundered in her chest. Her hands shook as she gripped the edges of the sink. She looked her head over carefully, whishing it would just go back to normal when suddenly the spikes shifted shape and returned to a more geometric form of her regular hairstyle, colored deep glacial blue and bright white rather than black and purple.

She staggered backwards as this happened before moving close to the mirror again to look at herself.

After losing herself in the details of her reflection, she thought about changing her hairstyle again, this time to something longer. She was only slightly less surprised as her ice hair responded to her thoughts. She played with this for another fifteen minutes before she could hear her father coming around in the next room, starting to grumble and shout through his gag.

She quickly dressed herself, grabbed her duffel bag and the money, threw the hood of her sweatshirt up to hide her new hair, and sprinted for the door.

She ran to get clear of the house then moved the pace down to a brisk walk, so as not to attract attention. Running down the street with her hood up and a stuffed duffel bag over her shoulder in the middle of the night was not her ideal way of being non-chalant.

She walked a good distance before thinking about a destination. She had no real friends; at least none to whom she would reveal her strange new secret. She had no close relatives and she would certainly not be making the trek to her mother's doorstep. The only place safe that she could think to go was the home of Chaucer's family.

An hour later, she knocked on the door. His mother answered, telling her through the small opened crack that Chaucer was very sick and was up in his room. It was better, she said, if Zoey came back later.

Zoey explained what had happened, spilling everything regarding the accident, her father, the liquor bottle, and the bathroom pulling back her hood to reveal the stylized ice which replaced her hair.

Chaucer's mother was not surprised. She opened the door the full way, revealing a white apron covered in blood which was tied around her waist. She lead Zoey upstairs to Chaucer's room where they both jumped at a scream of pain coming from behind the door. His mother nodded to her and Zoey entered the room, nearly feinting at what she saw.

Chaucer was a bloody mess. Portions of his bones were growing out of his body in large spikes and plates. His now unfamiliar face was contorted in a grimace, trying to repress the cries of agony. A triceratops like plate was growing from his forehead and back along his scalp in a bloody bone Mohawk. One side of his rib cage was pressed hard against his skin, trying to force its way out. She didn't know if it was the lighting in the room or because of his condition, but his skin looked green in parts.

Zoey ran from the room, past Chaucer's mother, and into the bathroom. She closed and locked the door and sat on the floor, wrapping her arms around her shins. She started to cry, but the tears froze along her face, leaving icicles at the edge of her cheeks.

She didn't know what was happening, but she had seen enough superhero movies to realize what this probably was. She knew that there was always a dark side to an origin story. She never thought she would be living through one.

## VII

"Water didn't work?" she asked.

"Of course it didn't," he answered, "Made it a little less noticeable, but only while I stayed in the shower."

"Soap?" she asked, "Shampoo?"

"No," he said, "They both made smoke bubbles. I got so mad the second time that my head exploded and I burned off all the lather."

"It's crazy," she said, moving her hand through the smoke that used to be his hair, "I still can't believe this is real."

"Believe it," Justin said, "I'm still coming to terms and it's happening to me."

Justin took another drag from his cigarette. The exhaled smoke mingled with his ever-smoldering scalp before dissipating into the air. He was sitting next to Lisa, his long-time friend and confidante, on the steps of her front porch. She listened patiently over the past few days as he told her the entire story – from the short walk to the bar through the trip to the morgue with Steph and Char's Mother to pick up the possessions of the deceased.

"Thank you," he said, sighing.

"For what?" she asked.

"For being here," he said, "For listening to me. For letting me cry on your shoulder."

"You don't ever have to thank me for that," she said, "We're friends."

"Thank you, anyway," he said, "You have no idea what it means to me."

She spent the last few days very close to him during Char's closed-casket layout at the funeral home. He was very grateful for this. She was his rock in a room full of blubbering friends and relatives. She held his hand and squeezed hard when he would start to lose it. He knew that, like her, he would have to be strong and stoic as what seemed like everyone they ever knew cycled through the dimly lit parlor, crying and lamenting a life gone far too soon.

"You're welcome," she said, smiling.

They stared out into the suburban street, the bite of the yet-snowless winter was creeping in on them.

"I'm surprised I could keep this hidden," he said, motioning to his head.

"You've done a pretty good job of it at the funeral home," Lisa said.

"Yeah, with a fedora duct taped to my scalp," he said, "Do you know how many weird looks I was getting for wearing a hat inside a funeral home? It's going to be even worse at the service. I would get less dirty looks if I went into a church with smoke hair than I would wearing a hat."

"What about a bald cap?" Lisa said, "We could play it off like you were so depressed you went and shaved your head."

"It would probably just inflate," Justin said, "I would look like an alien."

They laughed. It had been a while since that happened before.

"We have to figure something out," Lisa said, "Otherwise, you'll never be able to leave your apartment. Hats seem to do pretty well."

"Or," Justin said, "I could just take all that money the government gave me, build a big house, and never come out."

"Oh, come on," Lisa said, "Stop being a baby. What kind of life would that be?"

"A safe one," Justin said, "One without repercussions; one where those government guys stay away from me. One where I don't have to be a pariah because I'm a fat geek with smoke for hair."

"Knock it off," she said, "Or, I'm not going with you today. I've had enough of you feeling sorry for yourself. While I sympathize your loss, you can't let this keep you down."

"Fine," he said, "I'll try, but I guarantee nothing."

"What happened to the superhero idea?" she asked.

"I don't think I have that in me," Justin said, "Especially not now. I'm defeated. As far as I'm concerned this is the worst thing that's ever happened to me. It's definitely the worst thing that's ever happened to Char's family."

"Stop," she said, "You're going to wind up blaming yourself and that's not what you should do. It's not what she would want you to do. Don't you think she would have wanted you to take this and make something good out of it?"

"It's pointless," Justin said, "I'm not a comic book character. This stuff only comes second nature to me based on what I read. I'm not the hero-ing type; I'm the type who reads about hero-ing. What am I going to do to the bad guys? Smolder at them?"

"You've got better," she said, crossing her arms, "Show me."

"I showed you the lighter trick," he said, taking another puff of his cigarette, "That's all I'm good for."

"That's a sad batch of crap, what you just said," she said, "Do better or I'm not going with you today."

"You can't keep using that as a threat," Justin said, "It's not fair."

She stared at him, dropping her hip and tapping her foot.

"Fine," he said, walking across the porch to her charcoal grill, "But, stay back. I'm not sure what's going to happen."

She stayed where she was, about five feet away, but pulled her wavy red hair back just in case.

After a few moments of concentration, a small fireball grew in Justin's hand. He looked back at her as she took a curious step forward. He tossed the fireball into the remains of the charcoal and it offered a tiny explosion, spreading the flames around the bowl of the grill.

"Seriously," she said, "You can throw fireballs."

"I haven't really practiced much with it yet," Justin said.

"But, you can throw fireballs," she said, "Like, for-real fireballs. Obviously, they don't hurt you either. Does fire even effect you?"

Justin shrugged and stuck his hands into the small flames remaining in the charcoal.

"Guess not," Justin said.

"So, what you're saying is: you can throw fireballs and you can't be burned, but you don't want to be a superhero."

"Not today, I don't," Justin said, "Now, are you riding with me? We don't want to be late."

Lisa smiled at him and straightened his tie.

"Stop putting yourself down," she said, "Game face. This is going to be a rough day."

Justin pulled the fedora tight onto his head and they walked to his car.

The ride was silent. Justin was lost in thought.

This was bound to be the most difficult challenge he would face in his life; delivering his girlfriend's eulogy. He could feel the tears welling up in his eyes as he went over the words in his head, prompting Lisa to grab his hand and squeeze. He took a deep breath and felt slightly more grounded.

He and Char had been together for a very long time. By all convention, they should have been married. They had been with each other their entire adult lives and co-habitated for more than half of that time.

They often argued, but always over stupid things. They talked about marriage. They would have likely gone through with it in the next year or so if the accident didn't happen. Their future had been cut short by fate and had left Justin disfigured. He felt cheated. Angry.

He missed her more than he understood. He had issues being home alone. He could barely sleep without her next to him. Insomnia had taken hold and it showed in his bloodshot eyes and stubble in the spots he kept smooth adjacent to his goatee. His suit was, unlike his face, neat and clean; pinstriped and pressed and would draw attention away from his sad visage.

When they arrived, Justin pulled the fedora tight to his head.

"You can't get away with wearing that in church," Lisa said.

"I don't have a choice," Justin said, "People are going to think I'm rude for doing it, especially at a funeral, but I figured I could work something into the eulogy as an excuse. I have to wear it or the secret is out. I'm practically a widower. I don't think anyone is going to yell at me today."

"Ready, then?" Lisa asked.

"No," Justin said, "I don't think I could ever be ready for this."

\*\*\*

"13-A, this is 13-Prime, come in."

He didn't respond. His mouth was full.

"13-A, this is 13-Prime. Respond now."

The large bald man sat on a park bench, eating a small bag of popcorn a kernel at a time. When he swallowed, he tapped at the small XIII logo pinned to his lapel.

"Thank you for choosing 13-A," he said through his deep southern drawl, "What can I get for you today?"

The line went silent for a moment.

"Agent Moorsblade," said the stern voice on the other end of the radio, "Please take this seriously. You are setting a bad example for your fellow agents, especially those who are more impressionable."

"It was a harmless little joke," said Moorsblade, "Don't get your panties in a bunch, boss man."

The line went silent again and Moorsblade smirked. He pictured Agent Williams' face turning red which, in fact, it was. After a moment of cool-down time, communications resumed.

"Do you have a visual on the package?" Williams asked, sounding markedly frustrated.

Moorsblade surveyed the scene casually, popping another kernel into his mouth. From behind his sunglasses he watched a crew of people as they finished setting up a stage in the center of the park. He shaded his eyes from the noon-time glare as he turned to look at the road as men in black suits not unlike his own began lining the cordoned and red-carpeted path leading from the sidewalk to the stage.

A large crowd was assembled. A marching band assembled on stage and waited for their cue. A black limo slowed to a stop, perfectly aligned with the red carpet.

"Prime, this is 13-A," said Moorsblade, "Package is in transit and about to be delivered."

"Maintain your visual," said Williams, "13-F, confirm eyes on delivery."

"13-F here," said a female voice, "I have it."

\*\*\*

No one said a word about Justin's hat. It was too somber an occasion.

He was in a pew at the front of the church, crying into Lisa's shoulder. She patted his back as Mike kept his hand on Justin's other shoulder, tearing up himself. Lisa was almost crying, but had given herself a hard pinch on the leg to stay straight. She hated to cry for anything and she knew she needed to be strong for Justin.

This breakdown was prompted by Justin's delivery of the eulogy. It was very eloquent and well-written, as to be expected. It inspired more than a few sobs from the crowd. He started to waver toward the end and, for a moment, Lisa thought she would have to step up to her earlier promise that, if he could not complete his reading, she would finish for him. She was thankful that he only lost control at the very end, running back to their pew before bursting into tears.

The casket was closed in the center of the aisle, as it had been throughout the entire funereal process. The funeral director stated that her body was covered in severe burns, enough that there was not much recognizable nor much that could be done to make it so.

The priest move to the head of the casket and began to close the service. His words were lost to Justin. His crying had subsided and his mind wandered back to those strange times had by every couple – lying in bed and speaking in hypotheticals, asking each other what they would do if the other died. He hated these situations. He never wanted to think that something so terrible could happen. For the first time, that childish sense of invulnerability and immortality had been broken. Before now, he thought it preposterous that anyone, let alone Char, would die any time soon.

"My friends," said the priest, "Before we send Charlene to her rest, please join me in the final prayers for the departed."

\*\*\*

*Hail Mary, full of grace…*

She took the binoculars down from her eyes and dropped to one knee on the gravel-covered rooftop.

She pushed back her olive-drab cloak. It fluttered over-dramatically in the wind of her high-altitude position. In her head, an action movie soundtrack played as she removed a high-tech pistol from the holster on her back and set it down. She reached with both hands to an elaborate harness which ran from her neck to the small of her back, built-in to her tight black jumpsuit.

*…the lord is with thee…*

With a flourish, and with the imagined crescendo of the pounding guitar illustrating that the hero was preparing to get down to business, she snapped an extended stock on to the back of the pistol and an extension to the front which, her weapons briefing told her, would convert the pistol shot into a shotgun-like blast.

The next piece, a long barrel extension with a suppressor at the end, converted the weapon into a large-bore sniper rifle; extremely deadly in the proper hands. As the music in her head hit another series of jammed power chords, she was confident that hers were the proper hands.

*…blessed art thou amongst women…*

The last piece to attend to was the scope.  She was told when first briefed on her weapon that this was the most powerful electronic magnifying device ever created for this purpose.  Not only would it show her target from miles away, but it would also compensate for wind and bullet drop before rendering a visual.  All she had to do was put her target in the center of the reticule and the rifle would hit within 10 micrometers, which she assumed was a very small margin of error.

She closed one of her solid jet black eyes and raised the rifle, looking down at the park.

"13-F to 13-A," she said, "Peek-a-boo."

*...and blessed is the fruit of thy womb, Jesus...*

The scope pinged Agent Moorsblade, outlining his form in red and showing a brief portrait to let her know he was a friendly.  She tapped at a button above the trigger to zoom in on him.  He smiled, waved, and continued eating.

"What's with the popcorn?" she asked.

"We didn't get lunch," he said, "We've been at this all day and I'm hungry.  Guess the scope checks out, then."

"I can hear you chewing," she said, "It's gross."

"You think that's gross, rook," he said, "You ain't seen nothing yet."

"Prime to all" said a different voice in her ear, "Keep this channel clear.  Mission-specifics only.  No chatter."

"Sorry, sir," she said.

"Whatever," said Moorsblade.

She flipped a small stand into position along the barrel of the rifle and laid down, setting the stand on the edge of the building.  She adjusted her view, putting the upper portion of the podium in the center of her site.  From here, she could see the Seal of the President clearly.

"13-F to 13-A," she said, "F-O-F established."

"Sweet," said Moorsblade, "Wait for my word, then drop it like it's hot."

"Roger," she said.

*...Holy Mary, Mother of God...*

A young, well-dressed man approached the podium.  She centered the crosshairs on him as he looked toward the end of the red carpet, waiting.

"Bang," she whispered to herself, "Headshot."

She looked over the scope and could see the crowd stirring.  From here, they looked like an excited ant colony.  She felt adrenaline kicking in.  Back through the scope, she saw the young man acknowledge a signal and lean forward to the small pack of microphones.

"Ladies and Gentlemen," he said, "The President of the United States."

The band kicked in to a rudimentary version of Hail to the Chief as the crowd went crazy. A gentleman exited the limousine flanked by four of the black-suited men, walked down the red carpet tossing waves and greetings to the crowd. Cameras flashed as he mounted the stage and moved to his place behind the podium.

*…pray for us sinners…*

"13-F, this is 13-A," said Moorsblade, crunching another piece of popcorn, "You are cleared for take-off."

The target moved right into her crosshairs. She tapped the button to zoom in further, close enough to see the beads of sweat on his forehead. She could feel her heartbeat slowing. She took a deep breath.

*…now and at the hour of our death…*

She slowly exhaled as she pulled the trigger. His mouth had just opened to begin his speech. He didn't get a word in before the impact.

The shot was not heard. The projectile en route to him was too fast to be noticed by the naked eye. Through the scope, she saw the nickel-sized circle of deep red appear on his forehead as the contents of his skull were emptied out through a much larger exit wound onto the stage behind him.

Blood spattered across the uniforms of the marching band. The projectile was so fast and efficient that he barely moved. For a moment, he stood with a confused look on his face. The crowd was frozen in a moment of comprehension. To her, this happened in slow motion. The blink of an eye between the shot and the realization of the result lasted an eternity.

Someone in the crowd screamed as the President collapsed in a heap. The crowd panicked and started to flee in a frenzy.

*…amen.*

Secret Service agents leapt, a moment too late, to protect the President. They were clueless and shocked. There was no visible assailant and no sound of gunfire. In the small area between the stage and the crowd barrier, agents with their weapons drawn were surveying the crowd for suspects.

One of the agents pressed two fingers to his ear while speaking into the cuff of his shirt. Typical, she thought.

She heard the whir of helicopter blades. They had likely been on standby in case something like this happened. This was usually the first step – closing airspace and establishing superiority. She rolled over in her prone position so she could watch the sky, clutched her rifle tight against her chest, and concentrated. She and her rifle both disappeared from sight.

*Our father, who art in heaven…*

"Control, 13-F," she whispered, "Confirm package drop."

"Package drop confirmed," said the calm voice of Control, "Package registers no vital signs. Operation 26113F, objective one, complete. Proceed to extraction point."

"13-F, this is Prime," said the radio, "Excellent shot. Be aware that aerial surveillance is inbound to your location. Remember to remain perfectly still or your chameleon ability will shift and may give up your position."

"She knows what she's doing," Moorsblade interrupted, "Let her go her own way."

"13-A," said the other voice, "Mind your place. 13-F, continue to extraction when you are satisfied that you have avoided surveillance."

"Roger, Prime," she whispered.

*...hallowed be thy name...*

Two Blackhawk helicopters buzzed over the building, hugging close to the rooftop. She shut her jet-black eyes tight as they kicked up dust and gravel. They headed off toward the park. She was confident that she was not seen.

She slowly rolled over and watched as they lowered to get a closer view of the scene. They started sweeping in a spiral pattern out from the park.

She got up, crouching, and moved very slowly toward the access door through which she had entered.

She was virtually invisible while standing still, but a strange silhouette of her figure could be seen while she was in motion, like looking through water. It reminded her of a movie; something about a jungle and a bunch of beefy dudes being hunted. She couldn't remember the name, but she knew she'd at least seen clips of it. She could see herself thermographically with the improved vision of her black eyes, but thermographics were hard to come by for the average on-looker and her ability made it easy to disappear.

*...thy kingdom come...*

She deactivated her ability once she was inside and the door was firmly shut. This was the upper machine room for the elevator system and, it being the weekend, she knew no one would be up here to see her. Tugging at an area on the stock of her rifle revealed a strap. She connected it near the barrel and swung the rifle across her back.

Banks of large electric motors hummed and creaked as the thick cables spooled around them. She approached one of the motors and opened a hatch in the floor.

She dragged her fingers across the large metal bracer that covered most of her left forearm causing it to light up and reveal its mirrored screen which immediately gave her read-outs on her vitals, the current radio frequency she was monitoring, and other assorted environmental data. She tapped an icon in the lower right hand corner which brought up a keypad emblazoned with symbols and colors. She punched in a sequence and a flat piece of metal ejected from the area near her wrist.

She pulled the metal strip from the bracer revealing that it was a foot-and-a-half long, a few inches wide, and flexible. She wrapped the metal around her right hand and grabbed the top of an elevator cable.

When she was sure of her grip, she dropped down and clamped her feet around the cable as well. She closed her eyes and opened her grip. The metal soles of her boots sparked as she rode down, using the metal on her hand as a brake. Her short red hair was tossed around her pale face as the sparks became more intense.

*...thy will be done...*

There was soft thud and a light clank of metal-on-metal as the soles of her boots met the top of the elevator car. She had left it stopped between the third and fourth floor. Looking back up the shaft, she could not believe that she free-climbed thirty-six stories of elevator cable to reach the roof. She had a harder time believing that she'd slid back down to a soft landing.

She dropped down into the car through the access hatch and knelt down before a black briefcase and a pile of neatly folded clothes. She opened the case and disassembled her rifle. Every component had a fitted foam area except for the base pistol, which she placed on the floor. She removed her olive cloak, folding it neatly, and placing it over the components before attaching a false top which gave the briefcase the appearance of carrying documents and a cell phone.

She dressed in the folded clothes she'd left behind, wearing the black-and-white company suit over the skin-tight field suit, and tucked the oversized pistol into the back of her waistband. Sunglasses covered her strange black eyes as she fixed her hair in the mirrored walls of the elevator car.

*...on Earth as it is in Heaven...*

Pushing up her sleeve to reveal the bracer once again, she tapped at the screen causing a small cable to unravel from it. She connected it to the open emergency panel of the elevator and tapped a few more times. The elevator's lighting changed from the dim emergency stop to the bright fully operational and began to descend.

She rolled her sleeve back down and adjusted the collar of her fitted suit coat, making sure that her lapel pin, the XIII logo, was facing upright.

As the doors opened, she grabbed her briefcase and walked down the hallway tossing a nod to the security guard at the main desk. He didn't notice. He was busy watching breaking news on his tiny television about the President's assassination.

*...give us this day our daily bread...*

She had hoped to blend into a crowd and disappear but the streets outside were nearly abandoned. No one was in her immediate area. She could hear the thrum of panic coming from the park, blocks away. Any people on the streets seemed to be going inside or at least moving away from the scene. Her extraction point was on the other side of that mess and she didn't have time to circumnavigate. She would have to pass through the main area of investigation where someone had just shot and killed the leader of the free world. She was not anticipating a fun trip.

With a sigh, she set off toward the park, trying her best to look convicted and businesslike; as if she were late for some important meeting. It was the weekend, however, and it would be difficult to convince anyone that this was the case. Confidence, she told herself, would get her through. All she had to do was keep her chin up and give no one reason for suspicion.

*...and forgive us our trespasses...*

"Excuse me, ma'am," said a voice behind her.

She kept walking. Confidence. Look too busy for it. Just keep charging through.

"Ma'am," said another voice, "You can't be here. This is a closed perimeter."

She glanced in the mirrored inside edges of her sunglasses and saw two men, black suits similar to hers, wearing earpieces and sunglasses, approaching her quickly.

"You should have been told to stay in your building," said the second agent, "Haven't you heard, the President has been shot."

Say nothing, she thought. Keep going. You know where you have to be. If you ignore them, maybe they'll go away.

They called after her, jogging to gain. They were within arm's reach when she decided the whole confidence thing was for suckers and started to sprint away.

The agents were faster. She saw one of them lunge to grab her and dodged by leaping into a high-arcing front flip. The agent grabbed only air and stumbled underneath her just in time for her to bring the heel of her steel-soled boot down onto the back of his neck. He crumpled to the ground in a heap beneath her foot as she landed, sliding three-feet across the pavement as he hit.

The other agent was lunging as well, having no time to react to his companion being stomped. Her back was to him and she saw it coming with time enough to wheel around and catch him in the face with a steel-toed roundhouse. The second agent collapsed to the ground like a rag doll. She turned on her heel, likely grinding into the vertebrae of the agent she'd stomped, and continued running.

*...as we forgive those who trespass against us...*

As she continued, she looked around for their backup. When she was sure no one was following her, she activated her chameleon ability, leaving a trail of optical distortion behind as she ran.

Agents, SWAT, and even some armed military stood at police barricades at the roads leading into the park. She stopped, then slowed to an almost painful crawl, making it through the barricade.  Once she was inside, she ducked behind a large tree.  She rolled up her sleeve and tapped in the same command that gave her the wire to interface with the elevator.  She pulled on it until it popped out of her bracer.  She curled it around her little finger and jammed one end into her ear, giving her a similar appearance to the other agents wandering around the scene.

She moved quickly, but carefully, not getting too close to anyone, but nodding to a few of the other agents.  She was afraid of being recognized, but this was much faster and beat the hell out of sidling along walls until she reached the opposite end of the park.

Once she made it through, it would be just a few quick blocks to the extraction point.

*...and lead us not into temptation...*

"13-F, this is Prime," said her radio, "Secret Service radio traffic reports two men down, assailant matching your description.  What is your status?"

"Prime, 13-F," she said, "I've made it through the park.  I have not been identified."

"Don't be so sure, girl," said the voice of Moorsblade, "These ain't rookies you're dealing with."

She ducked off into a side alley when she was a block from the park.  With her ability active, she scaled a fire escape and sprinted along the rooftops, making good use of the parkour skills she learned.  She shocked herself when she made the leap over a four-lane cross-street.

When she reached the street of the extraction point, she jumped down, deactivated her chameleon ability, and casually walked along the sidewalk toward the black panel van which was her designated pick-up.  She sighed, satisfied.

"Freeze!" a voice screamed, echoing around the empty canyon of the street.

She stopped in her tracks, once again looking at the rear-view reflection in her sunglasses.  A dozen agents surrounded her, all on foot, all leveling large caliber pistols at her.  She sighed again, this time out of frustration.

*...but deliver us from evil...*

Without a thought, and with lightning speed, she drew the pistol from her back, spun and dropped five of the agents on her left with headshots before they could even think of pulling the trigger.  The other seven agents had aimed, but her chameleon ability kicked in reflexively with the danger.  She sidestepped her position as this happened and seven shots came so close to her that she could feel the wind from the bullets.  She pulled her trigger seven more times, each shot catching its targeted assailant in the center of the forehead and dropping them to the ground.

She became visible again and walked gingerly in reverse toward the rear doors of the van. Her gun was still smoking as she turned and leapt into the vehicle just as the doors were opened.

...*Amen.*

"Prime, 13-A," said Moorsblade, now in front of her, still eating his popcorn, "Delivery girl's back."

"Copy," said the radio, "She has some explaining to do."

"Control, 13-A," said Moorsblade, "All objectives complete. Analysis."

She tilted her head at Moorsblade.

"What did I do wrong?" she asked.

"Analysis complete," said the voice of Control, "Main target neutralized at time signature 00.00.57.49. Operative extracted at time signature 00.01.36.45. Mission called complete by Senior Operative at time signature 00.01.36.56. Collateral property damage: zero. Collateral casualties: twelve deceased, two severely injured."

"Care to explain the twelve dead Secret Service outside the van, darlin'?" asked Moorsblade.

"They got the drop on me," she said, stuttering, "I... I didn't know what to do. I just did what came naturally."

"That so?" said Moorsblade, "Those people weren't the target. You eliminated the target. You beat them up, you knock them out, you do what you have to do. What you don't do is leave a trail of bodies leading right back to your extraction point."

He was frustrated. His accent came out more when he was frustrated.

"I just," she stammered, "I didn't know what to do. I was scared."

"Scared?" he said, scoffing, "Sweetheart, I've been with this outfit for a long time. The first thing I learned was to forget about fear. Looks like we're going to have to run it again to teach you that lesson."

"Again?" said a woman's voice from the front of the van, "Christ, Johnny, she's run it eight times already. I think she gets the gist. She didn't really have much choice with that last little surprise. Twelve armed Secret Service at the last second? You can't tell me you wouldn't have done the same."

"I wouldn't have, Joey," he said, "And you know it."

"Yeah, well," Joey said, "Not all of us are bulletproof."

"We're running it again until we get it perfect," said Moorsblade.

"Give her a break, Johnny," said Joey.

"Prime?" Moorsblade called out.

"She runs it again, Agent Briggs," said their radios, "Control, reset scenario. Variable group 17R/Delta. For the record, Agent Gentile, good job. And, nice shooting."

"Thank you, Agent Williams," she said.

"Remember, Char," said Moorsblade, "No fear."

"No fear," she said, dropping the magazine from her gun and loading a fresh one, "Right."

Moorsblade opened the doors and Char leapt out of the van.

"Control," said Moorsblade, "Begin mission timer."

\*\*\*

The sun was setting. Purples and oranges played across the horizon. The cold winter wind made his long leather jacket ripple and disturbed his smoke hair.

Justin stared at a pile of dirt in the middle of the large cemetery. This pile, he was told, would have to wait until spring to be tamped down, leveled, and seeded. Warmer weather would allow for more manipulation of the dirt and the placement of her headstone. It would be well into the summer before the grass would grow and this patch of land would become just another plot. For now, his girlfriend's grave site stood out from the rest; a testament to his feelings for her.

"You would have liked the ceremony," he said, "People had so many nice things to say. Some people you wouldn't even expect. They wanted me to let you know they'll miss you. Horribly."

His throat tightened. His eyes watered. The tears were absent. He felt weak, dehydrated, and drained.

"I wanted to let you know how horribly I'll miss you, too," he continued, "I know how much you would have missed me if this was the other way around. I miss you when I try to sleep at night. I miss you when I wake up in the morning. I don't know if I can handle it. I'm going crazy. But, I know you would have wanted me to keep going. I know you wouldn't want me to quit just because you're gone. I know you'll be out there, watching me. I know we'll be together again someday."

He placed a single rose on the mound, burying the stem in the dirt to prevent it from blowing away.

"I love you, Char," he said, "Goodbye."

## VIII

Jess was being watched.

She didn't know how she knew it, but she was sure. Chills ran down her spine constantly. She couldn't focus on what was making it happen, but when she did, she got a terrible feeling.

Jess had been teaching herself to focus her psychic abilities through meditation. The Nerd Corps of comic-book-reading, role-play-gaming friends who surrounded her believed it to be the next logical step. All of the most powerful fictional psychics - of which she found there was a surprising laundry list – meditated to better themselves. As there were no real world examples to follow, this was the best guidance she had.

Justin stepped up with a book on transcendental meditation he'd had for years but never honestly implemented. He didn't have the patience for it. He told her the little he'd learned and left it in her much more capable, if not anxious, hands.

A few days into her experimentation, she found that she could tap into a sort of psychic radar. It was something straight out of a movie; she could locate people within a pretty large radius and tap into their minds. Once she discovered this, it raged out of control, her nose bled severely, and she caught a high-level migraine from hearing the thoughts of thousands of people at once.

She refined the technique and started to visualize every mind as an individual point of light on a black field. She concentrated on reaching out to touch but one of them and, when she did, she was inside that person's mind. She could hear their thoughts, she could see their memories, and she could see what they were doing at that moment.

This proved to be extremely awkward as the first person she tapped happened to be masturbating in front of his computer. It was at this point she realized she could manipulate them as, when she thought he should stop, he did so mid-stroke, stood up, put his junk away, and left the room to go about doing whatever he was doing before he sat down to rub one out.

She freaked out inside. She could manipulate people into doing whatever she wanted and she wasn't afraid to continue practicing it. She tapped into random people and made them do simple things – make a fist, raise your arm, walk over there – but she told no one. She knew if the rest found out this particular capability, they would definitely look at her differently. She figured she'd have to tell them eventually but being a psychic already had the rest of the group on edge.

The guys also helped her to find her telekinetic abilities. This largely involved studying Star Wars related properties, which was not entirely unenjoyable to her. The first day, she had things flying through the air. By the third day, she was doing some more intricate manipulations like remotely typing on a keyboard. She wasn't sure how much more she could develop this, but she was sure she could get creative if necessary.

None of her abilities helped her to dispel the strange feeling she was currently experiencing. It was like someone was staring over her shoulder, observing what she was doing. She wondered if this was what it felt like when she entered someone else's mind.

The lights on the black background began to fade and darken. Her radar was faltering. The only thing that remained was one bright light and it began moving toward her.

Hot fear dropped in her stomach. She wanted to break the meditation but something was holding her back, like trying to awaken from a nightmare. She was trapped. She held her arms up in front of her as the light approached, still trying to pull herself away. It charged at her like a train in a tunnel and, as it was about to strike, she screamed.

It wasn't until she hit her head on the edge of the coffee table in Kurt's living room that she realized she had been floating a foot or so above the couch where she started her meditation. Now on the floor, she rolled onto her back, opening her eyes. The room was spinning. She had a terrible headache and could taste copper in her mouth. She wiped her upper lip and saw blood on her fingertips, likely from her nose. She felt the chill of the cold sweat in her hair and on her body.

The silhouettes of three people appeared in her vision. It took her a moment to focus before she realized it was Justin, Josh, and Kurt. She sat up and put a hand against her throbbing temple before putting the other one on the spot on her forehead where she impacted with the table.

"You ok?" Kurt asked.

"No," she said, "My brain feels like it's going to explode."

"Tell me exactly what happened," Justin said.

"I," she stammered, "I don't know for sure. I think I might have been concentrating too hard. Don't worry, I'll be fine. It's nothing."

"It's not nothing," Kurt said, "You screamed like you were being stabbed in the back."

"I just overstretched myself," she said, pushing the comforting hand of her boyfriend away before it could touch her, "The scream was probably a reflex or something. Seriously, I'm fine. I just need to get in the shower. I feel disgusting."

She stood up, shrugging off their help. The room was still spinning but she managed to get her balance without assistance.

Josh opened his mouth to comment.

"No, Josh," Jess said, cutting him off, "You can't join me."

"Can you stop being psychic for a minute?" Josh asked, "You'll ruin all the one-liners."

She rolled her eyes and walked away, leaving the three of them in the living room.

Kurt stared at Josh, narrowing his eyes.

"What?" Josh said, "It was a joke, man, relax."

"Anyway," Justin said, "What was this incredible thing you wanted to show us?"

"Oh, right," Josh reached into his pocket and produced a box of playing cards. He held it up for the other two to see.

"Don't tell me you made me drive you over here so you could show us a stupid magic trick," Justin said.

"Come on, man, think about it," Josh said, "I swiped this from the hospital, remember?"

"Oh, right," Justin said, "That pack of cards I ridiculed you for swiping. Is this supposed to remind us that you'll take candy from babies if you see fit?"

"I didn't steal playing cards," Josh said, "I took the box they were in."

"Surely a crime for the ages," Kurt said.

"Would you guys lay off me and let me explain?" Josh asked.

"As long as we can get to the point soon," Kurt said.

"Fine," Josh said, "I'll let this speak for itself."

He opened the card box and threw a wad of taped –up gauze onto the coffee table after which he sat back and spread his arms over the back of the couch as though the other two should recognize it as something of incredible importance.

Kurt and Justin looked at each other.

"Let me guess," Justin said, "You're cutting yourself and you need us to help bandage your little emo wounds."

"No, dick," Josh said, "Open it up."

"Dude, we're not interested in your medical waste," Kurt replied, "Just tell us what it is and spare the suspense already. I'm not going to play guessing games all day."

Josh sighed and leaned forward. He removed the tape from the gauze and revealed a cotton ball on which was crusted a small black stain.

"You're bleeding black from your little emo wounds?" Justin asked.

Josh casually reached and touched Justin on the forehead, shocking him. Justin jumped and swung to smack Josh's hand out of the air only to be shocked again.

"This is it," Josh said, frustrated, "This is the stuff. The black goo from the accident."

"How the hell did you get that?" Kurt asked, "They decontaminated us so thoroughly most of us are still down a few layers of skin."

"You guys didn't have it in your eyes," Josh said, "When I woke up, that Agent Williams guy was too busy scaring the crap out of me to notice that I pocketed this. I stole the card box because I needed somewhere to put it that it would be safe and wouldn't get contaminated."

"What are you going to do with it?" Justin asked.

"I've got a friend who's a doctoral chem student," Josh said, "Thought I'd have them analyze this and see what it is. Maybe we could find a cure or something."

"Cure?" Kurt said, "Why would any of us want a cure? This is the greatest thing that ever happened! We have super powers! I thought this was something you guys always wanted! A cure would be wasting all the potential we've just been given!"

Justin and Josh looked at each other before turning back to Kurt.

"Speak for yourself," Josh said, "I can't touch anyone without zapping them unless I'm wearing gloves."

"Not to mention that some of us can't go out in public without specialized headgear," Justin said, "Also, the girlfriend I've had since high school is now dead. Beyond my mourning, I'm being forced into a comic book archetype that I'm not really looking forward to satisfying, so the sooner we could cut this off, the better."

"You think you're being forced into an archetype," Kurt said with a huff.

"Yes," Justin said, "I'm the reluctant one who is supposed to be spurred on by the death of a loved one. The audience sympathizes with me because of my physical deformity and because, behind all of my cynical running commentary, I'll always be intensely remorseful over the death of my lover."

"And you think avoiding this is worth stripping yourself of what is essentially a miracle," Kurt said.

"Yes," Justin answered, "Because I will likely be the comic relief which means I will either be dead before the end of the story or watch many of my friends suffer or die which would darken my personality, likely making me more of an anti-hero and even further endearing me to the audience and giving me a bigger role in the sequel."

The others stared at him.

"You have seriously lost it," Kurt said.

"No, I haven't," Justin said, "Stereotypical origin story, stereotypical government agency, stereotypical future. It's logic."

"Based in fiction," Josh said.

"Life imitates art," Justin said, "Don't worry, when things like that go down, I'll say that I told you so."

"Honestly, I'm just upset that I can't touch my girlfriend," Josh said.

"That makes sense to me," Kurt said, pointing at Josh, "And, if you're that upset, maybe you should get your guy to cook up some antidote. I won't be joining you, of course, and I don't think Jess will be either."

"Antidote is a bad idea," Justin said.

"You just said that you wanted it!" Kurt shouted.

"I didn't say I wanted it," Justin said, "I was making a case for why we should want it. If any of us keep going with this whole hero thing, an antidote could be used against us. Not to mention the fact that if Sparky the Wonder Dog here hands a sample off to someone and they make batches, even to test, the gig is up and we're going to have problems from the stereotypical shadowy government organization. Someone will figure out what it does and that's how super villains are made, boys and girls."

"So, do you want the antidote or not?" Josh asked.

"I don't want whatever gave us super abilities out in the open," Justin said, "I want the antidote, but not at that cost."

"It's not like we can generate this in-house," Kurt said, "Last I checked, none of us were lab-grade chemists."

"The minute anyone says anything about this," Justin said, "We're done. If they blog about it, post it on Facebook, tweet it, or make a YouTube video showing something crazy, it's all going to end. The government will step in and write it off as a special effects-based hoax and trace that guy right back to us at which point it's all black bags and lock up before they systematically vivisect every last one of us to figure out what makes us tick the way we do."

"That's dark," Josh said.

"It's not wrong, is it?" Justin asked, "You can call me paranoid all you want, but you should have that kind of fear at least in the very back of your mind. Better alive and dealing with this situation than cut to shreds in the most painful death imaginable."

"Fine," Josh said, putting the cotton away, "Maybe I'll just learn to control my little problem. I can hash that out. I feel sorry for you and Budda, though."

"Pity us, then," Justin said, "I'll find a way and so will he."

"I guess that's that, then," Kurt said, "Now, there's something I want you guys to see while you're here. Come on."

He stood up and almost ran through the kitchen to the basement stairs. Josh and Justin followed slowly behind.

As they came down the stairs, the evidence of Kurt's super ability was amazingly tangible. Half of Kurt's basement had always been dedicated to storage and laundry but the other half was reserved for music. Many times both of them had been down here and none of those times did the place look even remotely serviceable as the studio about which Kurt had dreamed ever since he became a homeowner.

Now, the place was amazing – a bevy of flashing lights, speakers, and instruments behind soundproof glass with egg crate lining the other walls. It was everything he'd ever talked about and, now that he had the money and the innate ability to understand any piece of technology he touched, it was real.

"This is awesome," Josh said.

"Impressive, even," Justin said.

"Yeah," Kurt said, dismissively, "But that's not why I brought you down here."

He pulled away a rug near a basement door that lead to the backyard revealing a skinny wooden trap door in the middle of the concrete floor. It had been painted over many times along with the floor and looked as though it would be stuck shut.

"I never tried to open this thing before," Kurt said, "The realtor told me it was an old coal cellar and the previous owners of the house had it sealed shut to prevent a draft from coming up from below. I was never really curious about it until I started building too much studio and was losing room for storage, so I pried it open."

Kurt reached down to a small metal ring and pulled up. With a bit of effort the door creaked open and revealed a set of old wooden stairs. They would need to descend sideways as the opening wasn't really wide enough for a normal person's shoulders and Justin was slightly overweight as it was.

"We're going to need some light for this," Kurt said, standing up.

With a whoosh, Justin's fist burst into flames. He held it at his eye level.

"We're good," Justin said, standing up and going down the stairs first.

The others shrugged and followed him.

They emerged into a small sub-basement. The walls were rough stone, carved out and one piece. It was more of a cave with stairs than any coal cellar they had ever seen.

"Awesome," Josh said, "You have the Temple of Doom in your basement."

"It's a little small for the Temple of Doom," Justin said.

"Yeah, but it's huge for a coal cellar," Josh replied.

"If we're going to be crime fighters," Kurt said, "We're going to need a secret base, right?"

Justin and Josh exchanged eye rolls.

"Seriously?" Justin said, "This place is big, by the rust-belt coal-cellar standards, but this is hardly fit for the living, superhuman or otherwise."

"I'm almost scraping my head on the ceiling," Josh said, "And how is Budda supposed to fit in here?"

"We can widen the entrance," Kurt said, pointing at one of the walls, "And we can start digging that way. Toward the street. This house is near the bottom of a large hill and faces further elevation, so if we dig that way we should be below any utility lines or pipes. We might even be able to dig further into the hill if our needs expand."

"He sure sounds serious," Josh said, looking at Justin.

"Dude, what's wrong with basing our operation out of your living room?" Justin asked, "Or even my living room? Anyone's house?"

"If we were at someone's house, it would be a huge inconvenience and we would wind up watching TV all day or playing video games," Kurt said, "Also, the supercomputer would never fit."

"The what?" Justin asked, flatly.

"The supercomputer," Kurt said.

"Supercomputer," Justin repeated.

"Yes," Kurt said, "Su-per-com-up-ter. You're fairly tech-savvy, you understand the term, right?"

"Where the hell are you getting a supercomputer?" Justin asked.

"I'm going to build it," Kurt said, "But that's beside the point. I want a place that we can fortify. Somewhere that's out of plain sight. Somewhere we can work and plan and build in secret."

"You want a bat-cave," Josh said.

"Essentially," Kurt said, shrugging and nodding.

"This is getting stupid," Justin said.

"Says the man who thinks he can predict the future based on pop-culture stereotype," Kurt responded.

"You're playing into it right now, man," Justin said.

"Hey guys," shouted a voice from the hatch, "You down there?"

"No, Budda," Josh said, "We're just a bunch of ghosts who are having an argument."

Budda's head appeared in the opening at the top of the stairs.

"What are you guys doing?" he asked.

"Wait, how the hell did you even get here?" Justin asked, "You couldn't possibly drive like that."

"Steph's mom has a mini-van," Budda said, "We had to take out the middle seats, but she gave me a lift. I had to go in through the tailgate. I ran straight around back as soon as I got here so no one would see me."

"Smooth," Justin said, face-palming.

"So, what's going on?" Budda asked.

"We're thinking about using this space down here as a base," Kurt said.

"What, like a bat-cave?" Budda said, "Sweet!"

"At least someone's on-board," Kurt said, "Do you think you can get down here?"

"No way, dude," Budda said, "I'm too wide for this door."

"Then punch it," Kurt said.

Justin and Josh looked at him confused.

"What?" Budda asked.

"You heard me," Kurt said, "Punch the floor next to it. Give it everything you've got. Call it a test of strength."

"Uh," Budda said, the gears of his mind audibly grinding with consideration, "Ok."

"Dude," Justin said, "You're going to let him punch into your basement floor?"

"I want to test our digging equipment," Kurt whispered, "If he can't punch through, it's going to be a much harder time."

There was a loud impact from above.  Dust shook from the ceiling.  He had punched the floor along the wall side.  A small crack was visible through the stone.

"Oh, come on," Kurt said, "You can do better than that.  Don't hold back."

"I didn't want to mess up your floor too much," Budda said, "I kinda spider-webbed it."

"Don't worry about the floor," Kurt said, "Hit it in the same spot. Go as hard as you can."

There was a pregnant moment of anticipation, then a loud grunt, then the room shook beneath their feet.  The impact was loud and caused small pebbles and debris to shoot out and hit them.  A cloud of dust like billowing smoke was now next to what was left of the stairs.

When things began to settle, they could see a crater widening the original door.  Light streamed in from the basement.

"What the hell was that?" said Jess in all of their heads.

"Nothing," Kurt said, out loud, "We were just testing something."

"The whole house shook," she said, "Car alarms are going off outside."

"Sorry," Budda said, "My bad."

He slid into the cellar through the newly formed hole and was nearly bent in half by the height of the ceiling.  As he walked around, looking at the walls, an audible stone-on-stone noise could be heard.  It sounded like a temple door opening in an old adventure movie.

"Wow, it's awesome down here," Budda said.

"Think you could help us dig it out?" Kurt said, "Maybe not as loud as that?"

"Yeah," Budda said, "That was fun."

"Good," Kurt said, "Well, we're all dirty already, why don't we get started?  I think I have a pickaxe in the shed."

Josh and Justin stared at each other, looking disappointed.

"It was your idea to come here," Justin said.

Josh sighed and pushed up the sleeves of his dirt-covered thermal undershirt.

It was late by the time Josh made it home.

Emma was awake and at her computer with a steaming cup of coffee next to the keyboard.  She pulled her leopard-print robe closed as the door opened.

"What the hell have you been doing?" she asked, disgusted.

Josh was covered head-to-toe in dirt.  The clothes he set out with now looked like the worst examples shown in the best laundry detergent commercials.  His spiky blonde hair was matted brown and mud – dust mixed with sweat – clung to every inch of exposed skin.  His glasses, however, were surprisingly clean.

"Digging out the bat-cave," Josh said, "Don't ask."

"Some guy stopped by looking for you earlier," she said, "He left a package for you.  Said it was important, something you two were working on."

Without looking up from what she was doing, she waved an errant finger at the couch.  A sealed manila bubble envelope sat on the armrest.  Josh's name was written on the front in black permanent marker along with a large red stamp reading "urgent".

He stopped for a minute, realizing what this was and why he had set out to Kurt's what felt like so long ago.

He had kept one of the cotton balls to show the guys but he had sent the other one ahead to begin the lab tests.  He figured they wouldn't have a problem with it but now he felt guilty at the thought.  They were so adamantly against his idea and here he was with the potential cure in his hands.

He moved to sit on the couch.

"Get out of the living room," Emma said, still not looking up, "Go take a shower.  You're disgusting and you stink.  Don't touch anything we own until you're done."

He moved from his half-sitting position and took the envelope with him into the bathroom.

He started the shower but didn't even get undressed before he opened the envelope.

Inside was a translucent vial with a white label listing many unintelligible numbers and symbols written in pen.  The only truly legible word was the largest: Unknown (?).

A note fell out of the envelope.  He picked it up, putting large dirty fingerprints in the margin, and read the same scribbly shorthand which annotated the vial.

*Josh,*

*Was able to duplicate the sample you gave me.  Had to "borrow" the main catalyst (very, very rare) from cold storage to finalize formula (read: you owe me one).  Other unfamiliar elements also present. Strange combination of chemical and biological components.  Was not able to identify certain other reagents but when small sample of original substance was added, composition matched.  In other words, the sample could not be completely lab-replicated without using the sample itself. What you see is what is left after extensive testing.  Could not produce more due to lack of original material as well as main (and rare) reagent.*

*Substance does not appear to be a pathogen nor does it appear overtly harmful.  Tests inconclusive for most part.  Could not synthesize antigen or antidote as it contains no base toxic or harmful properties.*

*Apologies if this puts you out.  Kept a lid on things to the best of my ability.*

*Again, you owe me one.*


Josh turned the vial over in his hand and could see the viscous black fluid rolling around inside.  He was having trouble believing that what killed Char, what gave all of them these insane powers, could be looked at by a professional chemist and dismissed as harmless.

He undressed, got into the shower, and closed the curtain.

As he scrubbed, he could hear Emma enter the room and put the toilet seat down.

"What's this?" she asked.

He peeked out from behind the curtain and saw her holding the vial.

"Something the guys said they didn't want me to do," Josh answered.

"Anything else you can tell me about it, Captain Clarity?" she asked.

"It's a reproduction of the chemical from the accident," Josh said, "I wanted to see if he could make a cure but…"

"…it's not a pathogen or overly harmful, blah blah," Emma said, "I found the letter.  He seriously thinks this stuff is ineffective?"

"Apparently," Josh said.

"Did you tell him anything else?" Emma asked, "People dying, getting powers?"

"No," Josh said, "I didn't want to sound crazy.  I just wanted to see what he would come up with."

"What are you going to do with it?" Emma asked.

"Don't know now," he said, "I was hoping for a cure so that I might be intimate with my girlfriend again."

"It's not my fault you shock everything you touch," she said.

"I know," he said, "But, seriously, I don't know what to do with it.  The guys didn't want me to send it for analysis for this exact reason.  They didn't want any of this out in the open.  Justin kept screaming about supervillains and using it against us and stuff."

"Let me have it," Emma said.

Josh quickly pushed back the shower curtain.

"What?" he shouted, "No!  What if you take it and, like, turn into a puddle of goo or something?  You don't know what could happen!  You could wind up like Char.  This isn't something fun, it's incredibly dangerous."

"Not to use, dumb ass," she said, "Let me have it and I'll hide it.  That way, when you become these big-time superheroes, the bad guys can't find it and make kryptonite or whatever."

Josh tilted his head.

"You know," he said, "That's actually a really good idea."

"What can I say," Emma said, "I read a lot of comics."

She flushed the toilet and walked out. Josh shouted as the cold water hit him.

"Night, honey!" Emma said, shutting the bathroom door.

## IX

He was lying in bed, reading the top book in a large stack of hardcovers that sat near his nightstand. It was difficult to turn pages. His fingers were much larger than before and his fingernails had grown into thick claws. He eventually figured a way to put the sharp point of his index finger claw on the upper corner and gently slide it across the book. He had shredded multiple pages this way. It took concentration to restrain his strength.

After the first chapter, he tossed the book to the floor where it landed on a pile of other volumes that he didn't care for or deemed useless and grabbed the next book on the stack.

He was looking for something; an answer as to what he had become. This proved to be difficult research.

Before he opened his latest attempt, he stopped and stared at the back of his hand. He positioned the bright reading lamp on his headboard and looked closely.

His skin had gone from mocha brown to pale green. Dried blood was crusted around his knuckles which had extruded from his hand into sharp spikes. The back of his hand was now lumpy with overgrown and displaced bones. He dropped the book onto the bed and made a fist. The skin tightened up. It was thick. It looked more like elephant or rhino skin than anything human. His spiked knuckles looked like a weapon.

He remembered his long thin fingers. He thought about dribbling a basketball, curling his hand around a pencil, touching his girlfriend's body. None of that would be the same again. He was having enough trouble turning pages in a book. The idea of any fine motor skills seemed so far away now. He closed his eyes and wished it wasn't happening. He prayed it wasn't real and that he would wake up back into his normal life.

"Chaucer?" said a timid female voice from the other side of his closed bedroom door.

He opened his eyes and looked down at his hand. For a moment, he thought his prayers worked.

"What?" he shouted.

"We're worried about you," she said, "You haven't come out of your room since this started happening."

"I'm not going to, Zoey," he said, "I'm some kind of monster now. You don't need to see me like this. Neither do my parents."

"Chaucer, let me in," she said, "I want to see you. I want you to know you're not alone."

"No," he said, sitting up and looking at his hands, "You don't want to see this."

"I love you, Chaucer," she said, "Whatever is wrong with you, we can deal with it."

He stood up.  The floor creaked under his massive clawed feet. The long spikes shooting up from his shoulder blades touched the ceiling even though he crouched down as he'd grown a foot or so in his transformation.

When he reached the door, he fumbled with the lock.  He found himself again fearing that his fine motor skills had taken a permanent vacation.

When he was able to undo the lock, he grasped the knob and twisted with such amazing strength that it crushed like an aluminum can in his hand.  He left the door to swing open and stood in the middle of the room.  As Zoey entered, the reading light drew her attention to the empty bed which looked like a gigantic dried scab.  Blood pooled and crusted on his sheets every time another bone decided to protrude from his body.  The bed was shredded down to the mattress springs from his sharper edges and had been soaked through to the box spring.  Looking at this, Chaucer was amazed he didn't bleed out and die during his ordeal.

"Oh, God," Zoey said, covering her mouth as she stared at the imitation murder scene.

He sighed.  She turned to him and gasped, her eyes growing wider still.

"I know," he said, lowering his head, "It's terrible."

She reached out and touched his face.  His forehead had sprouted a cross between a triceratops plate and a bone Mohawk.  All of his hair had fallen out.  His jaw was now wide with a large underbite, enough that his larger lower canines stuck up from it and over his top lip. Small spikes replaced his eyebrows and two long ones jutted out from the corners of his chin, almost like a goatee.  His nose shrank and was now upturned, more like a snout.  Her eyes showed her reaction.

"Are you..." Zoey started.

"No," he said, "I'm not. I'm not anything; hurt, ok, feeling better, feeling worse... I'm none of the above."

He looked up and noticed something different about her as well.

"Your hair," he said, "What did you do to your hair?"

It wasn't her regular style.  In the low light of the room, he could see it was spikes of blue and white going up at an angle away from her face.

"Oh, sorry," she said, her hair changing to its regular style and shifting from mostly white to a dark glacial blue right before his eyes, "I haven't been doing it in the morning."

His large jaw dropped.

"What happened?" he asked.

"Something like what happened to you," she said, "It must have been the accident."

He closed his eyes again.  Tears rolled down his face.

"I should have called you, baby," he said, "I should have done the right thing. If I wasn't down there that night, everything would be normal. If I didn't ignore you; if I didn't make you come looking for me, everything would have been fine."

She lightly stroked his cheek with her hand. The tears froze as they touched her.

She stepped into him, hugging him around the waist which was now at her eye level. Half of his ribcage, along with his sternum, now stuck out from his body. There were sharper bits and spikes but she was careful to find fleshier parts to cling to and held him tight.

He gently closed his arms around her, making sure that the protrusions did no harm, and stroked her ice hair with a feathery touch.

"You stink," she whispered.

"Thanks, baby," he said, chuckling.

"Seriously," she said, "You've been up here for a week covered in rotting blood. I think it's time for a shower. You should clean up and come downstairs. Your parents are worried about you."

"Have you been here the whole time?" he asked.

"Yeah," she said, "I can't really go home after what I did. Your mom has been letting me use the guest bedroom. She knew you didn't want to be bothered. I went out and got everything you asked for and let her bring them in. I didn't want to add to your stress."

He smiled. The way his teeth had twisted and grown, he imagined it wasn't a particularly pleasant sight and he quickly wiped the expression from his face.

"Come on," she said, "A hot shower will do you some good. It'll do everyone some good. The whole upstairs hallway smells like an abattoir. If you're going to keep holding me, I don't want you stinking like a zombie."

Within a few moments, he was hunched down in the shower. His body had grown wider as well as taller, forcing him to turn from side to side as the water ran over him in halves. Streaks of red mixed with soap slid into the drain as he tried to address every new crevice. There were places behind his bony plates that were in serious need of cleaning. His loofah shredded on the many hooks and points and became useless within the first ten minutes. He called out to Zoey and had her bring him a kitchen scrub brush instead.

After an hour or so, he smelled almost human. He dried himself delicately, trying his best not to shred the towel. He found a large pair of boxer shorts and track pants waiting for him as he finished. Thankfully, they both slipped easily over the large curved spikes that sprouted from his kneecaps and the spiny plates that emerged from his shins. The waists of the clothes were enough to accommodate the outgrowth of his hips as the top of his pelvic bone on both sides now covered his side and lower back like a plate of armor.

Looking himself over in the mirror, he realized that most of the bones now outside of his body served some sort of greater purpose. The knuckle-spikes, the claws which were now his fingernails, the spiked plates on the top of his forearms, the large spine jutting out from his left shoulder, even the plate on his head seemed designed for either offense or defense. For better or worse, he had evolved.

This realization did not dissuade his mind from wandering to the negative points. He would never play basketball again. There was no way he could ever finish college or hold down a full time job. He wanted to go to law school. He wanted to do something good with his life. Now, he thought, because of the girl he loved, he would never get to truly live his life.

His rage was building. As he stared at himself in the mirror, he could see his eyes narrowing. He wanted badly to put his fist through his own reflection. He clenched his fist. He could feel his claws digging into his thick skin.

"You look like a new man," Zoey said, standing in the doorway of the bathroom.

"I look like a monster," he said, not turning away from his scowling reflection.

"I still love you," she offered.

He turned to her, the rage still burning inside him. This was all her fault, he thought. As soon as their eyes met, the rage began to fade. He realized how beautiful she was, even dressed down in a t-shirt and jeans. He couldn't help but look her over and sigh.

"I love you too, baby," he said, turning back to the mirror, "But this is too much. The pain was unbearable. Moving on will be unbearable. I've got to leave everything I ever wanted behind and start over. Like this."

"It's not all bad," she said, "I'm still here."

"You won't want me," he said, "Sooner or later, you're going to want something normal. You can still have that."

"I can't," she said, "I can't have normal, the same way you can't have normal."

"What, because of your ice-hair?" he asked, "You can hide that. It doesn't look strange for you. I can't hide this. I can't go out in public as a green-skinned, spike-covered monster."

"I've been reading a lot of comics," Zoey said, "Kind of like research. You could use a reverse disguise. Trench coat, hoodie, that kind of thing. We can dress you up so that all the stranger bits are covered."

"How do you explain an eight-foot tall guy dressed in a trench coat with spikes coming out of his back?"

She sighed and stared, unsure what to say next.

"I should be back at school right now," he said, his voice growing louder, "I should be practicing with my team. I'll never be able to go back. That whole reality, my entire future, was ripped away from me because of this. Because of some stupid accident. Because someone over-reacted when I didn't pick up my cell phone. I'll never be normal again. I'll never be anything!"

She spoke to him, but he didn't hear it. The rage was deafening. He stared at himself in the mirror, his eyes locked on the disfigured face which he barely recognized as his own. With a roar, he pulled back his fist and slammed it through the mirror. The full extension of his arm carried his fist through the medicine cabinet, the bathroom wall, and the interior wall of his own closet on the other side.

Zoey stood still. She had stopped speaking in mid-sentence, but he didn't hear what she was saying anyway. Her face was locked in a shocked expression. There were a few moments of silence where the only thing he could hear was his own labored breaths.

He pulled his arm out of the wall. Jagged bits of glass and tile stuck in his hand but did not penetrate the skin. He didn't feel any pain even after putting his fist through four or five layers of different material. He opened his hand and shook it over the sink, clearing most of the debris from it.

He looked down, then closed his eyes.

"I'm sorry," he said, "I have to go."

"Go?" she asked, stepping out of his way as he charged out of the bathroom and around the corner to his bedroom, "Go where?"

"I just," he started, thinking about things as he rummaged through his closet, "I just have to go."

Hanging in his closet were new clothes, things she must have picked out for him; an oversized black hoodie and a very large coat. He augmented these with a stocking cap and gloves, both of which were stretched to their limit and shredded by his spikes, but they would do the job of covering his head and hands.

He wrapped a scarf around his face to cover his misshapen jaw and his pug-like nose. He didn't bother with shoes. If he didn't bleed after punching his way through the bathroom and if he couldn't really feel the heat of the shower, he figured tromping around in the snow with his gigantic clawed feet would likely not bother him in the slightest.

Zoey plead to him from the hallway, but he stopped listening. He needed to get out of here. When he was dressed, he put up his hood and ran down the stairs. She chased him as he crushed the front door knob and walked out into the night.

Zoey trailed him as he started down the snow-covered sidewalk. A semi-circular wall of ice shot up from the snow, surrounding the yard. It was thick, opaque, and tall. He tried to reach the top to hop over, but it grew higher.

"Are you doing this?" he shouted back at her, "Is this what you got out of this deal?"

"Chaucer," she called to him from the bottom of the stoop, "I don't want you to go. Let's talk about this."

"I don't want to talk," he shouted back, "I need to get out of the house. I need to get my head straight. This is too crazy."

"What if someone sees you?" she asked.

"I'll make sure that ain't a problem," he said, putting his right hand on the wall.

He pushed, but it wouldn't budge. It was solid and was closing in, pushing him back toward the house. He looked back at Zoey. Her eyes begged him to reconsider as she stood barefoot in the snow. He felt a tug on his heart for a moment before he remembered that this was all her fault. He reared back with his right hand and punched the wall with all his strength.

The section of wall in front of him spider-webbed. He punched again with his left hand, causing more damage. When he pulled back for his second right hand, the wall lowered back into the snow. He looked back at Zoey again, straightened his hood, and walked onto the barren early-morning streets.

The temperature was too cold and the snow too deep for the usual crop of wanna-be thugs who usually haunted their small ghetto suburb. This disappointed him. The rage ran strong. He wanted a fight. He wanted someone to start something that he could finish. He hoped to find the normal gangbanger trash, most of whom he knew from high school, out skulking and pretending to be bad but found no such relief.

He crossed the large park near his house, figuring that the nuisance bar a few blocks away – notorious for violent fights and shootings – would be the perfect place to let out his aggression. As he approached, he heard a woman scream from the alley between a row of houses and the police station.

He stopped before rounding the corner and peered around the wall. A shaggy haired man with a knife had a woman pinned with her back to the wall of the police station. She struggled and cringed as his free hand worked to undo his belt before he started tearing open her pants. The man's boots slid across the icy back alley as he shushed her and continued his grim work.

Chaucer stepped into the alley. Briefly, he thought about shouting to the man, giving him the warning that sets the scene for most heroic rescues. The thought was very brief as his legs were already in full motion with his right arm pulled back and ready to strike. He closed the hundred-or-so-foot gap and was halfway into his swing before he thought of something to say. He slipped on the puddle of ice behind his intended target and his spiked knuckles merely grazed the back of the man's head. Chaucer tumbled to the ground and slid to a stop where the pavement dried out.

The attacker put his free hand on the back of his head and looked at the drawn blood. He turned away from the woman who collapsed shivering and crying against the wall. The man stared at the pile of Chaucer on the ground.

"You cut me!" the man said, looking outraged.

Chaucer sat up. His hood was down and his scarf had fallen away, revealing his green face and the spikes from his bone Mohawk sticking up through the stocking cap. He stood up as the man approached pointing the knife at him. The attacker paid no mind to Chaucer's freakish appearance and slashed across Chaucer's chest when he was close enough.

The blade cut diagonally across Chaucer's sweatshirt and exposed some of his extruded rib cage. Chaucer felt the knife hit his skin but felt no pain or cutting, only the pressure of the blade.

He grabbed the attacker by the top of his head, palming it as he would a basketball, and lifted him to his eye level. The attacker dangled two feet from the ground, wildly slashing the knife at Chaucer's arms, trying to set himself free. The sweatshirt was being shredded. Chaucer felt nothing.

The way in which he was being held was taking its toll on the attacker. His arms continued to flail and he dropped the knife to the ground. He attempted to support himself another way by grabbing on to Chaucer's forearm where his hands became impaled on the plate of spines which had grown there for what Chaucer believed to be defensive reasons. The man screamed as his right hand caught one of the larger hooked spines through his palm. Evolved that way because, Chaucer would later justify, it prevented his prey from escaping.

The attacker's eyes, once burning and crazed, were now very sober and fearful as he gave a pleading look to Chaucer.

"Run," Chaucer shouted, turning to the woman in a heap off to the side of the alley.

She panted and whimpered, looking at him with the same fear as her attacker.

"I SAID RUN!" he roared, the scarf falling from his face to reveal his twisted teeth and jaw.

The woman stumbled quickly down the alleyway and out into the street.

"Please don't kill me," the attacker begged, "Please, I swear to God I'll never do anything like this again. I'll stay off the streets. I'll get clean. Anything, just please don't kill me!"

A deep growl crept out of Chaucer's throat as he narrowed his eyes, turning his attention to his attacker's pleas. It occurred to him that this man's life was literally in his hands. Though his facial expression didn't change, causing even more intimidation to the attacker, he thought for a moment on what it would mean if he took this man's life. He wondered what it would mean for him if he killed somebody.

"Don't," said Zoey from behind him, "Please, Chaucer."

"You followed me?" Chaucer said, not looking at her.

"Don't do it," she said, "Let him go."

"You don't know what he's done," Chaucer said, "He was going to rape and probably murder a woman. He tried to cut me up. He's obviously a drug addict. I should just kill him and spare the world another parasite."

Every word he said was spoken with the best annunciation and diction that he had to offer. He thought it made him sound righteous – like one of the good guys.

The attacker continued sputtering and pleading to be let down and let go.

"Chaucer," she said, circling around to look him in the eyes, "Think about this. We're right behind the police station. We could go right around the corner and turn him in."

"And then what?" Chaucer asked, "They hold him overnight because he's clearly intoxicated. He won't say a damn thing about trying to rape someone in an alley and I'm sure as hell not going to stick around to tell them because the cops aren't going to take it on the word of a big green monster. They'll ask him where he got the injuries and he'll describe me. They'll laugh at him and let him go because he's just some crazy dude with a substance problem. Unless he's got a record already, they'll turn him loose tomorrow morning after he sleeps off whatever he's on and he'll be right back on the streets doing this again."

"No!" the attacker shouted, "No, no! I won't!"

"Shut up," Chaucer said, pulling the man nose to nose with himself, "You are worthless. Why would anyone waste their time on you? You think you've reached some kind of moment of clarity now that an ogre is about to crush your head, but it doesn't matter. You'll be right back out here tomorrow night if we don't do something about it now."

As Chaucer had been monologuing, the man scrambled with his non-impaled hand, grabbing at his back. When he found what he was looking for, he pulled it. Chaucer heard Zoey, almost in slow motion, shouting "GUN!"

The man's free hand whipped around. The .38 popped a shot into Chaucer's chest. At the moment the gun fired, Chaucer squeezed without a thought.

His head crushed like a grape. Blood spurted from every orifice as Chaucer closed his hand. The body twitched and wriggled and eventually went limp. Red covered him again, so soon after cleansing himself of his own. The man's head was now just a lump of limp flesh. Chaucer tore the man's other hand from the barbed arm spike and dropped him to the ground.

He saw Zoey standing there, both hands over her mouth. Her eyes were wide and she was making tiny squeals as she breathed heavily. Blood was spattered across her clothes. A bit stained her cheek and was now frozen there.

"Let's go," Chaucer said, grabbing her arm in his bloody hand and pulling her back to the main street. When he realized her feet were being unresponsive, he lifted her up awkwardly and ran away from the scene, stopping in an empty alley near a church a few blocks away.

Setting her down, he saw that her eyes were still wide. She looked like she was hyperventilating. She doubled over, her hand on her stomach, still huffing her breaths. She stood against the wall and vomited.

"Calm down, baby," he said, crouching to her eye level and reaching a large hand to touch her face.

She pushed the hand away with both of hers.

"Calm down, baby?" she asked in a low shout, "Calm down, baby? You just killed a man by crushing his head with your bare hands behind a police station and you're telling me to calm down, baby?"

"He shot me," said Chaucer, "He tried to rape that woman and then he tried to kill me."

"Well, he failed at both," she said, "Are you even hurt?"

He unzipped the now useless hoodie and there, flattened against his exposed sternum, was the slug. He picked it off with his clawed fingernails and held it up. It left a small chip in the bone where it impacted, but never even touched his skin.

"You killed that man," she said, "You killed him for nothing."

"I killed him because he was a rapist and obviously prone to violence," he countered, "He was a drugged-out psychopath. The world is now that much better without him."

Her face looked as blank and shocked as it did at the scene. He sighed. He knew she wouldn't understand and he could feel the debate coming.

"Who are you to judge who lives and dies?" she said, "You didn't know that man."

"I knew enough," he said, "I knew he was bad."

"He could have been rehabilitated," she said, "He could have served time for what he did."

"This ain't the comics, baby," he said, "Superheroes can't just drop villains off at the police station and expect justice to be done. The cops don't send someone off to jail just because a vigilante says they're guilty. The real world has due process and a slow-moving justice system. Even if the cops arrested him, he could get out on bond and continue wandering the streets until his court date in a few months, maybe even a year. Allow more time for sentencing. It would take forever for that guy to go away. We saved the legal system time and money by taking him out."

"'We' didn't do anything," Zoey specified, "'You' killed a man."

"He wasn't a man," Chaucer said, "He was an insect. He was a horrible crawling thing. He was part of an infection. People get shot in this city every day. People get raped, drug deals go down; home invasions, robberies, muggings, arson.  The cops can't track them all.  Even when they get one right, they might never gain a conviction even if there is eyewitness testimony.

"If they send a guy to jail, once he's out, he's going to be right back on the street doing what he did before.  I have no faith in the rehabilitation of prisoners.  Crime is just an endless cycle and I want to do my best to stop it by any means necessary.  I may not be able to become a lawyer now but I could become a hero."

"Justifying murder doesn't make you a hero," she said, "I have a man's blood on my clothes, Chaucer.  On my face.  You crushed his head right in front of me.  Murder is murder."

"For the greater good," he said, nodding.

"What happened to you?" she asked, "You were pre-law at Harvard.  You always talked about making a difference the right way.  You were never this bleak about humanity.  What happened to the man I fell in love with?"

"This is the part I have to play now," Chaucer said, "I look like a monster, I might as well be a monster.  All the blood, all the pain I waded through until tonight, it helped me focus.  I knew I'd never be able to go back to the real world and the only way to make a difference for the good would be to use my monstrosity.  Once people start getting hurt or disappearing because they've done wrong, maybe people will stop causing trouble."

"Ok, Mr. Wayne," she said, "You want to make yourself into an urban legend, fine.  My point is the man I knew to be kind, the guy who had it all in high school taking time out to talk to a  nobody, the person I was in love with just killed a man in front of my eyes and isn't the least bit remorseful.  If you do this, you're doing it without me.  I won't stand by and watch you kill again."

She turned to leave.

"Zoey, wait," he said.

She stopped.

"You're telling me that you don't feel the same way?" he asked, "You mean that out of the two of us I'm the only one who thought about using this power for good?  You said you were researching comic books.  None of that rubbed off on you?"

"Sure," she said, not turning around, "But I'm not willing to go that far.  Heroes in comic books do the right thing by the law.  The heroes who are darker, the ones who destroy and kill, are the ones who are hunted by other heroes or the police.  I don't think it should be done that way.  You can't walk around being judge, jury, and executioner or someone will try to stop you.  I don't want to be there when that happens."

She continued walking down the alley to the street, leaving him behind.

"Be real about this," he shouted, "Life isn't like it is in the comics."

"You're right," she said, before she rounded the corner, "In the comics, you would have ended up with the girl."

He moved to follow her and fell flat on his face. His lower legs were encased in ice and frozen to the floor of the alley. He punched at them to break free. By the time he made it to the end of the alley, she was gone.

It was the last he would see of her for a very long time.

X

The noise inside the house made Mike's pounding on the front door pointless.

The buzzing and whirring of power tools coupled with loud pounding made it sound like a smaller house was being built inside Kurt's already tiny house.

"Hey," said a voice from behind him.

He jumped as he felt a hand on his shoulder and turned around to find Jess.

"Where did you come from?" he asked.

"Oh, I'm not really here," she said.

"What?" Mike asked.

"I'm in your head," she said, "I've been practicing. It takes some concentration, but it's getting easier."

"Why are you in my head?" he asked.

"Mainly, to tell you that the door is open and they're expecting you," she said, "Secondarily, because I'm testing this ability. I think it makes people more comfortable than just normal telepathy. Hearing voices in your head can make you think you're crazy."

"Seeing people who aren't really there kinda makes a better case for crazy," Mike said.

"You wouldn't have known I was only in your head if I didn't tell you," she said.

He poked at her shoulder.

"Oh, I get it," he said, "Nice try. You're real, I can touch you. I can smell your perfume. You're messing with me. Funny. Next time come prepared."

"You gave me the idea," she said, shrugging, "You shouldn't be surprised that I put it to use. Honestly, I thought you'd be proud of me for taking this whole psychic thing and running with it. I'm kind of insulted you don't think I can do something this cool."

"Look," he said, poking her repeatedly in the shoulder, "I'm doubtful. You're real, there's no way you can't be. Nothing could be this convincing. You can't possibly be that powerful."

"I'm flattered that you approve of the level of detail," she said, "I'm more insulted you don't think I could be doing this right now. It's easier than you think."

"Whatever, you can't fake me out," Mike said, opening the door and stepping aside, "I still say nice try. After you, my dear."

She walked in ahead of him, sighing.

Inside, a junk pile nearly reached the ceiling. It was full of scrap metal and electronics from toasters to laptops all of which were in complete disrepair. Kurt stood in the center, surrounded by power tools and currently using a table saw to divide a long piece of metal in half. When he was through, he looked to the door and saw Mike walking in.

"Close the door behind you," Kurt said, popping an earplug out of his ear, "They've been waiting for you downstairs."

"Where's Jess?" Mike asked, Jess stood next to Kurt and smiled.

"In the bedroom, meditating," Kurt said, "Why?"

"Really?" he asked.

"Yeah," Kurt said, looking up from his work, sounding frustrated, "Really. Why? What do you need with my girlfriend?"

Jess moved around to stand directly in front of Kurt's eyes. She danced, rubbing herself against Kurt in a fashion that made Mike feel awkward. Kurt didn't flinch.

"He can't see me," she said, looking at Mike, "He can't hear me, smell me, or touch me either."

"You ok?" Kurt asked, "You're spacing out man. Quit staring at me like that."

"Watch this," she said, smiling.

Jess walked to the other side of the table saw and placed her hand on top of the blade. Kurt picked up another piece of scrap metal and turned it over in his hands before moving to start the saw again.

"Stop!" Mike shouted.

Kurt looked up at him.

"Seriously, dude," Kurt said, "I'm trying to work here."

"You don't see that?" Mike asked.

"See what?" Kurt asked.

"Go on," she said, "Tell him what you see."

Mike looked sternly at her, refusing to admit defeat. He honestly didn't believe she had power enough to do something so elaborate. He had been the game master to most of their group of friends for the better part of a decade and had what he thought was a very real idea of the scope of Jess' psychic abilities. This was something they'd discussed in theory that she may be able to do some day. He was convinced that this was just some kind of practical joke.

"You didn't measure," Mike said, trying to recover, "Don't you need to measure?"

"Yeah," Kurt said, "I've been eyeballing these things so far, but I guess I should be more accurate."

Kurt popped his earplug back in and searched through his tool belt.

Mike glared at her. She bent over and laid her arm across the table in front of the scrap piece about to be cut. It would be impossible for Kurt to push it through without first cutting off most of Jess's left hand. She flicked the blade with her right and showed Mike a bleeding finger as the blade slowly spun.

Kurt measured and marked the piece of scrap. He placed the push-block against the metal piece and pressed the pedal to start the saw. Most of Jess' arm was about to be removed as Kurt pushed the metal toward the blade.

"No!" Mike screamed, running across the room to push Kurt away from the saw.

"What the hell, man?" Kurt shouted.

"What do you mean what the hell?" Mike said, "You saw what was happening there."

"No he didn't," Jess said, "Go ahead, tell him."

"What?" Kurt said, "What was happening?"

Mike looked at Jess. It was an elaborate prank, obviously Kurt was in on it, and he would not be the one to admit defeat.

"You only measured once," Mike said, quickly, "You know what they say, right? Measure twice, cut once. Don't want to get anything wrong, do we?"

"Uh, thanks," Kurt said, "But please don't shove me when I'm standing around heavy equipment."

Jess put her arm back on the table, this time with the saw lined up closer to her elbow. Kurt was about to place the scrap back into position when he started looking around on the floor for something.

"Dude," Kurt said, "You knocked out one of my earplugs."

Mike shrugged and looked around on the floor near him.

Kurt grumbled and left the room.

"He's going to find another one," Jess said, "It's going to take him a while, trust me. I wanted us to have some alone time."

"Look," Mike said, "You're not going to get me. I'm not going to admit you're an illusion. I know you're playing Kurt as a puppet either with or without your abilities to make him not see you. I get what you're up to."

"You're saying that you believe I could exert total control over him without an issue, yet you can't believe that I am only in your head right now."

"You're right, it's` a bit of a stretch," Mike said, "You're probably not powerful enough to do that, either."

Jess scoffed at him.

"You want me to prove it?" she asked, "Fine."

She put her foot on the pedal to control the saw. It whirred around, waiting for material.

She slowly moved her open left palm toward the blade. Looking back at Mike the whole time.

"You're not fooling me," Mike said, "There's a safety on every one of those things. Once it hits human flesh, it'll stop and disengage the blade without even nicking you. Doing that won't prove anything except that you're real."

"Fine," she said, "You come over here and move my arm down. If it stops, you win. If it doesn't, you have to admit I'm right."

"Fine," he said, walking over and taking her arm, "Where do you want to be cut?"

"Surprise me," she said.

He waited for a moment, narrowing his eyes at her. Without any warning, he grabbed her hand and shoved it into the saw.

The safety did not disengage the blade. Her hand was separated from her body without much effort. She screamed and backed away as blood shot from her arm in great long spurts. Mike, left holding her severed hand, started screaming as well. He panicked, and backed away as Jess fell to the ground.

With her right arm outstretched, she reached for Mike, begging for help as her skin went noticeably paler. Mike leapt down to her, took off his belt, and tried to make a tourniquet. He sat her up against one of the scrap piles and tightened the belt as best he could. He could barely hear himself over his heart pumping in his ears as he apologized to her over and over. She cried and screamed, her sobs growing weaker. The tourniquet wasn't working, blood was still pumping from the spot where her hand once was.

Jess started to shudder. Mike called out for Kurt, then for general help. Jess looked him in the eyes right before they rolled back into her head and her body slumped forward. Mike openly cried and shouted apologies at the top of his lungs. He closed his eyes, unable to look at Jess anymore.

"What the hell?" Kurt said, arriving back in the room.

"I'm so sorry," Mike said, through tears, "Kurt, I'm so, so sorry. It was just a prank that went wrong."

"What are you talking about?" Kurt asked.

Mike opened his eyes. No Jess. No blood. Nothing but him lying on a pile of scrap sobbing like a moron.

Mike stood up and his pants fell down around his ankles. His belt was lying in a tight circle where Jess's arm would have been. Now, here he was, his commando status realized by Kurt and the rest of his friends who had come in response to his cries of help.

"Well," he said, wiping his tear-soaked face with the sleeve of his coat, "Where to begin."

"Begin with pulling up your pants," Justin said, "That would be a good start."

Mike did so, replacing his belt in the process.

"Jess," Kurt shouted, "You really have to stop messing with people like that."

She came out of the next room, dressed the same way Mike encountered her. She had two hands and was certainly not as dead as she had been just a minute ago.

"He doubted my power," Jess said, plainly, "For that he must pay."

"Apparently everyone must pay," Josh said.

"We've got work to do," Kurt said, looking at her, "If you want to help, fine. If not, stay out of the way."

"I've been telekinetically lifting rocks all night," she said, "My mind needs a break."

Now that the tears had cleared from his eyes and the fog of intense stress was starting to lift, Mike saw that Justin and in his own way Budda, were covered in dirt and sweat (the latter not in Budda's case). Josh was also there, but appeared to be cleaner than anyone in the room, save Jess.

"I think it's break time all around," Justin said, "Let's go back downstairs, Kurt said I can smoke in the cave."

Mike followed them, tossing Jess a sly middle finger right before he went out of sight. She responded by motioning at Mike's other hand, which he noticed suddenly had weight in it. It was a severed hand, her hand, with the well-manicured painted nail at the top of its middle finger standing alone as a reply. Mike tossed it aside and it disappeared. She smirked at him as he walked away.

When they reached the basement, another pile of scrap, this one mostly bare circuits and other open components.

"Jeez," Mike said, "This place is a mess. Where did he get all of this stuff, anyway?"

"Junkyard," Josh said.

"How are you so clean?" Mike asked, "Justin told me on the phone that we'd all be digging."

"Kurt has me helping him with this pile," Josh said, "I've been using my powers to test circuits."

"Yeah," Justin said, "They finally found a use for him aside from universal remote control and human hand-buzzer."

Josh reached to touch Justin's forehead and Justin slapped the hand away. The contact with Josh's skin zapped him anyway.

"What is all of this for?" Mike asked.

"He didn't tell us," Josh said, "It looks like something big, though."

"Down here," Justin said.

He led Mike down the coal cellar stairs and into the cave which had been tunneled out to a decent sized room. Construction lights had been staked into the wall and powered by an extension cord running up into the house. Justin and Budda both sat down on large rocks near where they had been working. Justin lit a cigarette with flames from his hand and took a long drag.

"We dug out the floor to give us about a nine-foot ceiling," Budda said, "Gives me enough room to move around freely."

"This place was tiny when we first saw it," Justin said, "We've come a long way, but Kurt wants us to do more. We figured your gravity manipulation could make things a bit easier, at least when we have to manually dig."

"You're doing something other than manually digging?" Mike asked.

"I'm glad you asked," Justin said, standing up, smiling, "Check it out."

He took a deep breath, made some flailing movements with his arms, cupped his open hands together and slowly drew them back along his waistline. As he did this, his smoke hair sputtered and caught completely on fire. Heat was building up between his two hands.

"This takes every ounce of my control," Justin said.

"To channel your powers?" Mike asked.

"No," Justin said, "To not yell HADOUKEN every time."

He thrust his hands forward and a blast of fire erupted into the wall. It impacted with a loud boom and shook the area. When the flames dispersed and the smoke cleared, a large round chunk had been taken out of the stone and left a glowing hot orange crater.

"Ok, that was awesome," Mike said.

"Check this out," Budda said, making it clear he would attempt to one-up Justin's feat.

He moved a wheelbarrow into position next to Justin's still-smoldering crater, pulled his fist back, and slammed it into the wall. The room shook again, significantly harder than with Justin's blast.

Budda extracted his fist from the wall and an avalanche of shattered rock poured out of the large hole into the wheelbarrow.

"Impressive," Mike said, "But it's so loud. How has no one called the cops about the noise yet?"

"I guess we're down far enough that no one notices," Budda said.

"You're shaking the ground," Mike said, "You don't think anyone has noticed this yet?"

"We've come pretty far," Justin said, "I think we're under the main part of the hill, beyond the houses on the other side of the street. That's well beyond anyone who would get disturbed by this."

"You mind if I take a crack at this?" Mike asked.

"Dude, you have gravity manipulation," Justin said, "What are you going to do besides make the physical labor easier on us?"

"I have a little more than just gravity manipulation," Mike said, "I've been going through gaming books, trying to figure out if I had any other abilities. I was testing my capabilities so I didn't have to find out about something due to some crazy act of self-defense."

"Like in every comic book ever," Justin said, "I see someone is coming around to my way of thinking."

"Actually, I really did it so that something wouldn't accidentally explode or be destroyed," Mike said, "I didn't want to find out about my abilities the hard way. Anyway, this is what I came up with."

To Justin and Budda, what he did next looked like a strange pantomime until they saw the final result. Mike extended his arm, palm out flat and facing the ground, raised it to chest level, then thrust it forward. Small rocks lifted off the ground and started to orbit him. He closed his fist and a thin round crack appeared in a large circle on the wall. The rocks around him dropped to the ground and he looked toward Justin.

"That's it?" Justin asked.

"Budda," Mike said, pointing, "Thump the wall right there. Gently."

Budda shrugged and did as he was asked. A hemisphere of rock slid down its own curve and came to rest, hanging half outside of its crater. Their jaws hit the floor as Mike smiled.

Justin walked up to it and reached out to its perfectly smooth surface.

"How the hell did you do that?" he asked.

"Forcefield projection," Mike said.

"No way," Budda said, "Dude, that's awesome."

"I don't know how precise I can be," Mike said, "But I can create pretty tough forcefields, invisible of course, in any shape. I can move them around, too. I started with a flat surface, used my gravity control to help drive it into the wall, and when I closed my fist to make the field a sphere, it cut anything in its way."

"Dude," Justin said, "You could sever people's limbs and stuff with that. You're freaking deadly now."

"It won't cut organic matter," Mike said.

Justin tilted his head, concerned.

"Don't ask," Mike concluded, "Let's just say I found out I can encase living things, but I can't crush them."

"That solves the bulletproofing problem, then," Justin said.

"Not really," Mike said, "If I put you in a bubble or something, you'd only have the air that went in with you, so you'd eventually suffocate. It's not safe. Again, before you give me that look, don't ask."

"Oh well," Budda said, moving down the wall, "Enough talking. Time for round two."

With that unnoticeable warning, he pounded his fist into the wall again. The room shook as Budda pulverized his area once more causing the large boulder Mike had just created to teeter. Before Mike could shout out a warning to Justin, who was standing right under the rock, it fell on him. Justin raised his arms as if to block it or catch it but it was obvious that this rock could not be stopped. With another loud slam, the boulder hit the floor and a dust cloud rose from the impact.

"You moron!" Mike cried, "You just crushed him!"

"What?" Budda said, finally looking, "Oh, damn."

"I have to go get Kurt," Mike said.

"Already here," said Kurt, running down the stairs, Josh and Jess hot on his heels, "Jess said she sensed danger and checked on you guys."

"Spider sense," she said, pointing at her head, "What happened?"

"Budda pounded the wall and made a boulder fall on Justin!" Mike said.

"It wasn't my fault," Budda said, "I didn't know that would happen."

"Shut up and lift the rock, genius," Kurt shouted, "He's still under there!"

Budda threw the boulder aside easily and they were all shocked at what they found: Nothing but the crushed cigarette Justin had been smoking when the boulder fell. Budda checked the underside of the rock and, to his dismay, did not find a flattened cartoon version of Justin on the bottom.

"What happened?" Josh asked, "Where is he?"

As if on cue, the large dust cloud began to gather together into a humanoid form. When it finished gathering, it looked like an ethereal version of Justin.

"No way," Mike said.

"Oh my God," Budda said, "It's Justin's ghost!"

There was a collective sigh. Even the smoke form shook its head.

"You can turn into smoke, then," Kurt said, addressing the smoke.

The lips of the form moved, but nothing came out. The communication ended in a shrug.

"We can't hear you," Jess said, "I can't communicate with you telepathically, either."

The form appeared to sigh.

"You've got no vocal cords," Josh said, "Nothing you're saying is making sound. Can you get your real body back?"

The form shrugged, then clenched his fists and concentrated. In a quick wave of flame from head to toe, the smoke returned to flesh and Justin was back to normal.

"Whoa," Justin said, "That was intense. Disorienting. What happened?"

"Self-defense," Mike said, pointing to the boulder, "Just like I said."

"Well at least I didn't explode just like you said," Justin rebutted.

"I guess we're all underestimating each other's power today, aren't we?" quipped Jess, staring at Mike.

"Can you do that again?" Kurt asked.

"I can try," Justin said, closing his eyes and concentrating.

After a few seconds, his hair flared and kicked into a flame. His fists glowed orange and burst into flames. Mike reached an epiphany.

"Stop, stop," he told Justin, "Bring it down."

Justin relaxed and his hair extinguished to its regular smolder. The glowing heat of his fists cooled back to normal.

"Concentration isn't the key," Mike said, "It makes you hotter. If you relax yourself, maybe that's how you can trigger the smoke."

Justin shrugged and took a few deep breaths.

"Relax," Mike said lightly, "Let yourself go."

"Are you trying to get me to pee or change into smoke?" Justin asked.

"Seriously," Mike said, "If you calm way down, it'll probably just happen on its own."

"You are trying to get me to pee," Justin said.

"Just do it,' Mike said.

Justin shook his head and continued taking deep meditative breaths. After a moment, his body seemed to disintegrate into the smoke form again. He opened his eyes and looked himself over, then took another deep breath. The form collapsed into a low fog covering the entire floor. It seeped into every opening and rose around the ankles of the group. It shifted unnaturally and small tendrils popped up before melting back into the rest of the cloud.

It drew back together and Justin returned to flesh.

"That is amazing," Justin said, "When I spread out, it's like being everywhere in the room at once – like I'm seeing out of every part of my body."

"Find anything interesting down here?" Josh asked, "Mummy's tomb, dragon's lair?"

"Actually," Justin said, walking toward their demonstration wall, "I did."

He pulled his hands back as he had done before and launched a blast of fire into the wall revealing a man-sized tunnel with pitch black walls. Wooden braces straddled the sides of the visible portion with one bracing across the ceiling. The cave continued far into darkness.

Kurt walked to the new tunnel entrance and swiped his index finger along the wall. He sniffed at it then licked it much to the disgust of his friends.

"Coal," he said, "This is a coal shaft."

"Why is there a coal shaft down here?" Josh asked.

"Dude, we live in the former industrial capital of the world," Justin said, "There isn't a town within two-hundred miles that wasn't built on a coal mine, a slag pile, or a reclaimed mill site."

"What now, then?" Mike asked.

"Justin," Kurt said, "After you."

"After me?" he replied, looking into the black cavern, "Why me? I don't want to go first. There could be like giant death spiders in there."

"You were already in there," Kurt said, "Did you see any giant death spiders?"

"No," Justin said, "But I didn't go very far and giant death spiders usually get you from hiding. Besides, if the walls are coal, I don't think I should use my torchlight in there."

94

"You discovered it," Kurt said, "You explore it."

"Why don't you go first?" Justin asked, "You're so anxious to go into the den of the death spider, you go right ahead."

"I'm not really concerned with going first," Kurt said.

"Way to brush it off," Justin replied.

Jess grumbled, snatched a flashlight off of Kurt's tool belt, and walked toward the entrance.

"Where are you going?" Kurt asked.

"Where two grown men are afraid to go," she said, "Stop acting like babies."

She walked into the cave, prompting Kurt and Justin to rush in behind her. Josh, Budda, and Mike stood in the coal cellar and looked at each other.

"I'm not going in there," Josh said.

"I won't fit in there," said Budda.

Mike sighed.

"You, suck it up," he said pointing to Josh then quickly moving his finger to Budda, "You, hunker down. She's right. We're grown men. We shouldn't be afraid of a stupid cave."

"A totally dark narrowly confined cave with braces holding up the ceiling and where God-knows-what has been living for God-knows-how-long," Josh said, "Yeah, fear is totally irrational here."

Mike rolled his eyes, produced a small LED light on a keychain, and walked into the darkness. Josh and Budda followed shortly behind, not wanting to get too far behind the light.

"Guys, wait up," Mike called into the darkness. His voice echoed along the walls.

He almost tripped. Shining the light down, he could see short wooden ties crossing under metal rails.

"Careful guys," he called back to the last two, "Mine cart tracks. Don't trip."

"Mike," Kurt called, "Just keep walking. You have to see this."

As he got further in, a bright flash hit his eyes. Jess had turned her light to see him. He shined his back as he heard Kurt speaking.

"No, keep that over here," he said, "I've got to get a better look."

The flashlight turned back to the wall where Mike could now see, through the spots in his eyes, they were staring at a large antiquated lever switch.

"Whoa," Mike said, "Paging Dr. Frankenstein."

"I know, right?" Justin said.

Kurt was crouched down, messing with two thick insulated cables. Their ends were frayed and had the green patina of old copper. He tapped the two exposed parts together and a loud zap echoed through the cave accompanied by a bright flash that sent some smoldering dust to the ground.

"That answers that question," Kurt said, lifting the cables carefully one at a time and placing them into the screw-down brass fasteners to which they must have been once attached. He took a pair of rubber gloves from his tool belt before producing a wrench to tighten the large screws down.

"Are you seriously doing what I think you're doing?" Mike asked.

"Sure," Kurt said, "The wires are still live. Might as well see what this thing does."

"So, you just find a strange steampunk-looking switch inside a hidden cave and you're going to flip it without even caring?" Josh asked.

"That's the idea," Kurt said.

"Have you never played a role-playing game in your life?" Josh asked, "You never hit the creepy-looking unmarked switch in the dungeon. It's always bad news."

"He's right," Justin verified.

"Look, this isn't a game," Kurt said, "Someone put this switch here for a reason."

"Giant cage from the ceiling," Josh said.

"Hatch in the floor drops into a spike pit," Justin offered.

"Mist of acid spraying from the wall," Mike suggested, "Just to be thorough."

"Relax, nerds," Kurt said, "I used my powers, I know what it's connected to and it is in no way a dungeon trap. I just hope everything still works."

Throwing the switch caused a loud clank which was followed by a low hum. Banks of lights turned on with loud bangs as the power reached them. When their eyes adjusted to the light, they could not believe what had been uncovered.

"Well," Budda said, "I think we're finished digging."

They were standing on the bottom of a large round room. The ceiling stretched almost a hundred feet up in a curved cone, almost like a bullet. The top was narrow, but the base was huge and mostly level stone aside from a few hopeful stalagmites which hadn't quite made it past the budding stage and sets of tracks leading into some of the caves.

Caves stretched off from the room in regular intervals and in spots higher along the walls. This room represented a former hub of activity with a main pillar of scaffolding housing a weight-and-pulley powered wooden elevator at its center to help mine carts rise to the elevated tracks positioned on narrow and largely unreliable catwalks crisscrossing the areas over their heads.

An old drafting table made its home here. It was covered in diagrams and maps and other undeterminable stacks of yellowed paper. Mine carts stood empty of their lode but still black on the inside from years of use. One must have been left on a higher track as below a broken bridge lie a single cart on its side.

Racks of tools were also present – pickaxes, shovels, sledge-hammers, stakes – all left behind.  They were caked with rust and likely useless, as were the mine carts.  There was no way of knowing how long these things had been down here.

"Monongahela River Coke & Coal Company," Kurt said, reading the corner of one of the maps, "1913."

There was a way of knowing how long these things had been down here.

"Wow," Mike said, "This place has been here for a hundred years?"

"Apparently," said Kurt, flipping through the documents on the table, "I can't believe that no one stumbled on this before.  These maps show tunnels going all through the hill, following coal veins."

"No one was digging under the street before, I guess," said Budda.

"Someone had to," Jess said, "They put a whole neighborhood up around this place.  There should be utility lines and stuff running all through this place."

"There's power," Josh said, "Maybe there's other stuff in one of these side caves, they just closed it off or something."

"It's not closed off," Kurt said, "They ran the utility lines along the mine tunnels as they built the neighborhood.  Apparently, the mine was still operating when the neighborhood started popping up.  There's a layout map right here.  Guess they didn't want to hit a gas line while they were digging."

"And no one's touched any of this in, like, forever," Justin said, "Suspicious coincidence, don't you think?  We just happen to find a large abandoned cave to use as a base right under Kurt's house.  It's all so stereotypical.  You'd think whoever is writing this would make it a bit more challenging instead of plopping us down into a gigantic set piece."

"Knock that off," Kurt said, "It's not mentally healthy."

"Origin story," Justin sang, tauntingly, "Just sayin'."

"Shut up," Kurt shouted, the noise echoing through the cave.

Everyone was silent, staring at Kurt and his clenched fists.  Most of them had no idea what the two of them were talking about before that outburst.  Justin was more than happy to explain it to them later, out of Kurt's earshot.

"Are those vents?" Budda said, breaking the silence and pointing up.

Kurt relaxed and flipped through the documents.

"Looks like," Kurt said, "Big grated ones.  Probably in someone's backyard or something by now.  They wouldn't have built over them because they look like they could be used for some kind of access.  We've got fresh air, power, and a map of the utility lines if we need anything else.  This place is perfect."

"So, what now?" Mike asked.

"Now," Kurt said, "We've got a lot more work to do."

## XI

She woke up in a cold sweat; gasping for air and frantically looking around.

In that moment where you're between a nightmare and reality, she didn't recognize the apartment she'd been living in for almost a month. Something felt wrong to her. This bed, this room, this place – it was not where she was meant to be.

Her heart was pumping. Gathering her thoughts, she wasn't sure that her nightmare was actually a nightmare. It was vivid and immersive but it didn't involve anything particularly dangerous or frightening. She was already straining to remember the details when the blare of her alarm clock caught her off guard.

The clear piece of thick plexiglass blinked red and beeped showing six-thirty on its surface. She touched the top with her pointer finger and the numbers returned to green. She took the rectangular glass surface out of the clock cradle and, with a touch, its display shifted to a remote control. She used this to turn on the lights.

Though the room felt unfamiliar at first, she sighed in relief as she recognized the place. Her bed was surrounded by three smoked-glass walls and one made of thick, cold concrete where her headboard was placed. She tapped at the clear glass screen in her hand and the windows became clear.

Lights activated as she swiped her finger. Her quarters were just as she had left them, though she still felt that something was strange. She was forced to shake it off as she glanced down at the glass display showing her daily schedule. Today, she was told, was very important. It was the annual progress review for her department. She was to be in uniform and on-point at precisely oh-nine-hundred and she couldn't disappoint, no matter how foggy she might feel.

She swung her legs off the bed and grimaced as her feet touched the cold metal floor. She would have to requisition a rug or something as this whole-body clench had become an unwelcomed part of her morning routine.

The door to her room slid open as she walked into the apartment proper – a loft style area with no walls. It was a nice apartment by her standards and contained a large kitchen with an island, small dining area, living room, bathroom, and a workout area which is where she was headed.

Almost every wall in the place contained mirrors which had a small clear dock, just like the one she used for her alarm clock stand. She placed the glass screen into the dock and the display transferred to the mirror. She turned on the news and watched during her half-hour high-impact workout.

Though her head was clearing and the alien feeling faded, she realized that her quarters were still very impersonal. She lived Spartan with no decoration or extras. Bookshelves in the corner near the living room screen were empty, towels near the workout nook and in the bathroom were the ones that came with the place. Pots, pans, appliances – everything was company issue. She wondered if the same went for the rest of her teammates. This place felt less like her own and more like an extended-stay hotel.

After her workout routine, she took the glass from its dock and placed it in the one in her bathroom mirror. She showered and, when she was finished, she caught herself staring at her reflection in the mirror. She was still getting used to the appearance of her eyes – solid, jet black with no other details, empty of expression. No whites, no irises, just the glossy black surface. She couldn't remember what her eyes looked like before she came here. She imagined that looking one's self in the eye was something that most people took for granted.

She left the bathroom and moved back to the bedroom, touching a button on the wall and revealing a large walk-in closet.

Inside were two rows of clothing; one side of the closet held six identical black suits with white shirts and black ties. The other side held six black jumpsuits and a few cloaks made of various types of camouflage. The back wall of the closet held an armoire containing company casual attire, undergarments, and an open rack containing six pairs of identical boots with metal soles and toes next to six pairs of black dress shoes. On the top shelf rested a black helmet which could be used to conceal her identity if necessary. It was the only piece of clothing which had so far gone untouched.

She dressed herself in uniform - a black jumpsuit with a pair of the metal-soled boots - selecting an olive-colored cloak to drape over her shoulders. After putting her boots on, she opened a drawer of the armoire which contained a metal safe. She pressed her hand to the top and, after a moment, it opened to reveal a large metal bracer which she placed on her forearm. The metal stretched and seamlessly sealed itself shut. The touch screen on the upper portion came to life, indicating that it was starting up. It showed her vitals - heart rate, blood pressure, temperature – and flashed to indicate the detection of elevated adrenaline levels. She swiped at the message to dismiss it with a sigh, realizing that she was still freaked out by her dream.

Also in the safe was a thin bracelet which she put on her right wrist and a belt which bore the black-and-red XIII logo in the buckle. Both of them matched the metal of the bracer on her left arm and both sealed themselves in the same manner after she put them on.

She double-checked herself in the mirror and swiped at her bracer to get the time. She had about an hour for breakfast then, as a pop-up message indicated, she would be needed for review in Conference Room D.

She walked across the apartment to the door, the footfalls of her metal soles making light clanking noises along the metal floor. She pressed a button next to her thick, pressurized, high-security front door. It hissed, pulled into the room a bit, then slid into the wall.

The hall outside was long and drab. The walls and floor were thick gray concrete. Thick cables and pipes ran along the ceiling broken up by banks of fluorescent lights every ten feet. The only color came from symbols painted on the floor attached to colored lines indicating paths to certain places and the occasional stenciled wording on the wall advising caution or restriction to certain areas.

Across from her door, a pale woman with dark hair stood. She was dressed in the same black jumpsuit with the same accoutrements. Instead of a cloak, she wore a small metal shoulder pad over her right arm. She smiled.

"Morning, Char," she said.

"Hey, Joey," Char said as the door closed behind her, "What are you doing here?"

"I was walking by and I knew you were on your way out the door," Joey said, "Figured I'd walk to breakfast with you."

Char looked puzzled then shrugged it off. She was still getting used to the idea of working with a psychic. She was not used to having someone know her every thought. She had nothing to hide, but it was tough to converse with someone who knew what she was about to say before she could even form a proper sentence.

"What's on your mind?" Joey asked, as they started walking, "Not that I don't already know, but I'm going to be courteous."

Char hesitated and stared down the hallway, trying to remember what she had dreamed. Nothing here could inspire her memory. If anything, it caused her to draw more of a blank.

"I had a dream last night," she said, "It was really unsettling. I can't remember anything about it, but it really got under my skin."

"I can see you trying to push it to the surface of your mind," Joey said, "I can't see it without going deeper. Would you like me to take a look?"

"Uh," Char said, "Yeah, I guess."

She was extremely curious to see what had her up and panicking before her alarm. She was anxious to know about the alien feeling and why everything in her life suddenly seemed out of place.

Joey motioned for her to come closer then reached out with her right hand placing her palm on Char's forehead. Her fingers fell to rest in Char's short, dark red hair. She closed her eyes before Char closed hers as well.

Char shook her head a bit, feeling dazed.

"Is it gone now?" Joey asked.

"Is what...?" Char muttered.

"The headache you were telling me about," Joey said, "Is it gone?"

"Oh," Char said, starting to recall the throbbing headache which woke her before her alarm this morning, "Yeah. Whatever you did must have fixed it. How did you do that?"

"Psychic trick," Joey said, "I've,,, borrowed… some skills from a neurosurgeon or two. I know just about everything there is to know about the brain. That includes headaches and how to get rid of them."

"Handy," Char said, her head still spinning. She wasn't quite sure what just happened, all she could remember from this morning was her headache.

"You're dehydrated," Joey said, "Make sure you drink extra orange juice this morning."

"You're the neurosurgeon," Char said with a shrug.

After a few turns through the nearly identical hallways, they arrived at the cafeteria. The room was large and open with a higher ceiling than the hallway. Metal tables and chairs filled the floor reminding Char of every prison cafeteria she'd ever seen in a movie.

The kitchens and the service line were off to the left side in a separate room. They approached the end of the line behind a few people in white lab coats bearing the XIII logo. They grabbed the standard-issue green plastic trays and waited for their turn.

"So, what's this whole review thing about?" Char asked.

"SecDef," Joey said.

"SecDef?" Char asked, "What's that?"

"The Secretary of Defense," Joey said, "The annual review is to check the progress of the Project to evaluate if our funding should continue. Problem is, the President just appointed some new guy, so we have to make extra nice."

"What am I supposed to do?" Char asked.

"Stand there and look pretty," Joey said, "That's what I do. Johnny and Agent Williams do most of the talking. Just speak if you're spoken to and you'll be all good."

"I hope he doesn't ask anything too complicated," Char said, "I'm still new here."

"Johnny will handle the important questions about the field team," Joey said, "You've got nothing to worry about. If you get stuck, I'll feed you some lines with telepathy. This guy won't know the difference."

After grabbing their breakfast, they made a straight line to their usual table where a humanoid bulldog was already seated. He wore a jumpsuit similar to theirs and had a napkin stuffed into his neckline, presumably to avoid getting any food or potentially drool all over his uniform.

"Ladies," he said in his typical gruff voice.

"Doug," Char said, smiling at him.

"You ready for SecDef today?" he asked.

"I just found out what this review means," Char said, "I had no idea we were meeting with someone official."

"Procedure," he said, sighing and shaking his head, "Military stuff, y'know. We're deeper than black ops, beyond top secret. Only SecDef knows we're here, so we have to prove ourselves to him."

"Is he going to want demonstrations?" Char asked.

"Don't know," Doug said, picking up a piece of bacon with his stubby-fingered paw and throwing it into his mouth, "New guy. Never met him before. Not a big fan of the current administration, so I imagine I won't be a big fan of him. Might want to see some results before he approves anything. Shouldn't be a big deal. I was in the Corps, I know all about this kind of stuff. Mostly they just want to see that your uniforms are crisp and your medals are polished."

"Great," Char said, "What am I supposed to do if he wants a demonstration? I'm no good at public performance."

"Don't get nervous," Joey said, "If he wants to see something, just do your chameleon thing or make the whole room quiet. He's not going to test your marksmanship and he's not going to ask for your training sim scores."

Char sighed. Her stomach clenched with the tension. She decided to start with one of the glasses of juice Joey recommended rather than digging in to the solid food just yet.

"Worse comes to worse, we'll give you a gun," Doug said, "You can clip his necktie from a thousand yards. That should shut him up."

He smirked. It made Char laugh. It was always comical to see his bulldog face make human expressions. It made her feel like she was in some kind of special effects-heavy summer blockbuster with a talking animal partner and it always cheered her up.

"Hey guys, hey guys," said a younger, much faster-paced voice as a skinny kid with an oversized robotic left arm and a metal plate over most of his head approached the table, "Whatcha talking about? You ready for SecDef? This is my first one. I'm ready. I've got all kinds of stuff to show him. It's going to be great!"

That entire sentence was spoken in a matter of two or three seconds.

The kid put down a drink carrier containing four cups with hot beverage collars.

"Ah, saved me a trip," said Doug, reaching for one of the cups, "Thanks, Chuckie."

Chuckie smacked Doug's paw away with his flesh-and-blood right hand.

"This is my coffee," he quickly rattled, pointing his finger at Doug, "Don't touch my coffee, this is my coffee, this is my coffee, get your own coffee, this is mine."

"Relax, kid," said Doug, "I'm just messing with you."

"You better be," said Chuckie, his eyes crazed and his finger shaking as it pointed at Doug, "I need my coffee. I need this for today. I can't go without it. Not on SecDef day. I've been waiting for this and if I don't have my coffee I'm not going to do anything right. Don't touch my coffee. I'll kill you."

Again, this series of statements set the land-speed record. When Chuckie talked, Char remembered those old commercials where the fast-talking guy was trying to sell children tiny cars. It was both funny and disturbing at times. The fact that he was the group's techie and would routinely try to explain new devices to them with the same cadence only made her scratch her head. Thankfully, Doug seemed to be able to translate and had a knack for using layman's terms.

"I thought you were going to try to lay off the coffee." Doug said.

"Pssh," Chuckie started, "Lay off the coffee? Why would I ever lay off the coffee? That would be a reckless waste of time. I was up all night working on some stuff. I wouldn't have finished if it wasn't for the coffee. Pulled an all-nighter. Figured with the meeting today I should just keep an all-nighter going into an all-dayer, get it?"

"You're fifteen," said Doug, "All that coffee is going to stunt your growth."

"Then I'll build a better body," Chuckie said.

"Don't you think you've done enough upgrading, robo-boy?" Joey asked.

"What?" Chuckie said, "Just because I cut off my own arm to install a better one and just because I had you help me with that brain surgery that one time because I developed a better technological frontal lobe with data ports in it? I don't think I'm finished yet, not by a long shot. You wait and see what I've got cooking. There's always room for improvement. Like this thing I was working on last night..."

"Save it for SecDef," Doug interrupted, "I don't think any of us really want to know what body parts you're upgrading next."

Chuckie thought for a brief moment before responding.

"I wasn't talking about a penis or anything," Chuckie said.

Char and the others just sighed and shook their heads.

"Unless you think that will help with SecDef," Chuckie said, his face very serious.

"I think that's one you should keep in the lab, kid," Joey said.

"Fine," Chuckie said, "But it wasn't a penis."

"Whatever," said Doug.

"Snap to, kids," said Moorsblade's deep southern accent as he approached, "Meeting's been moved up. Williams wants us in Conference Room D pronto."

Chuckie started chugging his coffee, his eyes watering with the heat, as the rest of them stood up and followed Moorsblade through a door on the other side of the room.

After a few turns through what Char believed to be an intentionally confusing labyrinth of corridors, they arrived at an elevator flanked by two guards with decidedly-not-standard-issue assault rifles and black riot gear displaying the XIII logo prominently on their shoulders. Char had seen guys dressed like this and carrying the same guns around the complex, but she'd never actually seen them standing guard over anything.

They boarded. There were no numbers to press in this elevator. She thought it might be voice activated but no one said anything. She felt no movement and as quickly as they'd stepped inside, they were on their way out to a different floor which was new to her.

This floor looked more like an office; deep red carpeted floors, softer lighting, a drop-ceiling rather than pipes and vents and cables, and actual doors which did not seem to be pressure sealed and multiple feet thick. At the end of the hall, directly off of the elevator, they entered a room labeled D.

Inside was like nothing she had seen since she joined the project; carpeted floors now patterned red differing from the one in the hallway, high-back leather chairs, three large presentation monitors and a black glass conference table in the center of the room. What was on the left-hand wall from the door was what interested Char the most.

Floor to ceiling windows beamed the sunlight of the morning into the room. The sun was rising over a forest whose canopy they appeared to be many stories high. A perimeter fence ran along the edge of the woods, giving way to a large and well-attended grass field some two hundred yards from the building. It was the first time she had seen the actual outside world in weeks, but she could not stare or bask in this fact for too long. The man in the dark gray suit and bright red tie sitting next to Agent Williams at the head of the conference table would make sure of that.

"Reporting as ordered, sir," said Moorsblade, offering a relaxed salute.

"You are right on time, Agent," said Williams, swiveling his chair and standing up, "Ladies and gentlemen, may I introduce the Secretary of Defense. He has come for a briefing and evaluation of the Project. Due to his newly appointed position, it is his prerogative to familiarize himself with programs classified top secret and above which currently benefit from the black-ops budget of our military. He is to return to our President with an assurance that said money is going to the proper programs and make cuts in that funding where necessary. I have informed him of the long-term goals of the Project and our ideals. He wished to hear from our current field team in person before making any decisions. Mister Secretary."

"Thank you, sir," said the pudgy, gray-haired man as he stood and Williams sat, "Let me first assure you that you may speak freely here. As SecDef, I hold rank over anyone else in this room. I expect complete transparency. That being said, I've heard you can all do some pretty extraordinary things. Tell me a bit about yourselves and what you can do. We'll start with you, miss?"

"Agent," Joey corrected him as he approached, "Agent Josephine Briggs, Psychological Warfare Specialist and Field Medic. I possess psychic abilities with a variety of functions including telepathy, memory retrieval, alteration, displacement, and erasure. I am also able to psychically track and remotely view targets. I've absorbed the minds of expert physicians including two neurosurgeons which grant me the medical capabilities of four different doctors combined, though I don't have the piece of paper which would allow me to use that title, much to my dismay. My most unique capability is that I am able to block and or overload the abilities of other psychics."

"Wait a minute," said the Secretary, turning to Williams, "'Other psychics'?"

"Have you not been read in to those reports yet?" Williams asked, "Psychic abilities are a naturally occurring, though exceedingly rare, phenomena. The CIA, NSA, and KGB have been at the forefront of psychic research for decades. Agent Briggs may not be the only psychic out there, but she is certainly the best-trained."

"Thank you, sir," said Joey, nodding to Williams.

"What about you?" said the Secretary, moving down the line, "The bulldog-man."

"Agent Douglas D'Angelo, sir," he answered, saluting, "Former Tech-Sergeant, United States Marine Corps. My MOS is weapons development and use, secondary is demolitions and disposal. I have heightened senses which also make me effective at recon and tracking, though I primarily use them to help further my research."

"And, why are you a bulldog, soldier?" the Secretary asked.

Doug looked to Williams before answering. Williams nodded to him.

"Genetic manipulation, sir," he said, "I was part of a previous derivation of the Project looking to manipulate the genome of a living human by adding certain animal traits; my heightened senses of taste, smell, and hearing originate from there as well as my increased muscle mass. The looks were just a side-effect. I'm much more handsome now than I was when I was a Marine, sir."

The Secretary laughed and continued walking down the line.

"That's an awfully big handshake you've got there, kid," he said, staring at Chuckie's gigantic metal left arm, "You look a little young to be involved in this whole thing."

"Age isn't important," Chuckie spit out, "I'm a genius and when you're a genius you have to do the things you have to do with the knowledge that you have. See, I'm the techie. I build things. Like, things that shouldn't be real or things that shouldn't even exist. Like, see those bracers everyone's wearing? I designed those. They're micro computers with GPS, touch-screen interface, an exclusive wireless network, medical monitors, and holographic projection capability. They're able to perform millions of different functions and they have built-in nanolathes which are able to generate small disposable items as needed, like little tools and stuff. Oooh, and I built this thing in my head that lets me interface with just about any kind of electronic device and boosts my memory and increases the speed of my thought process, like an overclocker for my brain. Then I built this cybernetic arm and it's got like super-strength and all kinds of hidden weapons and gadgets and stuff on it and I had to cut my own am off to attach it to myself but it's totally cool because this arm is seriously better than this other little weak fleshy arm except for when I'm working with small parts but then I have optional extensions that come out of the big hand that are like really small hands and they…"

While he was talking at his well-annunciated yet break-neck pace, Moorsblade had walked behind him and slowly put his hand over Chuckie's mouth to silence him.

"Chuckie," said Moorsblade calmly as the kid stopped talking beneath his hand, "Concentrate. Mr. Secretary here would like to know who you are. Please tell him your full name and title."

He slowly removed the hand, but kept it near in case the landslide began again.

"Agent Charles A. Richards, III," said Chuckie, "Like I said, I built most of this stuff and I'm going to keep building because I have all kinds of crazy ideas like…"

Moorsblade covered his mouth again.

"You may want to move on, Mr. Secretary," said Moorsblade, "He can go on for hours."

"I can only imagine," he said, "You, then. What's your special deal?"

He was looking right at Char. She was frozen and hesitant and her stomach burned with anticipation. She was never good with public speaking from what she could remember. She had no idea what to say. There was an awkward silence until Joey started telepathically feeding her lines.

"Agent Charlene Gentile," she said, "Recon, infiltration, and assassination. My enhanced vision lets me see in any spectrum allowing me to keep eyes on a target no matter the circumstance, even total darkness. I have the ability to cloak myself from view and make myself completely silent. I have enhanced speed and agility which, combined with my other abilities, can allow me to get anywhere without being seen or heard. I am also an expert marksman."

The Secretary seemed interested, but progressed down the line. She figured he became concerned when she mentioned assassination in her skill set. It wasn't something Joey prompted her to say, it just came up to the surface. She blamed one too many scenarios run in the training room.

"Ok, big guy," he said, getting to the end of the line, "I assume you're the leader of this group. What do you have to offer?"

"Agent John Moorsblade," he said, smirking, "I'm all you need."
He held his arms out, almost like a challenge.

The Secretary tilted his head and chuckled.

"Anything more specific you could offer, Agent Moorsblade?" he asked.

Williams shot Moorsblade a very stern look with his cold blue eyes. Moorsblade sighed.

"I'm practically invulnerable," said Moorsblade, his relaxed southern accent giving his voice an even cockier tone, "Strength heretofore unseen by mankind, flight capable of up to Mach four with running speed to match and physical endurance on the order of not really needing to eat or breathe, though I still do both out of a force of habit. Oh, and I got heat vision. I am a juggernaut of the most sincere order. I am a one-man army. In short, I'm pretty super, man."

"Funny," said the Secretary, "Quite the little group you've got here, Williams."

"Thank you, Mr. Secretary," Williams replied.

"Agent Moorsblade," said the Secretary, "Your team may be excused. I would like to speak privately with you and your superior."

Moorsblade nodded to the team and Joey lead them out of the room.

Joey lead them one door down from the meeting room. As they stepped inside, Char realized why they called this place the display floor. The room was massive and empty with very minimal lighting. Every door from the surrounding hallways led into this place. Piles of cubicle walls, rolls of carpet, and unopened crates of office supplies were scattered throughout in the event that they would have to put up a better front than just a meeting room.

The wall separating the large room from the conference room was translucent; enough that the whole team could still see and hear what was happening in the meeting. They all grabbed office chairs and sat near the edge of the wall. Char looked at Joey, confused.

"Hologram," Joey told her telepathically, "We can see them, they can't see us. Try to keep it down."

Char nodded and looked into the room just as Moorsblade took a seat across from Williams.

"You both seem to have things well in hand here," said the Secretary after a moment, "This whole thing is amazing, I have to say. When I was read in to the initial reports, I couldn't believe such a thing as super powers existed."

"We prefer not to use such outlandish fictional terms here," Williams said, "My people don't exhibit super powers, they exhibit abilities beyond that of normal human capacity. We call them extra-normal abilities. Imagine a normal person racing against an Olympic-level sprinter. You would not consider the sprinter's ability to run a 'super power'. It is merely above the standard to which the majority of the human population is held, therefore, it is extra-normal."

"Doesn't really matter to me how you spin it," said the Secretary, "I must say, it is impressive. However, we are not currently in a period where such a team would be needed for military purposes. Despite all of the exciting things and interesting people you've shown me today, I'm afraid it's already been decided to pull the plug on any large-budget black operations of this nature."

"Pull the plug, Mr. Secretary?" Williams asked, his voice retaining its calm and emotionless tone, "Why would you do that when you can see first-hand the progress we have made here? Our country is still waging a war on terror. I am in the process of gift-wrapping a victory for you which will guarantee public support for you and the current administration until the day you die."

"Just like you gift-wrapped Vietnam?" said the Secretary, "Or the Soviets? Or Iraq-One? Kuwait? Afghanistan? You may be black bag, but you've got a file as long as my arm in the DoD Vault. Don't think for a moment I haven't been reading about your endless project and all its iterations. Do you realize what could happen if you operation was brought to light?"

"Think about this, Mr. Secretary," said Williams, "My Project trains its Agents to be better than simple soldiers. They are operatives trained with subterfuge skills deadly enough to remove any threat to our great nation and its way of life. Agent Gentile can eliminate a target from up to three miles away with a single untraceable shot. Agent Briggs can read the minds of any captured insurgents. Agent Moorsblade can destroy an entire platoon on his own. My technology department is consistently creating things light years ahead of anything currently produced by the most advanced aspects of the military industrial complex and my Project is filtering those advances down as we move forward in a continuing effort to increase our quality of living.

"As our research continues, we will be able to create more amazing people and things like these. With power of such magnitude, the enemies of our great nation will have no choice but to surrender. The world will be free of terror, once and for all."

"You realize what happens if your team, if its methods, were to be leaked to the public, don't you?" asked the Secretary, "If our country has super-powered people..."

"Extra-normal," Williams corrected.

"Whatever," the Secretary said, "If we have these 'extra-normal' people running around in the open and anyone links them back to the US Government, we're going to face hell. You're going to start another Cold War, Williams - a superhuman arms race."

"We will not start a Cold War, Mr. Secretary," Williams said, "We are already in the middle of one. You may think that your file - 'as long as your arm', was it? – grants you a better understanding of my world.

You may think that you are in control due to this false understanding. This is exasperated by your newly appointed position of power. You may now know more about this nation's defensive capability than the President who appointed you but I assure you that you know nothing of what you're truly defending against."

Williams calm demeanor broke. The emotion in his voice, along with its volume, escalated.

"This Project has been operating, quite literally, since you were in diapers. This is its thirteenth iteration, each with its own threat in mind. It has served its country well in all those years by protecting the American people from dangers they never knew existed. If you were anything but an ignorant ass, like so many politicians before you, you would allow our work to continue uninterrupted and fully funded. You are not the first short-sighted appointee to tour my facility. The biggest disappointment of modern American politics is that the foolish continue to rise to positions of power."

"You are out of line, sir," shouted the Secretary as he slapped the table and stood up.

Moorsblade stood up as well, smirking at the Secretary as they locked eyes.

The Secretary appeared to have more words, but was intimidated away from them by the size of Williams' right-hand man.

"I am certain you were about to claim that I am addressing a superior and should not be so flippant with my words," Williams said, returning to his calm tone, "The fact is, sir, that you are in my facility; a facility which is legally able to detain your Secret Service detachment at the front gate due to their lack of necessary clearance. Your power here, as you will see, is null and void. This entire situation was a formality – an appeal to your better judgment. Now that we are sure said judgment is decidedly not for the better, we can handle things in a fashion to which I am more accustomed."

"Are you threatening me, Williams?" asked the Secretary, "I'll have your job! I'll shut you down and have you and your entire freak show thrown into Guantanamo!"

"Come now, Mr. Secretary," said Williams, with a rather out-of-character chuckle, "We both know that will never happen. But, the answer to your question is no, I am not threatening you. I do not threaten. In a different situation, I could have instructed Agent Moorsblade to remove certain parts of your anatomy in the most painful way imaginable, however, as you are a notable public figure, this would have been inadvisable.

"Should you have continued along your path of denying the funding of this Project, I would have crafted your life into a complete horror show. You would be publically discredited and dishonored. Your young wife would take your two children and leave you for fear of her association with your disgrace. You would be destroyed beyond all hope for redemption. Perhaps it would be you taking up residence in your charming Guantanamo facility."

"So," said the Secretary, sitting down, his tone changed from confident to fearful, "Why don't you?"

"I find it much more palatable to come to an agreement," said Williams, "While you are an insufferable, moronic, nothing of a man, you still hold the ultimate power to complete this transaction. While your qualities as any sort of true leader are untested and lacking, you are now a known quantity to me. As is said, I would rather deal with the devil I know than with the devil I do not. Now, the agreement will be that you continue funding this Project and we will continue saving the world. How does that sound?"

"Sounds good," the Secretary muttered.

"Very well," said Williams, "Now, as you would probably be broken under any amount of pressure when asked what happened here today and as your peers or your superior would likely attempt to shut us down after hearing of the intense pressure under which you were just placed, I am going to have my associate Agent Briggs remove the last bit of our conversation from your memory including the part where you urinated in your pants, likely out of fear."

The Secretary looked down and realized that Williams was right. It happened while Moorsblade stared menacingly, smiling while Williams talked calmly about the painful removal of body parts.

"Stay here," Joey instructed the others before walking through the holographic wall and into the conference room.

"For the record, Mr. Secretary," Williams said, "I could have had Agent Briggs, at any time, manipulate your mind into complete agreement. I wished to reach this agreement through conversation and demonstration, not through outright manipulation. With our conversation concluded and all implications in their proper place, I am sure I can have your word that this will be your last visit to my facility while you hold your position."

"Yes," said the Secretary without hesitation.

"Good," said Williams, "Agent Briggs will take care of a few details. We will have some new clothes replicated and brought to this room before you leave. As long as you can keep from embarrassing yourself from here to the elevator, no one, including you, need ever know about your little accident. Good day, Mr. Secretary."

Williams nodded to Joey. She put her palm on the Secretary's forehead with her fingers stretched into his hair.

"Anything else you'd like me to insert while I have him, sir?" she asked.

"No," Williams said, "He understands quite well."

This was the last the Project heard from the government regarding their budget.  It was also the last that anyone heard of the conference room chair used by the Secretary.

## XII

The first time was an accident.

Josh had been sitting at an old workbench in the back of the main cave, still sifting through the massive piles of electronics, utilizing his power to its most useful to date as a human circuit tester. He didn't have the technical knowledge to know what most of this stuff was but he knew Kurt had a purpose for it all. Every once in a while, Kurt would come out from the large tarp under which he'd been hiding – working on something huge – and taking components from the "good" pile before scurrying back under the cover and continuing the assembly of whatever.

The cave was busy enough that, when Josh did it for the first time, no one was paying attention. They all had their own parts to play in making this relic of a mine a habitable headquarters for whatever they planned to do in the future. It was Kurt's place, technically, and he had a vision for what it should become.

That vision involved everyone in their group doing as much as they could. Josh was happy that he didn't really have to break a sweat in his portion of the construction but continued to feel undervalued both in his abilities and his current position. Then it happened.

Most of the components Kurt had given him to test were long abandoned computer parts, bits of appliances, outdated cell phones – things which hadn't seen the light of day in forever. He purchased these from an e-cycling facility for double what they would get after the things were scrapped. Nothing that came through Josh's hands had a battery due to the green-minded people who didn't want alkaline or lithium crapping up the dirt. It was a common practice to remove the batteries from electronics before discarding them as they had to be disposed in a different fashion. This is why, Kurt insisted, Josh's job was so important. He could make sure things were in working order without actually powering them up.

It was a surprise when Josh stumbled across the remnants of an old portable radio with a pair of double-As still inside. The contacts on the first battery were corroded after he popped it out into his hand. The second one appeared newer and still intact. Josh held it by the contacts between his thumb and his middle finger and suddenly, he felt it – a rush of energy like he'd never experienced before.

He felt more awake and aware, like the effects of twenty cups of coffee had just snapped into his brain all at once. His muscles tensed up and suddenly didn't feel the fatigue of doing a repetitive task. He could feel the energy coursing through him. He knew right away what had happened and it bestowed him with a sudden glee and a renewed purpose.

As the energy flowed through him, he concentrated on channeling it to different parts of his body. He could feel it move at his command. The charge was waiting to be expended in one way or another. He narrowed his eyes at one particular circuit board sticking up from the top of the pile and pointed at it with is thumb extended up, like a gun. He dropped his thumb like a hammer and an arc of electricity leapt from his finger to his target, blowing it backwards and away from its companions.

The power had left him along with that energetic feeling, but he still smiled with the realization that he wasn't quite as useless as he thought he was.

"Hey guys," he said, standing up without thinking, "Let's go out."

"Out?" asked Justin, who was currently practicing welding with heat from his finger by building reinforced metal supports for the tunnels, "Out where, exactly? For one, it's almost midnight and for two some of us don't look quite human enough for the Friday night bar scene."

"Not what I'm talking about," Josh said, "Let's go out. Like, on patrol."

"Like, crime patrol?" Budda asked, setting down the large bunch of metal rods he had been hauling, "Seriously?"

"Is it that time already?" Justin asked.

"What time?" Josh asked.

"That part in the origin story where we go out on our first big bust only to have it blow up in our face somehow," Justin answered.

"I told you to knock that off," Kurt said from under the tarp, "It's not mentally healthy."

"Maybe minus the blowing up in our face part," Josh said, "But yeah. Aren't you guys like itching for action now that we've got all these powers?"

"Said the man with practically none," Mike said from one of the upper-tunnels.

"I don't know that we're all ready for that," said Kurt, poking his head out from under the tarp and staring at Justin, "Some of us need to gain more control with their abilities before they can be trusted in the field."

"You do know I never welded, ever, before today," Justin said, "Let alone while using my pointer finger in the place of a proper torch."

"You slagged the first dozen pieces of that metal," Kurt said.

"Because I've got no idea what I'm doing!" Justin shouted, "You just threw metal at me and wanted me to connect it using a power I have no real idea how to control! If I'm going to do my own trial-and-error on this, you can't be that upset with the results. We've got briefcases full of government money to throw around and you'd rather me sit here and do amateur hour. If you wanted them done well, you could have hired someone."

"Yeah, that would go well," Kurt said, "I'll just pick a random contractor out of the phone book and ask them if they can come down to my superhero cave for a major project."

"Whatever," Justin said, his hair flaring up around the edges, "Sorry that my brand new super powers aren't precise enough for you. Next time, I'll practice for a few months before agreeing to be your personal welding torch."

"Now kiss," said Mike, causing everyone else to giggle.

"Anyway," Justin said, raising his middle finger in Mike's general direction, "I'm not going out. While my work might not be good enough for Dr. Technostein here, I agree with what he's saying. We're not trained enough. I don't want to risk melting someone's head or getting shot for that matter."

"Whatever," Josh said, "Mike, you in?"

"I could use some time away from the cave, sure," he said.

"Budda?" Josh asked.

"Yeah, I'll go," he answered, shrugging.

"Jess?" Josh asked, not seeing her in the room.

"Someone has to make sure you stay safe," she said in everyone's heads, "Might as well be me."

"You sure you two want to stay?" Josh asked.

"I'm good," Justin said, "Don't really want to be there when the story takes that interesting, hopefully slight, turn for the worse."

"I'm staying," Kurt said, retreating behind the tarp, "Too much work to do."

"Fine," Josh said, "Let's saddle up."

"I'll drive," said Mike, "I think my SUV is the only thing that could possibly hold Earthshaker over there."

"Ha ha," said Budda as Josh began leading them out of the cave and back up to the house.

"Shouldn't we grab disguises or something?" Mike asked, "Ski-masks? Bandanas? Sheets with holes cut out for the eyes?"

"I don't think we'd need them," Josh said, "We're going to be dealing with street level stuff, not Doctor Doom. What's a thug gonna do? Tell the cops he got beat down by a bunch of people with super powers? They'd never believe it."

"I can always wipe their memories," Jess said.

The group stopped and turned to her, silent.

"What?" she asked.

"Seriously?" Mike asked.

"Well, yeah," she said, "I am a psychic."

"Dude," Josh said, "Remind me to keep your hands away from my head."

"There's nothing in there anyway, electro-boy," said Jess.

"Fine," Josh said, "But, seriously."

"I'm not going to erase your memories," Jess said.

"Don't do anything to mine, either," Budda requested.

"I'm not going to erase anyone's memories!" she shouted.

"You just said you'd do it," Josh said.

"To the bad guys," Jess said, "Are you a bad guy?"

"Um," Josh said, "Relatively, no."

"Then I'm not erasing your memories," Jess said, "I don't want to erase anyone's memories, but I will erase the memories of the bad guys if I have to."

"But," Budda muttered, "Then they won't know what they did wrong."

Everyone's attention turned to Budda with a collective huff of exasperation.

"If I could shock you right now," Josh said, "I would."

Mike opened the tailgate of the SUV.

"Ok," he said, "Everyone get in. All giant rock men get to ride in the back."

After a degree of manipulation including the removal of one of the SUV's rear seats, all of them were able to fit inside. Budda rode with his back to the driver's seat and his legs stretched out straight to the rear hatch and still had to hunch over to completely fit.

"Where to, then?" Mike said.

"I dunno," Josh said, riding shotgun, "Where there's crime."

"And where is that?" Mike asked.

"Y'know," Josh said, "Like, the bad parts of town."

"This whole outing just went full retard," Jess said, sighing.

"Ok, wait," Josh said, "Let me try something."

He put his hands on the stereo in the center console. Within a few moments, they were listening to the police band.

"How did you do that?" Mike asked.

"Police bands are radio signals," Josh said, "Just with different frequency ranges. I used my remote control powers to boost your car stereo to pick them up."

"That's," Jess stammered, "That's actually kind of impressive."

"Thanks," Josh said, "Can we stop at a convenience store or something before we get serious? I need to grab something to drink."

"Sure," Mike said, "As long as you promise to put my radio back to normal when we're done."

"I'll try," Josh said.


A few hours later, they were deep into the downtown areas of the city. Josh stared listlessly out the window, drawing power from the random assortment of batteries he'd grabbed at the convenience store. The drink was just a cover. The batteries were the real reason he wanted to stop.

The police calls coming over the radio were almost unintelligible; they didn't know the codes or the short hand. Mike said that he knew a bit about it, but couldn't prove it as they had not yet heard anything he recognized.

"I'm bored," Jess said, "Are we done looking for crime yet?"

"Yeah," Budda said, "This is kinda dumb. It's like three in the morning, dude."

"Even superheroes in the comics have slow days," Josh said, "They just never write those stories. Some nights, they probably go out on patrol and wind up swinging around on grappling hooks or wasting web fluid because they have nothing else to do."

"I guess sometimes they also wind up circling the same fifteen blocks in the Mystery Machine while waiting for the cops to announce some action over the radio," Jess said, "The hell with this."

"Wait," Mike said, cutting her off and turning up the volume.

According to the police band, a four-fifty-nine was currently in progress on the north side of the city.

"That's a tripped security alarm," Mike said, "Probably breaking and entering."

"I know where that is," Josh said, "It's not far. If we hurry, we can beat the cops there."

"Let's do it," Budda said.

Mike floored it. The wheels of the SUV chirped, and they were off.

When they reached the address stated over the radio, they saw that it was a jewelry store. It was a stand-alone building separated from the other row-shops by two very narrow alleys protected by fences and barbed wire. From Josh's observation, the front door and windows were all undisturbed. Through those windows, he could see flashlights moving around in the rear of the room.

"They must have gone in through the back," Josh said, "Go around the corner, there's a wider alley behind the building."

Without another word, Mike jetted them off and wheeled around the corner at the end of the block. He turned off his headlights and crept slowly down the alley, blocking the exit from the dead end with his vehicle. He stopped halfway down the alley and shut the engine off. Josh jumped out as soon as he was able.

"Wait," Mike shout-whispered as Josh ran ahead, "Wait for us!"

Josh stopped and absorbed more energy from his pocket full of batteries. He winced for a moment then started tapping his foot impatiently, waiting for the others. Budda was having a particularly difficult time passing between the wall of the alley and Mike's SUV and was being extra-careful not to scratch his friend's car.

Jess approached Josh and whispered:

"Be careful with that stuff," she said, "You don't want to turn into some kind of addict."

"What are you talking about?" Josh asked.

"The batteries," she said, "I know what you've been up to. I know what you discovered. I know you wanted everyone to come out with you tonight so that they could see you weren't helpless. I also know how the energy makes you feel."

117

"Quit," Josh said, pausing to think, "I dunno, quit being psychic. I thought you were going to stay out of our heads."

"It wasn't hard," she said, "A mind is like an open book when something is this important to a person. And, I promised I wouldn't erase your memories, I never said anything about not reading your mind."

"Just don't tell anyone else, ok?" Josh asked.

"Your secret is safe with me," she said.

"Well, before that it was safe with me," Josh glared.

"I'm just trying to protect you," Jess said, "I don't want anything bad to happen to you."

"Whatever," Josh muttered.

"We ready, ladies?" Mike whispered after Budda escaped his situation.

"Yeah," said Josh, tossing a final scowl to Jess.

They moved down the alley. Josh peeked around the next building to the wider center area, where the street ended.

The area was spotted with multiple dumpsters at the back of the surrounding buildings. The back door to the jewelry shop was wide open but no alarm was currently sounding A white panel van was parked here with its sliding side door open, engine idling, and the driver flicking at a lit cigarette dangling out the window.

"Must be a lookout," Josh whispered, "I'll sneak past him and scope the place out."

He dropped low and got behind the van. From there, he made his way to a small dumpster and, with his skinny frame, was able to squeeze behind it to avoid detection. The door of the shop was in plain sight. He stared at the driver and waited for an opening. When the driver looked away, he bolted for the door and made it inside.

The back room was a security suite. A small red light labeled "silent alarm" was blinking on a console. On a bank of monitors, he could see the two men in the main room with their flashlights focused on a spot on the wall, paying no attention to anything else. He also spotted himself in the monitor bank – the back of his head to be specific. He turned around and saw the camera staring at him. He casually raised his hand and shut it off with his remote control powers. The corresponding monitor went dark. He peeked around the corner and saw another camera. He made the clicking motion and shut that one off as well. Looking back at the monitor bank, six others were active. He waved his hand at the console and willed them all to deactivate. They obeyed.

His heart was pumping. There were bad guys right around the corner and he would catch them in the act. He put his back to the wall, took a few deep breaths, held his pointer fingers up as though his hands were guns, and made a flying action-hero leap into the main room.

The two men didn't notice him. He expected them to turn, guns blazing, forcing him to fire back. His action movie dreams were shattered as they continued working, undaunted.

He quietly stood up. He was across the room from them, behind the opposite counter. One was very tall and held a flashlight while the second, a shorter and stockier man now worked with both hands.

Josh was conflicted. He wanted to shout "freeze" but worried that it might cause him to get shot. The action-hero leap gave a much better chance that they wouldn't hit him. Now that he was standing still he didn't think getting their attention would be the best idea.

He slowly aimed his still-pointed fingers at the backs of the two men. This was it. Take them by surprise. None of the guys would believe that he could take out two thugs on his own. They would totally take him seriously after this. He smirked and dropped the thumb on his right hand.

A blue arc of electricity shot from his fingers and instantly impacted with the squat man's back. There was a loud crack as the energy jumped across the room and the victim fell to the ground in a heap.

"What the...?" said the tall man, turning around to see Josh, "Hey!"

The flashlight was on him now. He tried to pull the trigger on his other imaginary gun, but nothing happened. Josh felt white-hot fear boiling in his stomach as the tall man drew a real gun and started to speak. Josh took off through the back room and the open back door, returning to the alley.

"Guys!" he shouted, "Guys, help!"

"Hold it!" called the tall man behind him.

Josh stopped obediently and turned around to see the gun pointed at his head.

"What the hell did you do the boss in there?" the tall man asked.

"Nothing, I..." Josh started, "I zapped him."

"You what?" the tall man said, his face contorted in confusion.

"I zapped him," Josh said, "It was just a little jolt. It was supposed to stun him. He'll probably be out for a while. I was trying to stop him."

"Stop him from what?" the tall man said, "Deactivating the alarm?"

"Well, yeah," Josh said, taking a breath before he would explain everything.

"Is there a problem here, fellas?" Mike asked, walking out from around the corner, eliminating the possibility of Josh's explanation.

"Stop right there," said the driver, stepping out of the van with a gun on Mike.

"No thanks," Mike said, slowly walking toward him, "Don't think I will."

"Vinnie," asked the driver, "What the hell's going on here?"

"Vinnie?" Mike asked, "Seriously? Can you guys be any more stereotypical? I guess that makes Mr. Driver here Tony or Paulie or Silvio or something, right?"

"Relax, Jim," said Vinnie to the driver, "These guys ain't armed."

"No," Mike said, badly imitating Vinnie, "We sure ain't."

"You supposed to be some kind of comedian or something?" Jim asked, "Vinnie, what's going on? Where's the boss?"

"The blond kid says he tased him or something," Vinnie said, "Knocked him out. We were just trying to deactivate the alarm."

"Oh, that's all?" Mike said, "Trying to deactivate the alarm on a jewelry store in the middle of the night? Well, in that case, we'll just be on our way. Oh, no, wait; we have to take down some criminals first."

"What are you talking about?" Vinnie said, "Your guy busted in there and tased our boss. We didn't do anything wrong."

"Your boss?" Mike asked, "God, Justin was right. This is so stereotypical. Are you on some kind of mob heist or something?"

"What?" Vinnie said, "We work for Mr. Pesante!"

"Yeah, that doesn't sound like a mafia name at all," Mike said.

"He's right," Jim said, "We work for Mr. Pesante. This is all legit."

"Is that name supposed to mean something to me?" Mike asked.

"Mike," Jess said in his head.

Mike held his hand up to the hidden part of the alley.

Josh slowly slid his hand into his pocket while the two men were distracted by Mike. The batteries he bought had all been emptied.

"I would hope it means something to you," said Vinnie, "And your boy just knocked him out! Do you even know who he is?"

"I don't care who he is," said Mike, "Look, guys, you don't want to get hurt and we don't want to hurt you. Let's just put the guns down and everything will be a lot simpler."

"Mike," Jess said again, in his head. Mike ignored her.

Josh slipped his hand from his jacket pocket full of dead batteries into the front pocket of his jeans, where his cell phone was. He quietly popped the back of it off and absorbed the battery inside. The shock of power was the most he'd felt yet. It made him tense up, arch his back, and roll his eyes into the back of his head. His entire body clenched but he remained standing.

"What the hell?" said Vinnie, pulling back the hammer on his gun.

"Hey!" Mike called, anticipating a shot, and running toward Vinnie.

Vinnie turned and popped off two shots at Mike as he advanced. Mike stopped in his tracks.

Josh regained some control over himself as the shots rang out and fired a bolt at Vinnie's knees. Vinnie shook and fell to the ground, dropping the gun.

"Mike!" Jess shouted aloud.

"Vinnie!" Jim shouted, turning his gun on Josh.

Suddenly, Budda charged from the alley at Jim, his one massive hand batting the gun to the ground before the other wrapped around Jim's neck and pinned him to the side of the van. Budda looked down as Jim struggled to put his hands up in surrender.

"Mike," Jess called, running over to join the others, "Are you ok?"

Two flattened slugs hung in midair about an inch from Mike's chest.

"Well," Mike said, his breathing nervous as he swallowed hard, "Now we know that my forcefields are bulletproof."

He plucked one of the slugs out of the air and put it in his pocket before letting the other fall.

Jim struggled to speak against the pressure of rock on his throat.

"He's trying to say something," Jess said, "Let him talk."

Budda loosened his grip a bit, allowing Jim to rasp: "The sign..."

"The sign?" Mike asked, "What sign? What kind of cryptic crap is that?"

"The sign," Jim squawked, "The sign in front says Pesante Fine Jewelry. We work for Mr. Pesante. You guys just picked the wrong night to rob the place is all. Please, don't kill us."

"That's what I was trying to tell you," Jess said, "These guys belong here."

"Wait," Mike said, "You're not robbing the place?"

"No," Jim said, "You guys are, right? Go ahead and take whatever. Just don't kill us."

"So, I just zapped Mr. Pesante," Josh said, "The owner, right?"

"He's a cheapskate," Jim sputtered, "He's got this ancient alarm system and he won't spring for anything new. The freakin' security cameras still run on VHS. The thing goes off like every other night but he won't pay for repairs, let alone a new one. Happens so much that the alarm company just calls the cops and they call him. They don't even bother showing up anymore. Just take what you want and leave. I'm not going to try to stop you. Especially not with whatever the hell this is holding my neck."

"If that's Mr. Pesante in there," Josh asked, "Then who the hell are you guys?"

"Store security," said Jim, "I won't tell, I swear. I won't run. Please, I've got kids."

"Look," Mike said, "We're not the bad guys. We came here to stop a robbery, not to pull one off."

"Whatever you say," Jim said, panicking, his eyes welling up with tears, "Just take what you want and leave me alive. Please."

Jess reached over Budda's arm and touched Jim on the forehead. His eyes closed and his body went limp. Budda dropped him and he slumped to the ground with his back against the van.

"He won't remember the last half hour or so," Jess said, looking at Mike, "Sorry. He wouldn't have been receptive to anything you said; too much adrenaline and too much fear."

"Ok, then," Mike said, shrugging, "I guess we'll clean this up the easy way."

"Vinnie and Mr. Pesante are still alive, by the way," Jess said, looking with dagger eyes at Josh.

"Uh," Josh said, the rest of the group now looking at him, "Good."

"Budda," Jess said, "Grab these two, and put them in the van. I'm going to fix this."

She touched Vinnie's head briefly before going inside the store.

"So you can shoot lightning bolts now?" Mike asked.

"I guess," Josh said, "I just needed a little more power to make it work."

"That's pretty damn sweet," Mike said.

"Yeah," Josh said, yawning, "Takes a lot of juice, though."

Jess walked out of the back. A small drip of blood was coming from her nose.

"Don't forget the one inside, Budda," she said, wiping the blood with the side of her hand.

"Are you ok?" Josh asked.

"I just rearranged the memories of three innocent people who we attached for no reason," she said, "My head hurts, it's three in the morning, I'm standing in a dumpster alley, and my nose is bleeding. I'm freaking peachy. Just remember, I'm not always going to be here to clean up your messes."

She walked past them and continued to the Jeep.

They all wanted to just go home and forget this ever happened. They did, but not for long.

## XIII

Her stomach was bothering her. She knew exactly why this was happening but didn't want to tell anyone for fear of their reaction, especially not her boyfriend.

The last time she had seen everyone in the same room was at Char's funeral. Since then, the social life among their clique of friends had been relatively inactive except for whatever they'd been working on in the cave. No matter how bad her stomach felt, she resolved herself not to bring it up. She didn't want to bring everyone down after not seeing them for so long.

Josh led her through Kurt's tiny house, into the basement, and down the new coal cellar steps. He told her to be careful as they crossed the expanded original room and walked down a long, well-lit tunnel into what they were referring to as the main chamber. He'd told her about it, but she didn't believe how massive it was until she saw it with her own eyes.

The cave was finally complete and matched with every descriptor Josh had implied.

The ceiling stretched at least sixty feet up. Bridged walkways now replaced the old, rotten minecart tracks he described. The tunnels looked mostly clean of coal dust. New lighting had been added to some areas where the large overhead lamps didn't reach, including wires which stretched into a few of the tunnels. The floor had been leveled and was smooth to the touch. Josh hadn't told her how they accomplished that part, but when faced with questions about it she often assumed that it had something to do with super powers. Most things around here did.

Metal supports now lined the cave. Josh had told her about Justin's welding and Mike's forcefields supporting him as he worked. He told her about Budda widening caves by punching into the solid rock. He told her about his circuit testing and about Kurt's ongoing construction which was what brought them here today.

The giant object in the middle of the room under a makeshift tarp of bed sheets and plastic against the central pillar was the reason they were here. Kurt wanted everyone to witness the activation of what he was touting as the single greatest thing he would ever build.

"Impressive, isn't it?" Josh asked her.

"Yeah," Emma said, rolling her eyes, "It's a big cave alright."

"It's our Batcave," Josh said, "Our Sanctum Sanctorum. Our Avengers Mansion. This is where we are going to come to fight crime."

She had tuned him out. Her stomach was turning over again.

The rest of the group was standing in front of the tarp. Even Steph was here, standing next to Budda with a gentle rocky hand on her shoulder.

"Now that everyone is here," Kurt said, smiling, "We can get started."

"Could you please just do this already," Jess said, "I'm tired of sleeping alone at night while you're down here tinkering."

"Ladies and gentlemen," Kurt said, uncharacteristically overdramatic, "I present to you the heart of all we hope to accomplish: a way for us to look into any part of the world and see exactly what's happening. I give you... LENNY!"

With one swift motion, the entire tarp slid to the floor. Emma put her hand to her mouth as she saw what was revealed.

LENNY was a twenty-foot tall supercomputer which had been frankensteined together with parts from hundreds if not thousands of different machines. Though patchwork in spots, she could tell that a great deal of care for the machine's aesthetics went into its construction.

It was a monument of buttons, switches, lights, and monitors. Every bit of it appeared as though it were scrounged from something except for a few choice screens, namely the main screen in the middle - a brand new flat-screen which, if it had been someone's living room TV rather than a component in a crime-fighting computer, would take up most of the room and make for a rather ridiculous viewing experience.

Around the main pillar were a few separate terminals. To Emma, they looked like the places henchmen would sit in a supervillain's lair.

Kurt approached the main console and pressed a button. The dozens of screens and lights flashed to life for the first time. Emma let an audible noise of astonishment slip and watched as the lights flashed in a mildly hypnotizing pattern.

The words "LENNY is online" appeared in white writing at the top right of all the black screens followed by a blinking cursor. Everyone stared at this image for a solid minute before the silence was broken.

"You're kidding, right?" Justin asked, "That's it? 'LENNY is online'?"

"It's his first time booting up," Kurt said, "Cut him some slack."

"Him?" Justin asked, "You mean LENNY?"

"Yes," Kurt said, "Do you have a problem with him?"

"What does it stand for?" Mike asked.

"What does what stand for?" Kurt asked back.

"What does L-E-N-N-Y stand for?" Mike asked, "You have it there in all caps, I figured it was an acronym or something. So, what does it mean?"

"Uh," Kurt started, "Law... Enforcement... uh... Neutralization... um... N... You?"

"Great job," Jess said.

"Yeah, it was the first name I thought of," Kurt said, "I just thought it would look cool that way. All the supercomputers in pop-culture have acronym type names. HAL, WOPR..."

"GLaDOS," Justin continued, "Oooh! Is he going to speak to us in a cool computer voice? Please tell me he has a cool computer voice."

"No," Kurt said.

"Ok, first order of business," Justin said, "Program that thing to have a badass computer voice. One that relentlessly taunts people."

"Anyway," Kurt said, "LENNY is going to find the bad guys for us. He monitors television, radio signals, satellites, internet searches, even some cell phones. He searches for thousands of strings of keywords, compiles reports, and notifies us of the ones he thinks are of high importance. He assigns a rating to the issue and allows us to view the data he's collected on any one of his twenty-seven monitors."

"Spare us the jargon," Josh said, "Just tell us it's awesome."

"He's the most awesome system ever built," Kurt said, "He can do pretty much anything."

"Except speak with his own super-badass computer voice," said Justin.

Kurt glared at Justin.

"It's still not doing anything," Emma said.

"Not on the big screen," Kurt said, holding up a tablet, "I've got him under my command right here. Check it out."

He tapped at the screen a few times and the central monitor displayed a cable news channel. Other channels appeared on the smaller monitors on the main column of the machine.

"It's not just media, either," Kurt said, "I've hacked through to just about every system that isn't stand-alone which might be of some use - Department of Transportation, certain security grids, FBI files, local police computers, even the National Do-Not-Call List. It's all wired in to LENNY, ready to go whenever we need it."

"The more I hear about this," Budda said, "The more I think it's rabidly irresponsible."

"Why?" Kurt said, "This is the ultimate crime fighting tool!"

"It's also violating privacy in a manner usually reserved for the NSA," Budda said, "We wanted to stay off the government radar and here you are hacking into them. Don't you think someone is going to pick up on this?"

"Not a chance," Kurt said, "I've made sure that LENNY is absolutely trace-proof. I've got so much spoofing that no matter how they try they'll be tracking us back to a hot dog stand in downtown Tokyo."

"A hot dog stand in Tokyo?" Mike asked.

"Or some other equally obscure location," Kurt said, "It's random every time."

"And you're basing your security measures on your powers?" Justin asked.

"Yes," Kurt replied

"Powers we've only been using for a short time now," Justin continued, "You complained because I couldn't use mine to make precise spot welds without practice now you're claiming that your powers made an ultimate hacker out of someone who was essentially a luddite? Not only that, but you're claiming hacking feats which would only be accomplished in an early-90s movie. You can't just dial in to the school and change your info, Ferris."

"It's called Technopathy," Kurt said, frustrated, "I did my research. I can operate any machine I touch with expert proficiency. I can upload and download data with my brain like it was a hard drive. I can hack as fantastically as an early-90s movie because I innately understand everything there is to know about it. I don't write code, I just think of what I want to happen and it happens. So, please, can we put to rest any doubts about our safety and get on with our superhero careers?"

The room was quiet. Emma had never seen Kurt this angry before.

"As I was saying," Kurt continued, "LENNY has a filter which searches for key phrases. When the filter is active, he compiles all available data into a package, giving us access to video feeds, documents, reports, whatever is available. It ranks events with a number of stars; the higher the number, the more pressing the issue."

"Stars?" Josh asked, "You're giving crooks a wanted rating?"

"Actually," Kurt said, "It's more like a YouTube rating."

"So," Josh said, "Our entire crime fighting career is going to be predicated on the same system that gave us cats in shark costumes riding on roombas?"

"It's based on the coding," Kurt said, "It's not actually YouTube. I figured it would be a good idea to have the user interface emulate something familiar to everyone."

A pop-up box containing a small red exclamation point appeared in the lower left corner of the large screen with a ding. Kurt tapped at his tablet and the box enlarged. It read:

Borough Police – Car 3 – Domestic Disturbance Call – 347 Maplewood Dr. Action? y/n

"Pop-ups for crime?" Emma asked.

"Best way to keep track of the most current stuff," said Kurt with a shrug, "The cops call in a code for a crime, LENNY interprets it, gives us the info, and asks if we want to take care of it. Obviously, we won't be going on too many domestics."

"So much for the late night stakeouts," Josh said.

"Dude," Justin said, "Can we hook up an Xbox to the big screen?"

Kurt shrugged.

"Do whatever," he said, "Just don't touch anything I've already plugged in. The pop-ups will appear regardless of what's happening on the screen. I'm also going to be bringing some furniture in so we can be a bit more comfortable. Anyone who wants to stay here during their downtime is more than welcome. Pick a tunnel and furnish out a room if you want. This is like a fire house, though. If you're here, you're on call."

"I'm totally hooking up my Xbox down here," Justin muttered.

"Just don't touch any of the control panels until I get a chance to show you how to use them," Kurt said, "They're always gathering data and they're extremely sensitive."

"So you guys are really going to do the whole crime fighter thing," Emma said.

"We've put enough time into this place," Kurt said, nodding, "Would be a shame for it to become just a big clubhouse."

Pain shot through her stomach. She flinched and doubled over slightly.

"You ok?" asked Kurt.

"Uh, yeah," Emma said, "Y'know, cramps and all."

"Oh," said Kurt, dismissively, "Right."

It was the best excuse in the world for having these pains in front of everyone. She wondered how long she had until something else happened. She hoped that, whatever came next, it wouldn't be noticeable. She wondered if anyone else here had felt like this before.

"Hey Kurt," Mike said, "There's a big blinking exclamation point now."

He tapped at the pad and LENNY went into another mode. Things on the main screen shuffled around madly before it displayed:

!!! URGENT !!! Media Found – Facial Match Confirmed – Group Member Sighted In Action !!! URGENT !!!

The messaged flashed for a few seconds then cut to a feed of local news.

"An odd attempted break-in at a local jewelry store is baffling both police and the owner of the store on the North Side," said the reporter, "This footage was obtained from the scene and can only be seen exclusively on our station."

They cut to a still shot of Josh with his hand up as if he were holding a remote control.

"Police are on the lookout for this man: an unidentified white male with blond hair and glasses in his mid-to-late twenties. This video comes from an inspection of the security tape at Pesante's Fine Jewelry nearly a week ago. The break-in was discovered when the storeowner realized that his security system had been inactive since this video was taken. An inventory of the store revealed no missing property however the unknown man is still wanted for questioning with regards to the incident."

The clip came to an end and LENNY displayed a message asking if they would like to resume their program from the last paused point.

The room was silent for a moment.

"Sweet," Justin muttered, "He has DVR."

"Josh!" Mike shouted, "You told us you had this covered!"

"You guys knocked over a jewelry store?" Kurt asked.

"We thought someone else was trying to knock it over," Jess sighed.

"Then why would you shut off the cameras?" Kurt asked, "Everyone's going to think you were robbing the joint!"

"We had to shut them off," Josh said, "We didn't want to be seen. I had to go inside and I didn't want to be on video."

"And yet," Kurt said, "Somehow, you were."

"You shut off the security," Mike said, "But you didn't erase the tapes? Even after that one guy told you they were in there? On VHS?"

"I wasn't thinking about the tapes, ok?" Josh said, "I was thinking about plugging a couple thousand volts into two guys who we thought were robbing the store. Blame adrenaline."

"Whatever you choose to blame," Kurt said, "This is a pretty epic fail."

"We didn't take anything," Budda said, "Even the news knows it. The owner probably just wants to know what Josh was doing there."

"Even though Josh didn't erase the tapes," Jess said, "I erased the whole thing from their memories."

"You erased memories?" Kurt said, "Why didn't you tell me that this turned into such a cluster?"

"You didn't ask," Jess said, "And, when I tried to tell you, you asked me to leave you alone because you were working on this stupid thing."

She motioned to LENNY and turned her back on him.

"This was the biggest failure in superhero history." Kurt said, "Josh gets caught on tape, Jess erases people's memories…"

"I got shot twice," Mike said.

"You got shot twice?!" Kurt exclaimed

"Well, shot at," Mike said, "My forcefields got the job done, thankfully."

"What happened to you, then?" Kurt asked, turning to Budda.

"I'm fine," he said, complacently.

"So, did you stop the robbery?" Kurt asked.

"Turns out it wasn't a robbery," Josh said, "It was a late-night security check by the owner. I shut off the cameras and snuck inside. Managed to stun the owner with a lightning bolt."

"Lightning bolt?" Kurt asked, "You?"

"Yeah, I shoot lightning bolts now," Josh said, "Lightning bolts are cool."

"Whatever," Kurt said, "I don't really care about the story. You've ruined our chances of becoming superheroes before they had a chance to get off the ground. We're done here."

"Hey, lay off him," Justin said, "We're all rookies and it was a rookie mistake. Just because your abilities apparently allow you some flawless understanding of the universe doesn't mean the same goes for the rest of us."

"We're done, don't you see?" Kurt asked, "Those government people from the hospital are going to see him on TV and flip their shit. They're going to come looking for us and all of your worst paranoid delusions are going to come true."

"Delusions?" Justin said, "This whole time I've been predicting everything that happens just by looking at the tropes! I told them this was going to end badly before they even left the cave. The government won't move on this, it's not the right time yet. We're barely into the second act."

"Listen to yourself," Kurt said, "You're losing it."

"I think I'm finding it," Justin said, "Logically, I think we're going to be ok for now. The government guys didn't say we couldn't get on the news, they just didn't want anyone blabbing about the chemical spill. I guarantee there wasn't a masked vigilante clause in that giant contract we signed. There's no way they could have thought that far ahead. They would have black bagged us by now."

"People are looking for Josh," Kurt said, tapping at the tablet and bringing up the police database on the screen, "He's wanted in connection with an attempted robbery."

"Wanted for questioning," Josh said, adjusting his glasses and looking at the main screen, "There isn't a warrant out for my arrest. I didn't do anything and, even if they think I did, they can't prove it. I didn't leave any fingerprints in that place and any of the guys who would be able to identify me have no memory of it. If they ask me, I'll tell them I was there to repair the broken security system. Those guys said the owner is a cheapskate and the alarms go off by mistake all the time."

"And where are your credentials?" Kurt asked, "They're never going to believe you."

"You've got unlimited hacks," Josh said, "Can you just fake something?"

"LENNY was not built for breaking the law," Kurt said.

"I beg to differ," Josh retorted, "LENNY is already breaking the law. You hacked local, state, and federal government systems not to mention the cell-phone snooping capabilities you hinted at back there. Just because you want to use the information to do good things doesn't make what you did right."

"Josh is right," Jess said, "His fix works. We could just fake it. We file a bogus report in the police database, I go down to the station and mess with some heads and make them think they did an interrogation, and it's over. It's the simplest and easiest solution."

"You want me to reduce my masterpiece to petty forgery?" Kurt asked.

"Yes," Emma shouted, tired of staying silent in her pain, "Yes, you self-righteous moron. You cannot possibly justify all the laws you've already broken in pursuit of your stupid crime-fighting plans and then come up short when you have the opportunity to help one of your friends out of a jam – a jam that affects all of us, for that matter. If you seriously think that those Feds are going to be knocking on your door then now is not the time to worry about sullying the reputation of your 'masterpiece'. Fake the ID, fake the memories, fake whatever you have to fake, and keep the lid on the situation."

She took a deep breath and clutched at her stomach as she finished. It hurt worse than before, but she was tougher than most. She grabbed at Josh's shoulder to steady herself and did her best not to wince to noticeably. When the pain subsided, she started walking toward the door, stopping next to Kurt on her way out.

"And, if you didn't pick up on the hints," Emma said, "Your girlfriend is tired of you ogling that machine instead of her. Doesn't take a psychic to see that."

She walked at a quick pace out of the room and back up into the house. Josh chased after her.

"Where are you going?" Josh asked, catching up to her as the breached the basement floor.

"Home," Emma said, "This place just isn't for me right now."

"You want me to drive you?" he asked.

"No," she said, "No, I just… I don't want to be here. I'll walk down to the busway and catch a ride home. No big deal. Go back downstairs and make sure they straighten out this mess. You guys have work to do."

"It's not like we're breaking our backs anymore," Josh said, "I can ride you home."

"Just let me go," she said, "I'm frustrated and I need to cool down. I don't want to blow up on you as well."

They looked at each other for a moment. Josh seemed to understand.

She flinched as another biting pain ran through her stomach. She turned away from him and continued up the stairs into the house. He probably called after her, but she didn't hear it. She was just happy that he wasn't following her anymore.

Half-an-hour and one bus transfer later, she was back at the apartment she and Josh shared. Her stomach was now wrenching with pain.  She sincerely hoped that she hadn't given anything away by going with him to the cave tonight.  She wasn't sure if this was the natural progression of what was happening or not, but she didn't want to tip her hand by exhibiting some kind of tell-tale sign.

She staggered to one of the many bookshelves lining the walls of their small living room and pulled down a leather-bound copy of the Bible.  It was thick with gold-lined pages; one of the stereotypical sort of Bibles you always see in movies.

She dropped down on her couch and opened the book.  She flipped through the first few chapters until she reached the section she had hollowed out into a rectangular hidden compartment.  She believed that this was the all-time greatest hiding place.  If someone were ever in another person's house, the chance of them flipping through a book on a shelf was slim.  The chance that they would flip through a bible were next-to-none.

In the space was a vial with a while label and a black cap which should have topped it off.  Handwritten on the label was "Unknown (?)".

She removed the vial and clutched it in her hand for a moment.  She looked down as their cat rubbed against her legs, oblivious to the growing pain in her stomach.

Was this what they went through, too?  Were they all knocked out during this part of the process?  Josh was unconscious most of the time at the hospital, so he couldn't really tell her how it felt.  No one talked about any horrifying pains after the incident or when things started to change for them, so she figured it probably shouldn't hurt this much.  She was convinced that she had gone about this all wrong.

She lurched forward with a spasm in her midsection that felt more like a hard punch to the gut.  Her hand lost hold of the empty vial and it clattered to the floor.  The cat took immediate interest and batted it under the couch.

The pain grew.  It branched out from her stomach and spread throughout her body until it felt like she was going to implode.

She refused to scream as darkness started to creep into her vision.  She struggled, but her body forced her into unconsciousness on her living room couch.

***

Zoey had seen him before.  She remembered him from the hospital.  If everyone at the hospital that day had seen similar side-effects as she and Chaucer, then she supposed it was only a matter of time before one of them made the news.

It had been a while since Chaucer's crime fighter breakdown.  She had been staying with his parents in the guest room since then, but he never came back.  His parents asked what had become of him after that night.  Zoey was not quite ready to admit to them that her son had committed an extremely brutal murder, so she shrugged and made up a story about how he out-ran her and disappeared into the night. She told them that he thought himself to be a monster and that this was his primary reason for going away.

Things had become tense between them. They kept looking to her for answers she didn't have. Her phone did not ring. His parents received no communication. Every day that passed without him, the skies grew grayer. She knew that her welcome had been worn out.

His parents remained hopeful that he would return. This was driving a wedge deeper into their tenuous and unfamiliar relationship as Zoey knew that he would likely never come back.

They allowed Zoey to stay because they wouldn't let her go home to the abusive alcoholic she'd described as her father. And though they knew that she was old enough and certainly had the money to get her own place, they understood that she needed the support of a family with what she was going through, even if it was a strangely adopted one.

When she saw the guy with the spikey blond hair on the news that one night, she knew what she had to do.

They showed him as a small blurb on a crime watch feature. He was caught on camera in the back room of a jewelry store but didn't steal anything. He turned the camera off with a click of his fingers and, in that seemingly inconsequential moment, she knew he was using a super power.

She suddenly realized that she and Chaucer were not the only ones. She'd secretly known it before then, but now she could rest assured that more people, good or bad, were going through her same situation. She knew that someone else out there would understand.

She remembered seeing him with a large group of friends. The idea of an entire group with the same powerful malady gave her instant hope that there may be other people out there who didn't have the same primal ideas as Chaucer. Even though he was shown at a jewelry store likely doing something he shouldn't, the blond guy and his friends might be much more accommodating to her situation.

She packed up that night and left the next morning, assuring Chaucer's parents that she would be fine and that she would be in touch if she ever caught up to him again.

She set out thinking that she would find understanding without knowing exactly what she would be getting herself into.

## XIV

"Ok, run this by me again," Josh asked from the back seat of Mike's SUV, "Why am I emptying out my apartment?"

"You're not emptying out," Kurt said, "Just grab enough of your stuff that you can stay in the cave for a week or so without a problem. I think it's best if you stay hidden for a few days while this all cools down."

"It was never heated up," Josh said, "My picture was on the news one night and the cops said I was wanted for questioning. You took care of all of that with LENNY last night. Why should I still be worried?"

"Your picture was with the cops," Kurt said, "Maybe the Feds. Someone could still try to run you in for questioning and, if they get a chance to do the real thing, it could be game over."

"So, why are Mike and I here if we're just going on a clothing run?" Justin asked, his smoke hair hidden by a black fedora.

"Backup," Mike said, "In case these two can't decide whether Josh needs to bring formalwear or a bathing suit or something."

"In case," Kurt said, sternly, "Josh's house is under surveillance or something."

"So, wait," Justin said, "The three of us came along with Josh on a clothing run so that, in case his apartment is under surveillance, we can all get pinched? Doesn't seem like a very good plan."

"It felt logical at the time," Kurt said.

"Seems like this will be the perfect place for the second act game changer," Justin muttered.

"Would you stop it with the literary crap?" Kurt shouted, "You're killing me here."

"I've been right so far," Justin said smirking, "Just expect the unexpected."

"I expect," Josh said, "That we go into my apartment, get my clothes, and leave. It's not like I'm freaking Pablo Escobar. I showed up on a camera and the cops wanted to talk to me. Interpol has no idea who I am and I have done nothing the past to warrant any surveillance by any number of government agencies except for standing on a sidewalk during a chemical spill."

"It's the last part that worries me," Kurt said.

"No action until the third act," Justin mumbled, "Second act will end with a prelude, but that will be the first time we run into any real problems."

"Shut up!" Kurt shouted.

"Just telling it like it is," said Justin, "Origin story 101."

Mike pulled his SUV into one of the many visitor spaces of Josh's red brick apartment building. Josh keyed them in through the glass front door and ushered them quickly through the lobby to the narrow elevator. When they arrived at the sixth floor and attempted to enter his apartment, Josh found himself stuck.

He opened the deadbolt and the doorknob with two separate keys, but the chain had been left on the door.

"Emma?" he called in through the small crack, "Let me in, I'm home!"

After a moment, no one came.

"Emma!" he called again, "Come on, hon, open the door!"

"Did you check on her after last night?" Mike asked, "She was looking pretty ill. Maybe she's sleeping."

"Hang on, guys, I got this," Justin said.

He turned into smoke and slipped through the crack in the door allowed by the chain rematerializing on the other side. He shut the door, undid the chain, and opened the door wide.

Josh made a bee line for the bedroom, calling for Emma. Kurt and Mike entered behind Justin and stood in the small living room. Josh came out of the bedroom.

"She's not here," he said.

"How could she not be?" Justin asked, "The chain was across the door and it only leaves a tiny crack. The only way anyone could get in or out was if they could do something like I can."

Mike jumped and threw out an arm as he saw movement out of the corner of his eye. A black-and-white cat floated through mid-air struggling to stay afoot in an invisible sphere.

"It's ok," said Josh, "I don't think the cat is with the Feds."

Mike lowered the cat to the floor and released it. It immediately sought refuge under the couch.

"Her purse and cigarettes are still here," Justin said, pointing to the coffee table, "She wouldn't have gone anywhere without those."

"You thinking kidnapping?" Josh asked.

"No," Justin said, "She would have resisted. There's no evidence of struggle and there's no way they could have escaped. All the windows are closed and in one piece."

"Leave it to you to think like Batman," Mike said.

"I'm always thinking like Batman," Justin said.

"What if it was a kidnapping?" Kurt said, "It stands to reason that those government guys have super powered people, too. What if one of them was a teleporter or something and they jumped in and black bagged her? Would have been a no-mess kind of situation."

"What makes you think the government guys have powers?" Mike asked.

"Did you see the size of the dude who made us sign the contracts?" Kurt said, "Knowing what we know now, there's no way he's normal. They could have engineered someone to be the perfect abductor."

"They haven't bagged anyone else close to us," Justin said,

"Why would they bag her? Steph and Lisa both know just as much as she did. Why Emma?"

"They didn't black bag her," said a new voice from the hallway.

After the initial jump of the scare, reflexes had Justin's fists on fire and ready, Josh's hands jammed into his pockets, Mike's arms thrust out, and Kurt moving to get behind those three.

Mike used his forcefields to pin the stranger to the wall. He was dressed just like the agents at the hospital; black suit, black tie, white shirt, sunglasses, and a familiar looking lapel pin. He was average in height and build with slightly pale skin and black hair which was perfectly slicked back. He looked very much like the definition of a government agent, as if he could blend in with any crowd.

"Let him go," said another voice from the hallway, "We're only here to talk."

An agent identical to the first appeared in the room, his hands raised.

Mike looked to Justin, Justin shrugged, then spoke:

"You got any weapons," Justin said, nervous, "I suggest you put them on the ground now."

"No weapons," said the agent with his hands up, "You can check us both if you want."

Justin looked to Kurt.

"Anything on them?" Justin asked.

"How am I supposed to know?" Kurt replied.

"You've got that tech stuff," Justin mumbled, "Can't you detect weapons and crap?"

"It doesn't work that way," Kurt muttered.

"Look, boys," said the agent, "Just trust me here, ok? If I was going to cause trouble I could have done it over a month ago."

"What the hell are you doing in my apartment?" Josh asked, looking notably more intense than before.

"I'm just here to talk," said the agent, "I know who you are and what you can do, but I'm not here to hurt you or black bag you or whatever other malicious garbage you think is going to happen just because Captain Zap over there got a little bit of airtime."

"You're not making me feel any more comfortable about this situation," Justin said, his hair flaring around the edges, "Especially considering your uniform there."

"He's right," Kurt said, "You're one of them, aren't you? You're probably surrounding the building right now. This is all a giant trap."

"No, no, no," said the agent, "Kurt, right?"

"How do you know his name?" Justin shouted, the flames on his head getting higher.

"Relax, Justin," said the agent, "I know all of your names."

"We did print legibly and sign about twenty-seven dotted lines not so long ago," Mike said, "They also replicated the contents of our wallets. It's not really a stretch to think they know who we are."

"Oh," said Justin, "Yeah. Well, still..."

"Could you at least drop the forcefield on my associate?" asked the agent, "He's starting to suffocate."

The imprisoned agent was turning an interesting shade of blue now that they were looking at him again. Mike looked to Justin and Justin shrugged.

"Fine," Justin said, "But, if you move funny, I'm gonna start cooking."

Mike relaxed his arms and the agent fell to the floor, gasping. Justin covered them both with his flaming fists.

"I didn't know those things were air-tight," Justin said.

"Me either," said Mike.

"Look," said the standing agent, "We're here to help you. Let's all just relax, sit down, and talk."

"Where's Emma?" Josh barked, pointing his finger at them emphatically.

"We don't know," said the agent, shrugging, "We don't have her."

"Not buying it," Josh shouted, "You have her and you're here to take us, too."

"We can do this all night if you like," said the other agent, looking at Josh as he got to his feet, "You can point at me and posture, I can sit here and tell you I've got nothing to do with your girlfriend's sudden disappearance, you can posture some more and maybe even take a shot at me while giving absolutely no thought to the fact that you'd be murdering someone which would be a much worse rap than being in the wrong jewelry store at the wrong time, or, we can just sit down and talk like civilized people. That second one was my goal from the beginning and I vote for that."

The two identical agents, now standing shoulder to shoulder, merged together into one agent. He looked exactly the same as both of the others. He straightened his tie and sat down in the chair of the computer desk.

The group's jaw dropped. They had seen impossible things since the hospital, but nothing like that.

"It's your choice, of course," said the agent, "But I think you're going to want to hear me out."

Justin extinguished his flaming fists. His hair still flared around the edges before sputtering and going out completely.

"What are you doing?" Josh shouted, "This is one of the bad guys!"

"Let me assure you," said the agent, "I'm not even close to one of the bad guys."

136

"Josh," said Justin, "Let's at least hear what he has to say before electrocuting him."

"I'd recommend it," said the agent, grinning.

"You guys ok with this?" Josh asked, looking at Kurt and Mike.

"Yeah," Kurt said, tentatively, sitting on the couch next to Justin.

"I'll listen," said Mike, sitting as well.

Josh remained standing, his finger pointed at the agent's head.

"Come on, man," Justin said, "Give him a minute. He's got powers, too, and I'm sure he could have kicked all our asses like a million times by now without breaking a sweat, am I right?"

"One-thousand percent," said the agent, smiling.

"I'm keeping him covered," said Josh shaking his head, "He's an intruder in my house. I've got rights. I'm waiting for that one false move."

"Fine," said the agent, sighing, turning toward Josh, "That's fine. We can still talk and this is your house. It's your prerogative to keep it safe. Just do me a favor and keep your aim right here."

The agent tapped his temple.

"If you can hit it exactly, that would be preferable," he continued, "You've got the best chance of killing me there depending on how much voltage you're putting out and how accurate you are. You'll either kill me or stun me, both of which will allow you to make the quick getaway you're thinking you'll have to employ. I'd honestly prefer if you put everything you have into that one shot and fry me outright, though, because I'd rather not suffer the brain damage that might come after a stun. That is, if you still feel the need to do it after our conversation is over."

The agent's face was deadpan as he delivered the instructions. Josh waivered for a moment but kept his hand pointed and his eyes locked on the agent's sunglasses.

"Suit yourself," said the agent after a moment.

"So, who are you," Justin asked, "And why are you following us?"

"Call me Agent Phalanx," he said, "I used to be a part of the group you met at the hospital. I'm not anymore."

"What agency were you with?" Kurt asked.

"The blackest of all black ops organizations," Phalanx said, "It's called The Project. So dark and so deep that they report directly to the Secretary of Defense and, last I checked, he didn't really have any knowledge about it, either. Even the President doesn't know about it."

"What do they do?" Justin asked.

"I can't tell you everything," Phalanx said, "Not yet, anyway. The only thing you really need to know is that they've been engineering extra-normal entities for a very, very long time. The Project operating now is the thirteenth iteration. It was established to help give the free world an edge during times of war. The motivation has, of course, changed over time. No one is sure about their current goals save the Project's mastermind."

"Agent Williams?" Mike asked.

"Possibly," Phalanx said, "There was always an impression in my mind that Williams' strings were being pulled by a higher power."

"Any ideas?" Justin asked.

"No," Phalanx said, "Before you even think about it, I have no evidence on that, it's just an impression that I get. Let's stay on target. I'm just going to cut to the chase and tell you why I'm here."

"Ok,' Justin said, "So?"

"I'd like to offer you my help in becoming the greatest superheroes in the world," said Phalanx.

They looked at each other as Phalanx crossed his legs and tented his fingers. They were silent and looked at Phalanx in disbelief.

"Look, I saw your exploits at the jewelry store," said Phalanx, "That whole situation was awful. You came off too abrasive and you made a ton of mistakes, not the least of which was stunning the owner with lightning. It went poorly enough that your psychic felt justified in erasing the whole incident from the memory of the 'bad guys'. You went in unprepared and inexperienced and, if they had been actual criminals, you would have likely ended up dead. You need someone with the experience to teach you how your powers work; to show you both the full potential of your abilities and how to use them without hurting yourselves or innocent people."

"You're here," Kurt started, "Dressed like one of the agents who were trying to keep this whole thing under wraps – the guys who told us media coverage was a bad thing – and you want to make us into spotlighted superheroes?"

"I want to be your Ben Parker" said Phalanx.

"You want to instill your knowledge and hope for the world in us and then tragically die, forcing us to dedicate our lives to your ideals of power and responsibility and vowing to make the world a better place by fighting crime?" asked Justin, quickly.

"Not exactly," said Phalanx, "Bad example in a roomful of geeks. How about your very own Charles Xavier? Sound better?"

"Much better," Justin said, nodding.

"How do you know what happened that night?" Josh asked, "I shut off all the cameras. The only thing caught on tape was my stupid face."

"Did you check the roofline?" Phalanx asked.

Josh and Mike exchanged shrugs before Josh said: "No."

"In case you forgot from my introduction," Phalanx said, "I can be in many places at once. Trust me, I saw it all and heard it all. Total debacle, top to bottom. But, these are rookie mistakes and I want to help you guys go pro. By the way, when the cops found your impromptu dating service recording there, I went to them and had it eliminated. I got it cleared for you before they could run that report on the news. I didn't have time to kill the story, but I did have time to take the cops off your back even before Kurt here could do it for you. Nice play, by the way."

"Uh," Kurt said, "Thanks?"

Phalanx nodded.

"How?" Josh asked, still pointing at Phalanx's head, "Why?"

"Told them I was FBI," Phalanx said, "Told them that I was your handler. Made up some bogus stuff about your being some kind of undercover something and if they continued to pursue you they would be blowing a major investigation. They agreed and dropped the case, but not before the news got ahold of the footage."

Josh, confused, slowly lowered his hand from zapping position.

"The why is that I knew I would have to do something to gain your trust," Phalanx said, "Removing an APB on one of your people seemed like the most productive way to accomplish that. It doesn't benefit what we all want to do if you're wanted by the cops."

"What is it exactly you think 'we' want to do?" asked Mike.

"We want to make something legendary," Phalanx said, "To inspire. To be a force for good. To be the world's first real superheroes."

"I'm still having trouble believing this isn't some kind of eventual betrayal," Justin said, "Second-act characters who look friendly are usually the ones who will pull the third-act twist and stab you in the back right before the finale. Especially in an origin story."

"Sure," said Phalanx, "But what if the twist isn't actually a twist. What if there's a big build-up as if there's going to be a twist and the real twist is that there is no twist."

"Please don't encourage him," said Kurt, "He's bad enough already."

"His worries are viable," said Phalanx, "So far, everything has been playing out according to a typical origin story and you guys have been rolling right along with it, up to and including my introduction to you. Life imitates art in this situation because there is no other basis for this aside from what you know from pop-culture. You even found an existing cave under your house which has its own backstory. It's as convenient as it is stereotypical but it plays right into the scenario and keeps the whole idea of predictability going. It's wise to keep your eyes open for this kind of thing. The Project knows that this is the track you're taking, which makes you just as predictable."

"Where does it all lead, then?" Justin asked, "How does it end?"

"That's why I'm here," Phalanx said, "Consider me your Deus Ex Machina. I know quite a bit about The Project and still have a friend on the inside. You'll need my help, my insight, and my training, if you plan on surviving until the end of the story. I know it feels like breaking the fourth wall, but there's no fourth wall to break. This is all more real than you can imagine and, predictable situation or not, some of you may end up dead. I'm here to make sure you have the best fighting chance before that inevitable very bad thing happens."

"If you two are done talking about this like it's a graphic novel," Kurt asked, "I'd like to get down to the facts. Why aren't you with this 'Project' anymore?"

Phalanx sighed.

"I was tired of being their puppet," Phalanx said, "My ability being what it is, I was the most utilized Agent in the Project's history. I can make an unknown amount of copies of myself. Aside from being able to outnumber practically any opponent, it allowed me to master skills at an exponential level."

Two other Phalanxes split from the original and stood on either side of his chair.

"Every one of these guys I make is an identical copy of me. They act independently. Until the point that they separate from me, we are one mind. I can't mentally communicate with these guys, but they know from our thought pattern that they're only here for demonstration purposes. When they sit back down..."

They did, absorbing into Phalanx.

"I gain any knowledge they accumulated while they were away from me. The Project used this to tutor rooms full of my duplicates on everything you can think of - languages, martial arts, hacking, stealth, subterfuge – they made me into a walking database of skills and secrets, not to mention a death machine in a fight. I'm the ultimate spy and they used more of me than I can even remember I had."

"So, you went rogue," Mike said, "Didn't they put a price on your head? Why aren't they tracking you down and locking you up?"

"That's the fun part," Phalanx said, "At first, they came after me, but because my boys and I are all identical, they could never figure out which one was the real me. In all honesty, I don't even know that I'm the real me. I could be another duplicate because my duplicates can make duplicates. Even if they caught me, they could never truly end me. I try to stay pretty far underground. They'll never find me if I don't want to be found."

"Yet here you are," Mike said, "Spilling your life story to a roomful of people who you're hoping won't rat you out to save their own skin."

"You won't rat me out," Phalanx said with a smirk, "Because that won't get them off your back. If you don't think they know your capabilities by now, you're sorely mistaken. Your abilities make you an asset to the Project. Untapped, maybe, but an asset none the less. Williams never lets go of an asset. Even if you hang up your potential capes and do nothing with what you've been given, Williams will still have his eyes on you for the rest of your lives waiting for that moment he needs soldiers."

"So, we fight the Project?" Josh asked.

"No," said Phalanx, "If you went up against the Project right now, Williams would annihilate you. You'd be shelved in cold storage until he figured out what he could do with you. He collects extra-normal people. Sometimes they become Agents, sometimes he keeps them just to find out what makes them tick."

"Extra-normal?" Kurt said.

"The Project's term," Phalanx said, "It was Williams' idea. He thought 'super-powered' sounded too unbelievable to put into reports and proposals. He was pitching a military program, not a comic book. Plus, making up his own term for it made it easier to misdirect people. An Olympic-level weightlifter has extra-normal strength – as in, greater than normal. A comic book-style strong guy can bench press an aircraft carrier and that gives him extra-normal strength as well. The Project is only interested in the latter, but all the people who read his briefs would think it was the former. The term stuck even though he doesn't report to a senate sub-committee anymore. He still uses it with the Secretary of Defense."

"Makes sense," Kurt said.

"Anyway, back to the real subject at hand," Phalanx said, "Do you want to be superheroes or just vigilantes who make bad mistakes?"

The four looked at each other in turn. There was a moment of quiet contemplation, each knowing what the other was probably thinking. Justin spoke.

"What's the time frame on this?" he asked, "We've got a lot to consider first. I'm not a hundred percent sure we can trust you."

"I understand," said Phalanx, "You should discuss this with your other two group members before coming to a decision. Until then, to give you guys a little jump-start, take this."

Phalanx removed his lapel pin and motioned to Justin. Justin took the pin with some hesitation and looked at it closely. It was identical to the ones he'd seen on the agents at the hospital; a black Roman numeral XIII inside a black circle with a red background.

"This is garbage," Justin said, announcing the results of his quick inspection, "This is just a pin. How is this supposed to jumpstart anything?"

"This garbage," Phalanx said, "Is higher-than-high-tech. For someone who projects the image of a pop-culture geek, you're very quick to doubt that something like this could exist. Haven't you ever seen a James Bond movie? Pass it on to Kurt, maybe he'll have some more appreciation for it."

Justin shrugged and placed it into Kurt's waiting hand. He closed his fist on the pin and shut his eyes. They started to move rapidly behind the closed lids and, when he opened them a moment later, an amazed look washed over him.

"Told you, right?" Phalanx said, "Higher-than-high-tech."

"This thing is the real deal," Kurt said, "Advanced communication device beyond anything I've ever seen. There's a ton of data stored on here, as well, but it's encrypted."

"Unavoidable fact, I'm afraid," said Phalanx, "I couldn't just leave that out in the open, could I?"

"I doubt it would have been a problem," Kurt said, "Lapel pin drives aren't really available on the open market."

"I have confidence that you'll figure it out," said Phalanx, "And, when you do, you'll see that I'm not lying. I want nothing but to help you succeed."

Phalanx stood up. The motion was sudden and caused Josh to raise his arm again. Phalanx gave him a disapproving look and Josh relented.

"I'll leave you to it, then," said Phalanx, "Nice to meet all of you in person. When you're ready, I'm sure you'll find a way to get in touch with me. Good day, gentlemen. Please give the Rock and the Psychic my regards."

Phalanx walked out of the front door, closing it behind him.

There was a long, uncomfortable silence as they all stood to watch him go.

"What now?" Mike asked.

"I'd still like to know what happened to my girlfriend," Josh said, "She couldn't have just evaporated."

"She was sick last night," Kurt said, "You said you put her on a bus. Maybe she's in the hospital or maybe she didn't come home."

"She came home," Josh said, "Her bag, her keys, her phone… everything is here, right where it would be normally. There's even a fresh pot of coffee on."

"Total Mary Celeste scenario," Mike said, "Oooh, spooky."

"I thought that guy would never leave," said Emma from the doorway of the bedroom.

She was wearing a satin leopard-print robe and, from the state of her hair and makeup, looked as though she'd just woke up.

All of them jumped, assuming their defensive postures again.

"Sorry," she said, putting her hands up, "I was hiding in the closet. I think that government guy was pounding on the door before you guys got here. I heard voices outside and I got scared, so I hid."

"I checked the closet," Josh said, "You weren't there."

"Then I did my job pretty well," she said, "So, what did that guy want? I couldn't hear him from in there."

Justin, Kurt, and Mike went on to tell her about Phalanx and the plans for which he laid a foundation. Josh, however, was distracted when the cat batted something out from beneath the couch and into his foot. He knew what it was even before he bent over to pick it up – a translucent glass vial with a black cap reading "Unknown (?)" down the side. The black fluid once inside was now gone.

He turned his head slowly toward Emma. He could tell she was only pretending to listen to what the guys were saying. She'd seen him pick up the vial and he felt her heart palpitate with fear from across the room as he narrowed his eyes.

She turned her attention back to the guys, smiling and nodding as if she really hadn't heard the entire conversation. When they were through explaining, she looked at Josh again. His eyes were still narrow. His vision blurred with anger.

"Guys," he said after the conversation ended, "Head back to the car. Emma and I have to talk."

They spoke, but he didn't hear them. They filed out of the apartment, closing the door behind him. There was a hard silence as he stared her down.

"What?" she asked.

"You have to ask?" Josh said, holding the vial up.

She paused a moment, carefully deciding how to approach this. Josh was not so careful.

"You betrayed me," Josh said, "You betrayed my trust. All of our trust."

"Technically," she retorted, "You betrayed everyone's trust to begin with by having that stuff made."

"That wasn't expected," Josh said, "I wanted my friend to find a cure and he didn't."

"No," she said, "Instead, he gave you more of the stuff. You didn't want it to fall into the wrong hands, so I made sure it couldn't."

"By drinking it?" Josh shouted, "All those stomach pains, that whole act in front of everyone, running home without me – you were hiding the fact that you actually drank that stuff. You wanted powers, like us. You said as much. Now, you're going to come at me with a twisted, lame excuse about making sure it didn't fall into the wrong hands? You could have killed yourself!"

"But I didn't," Emma said, "I'm fine. The stomach pains were real, but they went away. I'm not a puddle of goo, I didn't sustain major injury, I didn't grow wings or horns or a tail. I'm still me and I'm still alive. More importantly, the stuff is gone and it can't be used against you."

"You honestly expect me to believe that what you did was in the group's best interest?" Josh asked.

She said nothing.

"That's what I thought," he said, "Look, this... us... we're done. I trusted you with something and you used it to get what you wanted."

"Seriously?" Emma asked, "You were about to electrocute someone because you thought they'd taken me no less than ten minutes ago, now you want to walk out on our relationship?"

"Don't play guilt games with me," Josh said, "You're the one at fault here. You took something that was extremely important to me – to all of us – and you did the selfish thing rather than the responsible thing.

143

More than that, you put your life in danger to accomplish that selfish goal. You've not only proven you're untrustworthy, you've proven you're crazy."

"No crazier than someone who runs out at night and almost gets themselves killed," Emma said.

"That whole thing was supposed to be a good deed," Josh said, "We're trying to be heroes."

"Emphasis on trying," Emma said, "Come on, this isn't that big a deal."

"That stuff was one of a kind," Josh said, "My friend may not have found a cure, but we would have had a sample in case we wanted to keep researching. Now, you've taken that chance away from Budda and Justin who can never really lead a normal life again. They got the bad end of all this and you drank their last hope to get their regular lives back."

"Who are you kidding?" Emma said, "You know as well as I do that Justin is in his glory right now and Budda will probably find a way to cope with it. I know Steph will, too."

"That's not the point," Josh said, "We're only at the beginning of all of this. We don't know how things will go from here. This vial may have been our only solution to future problems and you drank it."

"Come on," she said, "Don't you even want to know what powers I have now?"

"No," Josh said, "Look, I'm done with this. I don't' want to talk about it anymore. You betrayed me for your own selfish reasons and that's all I need to know. You took something away from the group that can never be replaced. You stole our cure. I'm out and I'm not coming back."

He walked to the door and out of the apartment without another word.

She sighed, transformed into a cat, and went back to the closet to lie down and think about what just happened.

Josh would not see her again for a very long while.

## XV

He didn't feel anything as the car crashed into him. He didn't move; he didn't even get jarred. It folded around him like it had hit a telephone pole.

He only just saw it coming as it came around a sharp turn. He froze in the headlights like an animal, unsure of what to do or how to react. He could see the look of surprise on the driver's face right before the airbag deployed and everything from the front bumper to the engine block was crumpled against his unmoving legs.

Until that very second, Budda was full of unanswered questions about his current state.

He'd been sitting in the cave watching TV while Jess sat meditating on the other side of the couch they'd moved in front of LENNY's main screen. He wasn't sure why Josh needed three other people with him as back-up to get stuff from his own apartment, but he supposed it had something to do with the paranoia surrounding Josh's current wanted rating. Four super powered people going to pick up a few changes of clothes seemed like overkill.

"I think I'm going to go for a walk," Budda said.

"A walk?" Jess asked, opening her eyes and turning to him, "Are you crazy? What if someone sees you?"

"I have a disguise," Budda said, "A big trench coat. Seventy-two extra tall. Beige. And a brown fedora. Just like Ben Grimm. Steph bought it for me."

"You really think you can get away with that?" she asked.

"It's dark outside and it's raining," he said, "Shouldn't be much of a problem. Besides, I'm going walk down near the busway, not a whole lot of traffic there in the evenings and there's no houses."

"Whatever, then," she said, "Try to be back before everyone else, though."

"Ok, mom," Budda said, his eye-roll unnoticeable due to his solid obsidian eyes.

"Seriously," Jess said, "Do you want Kurt or Justin busting your balls because you left the house unsupervised and unaccompanied?"

"Point taken," Budda said after a brief pause, "I won't be gone long."

After getting dressed, something he didn't do much of anymore, he walked out into the winter rain. He wished he could feel the drops falling on him. He wanted to feel the wind which played at the lower part of his coat and caused the empty tree branches to clatter together. He could not smell the moist cold air.

Losing three of his five senses was the most difficult thing about his transformation. He quickly adjusted to the height difference and the extreme physical strength.  Even the senses of taste and smell didn't matter as much, considering he didn't need to eat or breathe anymore. He had been a smoker and his brain was telling him that he still needed the chemicals he'd become dependent upon back in his normal life.  It cried out for caffeine, nicotine, alcohol... none of which could be obtained in his current state.  The pangs were slipping away, but slowly.

None of this compared to losing his sense of touch.

He didn't feel any pain, which he figured would be one of his greatest advantages should the group ever get into a fight.  At the same time, he couldn't feel the chill of the puddles as he sloshed through them with bare feet.  The legs of his pants were soaking through and he didn't notice.  The gravel and sharp detritus on the side of the road crunched underfoot but made no sensation.

He couldn't feel the soft skin of his girlfriend.  He couldn't feel when she kissed him or touched him.  He couldn't feel anything when they made love.

The sense of touch, he thought, was grossly underrated by humanity.  People went blind, people went deaf, people even lost their senses of taste and smell.  It was rare that his current condition occurred to flesh-and-blood people.  No matter what one's disability, the sense of touch was always taken for granted.

He tried to take a cue from Jess and attempted meditation to calm his mind.  It wasn't really possible without the rhythm of breathing. Without sensory input, he was starting to think he was just a walking brain.  An automaton.  A golem.

Other questions were left unanswered.  Without breathing, how could he speak?  No air passed over his vocal cords.  Did he even have vocal cords?  How did he see if his eyes were stone?  He imagined his guts were stone, did that mean his brain was stone, too?  If something hit him hard enough, would he actually feel pain?  These were the sort of conjectural questions the over-analytical comic book nerds asked to spark internet fights because they had no true answer other than the willful suspension of disbelief.

This was real life.  It was hard to suspend disbelief in something that was currently and actively happening.  He had resigned himself that it would take a long time to be able to make these determinations but he wanted the facts now.

In the middle of his existential crisis, he noticed something moving from the corner of his eye.  He turned around just in time to see the headlights streaking at him out of the rain and his brain stuttered.  He didn't even have time to brace for the impact.

\*\*\*

Her door was ripped from its hinges and tossed away.
"Are you ok?" shouted a strange voice.

146

The smell of burnt rubber and the powder from the airbag filled her nose and almost made her sick. Her head throbbed where, despite the best efforts of the car's safety measures, it had struck the windshield. Her vision was blurry and the lights of her dashboard were scrambled into a red and green lump. She touched her hand to her forehead to check for blood but couldn't make out anything.

"Are you ok?" the voice shouted again.

She looked toward the voice and saw the outline of a long coat and hat. The street outside was dimly lit and the rain wasn't helping her to identify this person. She felt dizzy. She tried to raise her hand to signal the figure near the door but couldn't manage anything. Words dribbled out of her mouth in an incoherent mess without her realizing she was trying to speak.

She remembered feeling like this when they pulled her out from under the tanker truck. The functional part of her mind speaking in the back of her head, told her that she probably had a concussion and that two of those in such a close span was probably not a good thing. Versions of this spattered out of her mouth as the silhouette reached out to her and everything went black.

"I know her," she heard another male voice say.

"Really?" asked the voice of the silhouette, "From where?"

"Well, I mean, I don't 'know her' know her, but I've seen her somewhere before. Can't remember where, but I have for sure."

"So, what's wrong with her?" asked the silhouette.

"From what I can tell," said a third male voice, "She's probably got a concussion. She took a nasty bump. At least it wasn't bleeding."

"What's with her hair?" asked the silhouette, "Did that happen in the crash?"

"Did you ever do any research on which specific genus and species of moron you are?" asked the third voice, "People don't get ice for hair from a head-on collision with a walking boulder."

"That's where I know her from," Justin said, snapping his fingers, "The hospital. She was in the accident. Her hair was a bit different that day..."

"It was likely a bit less frozen before," said Kurt, "I'd say that's 'extra-normal'."

She struggled to open her eyes, but her body wouldn't cooperate.

"Yeah, she's one of us," said the second voice, "She was the hot goth chick. Remember? The one I was talking about at lunch that day."

"We don't all have your infallible memory, man," said the silhouette.

"How could you not remember," said the second voice, "Look at her. She's gorgeous. She might be one of the hottest girls I've ever seen."

"She can hear you, you know," said a new female voice.

"Oh," said the second voice, "Well, uh… I'm just being honest. Sorry."

"Whatever, Casanova," said the third voice, "Is she going to be ok?"

"She's fine," said the female voice, "She's about to wake up."

Just as it was said, she willed her eyes to open.  She squinted at a bright light over her head and managed to put her hand up to shade her eyes.  Things were still blurry, but she now saw a blurry face with messy brown hair.  She recognized the voice as the third one in the conversation as he said:

"Hello?"

"Hell… oh?" she muttered.  Her mouth and throat were dry.  She coughed and someone put a straw up to her lips.  She sipped and felt the cool relief of water.

"Don't worry," said the silhouette, now attached to a blue-grey blur, "You're safe here.  How's your head?"

She groaned and reached for the injured area, feeling a bandage and an ice pack instead of her bare forehead.  She coughed out a laugh at the thought of the ice pack.

"You've had a concussion," said the messy brown hair, "You've been out for a few hours.  Are you feeling pain anywhere else in your body?"

She attempted to say no, but it came out as more of a groan.  She shook her head and found that her neck was sore, but nothing terrible.

"Wiggle your fingers and toes," said messy brown hair.

She did as instructed.

"Good," he said.

"You're lucky you hit me," said the blue-grey blur.

"Budda," said messy brown hair, "How exactly does hitting you make her lucky?  It did about as good as wrapping her car around a telephone pole."

"If it was some other guy out there," said blue-grey, "They would have been paste and she would have had to live with that."

She saw his logic.  Her vision was clearing.

"Whrrm I?" she slurred.

"You're in a safe place," said messy brown hair, now with a nearly blur-free face, "We're here to help."

"Car?" she muttered.

"I stashed your car," said blue-grey who was still too far away to make sense of visually, "I carried it off the road and hid it in the woods on top of the bluff.  What's left of it, anyway.  You nailed me pretty hard.  I don't think you'll be driving it any time soon."

"Sorry," she mumbled.

"It's ok, really," he said, "I can take it. You didn't even scratch me."

"Who are you?" she asked, slowly but coherently.

"Friends," said the voice who called her pretty, now seen as an olive-skinned man with what looked like smoke for hair, "We were in the hospital together a little while ago. After the other car crash. Remember?"

She remembered the other car crash, almost too vividly. Now that her vision was clearing she could see that, like her, his hair was definitely smoke and the blue-grey guy was made of stone. She felt a deep bolt of sadness, knowing that there were at least two more whose lives were changed as much as hers and Chaucer's. She closed her eyes for a moment and nodded to answer the question.

"Rest," said the messy brown haired man, "Lie back and relax. Jess is going to help you get some sleep. Remember, you're safe here."

He stepped away and a woman with dark brown eyes and auburn hair leaned into view. Her hands reached out and touched Zoey's temples and her vision went black again.

"Ok," Jess said, "We'll have to keep an eye on her. I don't know when she's going to wake up."

"What did you do?" Justin asked.

"Just induced sleep," Jess said, "When she wakes up is her body's choice. Someone should probably be here when she comes to. She's nervous and might over-react."

They were standing in a large carved-out room off to the side of one of the tunnels. She was lying on a small folding bed that Kurt kept in the house in the event of a guest. An end-table held bandages and a bucket full of ice which was the best they could do for her under the circumstances.

"What is she doing here?" Kurt asked in a whispered shout, moving toward Budda.

"She crashed into me," Budda said, "She was hurt. I didn't notice who she was, I just figured it would be a good idea to bring her back here."

"Oh yeah, pure genius," Kurt shouted, his volume increasing, "Bring a total stranger back to our secret – SECRET – base where the medical help amounts to me accidentally getting a scanned copy of a first-aid manual from the first computer I absorbed. Absolute brilliance. You're lucky she didn't have any serious problems or we'd be talking about a corpse right now."

"What was I supposed to do?" Budda asked, "Run her to the hospital so she could tell everyone she saw a giant rock monster? Call an ambulance and just run away and hope they find her? If I did either of those options, they would have freaked out about her ice hair. The government guys would have got to her for sure. She's one of us, we're sure of that now. We have to take care of our own, right?"

"She's not one of us," Kurt said, "She's a stray. We don't know her from Adam. The only evidence we have to go on is the fact that Justin saw her at the hospital and got excited."

"That's not fair," Justin said, "You guys saw her, too. You knew she was there, you knew she was part of this. There's no reason for us not to watch out for her. We're supposed to be superheroes, right?"

"You just want to save her because you think she falls into your imaginary plot somewhere," Kurt said moving from Budda to Justin with his shouts, "Is she another second-act Deus Ex Machina, like you thought of that Phalanx guy? Or is she some prospective love interest that you think you'll win over in the end?"

"Maybe the first thing," Justin said, "But the second thing is kind of insulting. That aside, she needed help and we're supposed to be helping people, aren't we?"

"We'll be picking up every random, injured passerby and bringing them here, then?" Kurt shouted, "If that's the case, get out of my house."

"It wasn't random," Jess interjected.

"What?" Kurt asked.

"It wasn't random," Jess repeated, her hand now touching the girl's temple, "She was out there looking for us. She recognized Josh on the news from when she saw us at the hospital. Based on that clip, she figured he was using a super ability to turn off the cameras and wanted to find us. She thought we could help her; relate to her."

Kurt and the rest turned to Josh, leaning on the tunnel wall outside.

"What?" he said, "It's not like I left a trail of breadcrumbs. They showed one clip on one local channel on one broadcast. It's not like they did a biography on me."

"He's right," Jess continued, "She went back to Duke's and asked the bartender if she knew us. She got a few names and looked online. We didn't exactly clean out our social media stats when we went underground, so she was able to find us easier than you'd imagine."

"Looks like LENNY has some jobs to do," Justin said, smirking at Kurt.

"I still don't like this," Kurt said, "How do we know she is who we think she is?"

"She's legit," said Jess, "Her story checks out. She came here on her own. Her only intention was to find others like her after she had a f-"

Jess stopped, her eyebrows raised, her skin paled and briefly turned green as she heaved and covered her mouth with her free hand as though she was going to vomit. It faded quickly.

"She had a falling out with her boyfriend," Jess continued, a more concerned tone in her voice, "He had powers, too, but he took off and she hasn't seen him in a while. She's just confused and looking for guidance. She knew we were the largest group at the hospital and she wants to be with people who will understand her. She wants a support network because she's never really had one before and she wants to do something meaningful with her powers."

Jess took her hand off of the girl's temple and shook it in the air, as if it were filthy.

"What happened back there?" Kurt asked, "You looked like you were going to puke."

"I just," Jess said, catching her breath as if thinking about it brought back the nausea, "I saw something gross is all."

"That bad?" Justin asked.

"So, what's wrong with helping this girl?" Jess asked Kurt, very purposefully changing the subject, "It's not like she crashed into Budda on purpose as part of some nefarious plot to infiltrate our secret lair."

"It could be just like that," Kurt said, "That's what's wrong with this."

"I read her mind," Jess pleaded, "What better proof can you get? Your psychic girlfriend is telling you that everything is ok. There's no need to be so paranoid about it."

"I still want to know a few more things," Kurt said.

"Call me old fashioned," Justin said, "But shouldn't we wait until she recovers, then just ask her stuff rather than poking around in her head?"

"This is more efficient," Kurt said, "I'm not going to take any chances. She could still be lying to us somehow and the last thing we want is a spy in our midst."

"You doubt my abilities?" Jess asked Kurt, "I know everything she knows now. Literally. It's like copying a file into my mind. I can tell you that from her earliest memories until now, she has never been a spy for anyone, even unwittingly. You seriously think you can't trust actual memory just because that Phalanx guy showed up and made you all paranoid."

"How did you know about Phalanx?" Kurt asked.

Jess raised her hand high in the air and pointed to herself emphatically.

"Psychic, duh," she said, "I was watching the whole thing through your eyes. I might as well have been in the room."

"Seriously?" Kurt asked, "Is nothing sacred?"

Kurt grumbled and stormed out of the makeshift recovery room and into the main chamber where Josh and Mike were already sitting and watching TV on LENNY's main screen. Jess and Budda followed close behind.

"You were taking longer than you should have," Jess justified, "I wanted to find out what was going on."

"You didn't have to invade my head to figure it out," Kurt said, "You could have texted me."

"What's the deal with the girl?" Mike interrupted, cutting off the argument before it could progress.

"Concussion," Kurt grumbled, "She's sleeping it off."

"She was looking for Josh," Jess said, "Well, us, I guess. She wants help."

"Did Phalanx send her here?" Mike asked.

"No," Jess said, "She's never seen him. She came on her own."

"Hold up," Budda said, "Who is this Phalanx guy you keep talking about and what happened while everyone was gone that you keep referencing him?"

Jess turned to face him, reached up, and placed one finger on his forehead.

He staggered back for a moment, then shook his head and regained his composure. Now it was as if he had been in the room as well.

"That was cool," Budda said, "Ok, so what do you think he really wants from us?"

"I don't know," Kurt said, reaching into the breast pocket of the work shirt he was wearing to produce the lapel pin, "I'm thinking we need to find out. He said everything we need would be in these encrypted files."

"How are we supposed to plug a lapel pin into a computer?" Mike asked.

"I can use my mind as a bridge," Kurt said, "I'll transfer all the files over to LENNY and we can look at them there, once I get them decrypted. Should be a good test of my abilities if this is really black-ops level stuff."

"What exactly does it do?" Mike asked.

"It's pretty awesome," Kurt said, sitting down at the main console, "Full communications suite with sound and video capability, quadruple-encrypted cellular transmitter, gigantic hard-drive, tracking device, Bluetooth ..."

"Tracking device?" Josh interrupted.

"Disabled," Kurt said, "Mildly comforting, considering the circumstances. Looks like the power for that system was bypassed."

"Someone disconnected the watch battery?" Mike asked.

"Actually, this thing has the battery capacity of a good laptop," Kurt said, "It's very impressive all around."

Kurt gripped the pin and put his hand on LENNY's console.

"Wait," Josh said, "Are you sure about this? What if it's a trap?"

"What kind of trap, exactly?" Kurt asked, "It's got no explosives, I can see all of its components, nothing is rigged for overload or self-destruction or anything like that. Near as I can tell, there's nothing that will immediately launch a drone to our location. It should be fine."

"You're being awful casual about this considering your psychic girlfriend just told everyone you're paranoid about Phalanx." Josh said.

"This is my element," Mike said, "This is what I'm supposed to be good at. I'm confident. I know what I'm doing."

"Just be careful, man," Josh said, "This guy knows more than our combined geek knowledge about the 'extra-normal' world. You don't know what could be in there."

"I'm not scared," Kurt said, taking a deep breath, "Ok. I'm initiating the transf-"

Kurt's face went blank and he fell forward onto the ledge of the console.

Shocked silence flooded the room.

"Dude," Josh said after a moment, "You'd better be faking."

Mike shook him by the shoulder then lifted his arm and let it go, watching it fall limp with a thunk onto the metal.

"He's out," Mike said.

Without warning, the constant hum of LENNY slowed to a stop. All of the monitors and seemingly useless blinking lights went dark except for the large main screen in the center. A loading bar appeared, bright green, casting an eerie glow throughout the cave. It moved from empty to full in a matter of seconds and changed into a row of numbers – 23:59:35 – and began ticking down.

"Ok," Josh said, "Giant green countdown clock. Probably not the best sign in the world."

"What happened?" Justin asked, walking in, "I saw the lights go down."

"Kurt was transferring the data from the pin to the computer," Mike said, "Then boom."

"He's in there," Jess said, suddenly.

"What?" Mike asked.

"He's in there," Jess repeated, "In the computer."

"How?" Josh asked, "It's not like he got TRON'd inside or something."

"His mind, moron," Jess scowled, "I don't know how it happened. I'm guessing but, based on fictional reference, it looks like his consciousness left his body and was downloaded into LENNY or something."

"Or something?" Josh asked, "What's 'or something'?"

"How am I supposed to know?" Jess shouted, "It's not like these powers came with a manual. It's my best guess, based on all those role-playing books you guys made me read."

"What's up with the countdown clock?" Justin asked.

"Stop asking me questions!" Jess shouted, "I know as much as you know right now."

The tide of shocked silence raised again, the group becoming spellbound by the numbers ticking away. Seconds disappeared into minutes with giant green gasps giving no indication as to what would happen at the end.

A wave of hopelessness hit next. No one asked questions. No one wondered. Justin made the only statement.

"Pop-culture dictates that this is something Kurt is doing on his own," he said, "I know he wouldn't like me saying it, but this is the part where he goes solo for an episode. We're not going to be able to affect anything with him until that clock runs down."

Jess pulled a chair next to Kurt's slumped body. She put a hand on his head and stroked his hair.

"What happens now?" Budda asked.

"We wait," Justin said, "And worry about it when zero comes."

## XVI

He opened his eyes to darkness.

He thought he was dead - no light, no sound, no feel of air or temperature, no smell of anything. He was sure he'd fallen into the trap alluded to by his friends. If this was death – alone in the dark with his thoughts – this must have been hell. He wished he could see something.

Immediately, he could see himself again. Some sort of spotlight shined down on him, illuminating a white floor beneath his feet. He was dressed in the same ripped jeans, worn t-shirt, and duct tape-covered sneakers he was wearing before everything went black.

The light was strange. It came down from above him but he cast no shadow on the white floor below. As he turned his hands over, looking at them, he realized there were no shadows at all. He looked up for the light source and saw nothing but the same darkness that surrounded him.

It was silent. He couldn't even hear himself breathing. The darkness surrounding him offered no reflections from the light. It was as if nothing existed outside of where he was standing.

He took a tentative step to the left. The light followed him perfectly. He took two steps to the right. It stuck with him on every motion. His legs remained illuminated as he made comically large steps, as if the light were conforming to him. He stopped, confused, and wished he knew where he was.

"Welcome, Kurt," said a somewhat familiar voice, shattering the silence.

"Hello?" he called into the darkness, surprised at his ability to speak.

Another figure illuminated a few steps away from him. Standing in an identical white-floored circle was a pale man in a black suit with slick black hair and sunglasses. He knew right away who it was.

"Phalanx," he said, "What are you doing here? What is this? Where am I?"

"Don't panic," Phalanx said, grinning, "You're currently inside of a computer. Most likely, you are inside your precious LENNY."

"Inside?" Kurt asked, "What do you mean?"

"If you're seeing me right now in the way I hope you're seeing me, you've transferred your consciousness into digital space," Phalanx said, "Seems a bit 90's 'internet' movie, I know, but it's actually a lot cooler than that. Don't be alarmed, you're supposed to be here. This is part of the reason I gave you the lapel pin."

"So, it was a trap," Kurt said.

"As we more than likely discussed in the real world, I'm offering to make you and your friends into heroes," said Phalanx, now walking in a circle slowly around Kurt, "I have the knowledge to teach you all how to use your abilities to their full potential and maybe even a bit beyond. The pin is merely a part of the proposition. You've done as I expected and that has brought you here. Congratulations on taking your first step toward claiming your true power."

"And, we're inside of LENNY right now?" Kurt asked.

"I've known other technopaths in my time. Most of them have had the ability to project themselves into a computer allowing them to download or upload information with their mind and, even more powerfully, giving them a visual and tactile operating system with which to encode data, decode data, and most importantly, program to the limits of their imagination.

"The pin contained more data than your mind could withstand. Being in contact with a computer allowed this jump-start of your transfer abilities as a sort of safety mechanism. In other words, I pushed you in here."

"More data than my mind could withstand?" Kurt asked, "What would have happened if I wasn't sitting at a computer right then?"

"Had you not been sitting at a computer," Phalanx continued, as though he didn't hear the question, "You would have had only five or so minutes to transfer the information before your brain hemorrhaged causing coma or death. It's a good thing you were prepared."

"Lucky me," Kurt muttered.

"This concludes the pre-recorded introduction," said Phalanx, "At this time I may now respond to limited questions."

"That was a recording?" Kurt asked.

Phalanx hesitated for a moment, the image stuttered, then it answered.

"Yes," he said, "This recording was made before I gave you the pin and placed here by another technomancer. It's meant to be a tutorial to help you get started with your new abilities and to help you unlock the data contained within this pin."

The image stuttered again before asking:

"Do you have any other questions?"

"Yeah," Kurt said after a moment, "I want out of here. How do I get that?"

A plain white door with a brushed metal knob faded into existence behind Phalanx. A red "EXIT" sign was above the jamb.

Phalanx stepped aside, gesturing to the door.

"What's this?" Kurt asked.

The image stuttered.

"The exit," Phalanx said, "If you pass through this door you will be back in your body."

"Where did it come from?" Kurt asked.

"You willed it into being," Phalanx said after another brief stutter, "This is your canvas to create. There is no formal keyboard interface to get in your way. There's no time of translation between what you think of and what you create. In here, you are in complete control."

Kurt cautiously approached the door, looking around its edges. The jamb was free-standing with nothing behind it; however, he had a suspicion that it would do exactly as Phalanx said. He gripped the knob in his hand.

"Before you do that," Phalanx said, "Consider the information you just transferred."

"I can access it from the outside," Kurt said, "I'm more comfortable in my body. This is freaking me out."

"Access is available from the outside," Phalanx said, nodding, "But you'll never be able to decrypt it. The encryption was written by another technopath. There's no conventional way from a programming or hacking standpoint that you'll be able to break it. It requires a more hands-on approach. Or, would it be hands-off approach? I don't know. I'm not a technopath. I'm just programmed to say this stuff."

Kurt tilted his head in confusion.

"At this point in my programming," said Phalanx after another twitch, "I'm supposed to remind you that you've got a time limit. The files, once transferred, will self-delete in twenty-four hours unless properly decrypted."

"Seriously?" Kurt shouted.

After a skip in the program, Phalanx raised his hands in innocence.

"Don't shoot the messenger," Phalanx said, "Remember, I'm a tutorial. I'm here to help."

Kurt sighed and looked around at the darkness. The door faded away as he let go of the knob as well as his desire to leave.

"Ok, Clippy," Kurt said, "How do I do this?"

Phalanx froze for a minute, then spoke.

"First," he began, "You'll have to create a technopathic operating system. Don't be daunted, it's easier than it sounds. All you'll need to do is imagine a sort of command center. Whatever you feel most comfortable with. Once you have some type of interface, you'll be able to access all of LENNY's resources. You just have to will it into being and it will do as you command."

The image of Phalanx stopped, paused, presumably until Kurt did what it asked.

He paced back and forth in the darkness, thinking. He stopped as an image came into his mind.

Behind Phalanx, he could see small dots of light. Banks of monitors and devices were activating. He could hear the white noise of electronics and caught a faint whiff of ozone. As things came alive, a giant war room was born as if someone raised a dimmer switch on reality.

The place looked exactly as he imagined it – like the bridge of a starship. The room was metallic and curved to the ceiling in a hemisphere. Hundreds of screens of varying size lined the perimeter with a dozen or more workstations, buzzing with strange holographic interfaces.  Each station had a high-backed black leather chair.

In the center of the room was a lowered circular area, below the ring of workstations, surrounded by railings on the upper deck.  Four small sets of stairs descended into the pit from each quarter of the room.  Light shined up from the floor of the sunken area and down from a central pillar hanging from the ceiling, stopping just above Kurt's eye level.  The half-pillar was surrounded by monitors near the top and orbited by holographic text crawls.  These were the first to display the green countdown clock, marking 23:50:59.  As he concentrated on it, the timer appeared on every monitor in the room.

Kurt smirked, impressed with himself.  Phalanx remained paused.

"Uh," Kurt said, "Ok, it's done."

"Excellent," said Phalanx, reanimating, then pausing to load, "Really?  You went with the starship bridge motif?  How typical.  I was expecting more out of you."

"How is a tutorial program critiquing this?" Kurt shouted, "I thought you were supposed to have limited responses!"

"I was prepared for many different design possibilities," said Phalanx after a pause, "Each option was programmed with a specific comment, most of them derisive.  If you'd like to hear them later..."

"No," Kurt interrupted, stopping the program, "Just tell me what's next."

"Next," Phalanx said, "You start decoding."

An iris at the bottom of the half pillar opened and spilled tens of thousands of small black and red bits into the middle of the pit until the light it generated was blocked out.

Kurt walked down the stairs from the upper deck and picked up one of the small objects.  It was a jigsaw puzzle piece; partially red, partially black, and no bigger than a quarter.  He closed his eyes and sighed.

"What is this?" Kurt asked, holding the piece up to the paused Phalanx.

"It's the file encoding," Phalanx said before pausing again.

"Really?" Kurt said, "I have to put together a giant puzzle to decode the files.  Now who's being typical?"

"Don't shoot the messenger," Phalanx said, his gestures and voice repeating an earlier response, "Remember, I'm a tutorial.  I'm here to help."

"Then help me put this thing together," Kurt said, "There's no way I'm going to sift through all this in twenty-four hours."

"I can't help you solve the decryption," said Phalanx, "My programming doesn't allow for it.  You do have it in you to help yourself, though."

The program paused. Kurt stared at the image of Phalanx, waiting.

"Well?" Kurt asked.

"Well what?" Phalanx said.

"How do I help myself?" he asked.

"Good question," said Phalanx, "Just the sort of thing you should ask a tutorial program. Remember, your imagination is the only limit. Think inside the box but, at the same time, think outside of it. Think of whatever you want and it will be here to help you. Good luck!"

The program paused again.

"That's it?" Kurt shouted.

The image did not move.

"Come on, that's it?" Kurt shouted, "I thought you were supposed to teach me how to use my powers here! What happened to that?"

"Don't shoot the messenger," Phalanx repeated, "Remember, I'm a tutorial. I'm here to help."

"Then help!" Kurt shouted.

"I can't help you solve the decryption," Phalanx repeated, "My programming doesn't allow for it. You do have it in you to help yourself, though."

Kurt grumbled and paced around the edge of the pit, noting that the clock was still ticking down.

"Ok," Kurt said, "Think inside the box, but outside too. I need more time for this."

"The passage of time in digital space is regulated by the processing speed of the computer into which you've transferred," said Phalanx, unexpectedly, "The faster the processor, the slower time will progress in the real world."

"Why didn't you say that when I asked you for help?" Kurt shouted, "That would have been helpful, don't you think?"

"Don't shoot the messenger," Phalanx repeated. Kurt ignored the rest of the statement.

"So, if I can overclock LENNY, then I'll get more time?" Kurt asked.

"The passage of time in digitals space is regulated by the processing speed..." Phalanx repeated.

While the program continued talking, Kurt concentrated on making LENNY faster. Based on what he'd seen and done so far, it should be a piece of cake. In his mind, he pictured a large red button under a hinged glass case labeled "overclock" just as one appeared on the console nearest to him. He laughed, opened the case, and pressed the button.

There was a loud whooshing noise, as if a large machine had started nearby, and the big green clock started ticking slower. He wished to see the comparative time in the outside world and the clock altered itself to 71:43:27.

"Triple-speed," Kurt muttered, "Not too bad. I'll have to do better when I get out of here."

He stopped for a moment as a thought entered his head. If he could do anything here, then he could simply will the puzzle to put itself together. He felt stupid for not having thought of it sooner and immediately began to concentrate.

The pieces didn't move.

"I noticed you were trying to will the data into being decrypted," said Phalanx, "To save you some time and possibly a stroke, I should let you know that, while you've taken the most logical course of action, it won't work. If data is encrypted by one technopath, another technopath cannot simply break the encryption by willing it to be so. While this will likely work on any other type of encryption, technopathic decrypting requires that you take that hands-on approach I mentioned earlier. This is why technopathic encryption can't be broken from the real world. You can will in the means for a solution, but you can't simply will the solution into being."

Phalanx went back to his idle mode. Kurt sighed and sat down near the large pile of pieces. He grabbed a handful of pieces and started sorting them. Some were red, some were black, some had both, and some were rounded on one edge. He set the rounded ones aside, assuming that they were the perimeter pieces.

Within ten minutes, he was frustrated. He couldn't take it. He wished he had something to do the sorting for him when he heard the whir of a small engine. A tiny wheeled machine with a dozer blade on the front was chugging along through the pieces. Behind it trailed a small container separated into four areas.

As the pieces were pushed into a small opening in the dozer blade, they were swept through a tube and deposited into containers for their proper edge or color category in the back.

The machine looked very art deco, almost steampunk, and contained many ambiguous lights and gauges which ticked and blinked to little more than cosmetic effect.

It was just what Kurt imagined.

He stood up, closed his eyes, and when he opened them the entire pile was being taken apart by dozens of the same tiny machines.

He smirked and stepped back to let them do the hard part for him.

\*\*\*

"It's been seven hours, Jess," said Justin, sitting on one end of the couch in front of LENNY's main screen, "He's not coming out of there until the clock runs down."

"I know," Jess said from the opposite end of the couch.

They were the only two still in the main chamber, their eyes glued to the ever-ticking clock. This was the first time either of them had said anything since the others left.

"You don't have to babysit him," Justin said, "You sitting here won't get him out any faster. I'm sure that, whatever he's doing in there, he's fine."

"He never expected anything like this to happen," Jess said, "I know that for sure."

"He'll be ok," Justin said, "Relax."

"What if it was a trap, like everyone thought?" Jess asked, "I watched that conversation happen at Josh's apartment. I could see into everyone's mind except for Phalanx. It was like he wasn't even there. I couldn't get any kind of psychic contact. He was a ghost to me. How am I supposed to know if we can trust him or not?"

"You don't," Justin said, "You have to go based on faith or doubt, like the rest of us. I'm sure he's got some kind of psychic protection being some almighty super spy from those Project people. Besides, it's not cool to storm everyone's brain to see if they're trustworthy."

"I don't like to wonder," Jess said, "My power is to know. And, I want to know."

"This whole psychic thing is really getting to you, isn't it?" Justin asked.

"What do you mean?" she replied.

"You can see all the answers," Justin said, "You know what people are going to say before they say it, so you think conversation is irrelevant. You know if people are lying or telling the truth just as they think it. You've got their whole life history before they can ever even approach you. Now, you're upset because there's at least one person in the world who you can't just open and read like a book. We're not that far into this and you're already forgetting what it's like to be a normal person."

"Because I'm not a normal person," she said, "I don't have to guess about someone's character or blindly trust people. I can see through everyone like they're made of glass. It saves me a lot of trouble. It can save all of us a lot of trouble. I prefer to know rather than be left in the dark. I know who they are, what they've done, and if they're lying to me and I'm better for it."

"Still kind of intrusive," Justin said, "It's really not fair."

"You encouraged this," she said, "You told me I should expand on my abilities. Now that I'm using them, you don't think it's the right thing just because I'm upset that I can't read the crazy superspy who suddenly pops in out of nowhere like one of the plot devices you're always going on about. I would think you of all people would want me to get as much on him as I could."

"I do," Justin said, "But, tell me you're not reading my mind right now. You trust me, we've been friends for years, you know I wouldn't lie

161

to you. Honestly admit you're not reading my mind right now and I won't ever bring this up again."

She looked away from him. He sighed.

"Look, I'm as untrusting as you are," Justin said, "The whole thing is just too convenient. If you're reading my mind, you know that I'm not crazy – I'm just addressing this whole situation in the only way I know how. Phalanx is a hit-or-miss plot twist in this story. He could be a deus ex machina or he could just kill us all in our sleep. You're right, we won't know before it happens if you can't tell us, but it's about trust and we'll figure that out as we go along."

"I still don't like it," she said, "I want to know for sure. Especially if this guy is supposed to be teaching us."

"It's really our only option," Justin said, "We're at the limit of our comic book and role playing knowledge. If we go much further, we might find something we can't properly control. Yeah, we're getting better with practice, but there's still a lot to learn about the outer edge of our abilities, not to mention combat and stuff. Last time we 'fought' someone, it didn't exactly go swimmingly. If we're going to do this right, we need an expert."

"What about this?" she asked, pointing to the countdown clock, "This doesn't seem much like help to me."

"He said there was information on the pin," Justin said, "Stuff that would get us pointed in the right direction. This has to be part of whatever he has planned for the future. He clearly has an agenda and taking one of us out can't work well to whatever end he has in mind, so I wouldn't worry about Kurt. He'll be back when this thing gets down to the buzzer and everything will be fine."

"Hello?" said an unfamiliar voice from behind them.

Justin spun on the couch and pointed his finger like a gun over a barricade. His hair changed from smoke to low flames.

"Don't move," he shouted, "I'll shoot."

"Relax, it's just her," Jess said, without turning around.

Still dressed in the dirty shirt and jeans with a bandage on her forehead, the girl with ice for hair put her hands up.

"Oh," Justin said, lowering his hand as his hair returned to smoke, "Uh, hey. How are you feeling?"

"A little achy," she said, rubbing her head, "But I'll manage. What happened to me?"

"You got into a pretty good wreck up there," Justin said, standing up and moving toward her, "You're ok now, just slightly concussed. The guy you hit is made out of stone, so he's ok, too."

"Your friend is made of stone?" she asked.

"Asks the girl with ice for hair," said Justin.

"To the guy with smoke for hair," she said, smiling.

He smirked.

"Justin," he said, extending his hand.

"Zoey," she said, pressing her palm to his. There was a slight hiss as their skin touched.

"So," Justin said, putting his hands in his pockets, "Why were you looking for us?"

"I remembered you guys from the hospital after the accident," Zoey said, "I was there with my boyfriend – well, ex-boyfriend. We were, uh, involved in the accident. I recognized the blond guy with the spiked hair on the news and followed a pretty long breadcrumb trail to track you down. You looked like a pretty tight group of friends, so I figured you'd all be together. I thought you guys would know a little more about what happened to us and what all this means."

"A car crashed into a tanker full of toxic waste at high speed," Justin said, "It covered us with black goo and the government paid us top-dollar to keep our mouths shut about it. Some people died… but those of us who survived got crazy super powers. That's pretty much everything we know."

"Yeah, I guess that about covers it," she said, "Impasses all around."

"Did anyone from the government talk to you about it afterward?" Justin asked, "You or your boyfriend?"

"Ex," she said, "Most definitely ex."

"Ok, ex-boyfriend," Justin corrected, "So?"

"No," she said, "We didn't talk to anyone about it except his parents and that was only because we were staying at their house until Chaucer and I had a… disagreement. He ran off and didn't come back. His parents tried to convince me to stay and keep things low key but I couldn't. Chaucer and I fought about how to use our powers for good. We were almost going to do the crime fighting thing until we discovered our outlooks on the justice system were slightly misaligned, to say the least."

"So you got into a fight about being super heroes?" he asked.

"We got into a fight about the morality of being a super hero," she said, "That's all I really want to say about it. Anyway, I heard you guys were messing around at that jewelry store on the news and I figured you'd be the ones to look up."

"How did you know we weren't robbing the place?" Justin asked.

"You guys all left the hospital with the same briefcase as I did," she said, "There would be no logical reason to go out looting and pillaging. I figured you wouldn't really need to go about creating a super-powered crime syndicate."

"So you came here to join us?" Justin asked.

"Sorta," she said, "I knew that if any of you were affected in the same way, you wouldn't look at me as a freak. That was enough to want to come here."

"Dig the spikes, by the way," Justin said, "Very punk rock."

She sighed and moved her hand around. Her hair shifted into a smoother, more swooping style though still sharp ice. The colors changed from a light blue to frost white with deep blue highlights. It looked strange, but almost real.

"Wow," Justin said, "Wish I could do that trick."

"You wish you could do that trick?" Jess piped up, "Do you have any idea how convenient that would be for a woman?"

"I know, right?" Zoey said, "I can have a different hair style at any given moment with zero effort. Probably the only good thing about my mutation."

"And you can look mostly normal," Justin said, "Closest I get to that is a hat that doesn't vent well."

A lull set in. Justin stared at the cave floor with his hands in his pockets feeling like a little kid trying to talk to a girl on the playground.

"Well?" Jess's voice prompted in his head.

"Uh, so," he said, "Were you in the bar with your boyfriend that night?"

"Ex," she corrected again, "And, no, I wasn't."

"Oh," said Justin, stopping in his tracks.

"Sorry," Zoey said after a moment, "It's just that it's sort of a sensitive subject. We'd been growing apart for a while and I went out looking for him that night. I saw him walking out, but I didn't get to talk to him until we went to the hospital. I had so much I wanted to say but then all this happened. He was in so much pain because of the way his powers manifested that I didn't want to burden him with any relationship garbage."

"What happened to him?" Justin asked, "I mean, when he changed."

She looked to the floor, closing her eyes tight as she put her hand on her chest.

"I'm sorry," Justin said, seeing tears forming in the corner of her eyes, "I shouldn't have asked."

"He got the worst of it," she said, after a long sigh, "His skin turned thick and green, his bones were growing out of control and pushing out of his body to make spikes and plates all over him. He felt every one push its way out, no matter how sharp or dull. He spent days screaming while I listened from a few rooms away. When it was all done, he wasn't the same person he was before."

Tears trickled down her cheeks and froze at the edge of her face in tiny icicles.

"Hey," Justin said, "You don't have to talk about it if it makes you upset."

"No, it's ok," she said, "I just... I haven't really talked about it out loud before."

She paused and took a deep breath before continuing.

"His parents were taking care of him day and night," she said, "They didn't tell me what was happening. I could hear them talking to him when I listened at his door. He didn't want me anywhere near. They wouldn't tell me anything about what was happening, I had to see it for myself. The night I did…"

She cried harder. Justin closed his eyes and sighed, feeling responsible for opening the flood gates.

Zoey sat down on the cave floor. Justin moved toward her and put his hand on her shoulder causing a low hissing noise.

"You're ok now," he said, "Whatever happened before, you're ok now. I know how you feel. I lost someone I loved in all this, too."

"I'm sorry," she sobbed, "I'm sorry for what I did to all of us."

"You can hardly blame yourself," Justin said, "It wasn't your fault, it was whoever was driving that little foreign car."

"Justin," Jess called.

"Whatever careless asshole was driving that car that night," Justin continued, "They're the reason we're all here as we are now. They're the reason that some of the people we love are gone."

Zoey sobbed harder.

"Justin," Jess called again, "Stop."

"That person is the reason your boyfriend is messed up," Justin said, "That person is the reason that my girlfriend is dead."

"Justin, leave her alone!" Jess shouted.

"I did it!" Zoey cried, "I did it! It was all my fault! I was driving the car, I wasn't paying attention, I smashed into the tanker. I did it, ok? I messed up Chaucer and I killed your girlfriend! I screwed the world up for everyone!"

She sprung up and sprinted away, her face covered in small rivers of ice. She ran back into the makeshift medical cave where she had been staying.

Justin could feel the rage building in him. He was doing his best to hold back, but his head was already on fire with anger. He felt something deeper building, something overwhelming and powerful. He was doing everything he could to keep it down.

His clenched fists were beginning to glow with heat.

"Justin," Jess said, "Don't fly off the handle."

"You knew," Justin said, pointing a glowing hot finger at her, "You knew and you didn't tell me."

"Yes," Jess admitted, speaking quickly, "I knew from the beginning. What she did was an accident, Justin. If I told you earlier then you wouldn't have trusted her. If you're going to argue about me being intrusive, then don't get angry at me when I don't tell you any detail."

Justin growled in frustration. He felt like his head was going to explode. He walked away, into one of the smaller tunnels. Jess continued to explain as he crossed the main chamber, but he was too

165

angry to hear.  He walked to the end of a tunnel and sat down, trying to meditate the anger away.

\*\*\*

The army of small robots deactivated one by one as their purposes came to an end.  They gave way to new robots more suited to the task at hand.  He didn't know how long he'd been inside the computer but a few of the original robots he'd thought up were still busily working.

The puzzle sorting battalion had now turned into one of assembly.  Each creation tested its pieces, one by one, moving around the unfinished areas until they found the right spot.

Kurt sat, bored, on one of the sets of steps leading to the pit.  The light emanating from the floor was almost completely covered by the assembled puzzle, save for the small patch near his feet.

"How's it going?" asked Phalanx, appearing on the steps opposite him.

"About fifty more to go," Kurt said, "And we're done."

The Phalanx projection stuttered for a moment.

"Impressive solution," it offered, "Not exactly impressive on time."

"What do you mean?" Kurt asked.

"Have you checked the clock lately?" asked Phalanx.

00:00:25:06

"What the…" Kurt started, "I thought the overclocking gave me more time?"

The image paused, then skipped into animation.

"A quick check of your systems indicate that your overclocking gave out over five hours ago.  Your solution must have been a massive drain on processing speed.  Even with overclocking, more than a few technopathic creations working at once creates quite a demand on a system.  Even one as advanced as yours."

"No warning?" Kurt shouted, "Nothing?"

The projection smirked.

"You were doing so well," it said, "I didn't want to discourage you.  Twenty-five pieces remain."

Kurt looked back up at the clock.  The time was speeding up.  It now read 00:00:15:21.

"You're new to this," Phalanx said, "You didn't know all the terms.  You simply overran things a bit.  Twenty pieces."

Kurt knew what the problem was.  With a wave of both hands, the robots vanished.  The clock slowed, showing 00:00:09:57.  He dropped to his knees at the end of the steps and started scrambling to put the pieces in place himself.  The smug face of the Phalanx projection stared down at him as he frantically tried to complete things.

With a time of 00:00:02:01 on the clock, the final piece was placed.

All edges of the puzzle sealed themselves together. The red and black coloring shifted and revealed the round XIII logo of the lapel pin.

The floor lit up brighter than before. Through the blinding glow, Kurt saw the iris in the bottom of the central pillar open. A thick bright beam of light shot up through it and into the central pillar with a loud hum. The beam subsided, the iris closed, and the lights in the room went dim. The giant puzzle was gone and the hundreds of displays and consoles slowly deactivated.

"What happened?" Kurt asked, turning to Phalanx as the image faded away.

The room went dark, just as it had been when Kurt first entered the system. The strange dead silence and unending black oblivion had returned.

He worried for a moment that he really was dead this time when suddenly, the room exploded back into existence. The displays around the war room were full of schematics, plans, equations, images, and videos. Kurt approached one section and started scrolling through the three-dimensional display with his hands.

"What is all this stuff?" he asked.

"Everything you need," Phalanx said, appearing next to him, "Just as I said it would be. The information here will allow you to create whatever your group may require to become superheroes."

Kurt paused when he reached the schematics of the lapel pin, taking a few minutes to look it over.

"This information can put you near technological par with the Project," said Phalanx, "As good as you are, Kurt, I don't think you'd have come up with most of these ideas on your own."

"There's no way," Kurt said, "I could never make anything like this. I'd need a lab that would be more out of science fiction than science fact. I'd need components that don't exist outside of a freaking alien spaceship."

"So improvise," Phalanx said, "I've given you the plans, it's up to you to make them real. You've got the data. Take your time. Experiment. I have confidence in you. You can make these things happen."

Kurt stared at the plans, slack-jawed and in deep concentration.

"Suit your friends up," Phalanx said, clapping him on the shoulder, "If anything, it'll give them a little more confidence."

Kurt nodded and continued dialing through the thousands of documents, realizing that he would have much more work to do than the two minutes left on the timer.

\*\*\*

Justin awoke in the dark. He had fallen asleep while meditating and didn't know how long he'd been out.

Dark was good. Dark meant that his hair was no longer on fire and his hands had stopped glowing. He was calm but still felt terrible about making that girl cry.

Jess was still sitting in front of the timer. They had a while to go. She could have sworn that time was being added on or looped around, but her eyes were too used to staring at the giant numbers to know the difference.

"You ok?" Jess asked without looking.

"You know the answer to that already," Justin said.

"Look, I didn't tell you because I knew you were attracted to her, ok?" Jess said, "If I didn't know you well enough to see it in your face and hear it in your voice, your surface thoughts were practically screaming it."

"Whatever," he grumbled, "Where is everyone?"

"It's just been you and I," Jess said, "The timer isn't done yet. They'll be here when it's time."

"Where's the girl?" Justin asked.

"Zoey came out about a half an hour ago," Jess said, "She went upstairs. She's still in the house if you want to talk to her."

Justin exited the main chamber and went up into the house. When he reached the small living room with no sign of her, he checked the two bedrooms on opposite sides of a small hallway. As he exited one, the door in the center of the hall, the bathroom door, swung wide. There, wearing only a towel and carrying an armful of dirty clothes, was Zoey.

She shouted in surprise as she saw him. He quickly turned away to hide his bright red embarrassed face.

"Uh, you were," Justin stuttered.

"Taking a shower," she said, "I figured no one would mind. I needed it. Not a big deal, is it?"

"No, no," he stammered, "Not a big deal at all."

"Were you looking for something?" she asked.

"You, actually," he said, "I wanted to make sure you didn't run off because of what I did."

"Well," she said, "I didn't."

"Ok," he said, "Good."

There was a silent moment. He had to restrain himself from turning around to look at her. He knew that if he did it would seem like he was ogling and he didn't want to be that guy.

"I hate to ask for something else," she said, "But, could I borrow your washer? I had a bag full of clothes, but your one friend moved my car and they were in the trunk. These are kinda rank."

"Sure," Justin said, "I mean, it's not my washer, but I don't think Kurt will care."

"You don't have to be so embarrassed," she said, "You can look at me. It's not like I'm naked or anything."

"I know, it's just," he stammered, "I don't want to look you in the eye because I know what I said earlier made you upset. Also, I don't want you to think I'm a perv or anything. I'm not a bad guy."

"No," she said, patting him on the back, "You're not a bad guy. You're the guy who's going to help me find the washer. It's ok, you can look at me."

"I might, uh," he started, his face flushing further, "I might stare. Guys tend to do that in situations like this."

"I know," she said, "I don't care. Just show me where the washer is, ok?"

"Yeah, ok," he said, "Follow me."

He walked without turning to look at her and lead her to the laundry room above the entrance to the cave. He pointed to the washer without turning to look.

"There you go," he said, "Have a blast."

She laughed as he turned his back to her when she walked toward the washing machine.

"You're really honestly embarrassed, aren't you?" she asked, smiling.

"Well," he said, "I wanted to apologize for my outburst. That was bad enough. The fact that you're half-naked is making it much more difficult. I don't want you to think I'm some kind of sleaze on top of being a jerk."

"You're not by far," she said, "I used to club around the goth scene. Those guys stare like they've never seen a short skirt before. I think it's cute that you're embarrassed."

"Whatever," he said, "I just want to talk to you. We can do that this way."

"I do my best conversing when I'm looking at a face," she said, "Can you please just turn around?"

"Fine," he said, relenting.

He tried to look her directly in the eyes and failed. She smiled as he looked her over finally arriving at her face. His cheeks were fire-engine red. This was the first woman he'd looked at with any degree of interest since becoming a pseudo-widower and it made him extremely nervous.

"So," she said, waiting.

"I'm sorry," he said, "I didn't mean to explode on you down there. I had no right. What happened, happened and it hurt you as much as it hurt me. I feel terrible that it was your first experience with me. I came off brash and angry and that's not always who I am."

"You were right," she said, "You were right to be angry. No one outside of me, Chaucer, and the black suits knew it was my fault. After what happened to everyone; your girlfriend and the other two who died,

Chaucer, your rock friend, even you… it was about time someone was angry with me. Chaucer didn't even blame me. At least, he didn't call me on it if he did. I think I needed someone to remind me that this was all my fault. If I hadn't been a stupid jealous girlfriend, none of this would have happened."

"You didn't do anything out of the ordinary," he said, taking a step toward her, "It was an accident. Plain and simple."

"It doesn't make me any less responsible," she said, "I've ruined Chaucer's life, your life and the lives of everyone involved. I've unleashed something horrible. Chaucer is a monster now. His first real action with his powers was to kill someone because he was already starting to lose his humanity."

"You also created heroes to stop the monsters," he said.

"Oh, come on," she said, tears freezing down her face, "You can't justify this. You shouldn't. Your life will never be normal again. You can't have a public life with your hair like that and neither can I. Neither can Chaucer or your friend who turned into a rock man. You'll never have the woman you loved back. I killed her. My stupidity – my arrogance – killed her."

She sobbed. Justin stepped closer, thought twice, but then put his arms around her. She grasped onto him and wept openly into his shoulder.

"Zoey," he whispered, tearing up himself, "It's ok. I forgive you."

She shuddered in his arms, gripping tight to him.

"Don't say that," she muffled into his shoulder, "You can't. None of you can."

"I can," he said, now crying himself, "We'll make it through. We'll be better for it. All of us."

"I tore your world apart," she said, "I tore mine apart."

"Zoey," he said, pushing her away so that he could look in her eyes, "It's ok. I forgive you."

Suddenly, she stood on her tip-toes, put her hand on his cheek, and kissed him deeply.

When they separated, steam rose from both of their mouths. Justin stared straight forward, dumbfounded.

"Thank you," she whispered before walking up the stairs, back to the house proper.

He was paralyzed. His mind raged with thought yet remained surprisingly clear at the same time. It would be ten minutes before he uttered to the empty room:

"You're welcome."

## XVII

It was cold, windy, and moist as they sat on the front porch smoking cigarettes. She wore a scarf and a stylish wool coat. He wore no layers beyond his clever black t-shirt and black pants. She shivered while he paced, leaving a trail of smoke in his wake.

"Then right when things get really intense and I'm trying to calm her down, she moves in and kisses me," Justin said, "I just don't get it."

"Well, was it just a peck? Like a thank you thing?" Lisa asked, "Or an actual kiss."

"Oh, it was a kiss," Justin said, "A fully full-on, straight-up, square to the lips, eyes closed, tongue in the mouth kiss."

"Out of nowhere," Lisa said.

"Totally," Justin confirmed.

"Wow," she said, "I'm not really sure what to tell you."

"Come on," Justin moaned, "You're supposed to be my insight into the female psyche. You have to give me something to go on."

"Why don't you ask Jess?" Lisa asked, "She's the psychic. She'd know for sure."

"She and I have a bit of a disagreement about how she uses her powers," Justin said, "Asking her to tell me what Zoey was thinking would be a giant contradiction of my point."

"If you want to know why she kissed you, there are only two people you can ask," Lisa said, "The girl who did it or the psychic who can read her mind. Your choice. If you don't do something soon, I know how you'll get. Your paranoia will take over and you'll keep speculating, overanalyze the situation, and wind up regretting something that could have been. You've got to buck up some courage and confront the girl. If you don't, you might wind up missing out on something good."

"Do I really want something good right now?" Justin asked, "I mean, I'm a pseudo-widower. Shouldn't I still be in mourning? Char's only been gone for a relatively short while. I shouldn't be running off to find something new already, should I? I don't know if I'm ready to be seriously involved with someone just yet."

"Relax," Lisa said, "You were kissed. It wasn't some kind of wedding vow. It may have just been a spontaneous outburst of emotion on her part. You were both very emotionally vulnerable at that point, maybe she just needed something to comfort her and kissing you was the first thing that came to mind."

"So, you're saying it's probably nothing, then," Justin said.

"No," Lisa said, "I'm throwing out a guess. You can plug me for answers all you want; I'm not going to have the real ones. I can only speculate, same as you. I'll say it again: You ask the girl or you ask the psychic if you want the whole story."

Justin continued pacing and taking drags from his cigarette. His hair and the burning tobacco both left trails in the cold air that made Lisa think of a train doing donuts on her porch.

"You're attracted to her, right?" Lisa asked, exhaling.

"Yes," Justin said plainly.

"Then be proactive for a change," Lisa said, "You've blown how many opportunities in your life because you speculated and stagnated. If you leave this one lie too long and she's interested, she's going to think you're not and walk away."

"I don't know if I'm ready to move forward with something like this," Justin said.

"So tell her that," Lisa said, "She'll understand. It's not like you're asking her to martyr herself for  you. Stop being so melodramatic. Man up and talk to her. It's been days since. She's probably waiting for you to say something."

"Yeah," Justin said, "I guess I should."

"Don't guess," Lisa said, "Just do. Show some balls. It'll do you good."

"Wait," Justin said, stopping in his tracks, "I just thought of something."

"What?" Lisa asked.

"Manic Pixie Dream Girl," Justin said, "Of course, why didn't I see it before?"

"Is that some kind of superhero name you picked out for her or something?" Lisa asked.

"No," Justin said, "It's a pop-culture trope. Lots of stories have them. They're usually love interest of one of the main characters or the most desirable female in the narrative. She's always short, attractive, quirky, fashionable, intellectual - basically, the perfect girl for the post-modern protagonist. They're the girl of your dreams who suddenly appears to make your life incredible and show the darker, depressed male lead that life is worth living. Think every character ever played by Zooey Deschanel. They almost share a name for God's sake."

"I get it," Lisa said, "But, why do you think she's some kind of pop-culture trope? This is real life, remember. Just because you think this is all going according to some pre-ascribed narrative doesn't mean that everything you come in contact with is another cliché."

"This makes too much sense, though," Justin said, "Why would a girl like that ever kiss a guy like me? I'm an overweight, beardy nerd. I'm no one's type. She proves my theory that we're stuck in some kind of origin story. Next thing you know, now that there's whatever sort of romantic interest, she's going to be kidnapped. In fact, I bet I get a call about it right… now."

He produced his cell phone from his pocket and waited. Lisa rolled her eyes and let the moment pass.

"You really need to stop it with that stuff," Lisa said with a sigh, "Can't you just accept that this girl is real, present, and unlikely to behave as some character archetype from a movie?"

"I guess," he said.

"And, no overanalyzing her," Lisa said, "Not with the kiss and certainly not with this Crazy Fairy Tinkerbell crap."

"Manic Pixie Dream Girl," Justin said.

"Whatever," Lisa said, "Don't think about it too much. Grow a pair, confront her about it, and get rid of the stress of it all from both angles."

"Fine," he said.

They both took drags from their cigarettes.

"Sometimes," Justin said, "I don't think I'd have a spine if it wasn't for you."

\*\*\*

Mike entered the long tunnel, this one much clearer and cleaner than the others. Around a long, sweeping curve he found the source of the grinding, cutting sounds and the ozone smell. A large workshop full of tools and piles of salvaged electronic devices, from cell phones to short-wave radios, had been established in this particularly large cave.

In the center of the mess sat Kurt at a wooden worktable which Mike recognized as one of the originals included with their abandoned mine. Welding goggles were perched atop Kurt's head as he currently disassembled an older-looking laptop with relative ease. Kurt did not yet know he had visitors. It was difficult to see anyone entering or exiting over the mounds of disassembled and waiting-to-be-disassembled technology.

"Dude," Mike said, causing Kurt to jump slightly, "What are you doing?"

"Building stuff," Kurt answered without looking up from his work.

"Duh," Mike said, "You got up from that computer incident without saying a word and started moving things in here. You haven't talked to anyone since. All you have to say for yourself is that you're building stuff?"

"Yes," Kurt said, still not looking up.

"What are you building?" Mike asked, "Iron Man armor?"

"No," Kurt said.

"Robot butler?" Mike asked.

"No," Kurt said.

"Holographic computer interface?" Mike asked.

"Is there something else you can be doing?" Kurt asked, finally looking up, "I'm busy."

"You need to come up for air," Mike said, "No one's even seen you in three days. Jess is starting to wonder if you're ever coming to bed."

"Well, she's the psychic," Kurt said, returning to his work, "Maybe you should get her to tell you."

"Dude, seriously?" Mike started, "Your friends – remember us? – we're worried about you. Your girlfriend is worried about you. At least let us know what…"

Mike was cut off by Kurt slamming his fists down on the worktable.

"Would you please just leave me alone so I can work in peace?" he shouted.

When he looked up again, Mike could see that he hadn't shaved, bathed, or probably slept since he'd been at this.

"Whatever," Mike said, turning his back and walking out.

Jess watched the whole conversation from Mike's perspective. She already knew that it would be a mistake to try and speak with Kurt, but Mike insisted. She warned him that it would go poorly.

When the countdown clock ended and he woke, he didn't even look at her. He didn't take time to appreciate the fact that she'd sat awake for twenty-four hours, waiting in vigil for him to hopefully snap out of it. He only muttered: "I have to get to work." After that, he spoke to no one, but moved quickly and constantly.

She followed him around, trying to ask questions about what happened inside only to get mumbled nonsense or dismissive one-word responses. He walked by everyone, not caring or noticing the concern expressed. He disappeared for an entire day coming back with a truckload of tools and components. He rigged a doorbell into the cave and quickly left his nest to answer the door always returning with a package or two – something he had ordered online was the only assumption.

She tried to read his mind, but it was clouded with schematics and diagrams. It was like he was thinking in ancient Egyptian. She couldn't translate anything. She tried to access his memories, but they were blurred and hazy because of the amount of thought he was devoting to his work.

After the first two days, she gave up trying to communicate with him in any way. She figured that, whenever he was done with whatever he was doing, things would go back to normal. He would probably be out of the workshop by the end of the day and everything would be fine.

At this, the end of the first week, she was starting to lose faith.

"He's impossible," Mike said, coming out of the cave, "I don't know, Jess. I don't know what to do."

She opened her eyes and sighed. She had been attempting to meditate in her usual spot – the couch in front of LENNY. It wasn't working.

"Waiting seems like all we can do," she said, "Everyone else tried and had about as much luck as you did. I've had even worse luck than that."

"I know how you must feel," Mike said, putting a hand on her shoulder.

"Thanks," she said, sweeping his mind quickly, "But I know for a fact you have no idea how I feel."

"Right," he said, shaking his head, "Well, I'm going home. It's late. Are you going to be ok here?"

"Yeah," she said, "Everyone's off doing their own things right now, but I'll be fine. See you tomorrow."

He nodded, waved, and walked out the door of the main chamber.

She attempted to resume whatever meditation she could manage. It was the closest thing to sleep she'd had since her vigil. She had gone to the bedroom in the house upstairs and attempted sleep twice but failed. She had become accustomed to sleeping next to someone and couldn't get comfortable without Kurt near her. She knew that he wouldn't want to waste his time sleeping and, when he absolutely had to, he certainly wouldn't waste his time coming upstairs to do it.

She felt haggard. She hadn't left the house since before this started. Normally, she was very self-conscious about her appearance and making sure she looked her best. She hadn't put on make-up or done anything with her hair aside from constantly retying a shoulder-length auburn utility ponytail. She knew she looked a wreck to everyone, but she didn't feel like caring.

Things for the rest of the group had progressed normally. They came and went as they pleased, continuing to reassure her that everything was going to be ok in the end. Looking through their minds, she could see their real opinions. None of them were hopeful that normal would return any time soon.

Down here in the cave, when things were quiet, she felt the volume turning down on her worries. It was dead silent save for the occasional clatter coming from Kurt's workshop. This made it very easy for her to drift into her meditative state.

The darkness of her empty mind became a star field; each glowing point of light represented a mind within her radius. She spent far too much time reaching out to these lights and digging into people's heads. She had become addicted to dirty little secrets and hidden agendas. From here, she could see through other people's eyes and experience things as they do. She could hypnotically suggest commands as simple as stand up or as complex as mental illusions complete with tactile sensations. She could make someone think they were getting eaten by a dinosaur and they would feel every sickening chew.

She hadn't gone that far yet, but she knew she had it in her. She scared the crap out of a traffic cop by making him see a velociraptor charging him from down the street. She let up before the attack would have happened. She was pretty sure she could kill with that ability, if not by fear alone, then by stimulating pain centers or even combining telekinesis with the illusion to give the full effect.

She had taken to using her illusion power to create an image of herself that would interact with people. She had done this before, tormenting Mike into thinking he had cut off her hand with a table saw. This time, her intention was more necessity than mental torture. No one seemed to notice a difference.

She also found that she could manipulate people into not seeing her. Psychic invisibility, the gaming geeks called it. It was pretty difficult to achieve as she had to manipulate the minds of anyone who could see her, but it was a great way to take her mind off of her current situation. If she was concentrating on not being seen, she didn't have time to concentrate on Kurt and his despondence.

"Hello, Jessica," said a strange voice.

She opened her eyes and saw a pale man with slick black hair in a black suit and sunglasses sitting on the other side of the couch. She fell from the levitation which typically accompanied her meditative state and landed hard. She backed away from him, nearly climbing the couch. Her heart pounded in her chest. For the first time since the accident, she was honestly frightened.

"Something wrong?" he asked.

"You," she stuttered, "It's you. You're not supposed to be able to see me."

"Yet, here I am," he said, "Seeing you. I suppose it's always unsettling for a psychic the first time that happens, but you'll learn to get over it."

"How?" she asked.

"Well, how you get over it is a matter of many different things. Time, for one."

"No," she said, "How can you see me?"

"Oh, that," he said, "Yeah, I can't be affected by psychic abilities. Little trick I picked up over the years. Comes in very handy in my line of work. Does it bother you?"

She stared blankly at him.

"I'll take that as a yes," he said, "I'm assuming you know who I am, right?"

She nodded.

"Sorry," he said, "Not very friendly of me to just assume you know who I am, is it? Formal introduction, then. I'm Agent Phalanx. Pleasure to meet you."

He extended his hand.  She stared at it.  Her heart was beating in her throat and white hot fear burned in the pit of her stomach.

He reached out with his left hand, gently grasped her right wrist, inserted her fear-chilled hand into his, and shook.

"You really are scared right now, aren't you?" he asked with a smile, "Why?"

She continued to stare.  She opened her mouth to explain, but couldn't think of anything to say.  She was more suspicious of him than she was frightened.  She wanted to know more about him, but...

"I get it," he said, snapping his fingers, "It's because you can't read my thoughts, isn't it?  It's because you can't turn my mind over like you're looking for something stashed in an apartment.  Don't worry.  You're not the first psychic who has been put off by me and you probably won't be the last."

He was right and she knew it.  His was the first mind she couldn't touch.  She had grown so accustomed to just knowing things that the mystery of this guy shook her confidence in a way she'd not felt in her life.

"I just came here to talk," he said, "I don't mean you any harm.  Please, take my word for it and try to calm down.  I've got some important things I'd like to discuss and it won't help much if you're velcroed to the back of the couch, paralyzed with fear."

"Sorry," she muttered before taking a few deep breaths and returning to a more conventional seating position.

"I understand," he said, "I really do.  More than you know.  You've been going on for a while now able to scour the minds of anyone within your sphere of influence to see their true intentions.  You know when people are lying to you and you've become accustomed to that.  Now, out of the blue, here I come – Mr. Tabula Rasa himself – a brick wall in a world full of open doors.  You must have been disappointed when you couldn't offer your friends any intel on me when they got back from our first conversation.  Scared you then, too, didn't I?  Doesn't help that I always turn up dressed like this."

"Why don't you dress a different way, then?" Jess asked.

"Do you think anyone would take me seriously if I showed up in a Hawaiian shirt and some cargo shorts?" he asked, "No.  People respect and fear the suit, especially when they've had run-ins with the people who usually wear this get-up.  Plus, this is the only set of clothes I have that can multiply."

"Multiply?" she asked.

"Never mind," he said, "Back to the task at hand.  I'm going to need you to do whatever you can to trust me.  I know you're just as suspicious as the rest of them about who I am.  More so, I'm sure, since you can't read me."

"Why do I need to trust you?" she asked.

"Because I want to work with you," he said, "All of you. You were privy to the previous conversation. I want to help you. If you want to play at being superheroes, I can show you how to become the real deal."

"And, you think if you can convince me," she said, "You'll convince the rest of them."

"Basically," he said, "You're the hardest target. Plus, they look to you for insight on who to trust. If you trust me, then it's likely they'll follow suit."

"I think you're overplaying my influence," she said, "Half of them get angry at me for reading people's minds. Plus, I already told them I couldn't get anything from you. I told them you weren't to be trusted because of that."

"I know," he said, "It is not irreparable. When he's ready, your man Kurt is going to come out of his little nest ready to believe whatever you say about me. I've given him everything that makes my former agency tick, technologically speaking. He's going to show an immeasurable amount of trust based on that alone. If you add your backing to that, then I'll be on board and trust me when I say that's exactly what you need to get where you want to go."

"Wait," she said, "Why am I listening to this? You want me to lie to my friends?"

"I don't want you to lie," Phalanx said, "I want you to tell them the truth. I want the two of us to come to a trustful understanding. Besides, what difference does it make if you lie to them? You've been lying to them since the beginning and they don't know it."

"What do you mean?" she asked.

"You're not just reading their minds, you're raiding their minds," he said, "You know every dark little secret their subconscious has tried to stash away. You're reading them like books from birth to current, analyzing and judging everything they've done and you haven't exactly been honest about it."

"There's no way you can know that," Jess said.

"Please," he scoffed, "I know more about psychics than you do and you actually are one. Oh, good. The coffee's here."

Jess followed his sunglassed line of sight toward the door of the main chamber. Another agent, identical to Phalanx, carried a tray in one hand and a small folding table in the other.

The identical agent set up the small table in front of them

"I borrowed your kitchen," he said, "Sorry, I probably should have asked. I brought my own coffee service, but I needed the stove. Hope you don't mind."

"How do you take yours?" asked the other Phalanx as he set the tray down.

"Cream and sugar," she stuttered, followed by a blurted out, "Please."

"Of course," he said, preparing it for her and handing her the cup and saucer. He poured another cup, black, before sitting down and merging with the Phalanx to whom Jess had been speaking.

"I do make a damn good cup of Joe, if I may say so," he said, picking up the saucer and sipping at the cup, "I always find these late-night sessions much easier when you've got a bit of caffeine to give you an edge, don't you agree?"

"Uh," she said, still confused, "Ok?"

She took a sip of the coffee. He was right. It was good.

"As I was saying," he continued, "There's not much I don't know about you. Even things that aren't in your file."

"My file?" she asked.

"You're surprised?" he asked, "The Project compiled files on all of you the minute you turned up at the hospital. You signed a rather lengthy document with their name on it stating that they had rights to surveillance if they saw fit, including, retroactively, keeping information on you in a file. They don't keep anything they touch too far out of reach."

"So, they're watching us?" she asked, the fear returning, "Like, right now?"

"No," he said, "They've got more important things to do at the moment. That's why I'm here. I'm quite content to stay out of their sight as long as possible. The only reason they'd be watching you right now is if one of you ran to the media. They don't like the spotlight. I mean, really, how would people react if they found out that our government has been researching and generating super humans for the better part of a century? They're buried pretty deep but, eventually, someone would find them and avoid the inevitable mind-wipe that comes with their discovery."

"Why leave us out in the open, then?" Jess asked, "Why not pull us in? I mean, if we really become superheroes, we'll be all over the media."

"They don't really care if you become superheroes or not," Phalanx said, "As long as your origin never gets out in the open, you're golden. They knew there was a remote outside chance one of you would gain an ability or two and their risk assessment data told them that, if that happened, you would either be complacent or work for the common good, either way no risk to the Project unless, again, your origin came out.

"Of course, they didn't count on everyone in the accident gaining abilities. Still, your group, though horrifyingly dangerous in its own right, is the least of their worries. I want to change that. I want you guys to become so big that it eventually draws the Project into a direct conflict with our team and we can take them down."

"You're saying you want us to become superheroes," she started, "So that we can eventually take on an entire government agency in a head-on collision?  Yeah, what sounds like inevitable death or imprisonment doesn't make it very enticing."

"That may be so," he said, sipping his coffee, "But, they need to be brought to task."

"Why?" she asked, "For what?"

He put his coffee cup down and leaned forward, looking much more severe.

"The end goal of the Project has always been to 'win the war'," Phalanx said, "Since its first iteration, the Project has had a hand in every major global conflict and political issue, every time with a new iteration and new ideas to out-think the enemy.  The atrocities Williams and his staff have committed over the years are inexcusable.  The horrors they made others a party to were sometimes that much worse.  Williams has devoted himself to a cause and as times change so do the parameters of that cause.  He has the science, the budget, and the manpower to take over the world.  It's only a matter of time before he sees the world as his enemy and indoctrinates those who follow him to see things his way.

"If you ever wanted a bad guy to face, you've got it.  The Project is a super villain factory of the highest order and they have to be stopped."

She sat staring at him, her head tilted downward in disbelief.

"And that's the line you want to go with?" she asked, "To inspire everyone to action?  Just giving them a 'super villain factory' on a silver platter?  You realize that will set off all kinds of red flags with the 'origin story' crowd, right?"

"I'm counting on it," Phalanx said, "It plays right into things.  Plus, a common enemy does wonderful things for team unity."

"Feeding them a line of crap, no matter how you candy-coat it, is still feeding them a line of crap," Jess said.

"It's not all lies," Phalanx said, "They really have done some horrible things in the name of both science and patriotism.  They're completely beyond reproach and have little to no morals when looking to achieve their goals.  That makes them extremely dangerous to, well, pretty much everyone."

"You're going to have to do better than that for me," Jess said, "I might not be able to read your mind, but I know you're glossing over something.  I don't even need to see your eyes to read it from your face."

He sighed and slowly removed his sunglasses.

She gasped as he opened his eyes.  They were solid white - no iris, no pupils.  She could tell by his body language that this was a symbol of trust.  She could tell by his face that he was very serious.

"I was inside," he said, "I know for a fact that these are bad people.  I didn't always believe it.  I was their soldier for a very long time but they're now my enemies.  As awesome as I am, I can't take the Project down on my own.  They know me and they have ways around and through me, even if I make an army of myself. Help is what I need from you and your friends. I want vengeance and in getting it I'll be removing a serious threat to the world as we know it. If I can help all of you deal with your current predicament and possibly create a force for good before I reach that end, then all the better. You have to admit that you could use the guidance."

She sipped her coffee, letting it all sink in.

"Where do we go from here, then?" she asked, "And why tell me all of this?"

"I'm telling you because you can keep secrets," he said, putting his sunglasses back on, "I also knew I wouldn't gain your trust unless I was up-front about everything. Where we go from here is into training, once everyone is on board."

"How are you going to train us?" she asked, "You don't have our abilities, you can't know how they work."

"I learned more than I should have during my time with the Project," he said, "I've seen extra-normal people burn out in a flash because they didn't learn control. Almost a thousand of them. I've seen a handful of psychics of your level stroke out or have aneurisms before they were even out of the gate. I saw at least five more drop in the field. Push yourself too far too fast and that's what'll happen. You really have no idea what kind of powder keg you're sitting on. If people lost control, it would be catastrophic."

They sat silently for a moment. The sudden gravity of Phalanx's offer was sinking in. She had seen Budda accidentally crush things. She had seen Justin's temper flare. She had propped herself up after feeling dizzy with a bleeding nose enough to know he was right.

She took a deep breath and exhaled slowly. She extended her hand to him.

"I'm in," she said, "What's next?"

## XVIII

Zoey rolled over and looked at a small digital clock. It was two-thirty in the morning.

She swung her feet off the edge of the bed and put them down on the stone floor. It was cold in the cave, but she couldn't feel it. All she knew was that she was thirsty and the pantry area, where they kept a bomb-shelter's worth of food and supplies, was on the other side of the main chamber from where she'd taken up residence.

She'd been living down here for over a week now. She tried to ask Kurt if she could crash here a while, seeing as it was technically his property. He just muttered whatever and told her to get out of his lab. It was Jess who set her up with a proper "room" in one of the larger caves.

Budda showed her where he'd stashed her car. She was able to get what was left of her luggage and, thankfully, the undamaged and undiscovered briefcase full of government-issue cash. The car itself was completely dead, but she didn't care. The only thing she lost by leaving it behind were very bad memories.

By her third day in the cave, she'd ordered a mattress and some furniture online. By her sixth day, the cave looked more like a proper room than an old coal chamber. Others were following her example and making their own quarters throughout the place.

She'd spent significant time with everyone in the group except for Justin. He avoided her at every opportunity. She figured he was still angry at her and, really, she wouldn't blame him if he was.

She asked Jess, with whom she'd grown fairly close, what his problem was. Jess told her that he was calming down about the accident but that he was also incredibly confused. Jess admitted knowledge of the kiss she'd given him and that he really didn't know how to react. Jess told Zoey about Justin's insecurities and about how this would likely leave him emotionally paralyzed for a while.

Zoey wasn't sure why she'd done it. As odd as passionately kissing a complete stranger would be, she did it without thinking because it felt like the correct thing to do at that moment. She didn't know if she was attracted to him, she hadn't spent any real time with him, it just felt like something that would comfort them both.

She hoped that, at some point, she could corner him and discuss things. She wanted to instill in him some understanding of her actions but, the way Jess talked about it, it might do him more harm than good.

She walked out of her cave, rubbing her eyes as the light of LENNY's main screen came into view. It was currently showing a Twilight Zone episode to no audience but kept the room dimly lit and decently visible for this time of night. She walked quietly across the main chamber and forgot which way lead to the pantry.

She guessed at a tunnel and started to approach it when her shadow suddenly appeared on the floor in a flickering oval of light. She turned with a start and was ready to throw a punch at whatever was sneaking up on her until she saw a flame covered fist which turned and started moving in the other direction.

"No, wait," she called.

The flames stopped and rotated.

"What are you doing?" she asked.

"Nothing," Justin said, "Just... thought I heard a noise. Sorry."

"It's no bother," she said, "I've actually been meaning to talk to you."

"About what?" he said with a huff.

"About the whole kiss thing," she said, "Jess told me it kinda messed you up and, well, I'm sorry if it did, but I..."

"I was going to go out on patrol," Justin interrupted, "You... wanna come?"

"Patrol?" she asked.

"You know," he said, "Like, hero patrol. Wandering around seeing if there's any crime to fight."

He stepped closer. She could see his face and the smoke of his hair. His glasses reflected the light from his fist-torch. She could tell that he was averting his eyes from her.

"Is there a reason you don't ever seem to want to look at me?" she asked.

"Every time we talk," he said, "You're half-naked. I told you before, I don't want to stare."

She looked down and realized she was still in her bedclothes; a pair of white panties with pink trim and the face of a cartoon cat in the center paired with a spaghetti-strapped white tank top. Her hair was probably a mess, too. The ice had a tendency to clump to one side and spike out when she slept. She blushed, knowing he was trying to be polite, and waved her hand to fix her hair.

"Stare if you want," she said, "I don't care; just look at me when you're talking to me."

He slowly turned his head toward her. The reflection of the flames on his glasses made it impossible to determine where he was looking.

"So, you wanna go with me?" he asked again.

"I was just getting up to get a bottle of water," she said.

"Sorry," he said, shaking his head and turning away, "Forget it."

"No, no," she said, quickly, "It's ok. I'll go out with you."

He turned back slowly.

"On patrol, I mean," she added, stumbling, "I'll go out on patrol with you. If you want. Let me get dressed and I'll be right back."

She passed him on the way back to her room. She could see the reflection of his glasses following her as she did. When she got back to her cave, she turned on her bedside lamp and looked at herself in the make-up mirror on her dresser.

She found herself remembering when she first met Chaucer. There was that awkward phase of getting to know someone of the opposite sex – someone to whom you were sort-of attracted – and all of those weird nervous feelings that came along with it. She had no idea why she felt this way when she was around Justin. Maybe it was the kiss. She still had no idea why it happened, but she wasn't opposed to it. Maybe they were both too emotionally vulnerable to handle what she'd done. She shook it off and got dressed.

She threw on a pair of jeans, a t-shirt, and a gray hoodie. Digging through her clothes, she found something she had picked up as a joke after the accident: a white domino mask. She put it on and changed her hair to be a more form-fitting helmet, almost making her look bald. It was cloudy white ice, matching the mask almost exactly. She put up her hood and walked back into the main chamber. He was waiting by her door.

"What do you think?" she asked, "Superhero enough?"

"It's perfect," he said, "Where'd you get the mask?"

"Costume store on a lark," she said, "Don't you have anything?"

"Yeah," he said, "But it plays hell with my glasses. I can't wear them both at the same time. I'm torn between my desire for anonymity and seeing with any amount of clarity."

"What about darker glasses?" she asked, "Mirrored ones. And a bandana or something to cover the bottom half of your face? That would probably do it."

"Not my first idea for a superhero look," he said, "But, I could make that work."

"We can't all be Batman, right?" she said.

He smiled as she noticed how appropriate the joke was. He was wearing a floor-length black leather trench coat, a black hoodie, black pants, and black fingerless gloves. There was an awkward silence as they stared at each other, her eyes locked on the reflection of the flames in his glasses.

"So," she said, "What now?"

"Well," Justin said, "I was just going to park somewhere downtown then walk around. See what happens. Street crimes are usually called in way after the fact, so there's no way we'd be able to use the computer to be effective."

"We can't just walk around looking like superheroes," she said.

"Then we don't use masks until something goes down," he said, "I used to work downtown late at night, trust me; no one looks twice at you unless they're looking for trouble."

"I know," she said, "I was in the club scene. I used to love walking around the city at night. It's quiet most of the time. You feel like you're the only one awake."

"Yeah," Justin said, "It's like the city is abandoned."

"No one watching," she said, "No one staring."

They had been moving closer to each other as they spoke. She realized this and her heart began to race. It seemed natural. They were an inch away from kissing again. She closed her eyes and waited for the inevitable.

"You guys are going out?" asked a voice from the couch in front of the main screen.

They were both startled and turned quickly to see who spoke.

"No," Justin said, "No, we're not going out."

"Really?" said the voice, now recognizable as belonging to a half-asleep Josh, "Sounded like you said something about patrolling downtown."

"Oh, that," Justin said, "Yeah, yeah, we're going out."

"Cool," he said, "Can I come?"

"No," said Justin.

"Yes," said Zoey, simultaneously.

"Rock," Josh said, sitting up, "I'll get my stuff."

Justin looked at her. She shrugged. She didn't know what to say to Josh. She was still confused and, even though it seemed strangely natural, she was worried that she was going to give Justin the wrong impression. She hadn't even had a full conversation with this guy yet, should she really want to jump right into a make-out session? Having a buffer there would make sure that things would stay in conversation mode rather than jumping to another conclusion.

"Ready?" Josh asked, approaching them.

"Dude," Justin said, "You look like a hobo Green Hornet."

Justin was right. Josh wore a trench coat and a pork-pie hat with a makeshift mask that looked like (and probably was) a black dress sock with two holes cut in it.

"So?" Josh said, "You look like a fat, olive-skinned Morpheus. What's your point."

There was a silent moment. She wasn't sure if they were going to fight.

"Fair enough," Justin said, "Come on, we're burning nightlight here. Sunrise is in like three hours. We have to make it out of town before the morning rush starts."

After a short drive in Justin's car, during which Zoey was largely disappointed that Josh had called "shotgun", they arrived in the city. The ride was quiet. Zoey wasn't sure if it was due to the presence of her invited third-party, nervousness about going out to fight crime, or simply because none of them had anything to say.

They parked in a twenty-four hour garage near the city center and exited through a back stairwell into the street. Zoey knew this area well. It was a strange overlap between the city's cultural and club districts. It was generally an unfriendly place to be after things closed up for the night.

"So," Josh said, breaking a long silence, "What's the plan?"

Justin shrugged.

"We walk around until we see a crime, then we stop it?" Justin offered.

"So, no plan," Josh said, "What if the cops see us like this?"

"Downtown cops don't usually stop anyone this late unless they see something really suspicious," Zoey said.

"Three people in masks walking down the street," Josh said, "That's not suspicious enough for you?"

"Look, Princess," Justin said, glaring at Josh, "If I knew you were going to get all excited only to whine about every little detail, I would have left you back in the cave."

"It's a valid question," Josh said.

"Can we just walk, please?" Zoey asked, "This is starting to get annoying."

She pulled up the hood of her gray sweatshirt and started off. The other two followed. Justin put up his hood as well. Josh removed his sock-mask. The winter chill in the air meant that their hoods wouldn't raise any alarms. Their apparent vigilance would only reflect their presence in this neighborhood at such a late hour. Their heads were on swivels, looking for some sort of action.

Within minutes, they passed by an alley where two men were loading large boxes from the back door of a building into the bed of a rusty blue pickup truck.

They crossed the mouth of the alley quickly. Zoey hoped they hadn't been noticed.

"Wow," Justin said, "Not more than a half-hour on patrol and we catch someone in the middle of a burgle."

"A burgle?" Josh asked, chuckling.

"Shut up," Justin said, "You know what I mean. They're burglars. They're burgling."

"Why aren't they robbers who are robbing?" Josh asked, "That way, we could catch them in the middle of a robbery instead of a burgle, whatever that is. Shouldn't you have said 'burglary'? I mean, burglars commit burglaries, right? Not 'burgles'."

"Whatever, burglary then," Justin whisper-shouted, "We caught people in the middle of a burglary. Does that make you happier?"

"Sort of," Josh started.

"Get serious, boys," Zoey said, "We don't know what's going on here. These guys could be armed."

"They could also be innocent," Josh said.

Zoey gave him a stern look.

"Seriously?" she asked.

"What?" Josh said, "It happened to me before, ok? Who's to say they're not making a night delivery?"

"Well," Justin said, holding his hand up and counting on his fingers, "One; they're loading things on to the truck, not taking them off. Two; it's three in the morning and, whatever your business is, no one gets a delivery this late. Three; that truck is a serious piece of junk if it's a delivery vehicle. Four; there are no lights on inside the store. And, five…"

As he extended his thumb to count the fifth thing, he slapped Josh in the forehead with the flat of his now open palm.

"They're robbing the place, Sherlock," Justin said, "This is not rocket science."

"Ok," Josh said, "Well, if we're going to this, let's come up with a plan of attack."

Justin grumbled. His hair flared at the edges under his hood. He stepped around the corner of the alley without another word.

"Hey there, fellas," Justin called out, "Need some help?"

The two men stared, watching him approach in shock, for a full thirty seconds before dropping the boxes they were holding and running toward the cab of the truck.

Zoey moved into the alley from where she had been watching and, with a wave of her hand, the puddles of snow melt in the alley stretched becoming a thick sheet of ice across the area where the truck was parked. With a flick of her wrist, the wheels were encased in ice as well.

"Nice," said Justin looking back.

"Thanks," she said, smiling.

The three of them approached the truck. Zoey and Josh were into a full jog to close the distance, Justin walked calmly forward.

Zoey stopped as she reached the ice sheet and thrust her fist into the air. A wall of ice, thirty feet tall, appeared at the end of the alley. Her smile grew as she saw the two men in the truck clamoring over each other, shouting, trying to figure out what to do. The driver locked eyes with her in his rear-view mirror. She waved to him.

Josh crashed down the alley behind her and dropped to a baseball slide to get beneath the lifted truck. It sputtered and choked as the driver tried to start it.

Justin, in his casual walk, finally reached Zoey at the end of the ice sheet.

"Well," Justin started, mid-yawn, "That was easy."

"That was intense," Zoey said, breathing heavily from the excitement.

Their eyes met and they smiled at each other.

A gunshot rang out. Both of them dropped to the ground. Zoey could see the passenger hanging uncomfortably out of the truck with a pistol pointed in their direction. Without any physical motion, a wall of ice shot up between the two of them and the gunman.

Another shot cut through the silence and impacted with the new frozen barrier, ricocheting off somewhere.

"You're shooting at us?" Justin shouted, "Really?"

He stood up and his hair burst into flames, destroying the hood of his sweatshirt. His clenched fists glowed red with heat as he approached the ice wall. His footprints melted into the sheet of ice on the alley floor. The ice wall melted around him as he passed through. He drew his fist back and thrust it forward causing a fireball to fly from the end of his arm. It went wide of the gunman and exploded into the ice wall in front of the truck creating a large arch to the street on the other side.

The gunman got out of the truck and made a break for the new way out. He slipped, unable to get traction in the icy alley.

Justin drew his arm back for another shot. Just as the gunman gained his footing, Justin nailed him in the back with his next fireball. The man fell forward, his face slamming hard onto the ice. The gun skittered away from him as his body went limp. Flames burned in a neat circle around the new hole in the back of the gunman's jacket.

The driver was still attempting, without result, to start the truck. Zoey stood back up and looked at the now panicking eyes in the rear-view mirror when they started to roll into the back of his head as he twitched violently.

Josh pulled himself out from under the truck.

"Is he out?" he asked, "Did I get him?"

Zoey ran to the driver's side door of the truck and pulled it open. The limp body of the driver spilled out of the vehicle. She gasped.

"Relax," Josh said, "I just tased him. Drained the battery of the car and sent the electricity through the frame of the truck to zap him unconscious."

She felt relieved when the driver moaned and squirmed but still bound his legs in ice as she'd done with Chaucer before.

She moved out into the alley and saw Justin, his head still mostly in flames, approaching the squirming body of the gunman. The floor of the alley looked like a hockey rink after a bench-clearing fight. Blood and teeth were scattered on the ice where the man fell. He moaned and gurgled as Justin flipped him over, quenching the flames on his back. His nose was clearly broken along with most of his face from his impact with the ice. Zoey kneeled down and turned his head to the side to let the blood drain from his mouth.

"Not bad, right?" Justin asked, "I didn't hit him with everything I had, but it was enough to stop him."

"Yeah," Zoey said, grimacing as the gunman coughed and spattered more blood onto the ice, "Enough to stop him eating solid foods for a while.

They dragged him by the shoulders to the side of the alley and sat him up. His head drooped, blood dribbling down his chin and onto his clothes.

"We really caught bad guys this time," Josh said, appearing at the back door of the store, "Security camera is broken, alarm's been disabled. The cops would have never known what happened unless they saw it in progress. This one was for real."

"As real as it gets," said a voice from the end of the alley causing them all to turn.

A man in a black suit with dark, slick hair and sunglasses approached them, slow-clapping through a pair of black leather gloves.

"What are you doing here?" Justin asked, narrowing his eyes.

"Who's that?" Zoey asked.

She'd never seen him before, but he looked familiar. Like one of those agents from the hospital. Justin stepped between her and the man's line of sight.

"My name is Agent Phalanx," he said, trying to peek around Justin, "Nice to finally meet you, Ms. Howlett."

"Howlett?" Justin asked, turning around.

"Yes," she said.

"Your last name is Howlett?"

"That's why he said 'Miz' in front of it," she answered.

"Like, the same last name…" Justin started.

"…that they gave Wolverine in his origin story," she said nodding and rolling her eyes, "And the movies, and the Ultimate line."

"I think I love you," Justin said, his eyes lighting up.

"Well, that's just wonderful," Phalanx said, "Can you guys resolve your little crush situation later, though? Time is limited, here."

Zoey felt her cheeks flush, though she didn't know if her cheeks could actually appear flushed anymore. Justin turned around to face the Agent.

"What do you want, then?" Justin asked.

"I came to observe," Phalanx said, "Sloppy, but you got the job done. A's for effort all around; substantially lower grades on execution. You'll be surprised at how much you improve when we start training."

"Training?" Josh started, "Dude, did you not just see us stop a heist in progress with no casualties? We don't need training, man. We've got this."

"You've 'got this'?" Phalanx said, air-quoting with his black leather gloves, "Dude, getting surprised by a gunshot in the middle of a robbery? Stopping to yawn? Baseball slides? Waving at the driver? You took time to taunt, they took time to panic and people in panic mode can do very irrational things. You have to be ready for anything at any time. You can't be a bunch of show-offs, especially since you don't know your full potential. This was the first time out for two of you and only the second time out for static-boy over there and you almost got yourself killed."

"He missed!" Justin said, "Dude was firing wild while trying to crawl out of a window.""

"Check the right side of your collar," Phalanx said, "You tell me how bad his aim was."

Zoey, still behind Justin, stood on her toes and saw the area Phalanx described. There was an indented white streak – a shallow, semi-circular valley – in the leather.

"So what," Justin said, "My coat got scuffed. Happens all the time."

"You got grazed," Phalanx said, shaking his head, "An inch to the left and your jugular would be dumping blood onto the ground while she cried over your body and lamented over all the time you could have spent together."

Justin took a closer look at his collar and met Zoey's eyes. She blushed more. She was sure it was visible now. She hoped he hadn't caught her.

"Preparation is key," Phalanx said, "That's lesson one in just about every line of work, if you want to do things well. I want to train your group and I want you to help me make this happen before that bullet makes it that extra inch and we don't have the chance anymore. You want to be comic book characters? You want to see the end of this origin story? You want your Manic Pixie Dream Girl? We've got to start yesterday."

"Hey," Zoey said, "I'm no one's Manic Pixie Dream Girl."

"Seriously?" Phalanx said, "Sweetheart, you need to look in the mirror and get some self-esteem. You're everyone's Manic Pixie Dream Girl."

"We've got this under control," Justin said, "We can do it ourselves."

"Man, your file is accurate," Phalanx said, smiling, "You really don't like being told what to do. You're a self-learner. You don't like asking for help. You need it, though, and you need to douse your pride enough to accept it."

"We've got it under control." Justin repeated.

"Then why is your hair flaring up right now?" Phalanx asked.

Zoey looked up and saw the smoke puffing into small flames, like lit matches, then disappearing.

"It happens when I get frustrated," Justin said, "So?"

"So what happens when you completely fly off the handle?" Phalanx asked, "All that rage, all that fire, will come spilling out and you'll wind up hurting people. Unintentionally, of course. Not like that guy against the wall."

Justin narrowed his eyes.

"You've all got weaknesses, Justin," said Phalanx, "You've all got strengths. I've got experience with this. Let me help you with both. This isn't the funny papers. This is real. You said so yourself at the beginning. Did all that go out the window because now you've got a girl to impress? If I remember correctly, you didn't want to get shot back when you were just a sad fat widower."

The flames on Justin's head began to grow. His fists were heating up, more than after the gunshot. Zoey stepped between the two of them and turned to face Justin.

"He's right," she said, "We need to learn how to control this. I'm not sorry for what we did to the people in that alley, but I've seen what happens when it goes a step too far. We need to train. We need to learn. If he can help us, we should let him."

She turned around and put her hand out to Phalanx. He shook it gingerly.

"Nice to see someone step up and do the right thing," Phalanx said, smiling.

"Justin," she said turning back to him, "It's the right thing to do and you know it."

She put her hand on one of his clenched fists. It hissed and released some steam, but didn't hurt either of them.

"I'm with it," Josh said, "I know I said we've got this, but I'd like to know what else I can do. I want to see my full potential."

"Come on, man," Justin said, "A week ago you were about to put fifty-thousand volts through this guy's head, now you want to be his Padawan?"

"Different situation then," Josh said, "I threw lightning once. I haven't since. I'd like to know how to do it right."

"I can help with that," Phalanx said, turning back to Justin, "Come on, don't you want to see what else you can do besides being an angry fireball machine? I'm sorry I said what I said back there, but it was only to prove a point about your emotions getting the better of you. We can work to control that."

"Fine," Justin said after a moment, "But I'm only agreeing because I don't trust you. I'm going to be ready for that third-act betrayal when it happens. Then, all that rage and fire is going to spill out on you."

"Whatever your terms," said Phalanx, "I'm happy to have you aboard."

Phalanx extended a hand to him. Justin reached out, his hand still glowing orange. Phalanx noticed this and removed his leather glove before shaking Justin's hand without flinching.

"I promise," Phalanx said, "I'll make you into a better person than this."

"Whatever," Justin said, "I promise if I find out you're betraying us…"

"I've heard it all before," Phalanx said, "You don't need to threaten me, Justin. If I'm betraying you, I'll submit to your wrath, whatever that may be."

Their hands separated. Phalanx quickly put his into his pocket.

"You should get back to the car," Phalanx said, "Get rid of all this ice and be inconspicuous. The cops will be on their way right about... now. You don't want to be here when they arrive. I'll see you soon."

He exited from the opposite side of the alley and was out of sight.

## XIX

A metallic ringing pierced the air.

"Again," said Phalanx.

Mike grumbled.

He waved his hands to guide a small, smoke-filled but otherwise transparent sphere through a set of metal rings on top of stands around the room. All of them were at a different height and the rings a different width. He moved the sphere around the course causing it to grow or shrink in size as needed. It swooped and dove in all directions to maneuver through the obstacles.

He bit his lip as he approached the last ring. The sphere clipped the edge causing the loud metallic ping to echo in the cave again.

"Dammit," Mike shouted.

"Again," said Phalanx, leaning against the wall.

An incense burner smoldered at the beginning of the course. Mike would create his force bubbles over it, capturing the smoke and making it visible. Mike moved his sphere quickly through the first parts of the course and threw his hands up as the sphere clanged into the final ring once more.

"Again," Phalanx said.

"Why am I even doing this?" Mike asked, "I know how to use my powers."

"Apparently not well enough to navigate this course," Phalanx said, "Again."

"No," Mike said, "No more. I've done this a million times and I don't need it. Floating a ball through a bunch of rings isn't teaching me anything about my powers that I don't know. It doesn't matter and I don't care."

Small rocks were lifting off the ground as his frustration built.

"Finish the course," Phalanx said sternly.

"I can make invisible bulletproof walls," Mike said, "I can crush things by increasing their gravity. I can wrap a person in an air-tight bubble until they pass out. Why the hell do I need to know how to float a stupid ball through a bunch of metal rings?"

"You've only flirted with this application of your power until now," Phalanx said, "This is key to unlocking your full potential. You couldn't even move your forcefield projections until we started working on this and now only the hardest part of this course is giving you trouble. I showed you that you could make tiny indestructible objects move at extreme speeds. That has to seem a bit cooler than walls and bubbles."

Mike got the point. When Phalanx finished talking, a small round hole appeared in the cave wall on which he had been leaning. Right next to his head. Phalanx turned when he heard the impact then calmly looked back at Mike from behind his sunglasses.

"That was rather uncalled for," he said.

"So is this exercise," Mike said, "You know what I can do. I know what I can do. This is pointless."

"Finish the course," Phalanx said.

"No," Mike replied.

"Finish the course," Phalanx insisted.

"No," Mike said, mocking his tone.

"You're saying you can't do it, then?" Phalanx asked, smirking, "You're just going to quit?"

Mike sighed and closed his eyes for a moment.

"I'm assuming you read my file or whatever," Mike said, "You're challenging me because you know I won't back down from it. You'll goad me into finishing by talking smack."

"Is it working?" Phalanx said.

"Yes," Mike said.

"Then finish the course," said Phalanx.

Mike muttered something under his breath and made another sphere.

\*\*\*

"Give me a cylinder," said Phalanx, "About an inch in diameter and about four feet long."

Zoey closed her eyes. From the frozen bucket of water in front of her, the cylinder sprouted.

"Break it off," he said, "Hold it up with both hands."

She did as he instructed, holding the frozen cylinder like a sword.

"Now, think of a weapon," Phalanx said, "Blunt or bladed, doesn't matter, whatever pops into your head. Make the cylinder into that."

The ice changed shape into a cloudy, translucent baseball bat.

"Good," Phalanx said, "Now, something more complex."

She closed her eyes again. The bat shifted into an elaborate katana. The blade was cobalt blue, like glacial ice. The small crossguard was snowy white. The wrapping of the hilt was a frosted light blue winding down to a snowflake charm hanging from the white pommel.

"Very nice," Phalanx said, sounding genuinely impressed. His voice conveyed more expression than his face.

"I'm pretty sure I'm a Green Lantern-type," she said, "Limited only by the power of imagination and sheer will."

He reached into his pocket and pulled out a small black cylinder. With a flick of his wrist, it became a long baton.

"You know how to use that thing?" he asked, using the baton to point at her sword.

Zoey felt her heart rate pick up as he idly twirled the weapon in his hand.

"Uh," she started, "Not really, no..."

He split himself into two.  Only one Phalanx had the baton and it approached her slowly.

She backed away, holding the katana in front of her with both hands.  She shook nervously and tried to keep a tight grip on the sword.  Her teeth clenched as the baton-wielding Phalanx assumed a combat stance and kicked over the frozen bucket as he closed distance.  He circled to her left.  She moved to match him.

"Look out," said the unarmed Phalanx.

The armed one rushed forward, the baton in his right hand swinging for the left side of her body.

She managed to twist the katana around and block the brunt of the blow.  A loud clang filled the cave as the metal impacted with the ice.  The force made her stumble sideways and fall over.  The blade clattered aside with the same strange ringing noise as her parry.

She flipped over and looked up at the armed Phalanx.  She was only slightly afraid.  She'd been roughed up pretty bad before, so she wasn't afraid of the pain.  She was, however, frightened that Phalanx would hit quite a bit harder than a drunken, middle-aged, failed artist.  She didn't want him to see that fear, but she was sure he did.

"Durable," said the unarmed Phalanx coming to help her up.

"Thanks," she said, "I've been beat up a lot worse before."

"Not you," he said, "The sword.  Honestly, I didn't think it would stand up to the impact.  I put everything I had behind that swing and it didn't even chip.  I thought you'd have a shattered katana and some broken ribs by now.  Did any of the blow make it through?"

He poked at her side.  She moved away.

"I don't think so," she said, lifting her shirt and looking for bruises on her pale skin, "But, why are we fighting?  I can make anything I want out of ice, why would I ever need to get into a sword fight?  I can just put a wall between me and a bad guy.  Or trap them in ice bars or something."

"What if it's the middle of the summer in an empty field?" Phalanx said, "What if you're stranded in a desert?  I like the non-violent approach and I can appreciate the kind of things you did in the alley, the actions of the other two notwithstanding.  Cartoonish bars and cute traps won't always be available.  Your power is limited by the quantity of the base substance."

"So what do you suggest?" she asked.

Phalanx reached into his coat and tossed her a clear plastic bottle.  She caught it and turned it over in her hands.

"Bottled water?" she asked.

"It's light, portable and you can fit it in a coat pocket," he said, "Anyone who doesn't know you won't realize you're armed.  Sixteen-point-nine ounces of water at your beck and call.  Your ability lets you create a greater mass of ice out of a small amount of water, which, beyond cheating laws of thermodynamics, means you can get more out of it. You won't be able to manage an effective wall or anything, but you can get a weapon. The more skilled you become with weapons, the less you'll have to worry about having an entire reservoir to be effective in combat.

"Now, make the katana again."

She concentrated and the bottle burst open. An exact duplicate of the katana now lying on the cave floor appeared in her hand.

"Keep a bottle on you at all times," Phalanx said, "Just in case. This way you can have your bat or katana or even a shield or armor or any other smallish object whenever you need it."

She concentrated and the katana twisted and flattened out, wrapping itself around her right arm. It became a translucent section of cobalt blue medieval-style plate armor, from shoulder to gauntlet. She flexed her arm around and, with another thought, produced spikes from the knuckles.

The unarmed Phalanx nodded in approval. The armed Phalanx, however, took his baton in both hands and brought a vertical swing down at her with all of his strength.

Zoey raised her arm just in time and parried the blow, staggering again, but not falling over.

Combat Phalanx backed away again as Zoey looked at her forearm. It was a strong hit, but the ice remained undamaged. Not so much as a scratch showed where the impact had occurred.

"I didn't feel a thing," she said, smiling at the more stationary of the two.

The armed Phalanx cried out, making Zoey go into a defensive posture. She saw him standing over the original katana.

"What happened?" asked the unarmed Phalanx.

"It's cold," said armed Phalanx, "Damn cold. I can't hold it without getting burned."

The unarmed Phalanx put a black leather glove on and touched her ice-clad arm with one fingertip. He yanked it back within a few seconds and waved his hand in the air. He then grabbed one of her armored fingers and pushed on it.

"What are you doing?" Zoey asked.

"I can't move it," he said, pulling his hand back again, "It's solid."

She flexed her fingers and her arm with no problem. The ice followed her every move without issue.

"That's unexpected," Phalanx said, "I guess it only moves for you. Bring the katana back if you could."

She obliged. The ice ran off of her arm in a fluid motion and reconstructed itself into the katana in her hand.

"Hmm," Phalanx said, rubbing his chin and looking at his armed duplicate, "What do you think?"

"I think she needs some proper training," he responded.

"Proper training?" she asked, "I thought this was proper training."

"No, no," said the unarmed one, "Not with your powers. You're everything we hoped for and more in that department."

"Tell me," said the armed one, "How do you feel about becoming a serious martial artist?"

She tilted her head, took a moment to think about it, then smiled. "When can I start?" she asked.

\*\*\*

"This sucks," Justin said, doubling over with his hands on his knees.

"No doubt," said Phalanx, his expression unchanging.

"Why am I not throwing fireballs right now?" Justin asked.

"Because you already know how to throw fireballs," Phalanx said, "That guy from the alley who is eating through a tube will attest to that."

"I know how to do this, too, man," Justin said, "It's giving me a headache. You don't know what it's like."

"When you clear it in a fast enough time, we'll take a break," Phalanx said, "Until then, you're going to keep it up. Now, do it again."

Justin sighed. Phalanx had constructed a maze of varying sizes of PVC piping. It twisted and bent in every direction with only one entrance and exit. The goal was for Justin to turn into smoke, navigate the maze, and come out on the other side as quickly as possible.

Justin took a deep breath, dissipated, and streamed into the tangle of pipes, spreading smoke along every path.

When he was smoke, he could see out of every tendril. He didn't know how many he could split into, but each one was another set of eyes. He was experiencing seven points of view at the same time in the maze and it was straining his concentration. When he eventually reached the end with one of his tendrils, he pulled the rest to him and exited the maze, reforming on the other side of the cave.

He became whole again in a flicker of flames and fell backwards onto the stone floor. He sat up and took a few deep breaths.

"Is it physically exhausting?" Phalanx asked.

"No," Justin said, "It's disorienting. Try looking in thirty-seven directions at once and see how that messes with your sense of balance."

"Get used to it," Phalanx said, "You have great potential as an infiltrator. You can get through vent systems, cracks in doorways, probably even locks. You can get places no one else can reach and then materialize. Jess can do something similar psychically, Kurt can do something technologically, but you can do it physically. If we need a button pushed or a lever pulled or something extracted without anyone knowing, you're the man."

"Great," Justin said, "Another job as a glorified button-pusher. Why did I even go to college?"

"You seriously underestimate your potential," Phalanx said, "For a group that's been gaming your whole lives, you guys really disappoint me.

"My potential is to light cigarettes with my fingers until I die of cancer," Justin said.

Phalanx sighed and shook his head.

"Ok," Justin said, "DPS. That should be my job. Just like any good fire mage."

"This isn't some MMO," Phalanx said, "This isn't a comic book, either. This is real life and here you can't DPS all your problems away. You can do so much more and you should."

"Tell me," Justin said, "When you were in all those classes back at your 'Project', did they ever give you one on sarcasm? If they did, you should get your money back."

Justin walked around the outer edge of the maze to the entrance. He could tell that Phalanx was narrowing his eyes behind those sunglasses and it made him smirk.

"Again, right?" Justin asked.

"Yeah," said Phalanx, "Again. Until you're not such a waste of my time."

Justin turned into smoke and cycled through the maze again. When he rematerialized, he was already sitting on the ground.

"Again," Phalanx said.

"Give me a minute," Justin shouted, his head spinning.

Phalanx stood over him, staring down derisively.

"I should have known you wouldn't take this seriously," Phalanx said, sternly, "Why am I even bothering with this? You out of all of your friends should have been decommissioned from the minute your powers exhibited themselves."

"Decommissioned?" Justin asked, "What are you talking about?"

"You're a danger to everyone here and you're showing no interest in controlling your ability," Phalanx said, "I'm trying to help you and you're sitting here whining about taking a break. For once I wish one of you would go against what it says in your file."

"Wait," Justin said, "Why am I a danger? And what does it say in my file?"

"That you're a hothead," Phalanx shouted, "Literally and figuratively. You're also lazy. You show tons of ambition but no desire to work for it. You start things and, when they get too hard for you, you just quit. Typical of your entire generation, really."

The smoke on Justin's head flared around the edges. His clenched fists were starting to heat up.

"And, this is why you're dangerous," Phalanx said, "You've got a temper. I told you back in that alley that your emotions are a problem. All it's going to take is for someone to say the wrong thing and you'll go supernova. Honestly, I'm surprised Zoey is still alive after you found out she killed your girlfriend."

"You'd better stop talking," Justin said, the flames on his head growing larger.

"Or what?" Phalanx said, taunting, "You're going to prove me right? You're going to show me that you can be a fiery murder machine? Your file says you make threats but don't back them up. I'm going to have to go with the record and say that you're just, for lack of a better term, blowing smoke. Nah. Knowing what I know about you, you're just going to stand at the end of your leash and bark."

Justin stood up. Flames were jumping up his arms. The t-shirt he was wearing smoldered at the edges. The fire on his head was growing taller.

"All that posturing," Justin said, "All that talk about wanting to help us. You just wanted in so you could disrupt everything. That was your angle."

"Honestly," Phalanx said, returning to a normal mode of speech, "No, that wasn't my angle. Really, I just wanted to poke at you. To see how the anger affected your abilities. Now, here you are, good and mad, and I can see what we need to work on."

"I don't appreciate being poked," Justin said, walking slowly toward Phalanx. The rubber soles of his shoes had melted and he left glowing footprints on the floor as he walked.

"Look," Phalanx said, backing up, "It was just an experiment. I didn't mean anything by it."

"We are not your toys," Justin said, slowly approaching him.

"Come on, now," Phalanx said, "Be reasonable. It had to be done."

"Reasonable?" Justin shouted, his eyes wide, his mouth spewing smoke as he spoke, "Reasonable?!?"

With a primal scream, a storm of fire erupted around Justin in a pillar. His smoke hair became a towering mane of blue-white fire. His fists and forearms were white hot. The rock glowed red beneath where he was now hovering above the ground.

His eyes burned like two small white fireballs, melting his glasses away. He took a deep breath and exhaled steam and smoke. His clothes, though singeing at the edges, remained mostly intact.

He raised his white hot hand toward Phalanx, his fingers outstretched, his palm centering on Phalanx's chest.

"Calm down," Phalanx shouted, "I just wanted to see how far this would go! I didn't think you would lose control."

"Who said anything about losing control?" Justin said, his voice deeper, his mouth belching flames as he spoke, "I'm just letting you know that the leash is off. The barking is over. Now you'll see me bite."

"I was trying to prove a point!" Phalanx objected.

"Point proven," Justin said, "Now let me prove mine."

A wave of flames swept over his body and coursed out of his open palm in an enormous white-hot blast. It was wide enough to encompass most of the cave and hit Phalanx directly. The section of the cave wall behind Phalanx exploded, creating a hole into the main chamber and shaking the entire cave complex. Stone and rock were completely incinerated by the heat from the blast.

When the dust settled, Justin floated slowly forward leaving a red-hot trail beneath him on the cavern floor. The edges of the hole were glowing faintly as the rock cooled down. He could see a crater on the other side of the main chamber where the blast had stopped. LENNY and the major facilities were not in the path of destruction noted by the glowing red trail leading up to the cooling crater.

"Wow," Phalanx said from behind him, "You completely vaporized me. You vaporized everything!"

Justin turned smoothly in the air, his hand raised and leveled at Phalanx once again.

"No, no," Phalanx said, cringing, "Not again, please. I get it. I made you angry. I'm sorry."

"How did you dodge that?" Justin boomed.

"I'm not the same Phalanx," he answered, "You burned the one who was taunting you into non-existence. Seriously: disintegrated him with fire. Pretty impressive considering the amount of heat it takes to burn bone to ash."

"Disintegrated?" Justin asked.

"Yeah," Phalanx said, "Killed, destroyed, caused to cease living, blew away. However you want to say it. Don't worry, it's not the first time and it won't be the last."

Justin closed his eyes and huffed a smoky sigh.

"I knew pushing your buttons would take you to a new level," Phalanx said, "But I never expected anything like this."

"Do you like what you've found?" Justin boomed, narrowing his flaming eyes at Phalanx, "Did this satisfy your curiosity?"

"Absolutely," Phalanx said, his voice almost giddy, "If we ever need a weapon of mass destruction, you are one-hundred percent it. You can practically erase people. There's nothing left of that other me."

"Nothing…" Justin said, lowering his hand and looking toward the hole, "I killed him."

"You killed him good," Phalanx said, "No evidence or anything. Completely incinerated him upon impact.

"What the hell was that?" asked another Phalanx, peeking through the hole.

"Yeah," said still another Phalanx, "What happened in here?"

His friends gradually appeared at the hole with their respective Phalanx teachers.

The blue-white tower of flames shooting from his head slowly shrank away and became a more conventional orange before extinguishing into smoke. His fists cooled quickly and his eyes returned to normal. He descended to the floor as smoke poured from his mouth and nose. He touched down and fell to his knees before falling forward onto his hands.

His clothes still smoldered at the edges like burning cigarettes. It left him with a half-sleeved t-shirt rising unflatteringly above his waistline, large holes in the knees of his pants right above what used to be the cuff, largely absent socks, and a pair of destroyed canvas tennis shoes.

He picked up what was left of his molten glasses. They were a lost cause.

"Are you ok?" Jess asked.

"Yeah," Justin muttered, some smoke still escaping from his mouth, "Yeah, I'll be ok."

"Dude," Josh said, "You totally went Super Sayan back there."

"We were training," Budda said, "And we felt an earthquake or something. Was that you?"

Justin didn't look up or even acknowledge him.

"Yes," said Justin's Phalanx, "He did that."

"What happened?" Zoey asked.

Justin lowered his head even more. He couldn't see that she was here but hoped she hadn't seen him as he was a few moments ago.

"Things got a little intense," said Justin's Phalanx, "It's ok now. Go back to your training, everyone. Phalanx, stay here with me for a moment. Head back to your rooms, we'll be with you in a minute."

Everyone filed slowly away. Zoey was the last to leave. Her Phalanx ushered her away.

Justin couldn't see what happened next. He could only see black and white blobs moving around and through each other without his glasses. There was no conversation between the duplicates as all but one filed out of the room. The remaining Phalanx approached as Justin squinted to make out his face.

"How did that make you feel?" he asked, kneeling down.

"I don't know," Justin said, looking down again.

"Powerful?" Phalanx asked.

Justin nodded.

"But not in the way you think," Justin explained, "I felt like I was overloading. Like there was something inside of me trying to erupt. I didn't want to let it. It wasn't freeing, like the comics say. It was constrictive. I had to try to hold it back."

"Didn't look to me like you were holding back," Phalanx said, "That was the most incredible display of elemental power I've ever seen from an extra-normal person and, trust me when I say, that's an accomplishment."

"Have you ever felt so angry that you thought you might explode?" Justin asked.

"Yes," said Phalanx without hesitation.

"Multiply it by a hundred and take it literally," he said, "You're not lying when you say I'm a weapon of mass destruction. If I access that higher level again, there's no telling what I might do."

"Don't take this the wrong way," Phalanx said, "This power, this higher level, you can't fear it. You have to explore it. Master it. Who knows what sort of potential you might unlock?"

"No," Justin said, looking into his sunglass-covered eyes, "I felt like I could set the world on fire back there. Felt like I wanted to. I don't want innocent people getting hurt because of me, least of all my friends here. I could have disintegrated someone else with that blast. Unknowingly. I would never forgive myself for that. I can barely forgive myself for your death."

"It's ok," said Phalanx, "I'm expendable. There's always more of me to go around."

"That's not the point," Justin said, sighing.

"Fine," said Phalanx, standing up, "We'll call it a day. Relax for now. I'll get you a new pair of glasses, rushed. We'll pick things up again when they come in."

"Whatever," Justin said, pulling himself to his feet.

He shuffled in his mostly melted shoes past Phalanx and out through the new, now cooled, hole.

For the first time since this started, he wasn't thinking about where the origin story went next. Instead, he thought of what could have happened; the friends he could have killed, the things he could have damaged, the greater amount of destruction he could have caused.

The story, whatever type it really was, could have ended here.

## XX

"Twelve," Moorsblade said, "All in the same week."

"How did something like this get so far without us knowing?" Joey asked, "Someone in monitoring must have blown it big time. Williams should be pretty angry."

Char shivered. It was either the temperature in the morgue or the fact that twelve brutally murdered bodies lay inside body bags on metal slabs only feet away from the three of them.

She had become accustomed to seeing death. She was even used to causing it, at least as realistically as the training exercises allowed. These corpses were slightly different than watching someone drop behind the reticule of a long-distance scope.

They moved to the first bag in the row. Moorsblade and Char stood opposite each other while Joey stood at the head. Char could feel her stomach churning with anticipation. The initial briefing didn't paint a pretty picture and she wasn't very excited about seeing what they described. The coroner's reports intercepted by the Project made the killings sound more like dinosaur attacks than traditional murder.

"Well," said Moorsblade, "Time's a wastin'. Let's see what we've got behind curtain number one."

There was a smirk on his face and an anxious look in his eye which Char found upsetting.

Char put her hands to her mouth and felt the vomit rising in her throat after Moorsblade undid the zipper with a flourish. She looked away.

"Who does things like this?" she said through her hands, "This is just…"

"Just what?" Moorsblade interrupted, "Terrible? Horrible? Awful? Disgustin'?"

Char turned to look at him. He sneered at her.

"Helpful hint, darlin'," he said, leaning toward her over the body, "Get used to it. You're being groomed as an assassin. If you can't take a little real-life carnage, how are you ever going to perpetrate it?"

"I don't care what orders I have," Char said, her hands still up, "I'm never doing that to anyone."

The head of the body had been completely crushed, leaving only the lower jaw intact. It was roughly torn open and gutted along the stomach. The left leg was ripped off at the hip, right out of the socket, leaving only dangling tendons and sinew.

Most of the ribs were crushed leaving the chest looking like a partially deflated balloon. Here and there, the broken ribs poked through the skin near severely bruised sites of impact. The right bicep had a rather large chunk out of it, resembling a bite.

Char glanced at Joey who was flipping through a document on a clipboard.

"Where's the leg?" Char asked, her voice trembling.

Joey flipped back a few pages and read.

"Wasn't recovered," She said.

"Oh," Char replied, closing her eyes.

"What's on the chart as cause of death?" Moorsblade asked.

"Wounds and markings consistent with large predator attack," Joey said, "Coroner speculates that it may have been a mountain lion, possibly a bear."

"It happened in the bad part of an urban neighborhood," Char said, clearing her throat and attempting to regain her composure, "The most dangerous animals are large pet dogs. It's not like wildcats or bears cruise through the ghetto at night."

"Obviously," Moorsblade said, "The fact that there are eleven others with similar injuries kinda throws the animal attack theory out the window. Unless we've got a very territorial zoo escapee."

"Most of them," said Joey, hesitating while flipping through the clipboard, "Yes, most of them – ten-out-of-twelve – had their skulls completely crushed. They're calling it blunt-force trauma, but…"

She put the clipboard down and looked into the bag.

"…I don't think so," she continued, "Looks more like a pressure crush to me, not a beating."

She pursed her lips and pushed up the left sleeve of her black business suit, revealing a metallic bracer. She dragged her finger across its surface to wake it, then tapped at the touchpad that appeared. After a moment, she flattened her right palm and a small device telescoped out of the matching metallic bracelet on her other wrist. She held the device near the corpse, moving it only to tap intermittently on the touchpad.

"However it was done, it was fast and violent," Joey said, "Must have been a terrible mess. The internals would have nowhere to go, so they would have gushed out of every orifice. Eyes, ears, nose…"

Char covered her mouth again, feeling the nausea creeping up as she used her imagination.

"Whatever it was, it would have happened all at once," Joey continued, "Honestly, it looks like someone crushed this with their bare hands. One hand, actually."

"Mountain lion, for sure," Moorsblade said.

"The coroner doesn't know any better," said Joey, "That's not a bad thing. If his final diagnosis had been 'head crushed and body mutilated by enraged extra-normal', we'd be in a very different situation."

"So," Moorsblade said, pulling up a metal stool and sitting down, "The victims ain't readily identifiable, bodies were all hidden so they weren't found by anyone walking down the street, but they ain't quite been disposed of in the traditional sense."

"Reports show nothing of value on their person," Char added, now flipping through the clipboard Joey once held, "No wallets, watches, money, car keys; nothing that would help establish identity."

"Wow," Joey said, holding her device out, "The hands have been skinned."

"No prints," Moorsblade said.

"Likely no dental, either," Joey said, "Most of the teeth have been crushed. The lower jaw survived, but most of the teeth there are missing."

Moorsblade sat back and crossed his arms.

"Who coulda done it?" he asked.

"No one we know," Joey said, shaking her head, "I've never seen anything this savage. Besides, anyone on our lists wouldn't be sloppy enough to kill twelve in the same area in the same week. It's too traceable. They would know we'd be on this."

"What about the accidents?" asked Moorsblade, "Coulda been one of them."

"Out of their jurisdiction," Joey said, shaking her head, "We're three-hundred-plus miles away from them and they don't usually leave their cave, let alone their city. Based on what I know, none of them would do anything this drastic, anyway."

"There were more involved than just that bunch of basement dwellers," Moorsblade said.

"Hang on," Char interrupted, tapping on her bracer, "I'm searching the coroner's database local to the chemical spill accident scene. Looks like shortly after the day of the accident, one of the smaller boroughs in the area turned up a body behind their police station. Guy was identified as an ex-con with prior drug and sex crime convictions. The report says his head was crushed in addition to some other superficial wounds. They attributed it to being run over by a plow since they found him buried in a snow bank. They think he could have been hit blocks away and just happened to fall off the blade behind the station. The snow's melted since then and there's been significant rainfall, so there would be little to no way to figure out where it actually happened."

"Cross-reference police reports," Moorsblade said, "Anything strange?"

Char flicked at the bracer, scrolling through pages of text.

"Here," she said, "Three days before the body was found, a woman was brought in as a vagrant. Says she wouldn't stop talking about a giant monster in an alley somewhere. When they pressed her, she had to be sedated. They identified her, contacted her family, and released her into psychiatric care."

"Fat lot of good that'll do her," Joey muttered.

"Field team, this is 13-Prime," barked the voice of Agent Williams in their ears.

"Prime, 13-A," Moorsblade answered, "What's shakin', boss?"

"Police in your vicinity have identified another victim and have an eyewitness account," he said, "Use cover F21-Beta and report to the scene immediately.  13-C, you are to recover the information and eliminate the source.  Is that clear?"

"Crystal, sir," Joey responded.

"GPS data transfer in progress," said Williams, "Prime out."

"Lucky thirteen," said Moorsblade, his smirk returning, "Joey, zip that guy up and let's roll."

***

"Seven?" Josh asked, "Why a seven?"

This was the first time their group had been together in a week and was the first time Kurt had decided to join them since retreating into his work.  Phalanx and Kurt both stood in front of the rest of the group, who huddled around the couch in the main chamber.  Luckily for all present, Kurt had decided to shower, shave, and change clothes from the mess he had become prior to their talk.

"Their number is thirteen," Kurt said, "Project XIII.  If we're going to be their opposite number, seven seemed most appropriate; lucky versus unlucky."

"Unlucky seven," Justin said, "Lucky thirteen."

"If that reasoning doesn't appeal to you," Kurt said, "Then I did it because there are seven of us."

"Does that mean you think the X-Men have their logo because there are ten of them?" Mike asked.

Kurt stared him down.  Mike was not intimidated.

"So, what does this thing do, anyway?" Jess asked.

Kurt plucked one of the items at which they had been staring out of its custom-fitted metal case.  He displayed to the group a one-inch button emblazoned with a roman numeral VII surrounded by a black circle over a red background.  It was almost exactly the logo of the Project.

"This," Kurt said, holding the button up, "Is this."

In his other hand, he held up the lapel pin he'd been given by Phalanx.

The room was silent.  A haze of confusion descended.

"And this means what to us, exactly?" Mike asked.

"This," Kurt said, holding up the lapel pin, "Is the most advanced communications device I've ever seen; triple-encoded VOIP transmissions over a clandestine and impregnable satellite-based WiFi network, direct transmission capabilities to any device on that network, HD A/V recording capabilities with onboard solid-state memory, and a GPS tracking device accurate to within twelve inches."

He held up the one-inch button.

"This," he continued, "Is everything I just said plus some nice little extras I worked in on my own."

"You spent all that time making radios?" Jess asked.

"It's not just a radio," Kurt said, "It's the smallest and most advanced piece of telecommunications ever produced outside of a government facility and I made enough for everyone."

"All that time," she said, her volume increasing, "All those nights I spent alone. All the worrying. All the times people came to check on you just to have you rudely turn them away. All the ignorance of your friends and the people you love and you were just making a stupid set of walkie-talkies?"

The room was silent. Kurt was stunned as Jess stared a hole through him. He turned away, seeing the fury in her eyes.

"I couldn't sleep," she continued, "I didn't sleep. For a month. All I wanted was for my boyfriend to put down his projects and stop acting like a robot for five minutes to come to bed. I thought you were working on something incredible; something world-changing. I defended you to everyone and justified all your cold, mean interactions and for what? Something we could have bought at Target for twenty bucks."

"Really," Kurt said, still not looking at her, "This isn't a toy here. This is seriously one of the most sophisticated communications devices ever, ever. I built them from the ground up, all by myself, and I made seven of them. I'm not sure if I can change my initial statements to sound more impressive, but if you continue yelling at me, dear, I'll sure try. For now, can we all just sit down and act like superheroes? You can scream about it all you want after we're done here."

The look on Jess's face was a cross between nausea, anger, and the threat of bursting into tears. She stormed out of the room without another word, practically running for the house upstairs. The entire group watched as she left and remained silent for a few minutes after she was gone.

"Moving on," Kurt said, cheerily, bringing the attention back to the button, "Each one of these pins comes with a micro-ear bud."

He held a small clear bead in his hand.

"Drop this in your ear and you'll hear everything that's transmitted," he said, "It's practically invisible and the technology is all plastic and silicon based, so it won't detect as metal. It's the ultimate in spy-tech."

There was a moment of awkward silence. No one really knew how to respond as he continued happily along after verbally shredding Jess, showing no signs of remorse. Eventually, when the silence was too much to bear, Justin spoke up to keep the subject away from the emotional.

"Did you figure anything out about bulletproofing?" Justin asked, "I mean, we've been out doing stuff without protection, which I originally didn't want to do. I've recently had a change of heart."

Kurt nodded.

"The Project team wears a top-secret ultra-light synthetic that will effectively stop a .45 caliber bullet at point blank range," he said, "It moves and breathes like regular cloth with next to no encumbrance. It's temperature reactive for all environments, going so far as to be freeze-proof and flame-retardant."

"Sweet!" Mike called out.

"We're not getting that," Kurt said.

A collective groan emanated from the rest of the group.

"The materials involved aren't exactly available to the public and can't be adequately engineered outside of a beyond-full-scale chem lab," Kurt continued, "This is about fifteen years away from being applied by the military, so, no, there's not much I can do about bulletproofing except to tell you that you're all sitting on giant piles of cash and there are a lot of people out there who sell things and don't ask questions."

"What else is there, then?" Zoey asked.

"Sorry?" Kurt said, "You are?"

"Zoey," she said, "We were introduced five times. Anyway, I'm kinda with Jess here: that's all you worked on? Nothing cooler or more important? Don't get me wrong, I like the walkie… communicators, but you have all the secret tech of the Project or whatever it's called up in your head. So, where's the Fantasticar? Where's the Negative Zone Projector? Where are the utility belts?"

Kurt stared blankly at Zoey.

"I don't have to take this from you," he said, his cheery demeanor changing as though a switch were flipped, "I don't have to take this from any of you. I'm doing the best I can with what I have here. I'm not working in a state-of-the-art black ops lab. I'm working in a cave in the side of an abandoned mine with as much stuff as I can buy on both the open and black markets.

"I know about some of their weapons, their armor, their computer tech, even their fancy bracers and their shoulder pads. None of it is even relevant to us at this point and it's all very tricky to build. Why can't any of you be impressed that I was able to produce something this incredible in a month, by myself, from nothing but some schematics? I know I can't shoot fireballs or dead-lift a school bus or make forcefields or any of that, but this is pretty damned impressive from where I'm standing.

"And you," he continued, slapping Phalanx in the arm, "You told me I'd have the secrets to everything if I helped you put your little puzzle together. You promised some endless font of information that would reveal everything about this Project who was tracking us or whatever. You lied. There was nothing there but a bunch of pipe-dream plans for devices, the one of which I decide to build and no one appreciates.

"Enjoy the radios, ingrates. You all make me sick. I'll be in my lab. Maybe, if I stay in there long enough, I'll be able to build something else on Captain Multiplier's Christmas list. Maybe something that will be slightly more impressive than communicators with the most ridiculous capabilities ever because apparently that's not enough for your luddites."

Kurt stormed off, back into the cave containing his lab. Again, the attention of the group followed the anger out of the room and waited until it was gone to speak up again.

"Swell guy," Zoey said, looking at Justin, "Just like you said he'd be."

"Not exactly the best first impression," Justin said, "Believe me, he was a bit grating, but he was never that bad before."

"For the record," Josh said, "I like the radios."

"So, what now?" Mike said, looking to Phalanx, "Back to training?"

"No," Phalanx said, taking another button from its case, "I have a better idea."

\*\*\*

"Whoever he is, he's acting alone," said Joey, "He's hiding somewhere in that section of the city and I can't find him."

"Is this not one of the main reasons you are on this team, Agent Briggs?" asked Williams.

"Yes, sir," she said, "I know, sir. Normally I can stretch my mind and find anyone once I've seen them. Something is different with this one, though. He's not on the grid, sir. I don't know how to describe it. The only way to find him at this point would be by coincidence, sir. I'd have to be monitoring someone's thoughts while they saw him and, well, he's a bit elusive as it stands, sir."

Silence rang through the large office as she finished her statement.

Agent Williams leaned against the deep, wooden window ledge and stared from his office into the early evening. The silence was broken by the clop of his shoes against the hardwood floor as he walked down the line of Agents at attention from Joey to Char to Moorsblade. He turned around and leaned against his massive yet relatively empty desk.

"You removed the police reports, I assume?" he asked.

"Better, sir," she said, "I removed the memories from the police at the scene. No report had yet been filed."

"And the body?" Williams asked.

"In custody," said Moorsblade, "Ready for the MEs in the lab."

"The witnesses," said Williams, "What did they see?"

"Humanoid," Joey said, tapping at her bracer for data, "Approximately eight- to nine-feet tall. Large shoulders, hunched back appearance, extremely powerful build. He was wearing a brown trench coat and a hood, enough to obscure most of the fine details. One witness saw spikes poking from the bulge in the back of the coat. Another reported claws at the ends of the fingertips. All report that he was covered in blood as he left the scene. No one gave chase."

Williams looked up at a clear display case hanging above and behind his desk. It contained a black leather body suit with a few armored pieces and a cowl attached at the neck. A pair of tonfa and a wide belt with a bevy of large pouches hung in the same case. The buckle of the belt was a red oval with a black outline divided in half by a single black vertical line. Char noticed Williams sighing as he regarded what looked like a relic from another reality.

"I want this thing, whatever it is, found and captured," Williams said, still focusing on the display case, "We can ill afford extra-normals on the rampage. If you have to sort through that neighborhood mind-by-mind, Agent Briggs, I suggest you get to it before we have to cover up another attack. Agents Moorsblade and Gentile, you will assist her in a ground search. Go to every scene, follow every conceivable clue, walk every possible trail."

"Sir," Joey started, "I've been heading up surveillance on the group of seven from the accident. Should I deprioritize my current investigations?"

"Yes," said Williams, "They are no longer high priority. We will deal with them when the time is right. From your reports, they are attempting to remain low-profile. They will not make as much noise as this creature should the killings continue. You have your orders. Dismissed."

They filed out of the office passing the massive bookshelves and glass-encased curios of indeterminable origin. The place reminded Char more of a museum than an office. Being the new person in the group, she didn't want to ask too many questions but she was very interested in whatever history was being kept here.

On the other side of the wooden double doors were the familiar dull gray concrete halls of the rest of the complex. She followed Moorsblade and Joey as they exited the area.

"Seriously?" Joey asked when they were a few turns away from the office, "We're supposed to just sit there and wait to catch this thing in the act? It's going to take forever."

"Won't be so bad," Moorsblade said, "We find somewhere to set up shop, start with a one mile radius from the highest concentration of attacks, and go from there. This guy obviously has a taste for the neighborhood. He might know the cops are looking for him but he isn't counting on us. Element of surprise."

"Why do we think he's going to stick to the same neighborhood?" Char asked, "Thirteen dead bodies with this thing's name on it and he doesn't think someone's going to start looking for him a little more actively? Nothing could be that stupid."

"Something could be that arrogant," Joey said, "From what I gathered from the witnesses, the latest victim wasn't a nice guy. They knew who lived in that house and he wasn't exactly a pillar of the community. He was dangerous and bad for the neighborhood. The kind of guy you don't rat out because he'll probably kill you for doing so. According to the memories I got at the scene, this wasn't the first bad guy to be taken out or disappeared in the area. I'm betting we could correlate most of those bodies in the morgue to missing thugs.

"This creature staked its territory and it's going to clean up the town. It thinks it's doing so much good here that it'll stay until the job is done, whenever it determines that might be."

"Then it's settled," Moorsblade said, "Joey get the rest of the team and…"

As he barked out orders, Char's head fogged over. She could hear him talking but it was distant and unintelligible. She saw Joey turn to her and caught a look of realization on her face as Char started to fall to the floor.

When she hit the ground, things became clearer. She was on her stomach with her cheek against the cold floor but she didn't feel hurt. She pushed herself up and realized as she looked around that she wasn't in the compound anymore.

The floor was the same drab concrete, but stretched on forever forming a horizon with an empty black sky. With her special black eyes, she switched between different types of vision. None of them gave her any clues as to what to make of this place.

When she looked forward, she saw someone sitting at a desk facing away from her. She wasn't sure if she had noticed this before or if it suddenly appeared. The glow of a computer monitor on the desk gave away only the silhouette of a high-backed office chair. The relentless clacking of a keyboard was her only realization that someone was in the chair, typing away.

She slowly approached the desk. The clacking of the keyboard stopped causing her to freeze in place.

"What are you doing here?" asked a woman's voice.

"I," she started, stumbling for an explanation, "I really don't know."

"Well, go away," said the voice, "You're not supposed to be here."

The typing resumed. Char tilted her head in confusion.

"Where is here?" Char asked.

"You're not supposed to know," said the voice, the sound of typing continuing, "Now turn around and go back the way you came."

"I don't know how I got here," Char said.

The typing stopped.

"Well, that's convenient," said the voice, "In that case, just think of not being here and you won't be here anymore."

"What?" asked Char, raising an eyebrow.

"Just do what I say," said the voice.

211

Char closed her eyes. She wasn't sure what to do at first but she pictured being back in her room at the compound. She tried her best but the sound of the keyboard clacking resumed. She cracked her eyes and realized she was still in the same place.

"It didn't work," Char said.

The clacking stopped. She heard a sigh.

"Something's wrong again," said the voice, "One way or another you keep finding your way back here. Tell that stupid little girl that she needs to put better locks on this place."

"I wasn't trying to get here," Char said, "I was talking to my team in the hallway, then I felt weird, then I fell. I must have passed out or something and I wound up here."

"Typical," said the voice, "Were you feeling particularly stressed or strained when it happened?"

"Not really," Char said, thinking of all the dead bodies and the anxiety they instilled, "Just a... busy day at work. That's about it."

"You don't have to speak code with me," said the voice, "I know exactly who you are Agent Charlene Gentile of Project XIII. This week has been your first field mission. Was there something in particular that got under your skin?"

"Not really," Char said, "I have been feeling kinda nauseous all day but that's probably because we spent half of it staring at mutilated corpses in the morgue."

"Hm," said the voice, "Could be a safety response, maybe. Retreating inward because you don't know how to react."

"Who are you, anyway?" Char asked, "How do you know so much about me?"

"Both very easy questions to answer," the voice said.

The chair swiveled to face her. She gasped and almost fell backwards.

An exact duplicate of herself sat in the chair. Exact, that is, except for the eyes. Her double in the chair had normal eyes with brown irises instead of Char's solid black orbs.

"You know I never get tired of that reaction," said the Char in the chair, "I'm always so shocked that I've been talking to myself."

"This has happened before?" Char asked.

"Many times," said the one in the chair, "In the beginning, this was practically a nightly routine. You'd pop in, be shocked that I was here, we'd talk things over, and you'd be gone by morning. Next night, same thing, as if you'd never been here before. Must have happened ten nights in a row before she found a way to fix it. She came to see me to tell me it was going to be harder for you to get in here but you still keep slipping in every once in a while. This is the first time in... well... in a long time."

"Who are you, really?" Char asked.

"I'm you," said the one the chair, "Before all of this. Before the Project, before the accident. I've been over it with you before but, really, the less I tell you the better. She erases everything I say and, I don't care what she says, constantly erasing your memories has to be bad for you. This is still my body, after all, and I'd prefer the least amount of brain damage."

"What do you mean 'before the Project'?" Char asked, "And, what accident are you talking about? I remember everything leading up to my recruitment. Nothing was locked away."

"You remember a life you never lead," said the one in the chair, "It's all implanted. Fake memories to keep you from asking questions. I'm not going to tell you about it because, for one, the memory erasure thing and, for two, every time I do, you get all weepy and start spouting off about how you made the wrong decisions and garbage like that. We'll skip that whole bit and I'll just tell you that everything you know about your past is a lie."

"They replaced my memories?" Char asked.

"No, they repressed them," said the one in the chair, "That's why I'm here. As good as that girl is with manipulating minds, she wasn't ruthless enough to outright erase your past. Maybe she felt guilty about it, I don't know, but she decided to keep me and the rest of your baggage hidden in the back of your head even though it wasn't really part of the bargain."

"Would you please stop making me ask follow-up questions based on the end of your statement?" Char asked, "Every time you answer, there's another question. Did I act like a bad TV show in my old life, too?"

"Hey," said the one in the chair, "That was uncalled for. They're making us more confrontational and I don't like it. Remind me to lodge a complaint."

"It was not uncalled for," Char said, "You're sitting there with all the answers, telling me you shouldn't say anything, and yet you keep dropping bread crumbs and tempting me to follow the trail. Stop trying to leave me with cliffhangers and just come clean."

"It won't matter if I do," said the one in the chair, "I mean, I could make you die with anticipation or I could reveal everything. It's all going to go away once you wake up. She's going to touch your head and all you'll remember is having a headache that's suddenly gone. Then, she'll throw you a line about the neuroscientists whose skills she absorbed and blah blah smoke and mirrors. Meanwhile, she's been taking things away to keep you focused."

"I get migraines," Char said, "Joey helps to get rid of them. She's my friend. Why would she be in my head adjusting things? How do I even know you're real? How do I know this isn't some kind of crazy hallucination?"

213

The one in the chair stood up and looked right into her eyes. She grabbed Char's head with both hands and held it steady.

"You only need to know one thing," said the one from the chair, "We wanted this. We asked for this. We did what was best for the greater good out of a feeling of obligation. Don't worry about what's down here with me, it's all gone. Embrace your new life, don't resist. Now, wake up. And, don't let her mess around too much. Remember, it's my head too."

She felt a waking sensation. The face of her duplicate from the chair faded and changed into Joey's as she returned to consciousness. The plains of nothingness dissolved to walls and a large observation window. Char knew immediately that she was in the infirmary.

Joey's cool hands touched gently against her temples. Char tried to speak but her mouth was incredibly dry.

"Is it," she rasped, coughing, "Is it all a lie?"

Joey's normally cold blue eyes took on a surprisingly compassionate look as she bit her lower lip.

"Yeah," Joey whispered, "Yeah, it's a lie, but it's for the best. For what it's worth, I'm sorry. I didn't think it would end up this way."

"Bet you say that every time," Char muttered.

"Not every time," Joey whispered, "I'm sorry, Char, but I have to do this again."

"Do what ag…" Char managed before a white light pierced through her mind.

She opened her eyes and shot up from her back. She wasn't sure where she was and looked frantically around for some point of reference.

"Char," Joey said, "You ok?"

"What happened?" she asked, her eyes darting around the room.

"You passed out in the hallway," Joey said, "Probably all the stress you've been feeling from being on your first field assignment and seeing those bodies. I know it's tough. I was in your shoes once, not too long ago."

"Yeah, I guess," Char said, rubbing the back of her head.

"Williams said that you should take the rest of the day off," Joey said, "Moorsblade and I are going to start lowering the dragnet in that neighborhood. You can catch up when you're feeling better."

"Ok," Char said.

"Lie down," Joey said, tapping at her bracer and lowering the lights in the room, "Get some rest. Doctor's orders."

Joey turned and started for the door.

"I wanted this," Char said, "Didn't I?"

"What?" Joey asked turning around.

"All of this," Char said, "The Project, the training… I wanted this, didn't I?"

Joey sighed, but looked up at Char smiling.

"You did," Joey said, "You asked for all of it.  Now, get some rest."

## XXI

Budda leaned against the concrete half-wall at the front of a row of empty parking spaces on the top level of the parking garage. It was twelve stories up and provided them a decent view over the streets of downtown. He could see the entire length of two of the busiest avenues just by crossing the empty rooftop. He periodically paced between the two vantage points to make sure he wasn't missing any action.

He sighed. He could see the wind blowing litter along the street. He saw the scarves and added layers of the few late-night passersby. It was the dead of winter and he stood on this rooftop, shirtless and barefoot, wearing only a pair of gigantic track pants to cover his dignity and a stocking cap so that his VII-logo communicator button had somewhere handy to be pinned. He didn't need the extra layers. He couldn't feel the biting wind. He was a rock and rocks didn't feel cold.

"Budda," said a voice, "Budda!"

"Huh?" he answered, looking down at Mike.

"I asked you a question," Mike said.

"Sorry, man," Budda said, "My mind was wandering."

"What else is new?" Mike said.

Budda almost laughed every time he saw Mike in his vigilante get-up. He wore a black pirate-style mask that covered his upper face and his hair in a bandana that tied at the back and flowed dramatically in the wind when he was standing. At the moment, he sat on the ground with his back against the wall over which Budda had been peering. He looked like a pirate.

"I was asking what Phalanx was teaching you," Mike repeated.

"You'll laugh if I tell you," Budda answered.

"I floated a ball through rings for days," Mike said, "Nothing could be dumber than that."

"Meditation," Budda said.

"That's actually pretty cool," Mike responded, "Why would you think I would laugh?"

"Because it sounds stupid," Budda said, "You'd think I would be punching through walls."

"No, it makes total sense," Mike said.

"It's harder than you'd think," Budda continued, "Meditation is harder when you don't breathe. It helps, though. I've been having some issues dealing with my three missing senses and my inability to sleep. He's been teaching me new methods and teaching me tai-chi."

"Wait," Mike said, "I thought you were only missing a sense of touch."

"No smell," Budda said, "And because of that, no taste either. It's tied into scent and breathing. Also, I don't need to eat, so those senses kinda don't make sense for me anymore. I guess whatever kind of evolution I'm going through got rid of my more useless systems."

"Dude, that sucks," Mike said, shocked.

"More than you can ever imagine," Budda said, calmly, "My brain still thinks that there's a human body attached to it. I get hungry and I can't eat. I get thirsty and I can't drink. I get tired and I can't sleep. My brain tells me I need these things even though my body doesn't.

"My change throws sand in the face of the most basic principles of nature; there isn't an organism on this planet which doesn't need to eat or drink or breathe, except me. My brain still thinks I'm flesh and blood. The meditation is to help my mind adjust and keep me from going completely insane."

"You've been dealing with that level of discomfort from the beginning?" Mike asked, "Why didn't you say anything to anyone?"

"Didn't want anyone to worry," Budda said, "We were so busy planning for the future that I didn't have time to care about it. Steph did what she could to help me, but it was hard for her, too. When I was home, I was twitching like a junkie. There are things you don't just take for granted but accept as sheer reflex. When you don't do them, it can make you buggy. I was pretty addicted to eating and breathing and feeling things when I was human. Now, they're just not there anymore."

"Speaking of Steph," Mike started, "I know this is personal, but can you still..."

"No," Budda said, cutting him off, "I literally can't feel anything. Steph kinda likes it, because it's also made of very rigid material, but it does nothing for me. It's infuriating."

"How have you not completely lost your mind yet?" Mike asked.

"I hid it from you guys," Budda said, "When I had a chance to channel my rage, I did it privately."

"And you're doing better now?" Mike asked.

"Phalanx said something about the meditation realigning my mind with my body," Budda said, "It's much better than it was in the beginning, but it's still very difficult."

"So," Mike posited, "He's really just teaching you to deal with the side-effects and not your powers?"

"We've been working a little on combat," Budda said, "When I need an outlet. Nothing overly intense. He's teaching me to box and a little MMA type stuff. He's also teaching me how to do it without outright killing someone with my strength."

"You can tone it down?" Mike asked, "I watched you punch through solid stone. I've seen you bend metal like clay. Must be hard to hold back."

"I've burned through six Phalanxes already," Budda said, nodding, "I'm starting to know my strength a bit better now."

"'Burned through'?" Mike asked, "What do you mean?"

"I mean smoked," Budda said, "Eliminated. Taken out. Squished."

"You killed Phalanx?" Mike shouted.

"Dude," Budda said, whispering, "Keep your voice down. And, yeah, six Phalanxes. No big deal."

"You killed someone," Mike whisper-shouted, "That's definitely a big deal!"

"Six someones," Budda said, "But it's ok. It was mostly accidental. Phalanx told me to do it. He said that I couldn't learn to control myself if I didn't know my limits."

"That's messed up," Mike said.

"But educational," Budda retorted, "He can make unlimited duplicates of himself that don't mind getting wiped for the greater good. If he says it's no big deal, I don't have a problem with it."

Silence set in again. Mike walked across the roof to look at the other observable street.

Budda knew he freaked him out. He wasn't sure if he should say something or not. He had a history of saying the wrong things at the wrong time and didn't really want to exacerbate things. Instead, he followed Mike to the other side of the rooftop.

"It's pretty messed up, y'know," Mike said, not turning around.

"What is?" Budda asked.

"This whole thing," Mike said, "You and me on a rooftop doing superhero patrol, having abilities that shouldn't exist, getting chummy with a super-spy secret agent who says he used to work for some super-secret government agency who has us under constant surveillance…"

He huffed a sigh before continuing.

"…You, a general pacifist, talking casually about murdering six people in God knows how horrible a manner and expecting me to accept it just because they're duplicates of the guy who's training you and he gave you permission to do it. I've been cool with everything up until now. I'm supposed to be cool because we're all nerds and this is something we've always wanted but I have to tell you, I'm starting to lose it. I was trying to get my mind around the whole thing and I really don't know if I can."

Mike's elbows were resting on the top of the barrier as he massaged his temples under his mask.

"I get what you're saying," Budda replied after a moment, "But, it's real and you have to accept it. I'm a rock, you can manipulate gravity, and we're here to patrol for crime."

"Listen to what you're saying," Mike said, "Did you ever think those kinds of words would be coming out of your mouth anywhere outside of a tabletop role-playing session? How can you, of all of us, be that dismissive of the situation?"

"I'm playing things for what they are," Budda said, "No matter how farfetched reality may be right now. It helps to keep me from freaking out. Do yourself a favor and just roll with it."

"I can't just roll with it," Mike shouted, "I'm a baker. I bake cookies all day. That's what I do and I do it extremely well. I own a very

218

profitable business based on that. I don't want to be a baker by day and a superhero by night. I don't think I can handle it. I mean, I'm a night owl and all, but I can't afford to be out all night until dawn every night of the week. Can't I just be a weekend superhero?"

"Everyone in the comics does it," Budda said.

"Everyone in the comics doesn't need sleep unless the plot says they do," Mike countered, "Not everyone in the comics has a nine-to-five where they're practically the only employee. They're all news reporters who are expected to be out in the field all day or eccentric billionaires who can afford to leave the operations of their company to a board of directors. I'm a small business owner. If I don't open up shop one day, that's a lot of lost income."

"We all got that big sack of money from the government," Budda said, "You don't even really need the bakery anymore."

"I have pride in what I do, Budda," Mike said, "That big sack of money is awesome but I'm not giving up everything I've built over the years. I can't just shut up shop and run off every time someone's getting mugged and I won't spend every night out here in the blistering cold waiting for something to happen. That's the part that the comics never show; when all the good guys are just swinging wasting web fluid or grappling line, tapping their foot and waiting for the next supervillain to try something stupid. I don't want to spend my nights like that when I could be doing other things."

"But, we're helping people," Budda said, "We're doing this so that we can make the world a better place."

"This is hour six of patrol one-of-one," Mike said, "We haven't been doing anything but staring down from the building-top onto empty streets and freezing our nuts off. Just because Justin, Josh, and Zoey happened upon a robbery doesn't mean we're going to see the same action."

"It'll happen," Budda said, "Eventually. Doesn't it make you feel like you're doing something good just by watching out?"

"No," Mike said, "It makes me feel cold and stupid."

Silence sat in as Budda just shook his head and stared down into the street.

"What kind of crime do you think we're going to stop?" Mike argued, "Most stuff aside from theft is stuff we can't prevent. Murder is usually very sudden, usually pre-meditated, and, most of the time, involves someone familiar enough to the victim that the cops drag them in within a day or two. Arson usually requires a lot of investigation which vigilantes like us won't be able to accomplish. Domestic disputes and general violence require context to solve, not a knockdown superhero brawl."

"But, when we see something," Budda said, "Like a mugging or a burglary or a drug deal, we'll be here to stop it."

"And, how often does that happen in this town?" Mike asked, "I know we're not in the nicest part of the city, but we're probably not going to see any kind of violence unless we start it ourselves. Face it; what we're doing is mostly useless in the long run. This city is a decent place with fairly decent people. It's not like we're a very high-crime area. Even stupid LENNY can only come up with car accidents, mild fires, and domestics most of the time. This town doesn't need a superhero, let alone seven of them."

"Maybe you're right," Budda said, "In the comics, when people are in Gotham or Metropolis or New York, things are always happening. Supervillains are escaping from Arkham or Blackgate or the Raft to launch some kind of world domination scheme."

"That's my point," Mike said, "Even if we were defending a bigger city, there aren't any supervillains. There isn't even a visible element of organized crime in this town. It's all underground and they don't usually bother anyone except the people who are in debt to the sharks or the bookies. We don't even get any natural disasters here unless you count blizzards and flooding, neither of which a bunch of battle-ready superheroes can truly assist with. So, no, I don't want to spend every night up here waiting for some schmuck to mug a passerby when I have to be up for work in the morning."

Mike turned his back to the street and leaned against the barrier with his arms crossed.

Budda continued to stare down, on the lookout.

Mike picked a few rocks out of the accumulated gravel in the corner of the lot. He placed a large one above his palm where it spun and added other smaller ones nearby, causing them to orbit the large rock.

"That reminds me," said Budda, breaking the silence, "I sent a sample of myself to the USGS to be analyzed."

"Really?" Mike asked, concentrating on the rocks, "That's a surprisingly good idea. What did they say?"

"It's unique," Budda said, "They've never seen anything like it before. They're keeping a sample but they want to send a field team to check out the site where the stone was found and, if I can prove there's more of it and it's naturally occurring, I'll get to name the new mineral."

"Name it after yourself," Mike said, adding another planet to his tiny solar system, "Moronium."

"Seriously, though," Budda said, "Not even the USGS knows what I am."

"Who cares what you are," Mike said, putting another rock into deep orbit, "You're a huge, super-strong, super-tough walking rock with an inflated sense of justice and no conscience when it comes to killing clones of your teacher. Do you really need to know more than that?"

Budda narrowed his eyes at Mike, who was now throwing pebbles at the orbiting objects and pretending they were comets.

When Budda turned back to the street, he saw a figure run around the corner of the nearest block and duck into an alley, where he leapt into a dumpster. Thirty seconds later, a police car rounded the same corner slowly, shining its spotlight into some of the darker areas. It stopped in front of the garage and an officer exited, walking into the lobby area.

Budda ducked back from the edge doing his best to hide his bulk behind the short wall.

"What's going on?" Mike asked.

"Cops," Budda said, "They just went into the garage lobby. Probably looking for this guy who just ditched into a dumpster in the alley."

"They didn't see him?" Mike asked, dropping his rocks and peeking over the barrier.

"Guess not," Budda said, "They were way behind this guy. Cops are probably asking the security guard downstairs if he saw anything."

Mike raised his finger after hearing something. Both of them remained silent as they heard the distorted voices of the police officers talking to each other echo off the surrounding buildings. A car door opened and closed and the idling engine of the cruiser revved up to a crawl as it drove off.

They both peeked their heads up a bit higher.

"That's dumpster right there," said Budda, pointing.

"Maybe he took off while the cops were inside," Mike said.

"No," said Budda, "I think only one cop went in. There was another in the driver's seat."

The lid of the dumpster lifted a bit, apparently allowing whoever it was to survey the scene. After a moment, he opened the dumpster and climbed out, casually making his way up the exit ramp of the garage.

"Let's get him," Budda said, standing up.

"'Get him?'" Mike asked, "We don't know what the cops wanted with him. Why would we just 'get him'?"

"The guy's obviously up to something or he wouldn't have ditched in a dumpster," Budda said, "And, he's smart enough to not go through the lobby because the cops probably just described him to the security guard."

"I'm not in the habit of chasing after innocent people," Mike said.

"Dumpster diving is a sure sign of guilt," Budda said.

"Maybe he's just a homeless guy," Mike said, "You don't know that's who the cops were looking for. Do you want another jewelry store incident?"

The sound of breaking glass could be heard from one of the lower levels along with a blaring car alarm. An engine started and tires squealed. Soon there were lights flashing on the buildings opposite the garage as a car sped down the spiral exit ramp.

"Ok," Mike said, "Now he's a car thief. Let's get him."

Budda smiled and put an arm on the ledge heaving his massive body over the barrier and off the building completely.

As he fell over ten stories, he couldn't feel the wind rushing past him. Because he wasn't worried about potential pain awaiting him below, he was able to prepare his body for landing and pray that he had timed his trick properly before he would reach the area where the exit ramp emptied into the street. He saw the front bumper of the car cresting the exit just as he was about to land.

He didn't feel anything as his feet crashed through the hood of the car. There was no pain as his weight and momentum destroyed the front of the engine, the radiator, the front axle, and everything attached. His feet cracked the concrete as he landed. The front end of the car now surrounded him and was rendered suddenly motionless where he planted his weight.

His back was to the driver. In an overly dramatic fashion, he stood up from his crouched landing posture and turned slowly around to face him, narrowing his eyes.

The driver, still recovering from the sudden stop and airbag deployment, scrambled to get out of the car. The exit ramp, however, was too narrow for him to open the driver's side door enough to get out. When he realized this, he produced a handgun from his waistband, screamed, and put a shot through the windshield into Budda's chest.

Budda grinned, leaned forward and gripped the front of the car's roof, peeling it back like a banana. With his massive right hand, he reached into the car and grabbed the driver by the hood of his sweatshirt. The young, scared man kicked and flailed. Budda pulled him nose to nose and sneered at him.

Dangling around three feet off the ground, the driver, pale-faced and frightened, lifted his gun and emptied the rest of the rounds into Budda's chest as fast as he could. He continued to pull the trigger a dozen times before Budda's curled up pointer finger flicked the gun out of his hands and sent it clattering into the garage. The driver flailed harder and screamed louder, punching and kicking at Budda to no result save for some bloody knuckles.

Budda lightly tapped the young man in the center of the head with enough force to knock him out, leaving the now unconscious driver with what would surely become the most storied bruise in his history.

"Dude," Mike shouted from the top of the ramp, out of breath, "What the hell?"

"It's ok, man," Budda said, setting the man back into the driver's seat, "I got him!"

Mike approached, his breathing heavy.

"I thought," he started, huffing, "I thought we talked about doing things quietly."

"He was getting away," Budda said, "I had to do something. I'll cop to the noise I made while landing, but this guy shot me like nine times. That's not my fault."

"Ok, well the cops are going to be here and soon," Mike said, "They couldn't have gone far and they had to have heard that ruckus. Come on, we have to get back upstairs."

"What about him?" Budda asked, pointing to the limp body of the driver.

"Leave him," Mike said, "The cops will sort it out. Now, come on!"

Budda crunched through the car and into the garage with Mike. He had to hunch down and carefully rush through the rear stairwell and back up to the roof. By the time they arrived, Mike now gasping for air, they could see the red and blue lights shining in the street.

"You ready?" Mike asked.

"Yeah," Budda said, "Let's go."

"Follow me," Mike gasped, "And don't look down."

Mike hopped onto the top of the roof's half-wall, on a side away from the street, and walked forward seemingly on air. Budda followed, unable to feel the smooth texture of the forcefield beneath his feet, allowing them passage over the tops of the shorter buildings and over streets and alleyways.

At the end of the invisible bridge, they reached the roof of another parking garage, this one containing Mike's SUV. Mike pressed a button on a remote and the tailgate of the vehicle opened. Budda rushed and jumped inside. Once they were situated, Mike drove off, exiting the garage and down the street, away from the scene which was now flooded with police.

"Are you ok?" Mike asked as he put the red and blue lights behind them and turned off the street.

"Yeah," Budda said, "Just a few dings. Nothing serious."

Budda picked at the crushed slugs which were embedded in his chest. It was disturbing yet empowering to think that nine shots at point-blank range couldn't do so much as chip his body leaving not much more than scuff marks behind. Not to mention the fact that he fell ten storied through the front portion of a car, engine and all, without a crack and without any sensation at all.

"Don't you feel like we should have done something more with that kid?" Budda asked, "Shouldn't we have left him in front of police headquarters or tied him up or something? Shouldn't we have left a note?"

"What flavor moron are you, exactly?" Mike asked.

"They always do that kind of stuff in the comics," Budda said.

"Tell me," Mike said, "What would the cops have done if we rolled up to one of their stations and dumped some random, tied-up, unconscious kid out in the middle of a cold winter night? First, they have

223

cameras, so they probably would have ID'ed my vehicle. Second, the kid might not be discovered, come to, and run. Third, if they found him, even if we left a note, they probably wouldn't arrest him or anything. I mean, we don't even know what he did, we just had an idea that the cops were looking for him."

"He stole a car," Budda said.

"Which you promptly destroyed," Mike shouted.

"He was going to get away!" Budda shouted back, "Also, he tried to shoot me. That's attempted murder."

"Self-defense," Mike said, "A giant rock monster just fell through the car he was driving and grabbed him up by his scruff. I think that's grounds for panic. Better that we left him there. The cops who were around the corner will likely take him in for whatever he really did, if they were even looking for him, and start the process."

"It's just," Budda said, taking a moment to think, "There's no closure, y'know?"

"Yeah," Mike said, "There's a lot less of it out here than there is in the comics. We can't risk getting caught. Just be glad we could do something regardless of how sloppy it may have been."

"I can't wait to tell the guys I jumped through a car," Budda said, "And stood up to a full clip of rounds."

"You'd better hope the guy in that car tests positive for drugs," Mike said, "Otherwise, we might have a problem."

"They'll just think he's crazy," Budda said, "It's not like the cops will come looking for us. That guy might as well say he was attacked by Bigfoot, it would get the same reaction."

"Let's hope so," Mike said, "We don't need the cops – or anything worse – coming after us."

Neither of them knew that it would happen on its own soon enough.

## XXII

"This is ridiculously high up," Josh said, looking down from the edge of the roof and feeling that sudden tingle.

"You wanted a watchtower," Jess said, "Here we are."

"I didn't think you'd lift us up forty-four floors," he said, stepping back from the edge, "Forty-five counting the mezzanine."

"Well, it's done," she said, "Deal with it."

He put his back to the city and slumped down along the wall at the edge of the rooftop, his legs skidding down onto the gravel.

This was one of the older skyscrapers in the downtown area; concrete and art-deco as opposed to the metal and glass of most of the surrounding buildings. The top of the building was a love letter to architecture which created one of the most memorable parts of the skyline – a large, stepped, concrete pyramid rising another ten stories or so above the occupied floors and crowned with a mausoleum, affectionately called The Beacon. LED lights caused each level of the pyramid to reflect a different color. Someone told Josh that it had something to do with the weather, but he didn't know the code to decipher it. One level, showing cobalt blue, must have been the air temperature because it was frigid up here.

"How are we supposed to fight crime from up here?" he asked.

Jess paid him no attention. She floated above the ground near the maintenance door, her legs crossed and her eyes closed in meditation.

"At the risk of sounding horribly cliché," Josh said, "The people look like ants from here, and it's the middle of the night. How are we supposed to see anything bad happening?"

"I've got it covered," she said, sounding annoyed, "I can see them all from here. Remember, this was your idea. You wanted to feel like a real superhero, perched on the edge of a skyscraper. Wasn't that what you said earlier?"

"Yeah," he muttered, "Now I'd rather look like an average grad student sitting in my car. I'm kinda nauseous up here."

She didn't reply. Her eyes were closed.

Jess wasn't really dressed for crime fighting or, at least, she didn't look the part. Full winter gear all colored some shade of pink wasn't the most intimidating of outfits, however, her choice of an Italian-style full-face white masquerade mask added a necessary level of creepy to her ensemble. He was happy she decided to take it off to meditate or he would have been freaking out even more.

He wore what Justin referred to as his "hobo Green Hornet" get-up, this time with a more traditional domino mask rather than a black sock with some holes cut in it. He wore it as much as possible. It made him feel more heroic.

No amount of heroism would get him over his sudden distaste for heights.

He reached into his pocket and drained a jolt out of one of the myriad of batteries he kept on him. He closed his eyes and held his breath for a minute as the power coursed through him. It was always a rush; better than any coffee he'd ever had and much more instant.

He hadn't slept more than one hour a night since the first time he drained a battery. He didn't feel the need. Phalanx questioned the wisdom of this during their training time and mentioned to Josh that, if he kept up like this, he was heading for a massive crash and soon. Josh disagreed. If devices could remain powered indefinitely with a bit of charging, he saw no reason the human body couldn't be run the same way.

Phalanx agreed with him, except for the indefinite part. He told Josh that he could remain awake and aware as long as electricity remained in his system but that he would have to remain vigilant with the level that remained in him. Doing things like throwing lightning bolts or – as he found he could do – powering devices without using batteries without being mindful might cause the crash, at which point all of his sleep debt would likely catch up to him at once.

He came close to passing out a few times while training but Phalanx would catch him on the nod and give him a chance to recharge.

He toyed with the idea of sticking his finger in a wall socket but Phalanx discouraged him. There was no telling how much power he would draw into himself and, if overcharged, there was no telling what would happen. He could simply overload the breakers of the house, he could potentially blow the entire city's power grid or he could wind up a crispy black stick on the ground. There was also the potential that he would explode, which even Josh couldn't deny was a down side to the idea.

The most power he'd had was when he slid beneath the truck in the alley and drained a poorly charged car battery in the dead of winter. Until they had time to experiment a bit more, Phalanx advised against going for the big stuff.

His remote control abilities didn't seem to require any of his charge and he used this ability to play video games without a controller late into the night. It helped to fill the hours and he routinely schooled anyone out of the group who went against him. His mental commands were faster than simple hand-eye coordination and gave him an almost completely unfair advantage.

He sighed. He felt the small amount of power he sipped from that battery fading. He put his hand back into his pocket, clutched at his bunch of batteries and panicked as nothing happened. There was nothing left. No more electricity. No more energy. He emptied his pockets, checking each battery one by one and tossing them to the gravel as they turned up spent. He was sure he'd brought enough to last him the entire night.

Paranoid thoughts and questions filled his head – did he use more power the longer he stayed awake? Would this be the reckoning to which Phalanx alluded? Was he going to pass out right now and not wake up for days? He couldn't have that. They were here to patrol. He had to do something.

Over Jess's shoulder, he spotted something. He stood up and moved around to get a better look at it. His eyes widened as he saw the black triangle enclosing a black lightning bolt painted on a metal box near the maintenance door.

He crept around Jess, his canvas sneakers crunching on the gravel. He didn't want to approach her while she was meditating. He knew that she would try to stop him if she knew what he planned to do.

He reached the box which was closed by four large bolts. He grabbed at one with both hands and tried to spin it loose, but it didn't budge. He thought for a moment and pressed his index finger to the head of the bolt, closed his eyes, took a deep breath, and dropped his thumb like the hammer of a pistol.

With a loud crack, the bolt was blown right out of the thread. The twisted metal of the corner of the fuse box remained and the bolt clattered against the wall before landing in the gravel.

He looked over his shoulder at Jess. Her back was to him as she remained floating and meditative. He thought she would have been alerted by the sudden racket. Figuring she was, luckily, off somewhere else and not paying particular psychic attention to his actions, he breathed a sigh of relief and pressed his finger to the next bolt.

After all the bolts were removed and the cover had been lowered to the ground, Josh felt the weakness creeping up on him. He looked back at Jess who remained amazingly undisturbed.

Inside the box, a row of large breaker switches presented themselves with yellowed labels stating things like "beacon" and "exterior LED" and "main power aux". Josh didn't care about their purposes, he only knew that by removing a fuse and jamming his hand into the contacts he would be able to get some precious electricity to keep him going. He was starting to lose his balance. His legs were turning to jelly. It was now or never. He reached for the fuses and...

"Don't do it," said Jess, suddenly standing right next to him.

"What?" Josh asked, turning to look and feeling extremely dizzy. He looked back to where she had been floating, expecting to see an empty space, but Jess still hovered there.

"Don't do it," she said again.

"What are you," Josh asked, "My conscience or something? I didn't think I would hallucinate when it got this bad."

"I'm in your head, dumb ass," she said, "We've played this game before, remember?"

"Oh yeah," he said, his voice starting to slur, "Why are we playing it now?"

"Because I don't want to break my meditation to tell you what you're thinking of doing is colossally stupid and completely insane."

"I know what I'm doing," Josh slurred, "I can take it."

"Phalanx wasn't so sure," Jess countered.

"What does he know?" Josh said, "What do you know? You're not me. You don't know what you're talking about."

"You don't either," said Jess, "You're being irrational because you're addicted. I told you this would happen and I told you to avoid it. I knew this would become a problem."

"It's not a problem," Josh said, "It's a solution. Everyone else gets to use their powers at maximum strength all the time. Justin goes ballistic, Budda pounds stuff, Zoey can make anything out of ice. Why can't I power up and see what it's like to be at my full potential?"

"Because it might kill you," Jess said, moving between Josh and the fuse box, "You're being irrational right now. Come sit and meditate with me. It'll take your mind off of things. If you crash, I can handle any trouble we find."

"Yeah," Josh said, "Just sit on the sidelines and let the real heroes take care of everything. I'm just the guy with the stupid powers who stays behind because he's useless. I am the Aquaman of this group. The Jubilee. I'm sick of being a joke."

"You're not a joke," Jess said, "You can shoot lightning."

"Not without juice," Josh said, "And, changing the channel and playing video games with my mind isn't useful in a fight. I can't turn into smoke. I can't mentally manipulate people. I'm not invulnerable. When I don't have any electricity in me 'shooting lightning' amounts to the strength of a few good foot rubs on the carpet and touching a metal doorknob. Powering up is all I've got and I need it, so just let me do this."

"Don't rationalize something that might kill you," Jess said, "Just calm down and come sit with me."

"I've been calm," Josh said, "I'm sick of being calm. On Mike and Budda's first patrol, Budda dropped ten stories through the front of a car to stop a bad guy while Mike made an invisible bridge so they could escape. Justin smashed a guy in the back with a fireball like it wasn't a thing. You're sitting over there meditating while you're projecting yourself to me mentally. It makes me jealous. I want to be a lightning-throwing badass, not some throwaway character. You have no limits, I shouldn't either."

"We all have limits," Jess said, "Phalanx says I could wind up stroking out if I push myself too hard. Budda lost whole senses in exchange for his powers. Justin almost blew the entire complex apart and himself with it. You do this and it'll be a very fast and harsh lesson about your own limits. Listen to Phalanx. You could wind up committing suicide in the name of an inferiority complex."

She looked him in the eyes, her expression earnest and worried. For a moment, he hesitated, but as his vision started to tunnel every inch of him was screaming to reach out for the fuses.

"Don't listen to your body right now," Jess said, "It's acting on behalf of your addiction."

"After all this time in my head," Josh said, "You still don't get it."

She sighed.

"I get it," she said, "I empathize but it doesn't make this right and I still don't agree with you. You need help, Josh. Let me help you."

"If I wanted your help," Josh grunted, "I would have asked you to undo the bolts."

He thrust his hand forward through Jess's immaterial body and tore a fuse loose with his last bit of strength. It sparked and sputtered in his hand.

Every muscle in his body instantly became tense. His eyes shot wide open and his teeth clenched tight enough that the grind was audible.

He could see the shocked expression on the face of Jess's avatar as it faded away and was replaced with the real Jess running into the periphery of his vision. She shouted things to him that he couldn't hear. His ears were full of white noise and his vision was starting to fade.

The lights along the pyramid dimmed as arcs of electricity jumped from the box to his skin, charring the sleeves of his coat and the legs of his jeans. The voice in the back of his head was suddenly in full agreement with Jess: this was a colossally stupid idea.

In his last conscious moments, he felt himself getting thrown backwards. His back collided with something hard before he collapsed onto what he could only assume was the gravel covered rooftop.

Everything went dark and suddenly gave way to a piercing white light. A floating sensation came over him. He felt no pain from his collision with whatever or his presumptive electrocution. He felt calm and good. Centered, as if he'd just awoke from a long nap. It worried him.

Before he had time to wonder if he was dead, his vision cleared as the white light dissolved away like static. The rooftop came back into focus and he saw Jess near the blown-out fuse box. Her eyes were wide and her hands covered her mouth. The LEDs lining the pyramid flickered and were extinguished.

The floating sensation and general good feelings remained but the look on Jess's face lead him to believe that something was very wrong.

"What?" Josh asked, "What is it?"

Jess took a few tentative steps closer, her hands still covering her mouth. He followed her wide, frightened gaze as she looked him over.

He put his arms out in front of him and saw the charred sleeves of his trench coat, smoldering and ruined enough to expose a layer of smoldering, ruined shirt beneath and down to his skin. He smelled burning rubber and looked down at his feet. Below his burnt jeans the soles of his shoes were molten and dripping onto the gravel below.

"I'm actually floating, aren't I?" he asked casually.

Jess quickly nodded, not removing her hands from her mouth.

"This isn't a hallucination, is it?" he asked.

Jess shook her head and moved her hands briefly to speak.

"You flew across the roof," she said, "There were so many sparks. And the look on your face... I thought you were going to die. You flew back and hit one of the climate control vents and went limp. Then there was this blinding flash and you were floating there."

He blinked his eyes. When he opened them, he and Jess were almost nose to nose. His feet were back on the ground. It happened so fast that it took Jess a full second to react and jump backwards.

"Holy..." she shouted, her mittens muffling her cry, "You just teleported!"

"Seriously?" Josh asked.

She nodded her head vigorously.

He turned around to face the city and focused on the rooftop of another skyscraper. He blinked and was looking back at Jess from the edge, three blocks away and a hundred feet below him. He blinked again and was now inches from her again making her jump a second time.

"Lightning," she shouted through her hands, "You turned into lightning."

"All I did was think about where I wanted to go," he said, "And, I guess I went."

There was a great amount of pressure in his chest. It caused him to double over and breathe heavily.

"Are you ok?" Jess asked, coming closer.

Josh held up his hand to stop her and took a few deep breaths. He could feel the power he'd absorbed trying to fight its way out. He was trying to contain it but...

"MOVE!" he shouted, causing her to run aside.

He thrust his arm out straight. Electricity coursed from his shoulder to his hand and unleashed a bolt of energy from his flattened palm. With a loud zap and a clap of thunder, it impacted with the climate control vent he'd previously dented. It was nearly disintegrated and the building's power flashed with the surge before blacking out again.

He felt relieved as though he'd just been sick. He took a few more deep breaths, then sighed.

"I'm ok now," Josh said, "I just needed to get that out of my system."

Looking down at his hands, small arcs of electricity jumped between his fingertips. He concentrated and produced a large arc between his two upturned palms. He could feel the power flowing through his arms like a circuit.

"You realize you're standing on melting rubber," Jess said, "And your clothes are smoldering. Do you feel any of that?"

"No," Josh said, "I don't feel any of it. I mean, I feel the texture, but it doesn't hurt. I don't even…"

He was cut off as the pressure built up in his chest again. He fell to his knees, gasping for breath. Jess ran to him.

"Get back!" he shouted.

He struggled to hold it in. He could feel the power trying to escape from every pore. His vision started to fade again. The static of the white light was creeping in and eventually blinded him again. He screamed and felt like he was going to burst.

After a loud crack and a whine of white noise, the white faded back again, clearing his vision. He realized he was no longer on the roof.

Still on his knees, he looked up at the sky. The stars were bright and many with no light pollution to interrupt them. As he looked around, the barren landscape was illuminated by the moon with a blue-white glow. Cacti and scrub grass surrounded him. His hands clutched dry, rocky sand as he collapsed forward onto them. The air was cool, dry, and clean. Wherever he was, it was both far away from people and far away from home.

The pressure was returning. He could feel the power welling up again. He hoped that his next outburst would take him back to where he was.

His vision faded to white.

There was another pop and a buzz in his ears. When his vision returned, he was back on the rooftop. Jess was sprawled out with her back on the gravel.

He slowly stood up.

"Jess," he said, "What happened?"

"What?" she shouted, climbing to her feet.

"What happened back there?" he shouted.

"I can barely hear you," she shouted, "You disappeared in some kind of energy explosion with a really loud boom then you came back the same way. My ears are ringing badly right now."

"Sorry," Josh shouted, "I didn't mean to do that."

"You need to get rid of this excess power," Jess shouted, "You obviously can't control yourself and you don't know what you're doing."

"No way," Josh said, "I've never felt better. I'm good now. I think I burned off enough that I shouldn't have a problem."

"Josh," she said, sternly, "Seriously, this is dangerous."

"This is awesome," he said, "I teleported to the desert. Like, four thousand miles from here. I can travel as energy. I can throw lightning whenever I want. I can fly. I'm a freaking God!"

He turned toward the edge of the roof and raised his hands, letting long arcs of electricity crackle from his fingers. The lights of nearby buildings flickered as the energy jumped to their steel frames.

"And now, young Skywalker," he said, imitating a voice and nodding, "You will die."

He laughed maniacally as he unleashed the power. Lightning flew through the night sky. The cement buildings were getting scorched by his discharge. Windows cracked and exploded into the air.

He felt powerful. For the first time since this entire thing started, he felt like he should. He felt like a man without limits.

He felt a sudden jarring sensation, as if someone was jabbing him in the side with their elbow.

"I'm Palpatine!" he blurted as he shot up in his seat.

"You're snoring," Jess said, "Loudly."

Josh raised an eyebrow, looking around to find that he was sitting in the driver's seat of his car. They were on the top floor of a parking garage downtown.

He quickly inspected his clothes - no charring, no smoldering, no molten shoe soles. He looked at Jess in the passenger seat as she stared, irritated, at him.

"Seriously," Jess said, "Anyone ever test you for sleep apnea?"

"What happened," Josh said, "How did we get here?"

"You drove us here hours ago," she said.

"We were on top of that building," Josh said, pointing to the rooftop, "I powered up. I teleported."

"We sat here," Jess said, "Because I told you how stupid it would be to go all the way up there when I've got the exact same surveillance capability right here. You whined about it and then you crashed out twenty minutes into our 'patrol'. I guess Phalanx was right about the sleep catching up with you."

"My clothes were burned," Josh said, "My shoes were melted. I shoved my hand into a giant fuse box and got electrocuted."

"You snored and quoted movies in your sleep for six hours," Jess said, "I know you were bound to crash, but next time, come prepared. We're supposed to be superheroes. We should at least try to stay vigilant."

Josh closed his eyes and sighed deeply, pinching the bridge of his still-masked nose.

"It was so vivid," he said, "My ears are still ringing from the teleports. I feel so drained."

"Probably because you forgot your batteries," Jess said.

Josh checked his pockets and looked at her when he realized they were empty.

"Seriously?" he said.

"Apparently," she answered, "You ok to drive, Sleeping Beauty? We should go home. Our shift is over."

"Yeah," Josh said, still confused, "Yeah, I'm fine. Let's go."

He took of his mask and reached to start the car. For a split second, he thought he saw some yellowish dirt on his palm. When he looked again, there was nothing. He shook it off, turned the key, and left the parking lot to get them home.

\*\*\*

"You did the right thing," Phalanx said, "Stop stressing yourself out about it."

"He was so happy," Jess said, "So excited. I had to take that all away from him."

"It was best," Phalanx said, "We didn't need him flying off the handle any more than he already was."

Josh was lying on the couch in front of LENNY, passed out and immobile as the two of them looked down.

"How long does he have to be out?" Jess asked.

"At least a few days until the power bleeds off," Phalanx said, "You did a good job manipulating him into thinking his clothes were still intact and that there was no residual damage to the area. Excellent thinking to make him believe he wasn't full of electricity, too. Everything I told him about potential burnout will make it seamless. He'll never know he wasn't dreaming."

"I don't like going behind backs like this," Jess said, "It doesn't feel right."

"You're a psychic," Phalanx said, "Get used to it. If you keep worrying about every time you lie or manipulate, you're going to drive yourself insane. Trust me, I've seen it happen."

"There's no way that will go unnoticed," Jess said, "There's going to be footage of it, not to mention the entire building was out of power. That's practically front-page in this town."

"I've set LENNY to media blackout mode for the event," Phalanx said, "If we keep Josh here after he wakes up in a couple days, it'll blow over like it never even happened."

"At least someone besides Kurt knows how to use that thing," Jess said, shaking her head.

"The only loose end is the two of us," he said, "You can't manipulate me, but I'm not telling. As long as you don't mention it, we're in the clear."

"He's pretty determined from what I could tell," Jess said, "This probably won't be the last time he tries to 'power up'."

"We'll cross that bridge when we come to it," Phalanx said, "Until then, keep it tight and try not to let him do anything stupid until we know he's ready."

"Fine," Jess said, sighing.

"It won't be easy," Phalanx said, "Being the psychic in a group like this never is."

She looked down at the floor of the cave and closed her eyes.

"Good night," said Phalanx, "Make sure you get some sleep."

To her, that was a more difficult proposition than anything else she'd done that night.

## XXIII

"You rang?" said Phalanx, pointing to the VII button he now wore on his lapel.

"I did," Kurt said, "Sit down."

Kurt's lab cave was as much a mess as his appearance, but had a few workstation stools not currently covered in electronic detritus. Phalanx took a moment to find one, brushed it off, and sat down.

"So," Phalanx said, "To what do I owe the pleasure? Your girlfriend can't even get an audience with you anymore. I feel almost honored to be summoned."

"Don't start," Kurt said, "I've been..."

"Busy," Phalanx interrupted, "I know. We all know. I can almost understand where you're coming from, but your friends are having a harder time with it."

"I'm not really concerned with being sociable right now," Kurt said, "I've just had a breakthrough and I wanted to run at least one idea by you, since you've been organizing the training activities."

"I'm listening," Phalanx said.

Kurt turned to a console and punched a few keys.

A small object on the table next to him came to life. It was a black dome with brushed metal trim around four inches in diameter. It emitted a blue glow and the whine of white noise. Once it warmed up, a six-inch tall hologram of Phalanx appeared. It looked like a small statue or action figure. It was opaque and the colorization was almost perfect.

"Impressive," said Phalanx, leaning in to take a closer look, "Good likeness, too."

"It should be," Kurt said, "I used the parameters of your avatar from the pin. Based on that, I can adjust the numbers and make it look like pretty much anyone."

Kurt put his hand on the keyboard and the small hologram shifted, becoming a likeness of a cleaned up, normal looking Kurt as he was before the accident.

"Wow, you've really got the details in there," Phalanx said, "Down to the ripped jeans and the duct-taped shoes."

"It's just a matter of programming, really," Kurt said, "No big deal with my powers. It can pretty much generate anything I can think of if I'm touching the controls."

With his hand on the cable connecting the device to the computer, it switched between three-dimensional portraits of the entire group.

"So, how does this fit in with the training regimen?" Phalanx asked.

"In a week or so," Kurt said, "I should have a few of these ready. With a few adjustments to the parameters, they can be programmed to project life-sized holograms, relatively indistinguishable from real targets.

I was planning on mounting them on some quad-rotor drones and letting the group do a large-scale training exercise. With my technopathic abilities, I can generate small-scale AI, equivalent to a video game, program the drones and the holograms to react properly, and we can have a live combat demo."

"That's," Phalanx started, thinking for a moment, "That's actually a brilliant idea."

"Thanks," Kurt said, "I know everyone thinks I'm just avoiding people up here, but what I'm working on is for the betterment of the group. I don't feel bad about neglecting my social obligations when I'm doing things to improve our situation. I'll need your help with some of this, of course. I don't exactly have much combat experience and I'll want input on what sort of scenarios and variables you'll want them to go through."

"Sure, sounds good," Phalanx said, nodding, "Do you mind if I leave one of myself here to help you out with that? I've got other things that need tending to."

"No problem," Kurt said, "Oh, and please tell Jess not to worry about me, ok?"

"That's not going to stop her," Phalanx said, standing up but leaving another one of himself on the workstation stool.

The VII button did not replicate and went with the one standing up to leave.

"Word of advice, by the by," said the Phalanx with the button, "If you're ever going to see your girl again, make sure you take a shower. It smells like something died in here and I'm pretty sure that's you."

"You'd be right," Kurt said, smirking and turning to the seated Phalanx, "I hope it doesn't bother you."

"Trust me," said the seated Phalanx, "I've had much worse. Your hygiene is your business. Let's get to work."

The Phalanx with the button nodded to them and left the room for the main cave.

His duplicate was being nice about the smell. It was putrid and he couldn't wait to get some fresh air. It stood to reason that the stench would be palpable as Kurt hadn't come down, even to use the bathroom (at least, not when anyone could see him), in weeks. He would wonder how he was surviving if it wasn't for the delivery of a palette of military surplus MRE rations which arrived not long ago.

Jess, Justin, and Zoey were standing near the cave entrance in the main chamber as Phalanx exited.

"Yes, he's ok," Phalanx said before any of them could ask, "He's working on something pretty awesome right now but he needs some time to finish which is when, I assume, he'll make his way out of his cave. If he sees his shadow, it's six more weeks of not bathing."

"Is it that bad?" Jess asked.

"Tear gas tests have proven more tolerable," he said, "But it can all go away with a good scrub. Oh, and he says you should all stop worrying about him."

"Like that's going to happen," Jess said.

"I told him as much," Phalanx said, "Anyway, he's building a better mouse trap in there. Best to leave him to it until he's done. You won't get much out of him if you try to communicate right now."

"What kind of better mouse trap is he building?" Zoey asked.

"The kind that'll improve the way we train," Phalanx said, "I don't want to give it all away. With the boundless enthusiasm you guys showed when he revealed the communicators, you'll pretty much break him if you're not truly amazed this time around."

"I thought we were done with training," Justin said.

"You can never be done with training," Phalanx said, "I think we rushed into the active patrol thing. There's been quite a bit of property damage and that could draw some unwanted attention. They don't like it when extra-normals cause random chaos for no good reason. That's the main reason we're not on their radar."

"They?" Zoey asked, "You mean the black suits?"

"The Project," Phalanx said, "Yes."

"How do you know we're not on their radar?" Justin asked.

"I have an infallible inside source," Phalanx said, "We're not on their to-do list. They've got more interesting things to worry about at the moment. This group – our group – has always been more periphery than priority. If we do good and don't drum up more attention than urban legends in doing so, things will stay that way. The minute our hijinks hit the headlines, they'll be on us like white on rice."

"And you know all of this for sure?" Justin asked.

"I did use the word 'infallible'," Phalanx said, "You've got a sizable vocabulary, I'm sure you know what that means."

"I don't know," Justin said, "I'm still waiting for that inevitable third-act betrayal."

"I'm so sad you feel that way," Phalanx said in an unsurprised monotone, "And after all the trust we'd built up."

"Seriously," Justin said, "I know it. We had the first act basic origin story and the second act discovery and training montage. We're nearing the end of the third-act and there has to be a conflict of some kind. I don't see that coming in the form of a threat from the outside unless someone is betraying us to an enemy. The fact that everything keeps coming back to the Project makes me think that they're some kind of Sword of Damocles hanging over us and, eventually, they're going to drop right on our heads."

"You're absolutely right," Phalanx said, "And, I mean that with all sincerity. They are absolutely a threat which could become very palpable at any given time. That's part of the reason why I've been advising you this whole time: to keep that from happening. If you're looking for a third-act betrayal, it's not going to come from me; that much I can assure you."

"I hate when they talk like this," Jess said to Zoey, "I can never tell if it makes too much sense or none at all."

"There's no way to be sure, though, is there?" Justin said, continuing his conversation, "At any moment, you could drop the dime to get back in their good graces; turn the tables on us just the same as we could have turned them on you back at Josh's apartment. Sell us out to save your own skin. You're the seemingly-benevolent helper character who gets introduced in the second act. You're the most likely candidate for a turncoat."

"What about your new best friend?" Phalanx retorted, motioning to Zoey, "By that logic, you have to suspect her, too. She was a second act character addition, just like me. Not only that, but she's your love interest – your very own Manic Pixie Dream Girl, pulled straight out of an indie flick. You said it yourself once. You don't think she's hiding something? You don't think she could possibly be poised to betray you?"

"She's not," Jess said.

"Wait," Zoey said, "Don't go dragging me into this. First: I'm nobody's Manic Pixie Dream Girl. I told you that in the alley that night. Second: I'm not going to stand for objectification here. Third: I've got no reason to betray anyone, least of all the people who took me in when my life disintegrated. Lastly: who ever said I was his love interest?"

"You're not?" Justin asked.

"She's not," Jess said.

"The traitor or the other thing?" Justin asked, turning to Jess.

"You're tailor-made for it," Phalanx shouted, turning to Zoey, "You're so far out of his league that you're not even playing the same sport! All you have to do is stand around and be attractive and any of the men in this group will give you exactly what you want. You could stick a knife into Justin's back at this point and he would smile and advise you on how to twist it."

"Don't try to use me as a deflection," Zoey shouted.

"Yeah," Justin said, his finger now raised into Phalanx's face as his hair flared around the edges, "Stop dragging her into this just to distract me. This is about you, Company Man, and how you wind up being the rogue agent in our midst right before the battle starts just to patch things up with your little agency."

"Stop saying that," Phalanx said, "You have no idea what they put me through and no idea what I am willing to go through to pay them back for every single indiscretion."

"Please," Justin said, "Like you couldn't be lying about that. You've been the one shepherding us through all of this. You're a big part of why this is playing out like the plot of a movie. As 'director', of course you're going to try to dissuade the audience from thinking it's you because you're the obvious choice."

"Your girl fits better," Phalanx said.

"I'm not his girl!" Zoey shouted, "I'm no one's girl!"

"Stop!" Jess shouted.

They all paused.  Jess wasn't sure if this was some manifestation of her power brought on by frustration or whether they were all legitimately surprised.  She took a deep breath and started to speak.

"Zoey, I don't want you to take this the wrong way, but I've been through your mind pretty extensively and I thought I had communicated to at least one other person earlier that you are most definitely not a plant, spy, or double-agent of any kind.  In fact, I've been through everyone's minds in our group, including those among us without powers, and I can safely say that we haven't been infiltrated by any number of implausible duplicates, replicants, pod people, androids, or straight-up traitors.  I can't say the same about Phalanx because he's unreadable for reasons he still hasn't explained and which I may not want to know.  I can say for sure that he's been pretty up-front with me about most things and I have even come to trust him to a degree.  So, can we please lay off the spy-game name calling and all the predictive literature stuff and concentrate on moving forward?"

The three others stared in silence at her, then looked each other over.

"Uh," Justin said, "Sorry, guys, I guess I got kinda carried away."

Phalanx straightened his lapels and fixed his tie.

"Completely understandable," he said, "You're actually smart to have misgivings about me.  And, Zoey, I'm sorry I pulled you into this.  I shouldn't have been so harsh toward you and I shouldn't have objectified you."

"Apology or not," she said, her eyes darting between Justin and Phalanx, "I'm not going to stand for it.  You keep using that literary term - Manic Pixie Dream Girl - treating me like I'm some kind of object or achievement.  Is that really all you think of me?"

Justin looked at her sheepishly, steeling himself and trying to choose the proper words.

"In the interest of full disclosure," Justin said, "As was mentioned, I did once use that term to describe you.  It was in a private conversation with a confidant and certainly not with any derivative of Agent Sneaky over here who was obviously spying on us for longer than we realized."

"That's not the point," Zoey said, "You still used the term to describe me; is that what you think I really am?  I'm not some quirky girl who's here to fix your sad, cynical world view with my 'carefree' attitude while we slowly but surely fall for each other.  In case you missed it, my outlook on things isn't exactly rainbows and unicorns.  I've got some very serious issues to work through and I'm too busy fixing  my own broken things to make your recovery from sad-sack land my sole purpose in life.

"When I kissed you, we were both in a really bad place. I saw an opportunity to shed a little light by doing something which would make us both feel a little bit better. I thought it was cute that you were so awkward about it and that did contribute to me being attracted to you but I am not by far anyone's pure ray of sunshine nor do I belong - or want to be - on a pedestal. If something develops between us – now or later – then that's wonderful but you should concentrate on fixing yourself instead of worrying about my place in your story and hoping that I'll do it all for you. It's too much pressure.

"I agreed with you when you said it was like we were walking around in an origin story. I've read enough comics and seen enough movies to know where things were going but it's just plain selfish to think that you're the well-written hero and I'm the just 'the girl'. If this is a story, didn't you give any thought to the other characters? Were you so self-centered that you remained, in your mind, the hero while assigning the rest of us stupid archetypes according to how you thought we fit? Phalanx is the traitor, Jess is the voice of reason, and I'm just 'the girl'? As if I have no characterization – no purpose of my own – aside from being a vapid love interest with my only reason for being to prop you up from the darkness and help you see the light again? Did it ever occur once in your narrative-driven mind that we've all got an equal share in this? That, for better or worse, we're all in this together? Did you ever even bother to contemplate that you're in a team comic and not a solo title?"

Justin was speechless. Quick and witty responses shot through his head at every turn of her speech but didn't have time to manifest as she expertly dissected his exact pattern of thought. He had been reduced to rubble, as if she'd gone into his head and kicked down all the columns that held up his brain. He had been called out before in his life but never so perfectly as this.

She gave him a full minute for a response. All he could do was stare, slack-jawed, at her as his mind puddled and leaked from his ears. Jess and Phalanx offered nothing, either. They were paralyzed by awkwardness and the fear that she could unexpectedly disassemble them in the same way.

When she realized none of them had anything to say in response, Zoey made a fist. She thrust it, upward facing, directly into Justin's line of vision. Her pale middle finger with chipped glitter-blue nail polish extended fully, five inches from the tip of Justin's nose.

"How's this for a third act betrayal?" she asked, keeping the finger in place for a moment before turning on her heels and heading for the entrance of the cave.

They all stared as she left in a huff.

"Don't worry," Jess whispered, "She'll be back eventually. She was just making a point."

"I should go talk to her," Justin said, quietly.

"You shouldn't," Jess said, "She gave you a chance at rebuttal and you didn't take it. Probably the smart move in the long run, though I'm sensing your lack of response wasn't really by choice. Let it go for now. She needs some time to calm down and you need time to figure out what just happened."

"What just happened?" Justin asked, echoing.

"All the crap got washed away," said Phalanx, "Harsh though it may have been; she made you realize the one thing you were missing: this isn't your story, it's our story, and maybe it's not a story after all. This is real and it just happened to conform to a standard. You sound dismayed when you're able to predict events and assign values to people based on pop-culture tropes but really it's the only way you've been keeping yourself from seeing how insane this situation really is.

"Example: you think you should go talk to her because that's what would probably happen in the next scene. By your estimation, once you catch up with her, you'll have a bit of an argument but you'll be able to redeem yourself in that instant by saying something clever. Then, you say something that makes her laugh. Then, the whole thing turns into a makeout session with the romantic theme of the movie playing in the background because that is the first step toward the climax of act three.

"That is not reality. No matter how much you want it to be. It's a poor assumption based on pure fiction."

"I've been right so far, haven't I?" Justin asked, his voice pleading, his face distressed.

"You didn't predict Zoey," Phalanx said, "Or her attraction to you, or her motive behind that kiss. You adjusted the path of the story in your mind once it happened and you started playing the part of the maladjusted post-modern protagonist. The reality of that is no matter how much respect you think you've given her to this point, you wanted her to be your Manic Pixie Dream Girl and you idealized her as such. You turned your own plotline from superhero blockbuster to mopey indie flick in one simple move.

"She's right, too. Ever since that moment, you've been treating this like you're the main character when you've got a party of six other main characters running along with you, Zoey included. If you keep thinking that way, you're going to wind up doing something stupid and your part of the story will be over long before the ultimate conclusion.

"She gave you a third act betrayal that played into your story. Maybe now you can concentrate on other things."

Justin's eyes were blank. He could feel his brain trying to regain its shape, but it remained a formless mush inside his head for the moment.

"I think I'm going to go lie down," Justin said, walking away to one of the side chambers and out of the room.

"That went better than I thought," Jess said once he was gone, "I was expecting explosions."

"You think we should keep an eye on him?" Phalanx asked.

"He'll be fine," Jess said, tapping her head, "I can watch him from here. He's just confused. You and Zoey did a pretty good job of breaking his entire world. He's going to need some time."

"He's got a week," Phalanx said, "We'll need him in top shape once the new training regimen is ready. If there's anything you can do to speed up his recovery, I suggest you do it."

Jess feigned a small salute as Phalanx returned to Kurt's lab cave.

Justin sat at the end of a row of folding chairs in the cave designated the "boys locker room" by the group. He was the first one here and was already dressed and ready to go.

He'd taken Zoey's suggestion from a while back and decided to mask only his face, leaving his smoke hair exposed and smoldering. He purchased "action glasses" for himself - a pair of welding goggles with tinted prescription lenses and heat-resistant metal – in light of what had happened previously with Phalanx. He didn't want to go blind in the middle of a fight.

Instead of a bandana to cover his nose and mouth, he used a high-end paint respirator painted gloss black with flames, like a hot rod. Thinking about it now, he planned the goggles out much better than the mask, which would probably melt if he had another episode. He would have to see if anything more high-test was available or if Kurt could work something out for him.

He sat staring at the wall, waiting for the others to show. It had been the prescribed week Kurt had asked for in unveiling his "surprise". It had also been a week since Zoey verbally eviscerated him and his ideals and he was still in recovery.

Reconfiguring his mind had taken up most of his time lately. He worked to adjust his perspective; to abandon the literary stereotypes which had been guiding his perception from the beginning. Mostly he was doing it because the pretty girl told him to but he couldn't shake the feeling that something big was still in the works and would happen soon. He was waiting for that I-told-you-so moment when he could say that he was right all along. Provided whatever it was didn't kill them first.

Phalanx entered the room with his usual smirking face.

"You ok?" Phalanx asked.

"I guess," Justin said, "It's tough thinking around it. Everything is still falling into place so perfectly, I can't see it any other way."

"I know," Phalanx said, the smirk turning into a more serious expression, "Believe it or not, I agree with you on this one. I can feel something coming, too. There's going to be a game-changing climax at some point soon. I just want you to know that, whatever happens, I didn't have a part in bringing it about. At least not directly or to my knowledge."

"I haven't really been able to sleep," Justin said, "Do you ever get over the anxiety?"

"No," Phalanx said, sitting near him, "When you know they're after you, you have every right to be paranoid. Even when you're sure the day is won, you never lose that edge. You can, however, learn to control it; at least to the point where it's not so outwardly apparent."

"I just want to get some rest," Justin said, "We're sitting here with some mystery hanging over our heads. It has to happen according to the narrative or else the end of the book is going to be a big letdown and there won't be a sequel. Either because we'll lose the reader's interest or we'll all be dead."

"When you put it that way," Phalanx said, "It does sound quite a bit crazier than I realized. Maybe you should lay off the literary end of it and concentrate on the now."

They sat in silence for the moment, Justin returning his stare to the wall.

"Why are we dressing up?" Justin asked.

"It's the first big training activity," Phalanx said, "If it's going to be as close to a real situation as possible, you might as well see how all of your costumes perform."

"Well, I'm ready," Budda said, walking into the room.

He wore a pair of track pants and a knit cap with his VII button pinned to his forehead. Nothing else.

"Not exactly much of a costume," Phalanx said.

"I don't need a costume to fight crime," Budda said, "I need a costume to go out in public. When I'm in crimefighter mode, I don't have to hide what I am. I look much more intimidating this way, anyway."

"You're not wearing any shoes," Phalanx said, pointing at his slate-blue stone feet.

"Rocks don't need shoes," Budda said.

"Apparently, rocks don't need shirts, either," Justin said, "Of course, you took your shirt off at any opportunity when you were human. Why should anything be different now?"

"You're just jealous of my chiseled physique," Budda said, striking a flexed pose.

"Never use that joke again," Justin said, plainly.

Mike and Josh arrived, both in costume save their masks. They had both decided to wear long black coats, as had Justin. It was an unofficial dress code and apparently Budda had missed the memo. They would eventually discuss the wardrobe choice as a reflection of pop-culture causing them to associate long black coats with unbridled badassery, but right now they had a little more to do to get ready.

Mike produced a mask which covered everything from the tip of his nose to the back of his head, including his hair. A white arrow streaked across the black cloth like a Mohawk with its point ending between the eyeholes. The ties of the mask fell long behind his head and, as Budda had seen in person, would flap dramatically in the wind when conditions allowed.

Josh set himself apart by wearing a brightly colored Hawaiian shirt under his coat. His mask was the same domino he'd been wearing on the streets along with a fedora. The guys would agree with Justin that he still looked like a hobo Green Hornet. Josh didn't care. He did find it difficult to wear his glasses along with the mask, but was never one for contact lenses. This left him constantly pushing his glasses up as they slipped down the fabric at the bridge of his nose.

"Gang's all here, then," Phalanx said, "Let's go meet the ladies."

The ladies, as it turns out, were already waiting in the main chamber. Their outfits set the collective males' jaws agape.

Jess wore a black punker-style jacket over a low-cut, bright pink t-shirt bearing a black broken heart logo at the low point of the neck. Her legs were covered by a matching short, pink skirt which showed off her fishnet-covered legs and the tall black leather boots which rose to her knees. Her face was covered in her blank-expressioned white masquerade mask which now bore the black broken heart logo in the center of its forehead.

Zoey, on the other hand, was using her ice hair to obscure her identity. It was formed into a medieval-style helm, slit with a thin T for vision and breathing. Her ensemble was a strange sort of nega-goth image – a white corseted top with a short white skirt and white fake-leather boots. She wore black-and-white striped stockings on her legs with a matching arm-warmer stretching to her elbow.

The boys were silent in their awe.

"Well," said Phalanx, finally, "You girls sure clean up nice."

"Thanks," said Jess, "Did you boys get a group rate on the trench coats?"

"Trench coats are the mark of a bonafide badass," Josh retorted.

"Yeah," Zoey said, "If you're in a movie in the mid-to-late 90s. I thought we were going for comic book, not poorly-scripted gritty reboot television show."

"Hey," Justin said, "I put in a lot of time on my look. And, I took your advice."

"I know," Zoey said, "It looks great. The matching trench coats make the three of you look like you're going to go out hacking computers circa Y2K, though."

"They're cool," Mike asserted, "End of story."

"In a retro-ironic way," Zoey said, "Sure. If it was only one of you wearing a trench, it would be cool. Right now you look like the three guys at Con who dressed as different versions of the same character."

"Can we concentrate on the issue at hand," Phalanx interrupted, "And worry about the wardrobe choices later? Kurt is setting up as we speak. We need to get to the site and get ready to go."

"What are we even doing, anyway?" Jess asked.

"Something very special," Phalanx said, "I promised not to spoil the surprise. You'll see when we get there. Now, let's roll."

Without much comment, they went upstairs and packed themselves into the back of a black panel van which ostensibly belonged to Phalanx. There were no full seats in the back of the van, only benches attached to the walls. This allowed for Budda to sit with his back against the rear door, his legs stretched forward.  Such were the perils of an eight-foot tall rock-man being on your team.

The ride was silent and slightly awkward.  Everyone had heard about what had gone down between Zoey and Justin last week and this was the first time the two of them had been in the same room for an extended period since then.  If that wasn't enough, they were sitting next to each other.

"You look," Justin started, moving his respirator away from his mouth, "You look awesome."

"You too," Zoey said, her expression unable to be seen through the thin slit of her helmet, "I'm glad you took my advice.  Leaving the smoke hair exposed looks very cool.  The goggles and the respirator give you kind of a steampunky feel."

"You've got a whole borderline renaissance faire thing going on," Justin said, "I really dig the helmet."

"Can we skip past the awkward part," Josh said, loudly and in full range of everyone present, "And just say you guys are cool with each other again?"

They both stared at him.  He glared back.

"Yeah," Justin stammered, "I guess."

"Sure," Zoey said, "Makes it easier for everyone."

"Good," Josh said, "Now kiss her or put your mask back on, Justin."

They both blushed, though it was impossible to see.  She did not retract her helmet, so he didn't make a move.  He didn't really feel now was the time, and put his respirator back on.  There were more important things to worry about than potential romance at the moment.

Josh's comment, which he thought would disarm the tension, actually made the ride to whatever site Kurt had arranged more awkward and silent.

Inside of an hour, the van came to a stop.  The Phalanx sitting in the passenger seat hopped out to open the doors for them.  The one in the driver's seat remained.

The side door of the van slid open causing most of the group to squint in the mid-day sun.

When eyes adjusted and everyone was out of the van, they looked over the burnt out industrial area to which Phalanx had brought them.

The ground was parched earth with a thick layer of dust and rocks, enough that they left footprints as they walked.  Large buildings were now empty of machinery which once helped turn the wheels of an empire.  Smoke stacks and boilers and a large blast furnace were forgotten relics left to rust in this patch of nowhere.  It was, in Phalanx's opinion, the perfect place for this.  Isolated, abandoned, and varied.

"Ladies and gentlemen," Phalanx said, "Allow me to introduce you to the next step in your training."

A very large man stepped out from around the corner of the closest long building. The black suit and the glint of red from his lapel caused him to be quickly identified, if his bald head and eyebrow piercings weren't enough.

The group was shocked to their collective core. None of them could process what they were seeing at this moment. The bald agent, the one from the hospital, was casually strolling towards them with a smirk on his face. He looked to be dressed for battle in a black jumpsuit with a large red metal shoulder pad above his left arm rather than the black suit they'd seen him in before. He stopped ten feet from them and looked to Phalanx.

"This," Phalanx said, "Is Agent Moorsblade - the current leader of the Project's field team."

They knew who he was. They just couldn't put thoughts into words. Some of them out of surprise, some of them out of fear, some of them out of sheer curiosity.

"Afternoon, folks," said Moorsblade, calmly, in his smooth southern drawl, "I take it from the looks on your faces that y'all might remember seeing me once before."

Finally, Justin turned to Phalanx and muttered:

"You son of a bitch."

"Oh, come on, now," Phalanx said, "It's not what it looks like."

"You son of a bitch," Justin repeated, louder, flames leaping from his head, "You lied to me! You lied to us!"

"Calm down," Phalanx said, frantically, "It was just a joke. Just a sample. We're messing with you. Kurt!"

Suddenly, Agent Moorsblade dissolved into digital interference and was replaced by a small quad-rotor drone hovering in place where his head had been. It was an unrefined thing; a simple toy with a camera and a black dome seemingly duct taped to it.

"Seriously?" Budda asked.

The drone lowered to a shorter height and an image of Kurt as he was before his self-imposed isolation appeared where Moorsblade once stood.

"Sorry," Kurt said, smiling, "I thought some of you might get a kick out of that."

"I should give a kick out of that," Justin said, "For a minute, all of my nightmares came true."

"Anyway," Kurt said, "This is the surprise. Holo-emitting drones. It's better than building something like a danger room because they're portable and independently programmable. Plus, these holo-emitters are very expensive and complicated to make, not to mention the complexity of the programming involved though that's really kind of a moot point for me. Long story short, it would be almost impossible within a small amount of time to prepare enough of these that I could simulate an environment and targets. I don't think even I have the capability to build a computer system to handle that many variables. So, here we are."

Six more drones hovered out from around various corners. The black domes strapped unceremoniously to them flickered to life and presented seven identical images of Kurt.

"These were all I could do on short notice," the Kurts said in chorus, "Some of the parts I've been using are now on backorder. I'm hoping to get more up and running as soon as I can."

Jess approached a Kurt and tried to tap it on the chest with her pointer finger. It went right through the image as if it wasn't even there. The image was so incredibly life like that it even showed the shadow of her finger as she poked.

"So that's how that feels," Jess said, reflecting.

"No forcefields or anything, unfortunately," Kurt said, "I don't have these things at Star Trek level yet. You won't be able to feel anything these things do to you. Their fists and whatever extensions they may manifest will pass right through you. I advise you, for the purposes of these exercises, to play along. I've rigged your comm-buttons to register hits, so I'll know when you're down. If you hit the bad guys, they'll react in kind. The only thing I ask is to avoid hitting the very top of the head."

All of the Kurts now appeared headless and the drones hovered there.

"That's where the sensitive machinery is and I won't be pleased if any of these get damaged," Kurt continued, "You shouldn't be practicing headshots anyway. We're not killers, we're super heroes. Go for the body until I can figure something out to keep the guts shielded."

"Dude," Mike said, interrupting the safety lecture, "This is incredible. This is video games in real life. That's what you invented."

"Well, that's not really the point," Kurt said, "But I see what you're saying."

"So, who are we playing against?" Josh asked, "Team Kurt?"

"No," Phalanx said, "We have something better lined up."

Six of the holograms, after some digital interference, changed into six figures in black jumpsuits. Three of them were familiar to everyone.

"This is the current Project field team," Phalanx said, "Agents Moorsblade, Briggs, and Williams you have seen before; the brute, the psychic, and the leader. These other three are new to you.

He walked down the line, stopping at the stumpy half-man, half-bulldog.

"This is Agent D'Angelo," he said, "Firearm and heavy weapon specialist."

He stopped at a very young looking man with thick hipsterish glasses and a gigantic robotic arm which looked like it would drag behind him on the ground.

"Agent Richards," he said, "Techie with a lot of gadgets at his disposal."

The last one was a female in a smooth black helmet, her face unidentifiable.

"Intel hasn't revealed the name or face of this Agent yet," said Phalanx, "All we know is that she is female and is extremely skilled in both long and short range combat. We're not entirely sure of her abilities, either. She's new and for whatever reason she's not yet fully on the Project's books."

"I'll be playing myself," Kurt said, "We're going to be doing a take-and-hold mission. This drone, as me, is going off to hide somewhere in the complex. Your goal is to find me and bring me back to your base, the van, before the Project team can do it. I've constructed rudimentary AI out of the little info we could get on them, so you'll have some decent opponents. It'll be fair, too; their programs run autonomously and they won't know where I am. Feel free to use all the powers at your disposal to accomplish the goal, just try not to destroy these little guys."

Josh raised his hand like a remote control and shut off all the Project drones. They clattered to the ground unceremoniously. He walked to Kurt's projection and grabbed it by the arm.

"We win," Josh said, smiling.

Everyone laughed except the Kurt projection who stared a hole through Josh.

"Seriously?" Kurt said as the drones turned back on and lifted back into their positions before resuming their projections. Now the entire Project team was staring at Josh.

"I know," Josh said, "I know. Stay in the spirit of the game."

"Please," Kurt said, "And don't think I won't know you're cheating, people."

The group finished laughing before Kurt's projection said:

"Come on, Mike, let my guys go."

Everyone looked at him.

"What?" Mike said, "Forcefields are my thing. If his guys can't move, we win, right? So, we win. Again."

"Spirit of the game," Kurt's projection cried.

"Oh, fine," Mike said, waving his hand, "I could also increase the gravity around your little drones and bring them down to the ground. You should be happy I'm not doing any real damage."

"Stick to projectile-based attacks for the time being, Mike," Phalanx said.

"Not much of a live-fire exercise if not all of us can use our full capability," Justin bemoaned.

"Yeah," Jess said, "Not all of us have projectile-based or hand-to-hand combat power sets. I can't do what I would probably want to do against holographic targets.."

"You'll have to think of something," Phalanx said, "Maybe some telekinesis."

"That's like giving a concert pianist a three-bar xylophone and asking them to play Liszt," Jess said, "I'm going to be so under-utilized."

"Deal with it," Phalanx said, unsympathetically, walking over to the projection of Joey, "If this were real, this one would be exuding a negative psychic field, blocking most of your powers anyway.  It's a unique little quirk she discovered that keeps her team safe from people like you."

"Great," Jess said, "So, not only will I be ineffective in this fight, I'll be ineffective in a real one, too."

"Try not to let it get you down," Phalanx said, rolling his eyes, "You can still manipulate the minds of ninety-nine-point-nine-nine percent of the populace.  Your puppet-mastering days are far from over."

"Any more objections?" asked the image of Kurt.

When the group was silent and shaking their heads to the negative, all the images except Kurt's blinked out and the six drones flew off into the abandoned industrial mess.

"Remember, first group to get to me and bring me back to their area wins," he said, "But you have to find me first.  Ready, set, go!"

Kurt blinked out and his drone whizzed off, too fast for any of them to follow.

"Ok, gang," Phalanx said, "Let's get to work."

## XXV

"We have to go," Mike screamed in his face, "NOW!"

"Budda," Justin coughed, his voice groggy from just waking up from unconsciousness, "Get Budda."

"He's gone," Mike shouted, "Get up, we have to go now!"

"He was moving," Justin muttered, "I saw it. You have to get him."

"Dammit," Mike said, shouting off behind him, "Someone grab rock boy, I've got Justin!"

"Yeah," Budda shouted, "Someone help me!"

Budda was crawling toward the gaping hole in the longhouse wall, doing the best he could for having only one arm. Zoey and Josh both grabbed his outstretched hand and started dragging him toward the van outside.

Mike had helped Justin to his feet, throwing Justin's arm over his shoulder and moving him as quickly as possible outside of the collapsing building, almost throwing him into the back of the black panel van. Justin nearly stepped on Jess's legs as she leaned limp with a vacant stare on her face. Josh and Zoey got what was left of Budda into the back as Mike shouted: "Go, go, go!"

The van sped off, skidding through the dirt with a rumble, kicking up gravel as it navigated the narrow alleys back to the entrance.

"What," Justin struggled, "What the hell happened back there?"

\*\*\*

"This place is pretty cool," Zoey remarked, "Lots of history here. Lots of art."

"Lots of tetanus, too," Justin said, regarding the copious amounts of rotting oxidized scaffolding left over from when the place had long ago been active.

"Be quiet," Jess said, "You want to give us away?"

"It's only an exercise," Justin said, "What's the worst Kurt can do with his little holograms?"

"Still," Jess said, "I'd like to win."

They crept through one of the long buildings which, judging from the large gantry crane high above at nearly roof level, used to handle a lot of the heavy lifting for this place. Train tracks imbedded in the concrete, untouched for years, billed this place as some kind of loading and unloading zone. Huge banks of windows, dusty to the point of being opaque, let light through in the many spots through which rocks had likely been thrown by any number of trespassers. Graffiti of all levels of artistry was plastered over every reachable and even less-than-reachable inch of the interior. Some of the pieces were so intricate it was difficult for all of them not to stop and take notice as if they were in a gallery. They had to remember the task at hand and Jess would continuously remind them about her desire to win.

Plants had sprouted from out of gathered dirt piles. There were ponds of orange water far below the holes in the sagging roof; refugee snow-melt which had made the long commute through the maze of metal it was helping to slowly devour. It was probably one of the most interesting places any of them had ever seen.

Zoey's ice katana clanged as it accidentally impacted with the upper part of a broken ladder whose bottom half they were now walking over. Jess turned and shushed her quickly. Zoey shrugged. She was on rear-sweep which meant she was walking backwards with Justin's hand on her shoulder to guide her. None of them knew that was going to happen.

They all stopped, now extra vigilant, waiting for some kind of retribution for the error of their loud sound.

As it came, Zoey saw it and broke contact with Justin in time for her to slice, cutting the hologram of the woman in the black helmet off at the knees just as she was about to put a fist into Jess's face on her blind side.

"Down," said Kurt's voice through the still hovering quad-rotor, "Returning to spawn."

"I didn't even hear her coming," Jess said.

"She's supposed to be able to move in complete silence," Justin said, "Isn't that what Phalanx said?"

"Good eye, Zoey," Jess said, "Thanks."

"Nothing doing," Zoey said, "I had the shot and I took it."

"Y'all sure are doing a lot of talking," said the southern drawl, entering the huge room from the back door, "Thought you were supposed to be stealthy and what not."

"That's the field leader," Justin said, "The one Phalanx called the brute. Moorsblade or something."

"Is that what he called me?" asked Moorsblade, "Brother, I'm so much better than a brute and, at the same time, so very much worse."

A chilling grin came over his face.

"Ok, this one is giving me goosebumps," Justin said, "I'll handle it. Pow, pow, pow!"

He held his hand up like a gun and fanned his thumb like a hammer. Three fireballs shot out and impacted on Moorsblade's chest.

Moorsblade looked down at himself. The black jumpsuit he wore had not even singed. He took a step forward.

"Hey," Justin said, "These things are supposed to go down when they get hit, aren't they?"

He fanned at his thumb again. This time, Moorsblade shifted and blocked the fireballs with the huge, red, metal shoulder pad on his left arm. He took another step forward.

"Kurt," Justin said after tapping his communicator, "I think your thing is broken."

There was no response.

"Justin," Jess said, "I think we've got a problem."

"Yeah, this thing is broken," Justin repeated, "I don't care what Kurt said, I'm frying the drone."

He aimed carefully down his finger and one fireball shot into the forehead of Moorsblade. Upon impact, Moorsblade blinked, then his grin turned to a frown.

"That actually hit you, didn't it?" Justin asked.

Moorsblade nodded.

"Aw, crap," Justin muttered.

In a streak of black and red, Moorsblade was in front of him. Justin's nose was level with his sternum. The girls slowly backed away. Justin didn't know what to do.

"A little bird told us," said Moorsblade, "That y'all were taking a little field trip to get some exercise. We figured that for an opportunity to stop on by and snatch you up."

"What little bird?" Justin asked.

"Oh, you know," said Moorsblade, "The kind that squawks. Anyway, we figured since you were all a bit far from civilization with everyone together, now would be the best time to get you all. See, the thought was that when one or only a few of you left, we couldn't take you because the others would wonder what happened. Also, we weren't about to raid your house and show our hand. We had to wait for an opportunity just like this. Thanks to our bird, we knew it was coming."

"Does that bird copy himself into identical other birds?" Justin asked.

"I can neither confirm nor deny that," Moorsblade said, grinning again, "Can't reveal the sources of our intel now, can we?"

"Johnny," called out a voice from the back door, "Leave them alone."

Phalanx stepped into the light.

"Well, as I live and breathe," said Moorsblade, turning around, "Speak of the devil and he shall appear. How you been, P.H.? Long time no see."

"What the hell are you doing here, Johnny?" asked Phalanx.

"Oh, are we still playing that game?" Moorsblade said, turning back to Justin, "Sorry, I just hate to ruin the surprise. Can you forget that last part I said about speaking of the devil? He's not the devil, he's your friend. There's no way he contacted us and arranged to trade y'all for his freedom. Oh, dang, I did it again."

"Stop it, John," asked Phalanx, "Why are you really here?"

"Keep playing dumb," Moorsblade said, "Nothing in the deal said you had to remain a hero to these guys and I don't really much care for lying. You called up, said you wanted to make an exchange, said we'd be especially interested in the psychic and the techie and maybe the elementalists. We told you we'd take the lot and you could go free."

"That's a lie," Phalanx said, "Don't believe him, guys."

The smoke on Justin's head was beginning to flare up.

"Oh, believe me," Moorsblade said, "Here, listen to the sound bite."

Moorsblade tapped at the silver bracer on his wrist.

"They'll all be there," Phalanx's voice said, echoing through the building, "Take me off your little 'most wanted' list and I'll give you the details. I know you've taken your eye off of them and you're not really paying attention, but there's some serious talent developing here that might go to waste otherwise."

"You sold us out to save yourself," Justin stated, his hair now burning tall, his fists clenched and heating up, "Just like I knew you would."

"Come on," shouted Phalanx in disgust, "That's so fake it's ridiculous! What did you do? Patch together a bunch of samples of my voice to get that?"

"He made the call directly to Agent Williams," said Moorsblade, his grin widening, "Yesterday. Told us it would be easy because you'd be fighting holograms of us. Told us we could sneak right up on you without you even knowing because the things were so damn realistic."

"That's a bunch of crap, guys," Phalanx said, "You should know me better than that."

"If you had the element of surprise, then why are you standing here monologue-ing?" Zoey asked, "Shouldn't you have just black-bagged us and taken us away?"

"I like to break things," Moorsblade said, smiling at her, "I like to watch people squirm and suffer. I wanted to break your spirit right before the end; watch the hope slowly drain out of you. What can I say, I'm an incurable sadist."

"I think you're underestimating us," Zoey said, "You're cocky because you don't think we can really take you guys."

"Us guys?" Moorsblade said, "Honey, all of you couldn't take little old me on my own, let alone with a team backing me up. Not even sparky here can really do anything to me."

"I don't want you," Justin said, his hair now a two-foot tall fire, "I want him."

He pointed past Moorsblade with a red hot finger to Phalanx.

"Seriously?" Phalanx asked with a sigh.

Moorsblade laughed.

"Well," said the very large Agent, "I suppose that wasn't in the deal. Guess I could give you a shot before—"

"Justin, get down!" Jess shouted, interrupting.

He dove to the side as Budda was in the air, his hands clasped together to deliver a flying double-axe handle to the bald head of

254

Moorsblade, like a wrestler jumping from the top turnbuckle. The two of them tangled up, large fists flying with incredible speed and power at each other. Each blow landing seemed to shake the building.

Justin stood up, turned away from the melee, and raised his open palm toward Phalanx who was still standing with a shocked look on his face near the back door of the building. Phalanx faced him with a look of resolve, straightened his tie, and said:

"If you feel you must."

Just as the pulse of fire was coursing through his body, Justin was doused by a hard stream of water, like a firehose, from the gantry above. He was knocked to the floor as steam and smoke rose from him, the water extinguishing his flames. Phalanx looked up, then ran out the back door.

Zoey leapt past the deadly entanglement of the two large super-strong men and slid through the water near Justin, creating an ice dome over the two of them. She then froze the oncoming stream back to its origin – a backpack based weapon being wielded by the bulldog-man who Phalanx called their heavy weapons expert.

With a squeeze of her fist, the backpack exploded into a giant block of ice causing the dog-man to be torn from the weapon's shoulder straps and knocked down. He backed away in a crab walk as large snaking spikes grew from the ice and attempted to nail him to the catwalk. He was quickly gone from her line of sight.

Justin was out. She was trying to wake him.

Jess stood, watching the entire scene unfold, feeling rather helpless.

She had tried to read into Moorsblade's head, but found that she couldn't. As a matter of fact, none of her powers, not even her telekinesis, were functioning. At first she thought it was nerves, but then she realized what Phalanx had said about the abilities of their psychic being able to negate other psychic abilities. She found herself breaking out in a cold sweat. It was the first time since the beginning that she couldn't touch anyone's mind.

"Weird feeling, isn't it?" said a woman who was suddenly standing next to her, "Happens to all of us. At first, there's too many voices to bear. Then, you learn to tune into more specific ones. Then, it all becomes white noise until you actually want to hear something but that white noise gets to be like a security blanket. You don't even realize it's there till it's gone."

"You're the other psychic, then," Jess said, still watching the futile fight of the two invulnerable giants.

"Joey," she said, "Joey Briggs. Always nice to meet another of our kind. We're not too common. Of course, we're slightly more common than evil Superman and the rock monster over there. Most of us die after exhibiting our powers for the first time. The noise, the nose bleeds, the overstretched boundaries."

"I had some help coping," Jess said.

"So did I," said Joey, "We're lucky. It's not like there's an internet support group for psionics."

"What now, then?" Jess asked.

"We wait until the action shakes out," Joey said, "I can't use any of my abilities while I'm negating yours and there's no sense in the two of us trading blows. I've absorbed the minds of more than one martial arts master and, based on our recon, I'd dust you in a second."

"So, we just watch?" Jess asked.

"Until there's a winner," Joey said, "Then we'll see."

Jess was unsettled when she saw the expression on the other psychic's face; a knowing smile. Suddenly, she didn't like her chances.


The two heavyweights traded punches, neither of them doing damage to the other save for a few small stone chips flying from Budda every once in a while.

They locked up like professional wrestlers; their hands on each other's shoulders in a classic test of strength. Moorsblade smiled at his opponent.

Neither of them were winded. Budda couldn't breathe and Moorsblade didn't need to very often. They'd been pounding on each other with their full strength for a while now and things didn't really seem to be reaching any kind of conclusion.

"You're tough," Moorsblade said, "I'll give you that. Landing some good punches, too."

"I know," Budda said, "That's why I'm going to win."

"See, that's where you're wrong, son," Moorsblade said, "I know what it is you need to keep up with me and I can take that away at any time. I let you get in your punches just to make you feel a little better about yourself before I bring you all the way down."

"Yeah, right," Budda said, "I'm a rock. Rocks don't' have weaknesses. What could you possibly take away from me?"

Moorsblade's fingers dug into the rock of Budda's shoulders with a sudden show of his full strength.

"Leverage," Moorsblade said, smiling.

He lifted Budda off the ground and hovered in mid-air,


Justin awoke, coughing up water as Zoey slapped at his back. He looked in time to see his friend getting lifted from the ground by the large agent.


"I'm so sorry about your friend," Joey said to Jess, not taking her eyes from the action, "I've seen this happen before and it does not end well."

"Bye bye, Rocky," said Moorsblade, "Shame we couldn't scrap a little longer. Been a while since I found someone could take a beating as good as you."

"You think dropping me is going to hurt me?" Budda scoffed.

"No," Moorsblade said, "But this might."

There was a loud snap as Moorsblade pulled Budda's shoulders in opposite directions. A crack was forming in Budda's stone running from the area between his right shoulder and his neck diagonally down to his left hip.

Budda struggled against it, grabbing Moorsblade's arms and trying to force him to stop as the sadistic smile grew bigger on his assailant's face. He kicked and shouted as Moorsblade's hands slowly grew farther apart. Moorsblade went into a screaming laugh as he used every bit of his strength.

There was a sudden silence as Moorsblade returned to the ground with Budda's head, left arm, and half-torso in one hand and his right arm, lower torso, and legs in the other. He tossed them aside and dusted his hands off.

"Not like we needed another strong guy anyway," Moorsblade sneered.

Jess covered her mouth. Her stomach churned and she choked back some vomit.

"Yeah," Joey said, "That's how it typically goes. Usually, it makes more of a mess."

Zoey backed away as she felt the heat emanating from Justin's body. The ice dome she made vaporized around them.

The water covering him was evaporating into steam. The smoke on the top of his head was sputtering to life and, as he got to his feet, he screamed and was engulfed in a pillar of blue flame. His clothes smoldered at the edges. The metal chains holding his goggles to his face were heating red. The respirator was slowly melting away. He hovered on a cushion of heat a foot above the ground. His arms were white hot from his fist to his elbow. His hair was now a flowing mane of blue-white fire. He stared at Moorsblade, his eyes glowing behind the tinted welding goggle lenses.

Moorsblade laughed.

"Nice light show," Moorsblade said, "You gonna come get me now because I broke your pet rock?"

"That was my friend," said a deep angry voice as smoke belched from Justin's mouth.

"Yeah, I know," Moorsblade said, "That WAS your friend. Tell you what - if you're feeling sore about it, I'll let you take your best shot. I won't move, you can go right ahead and use all of that righteous anger

257

you're feeling right now. Here's the deal, though: if you don't kill me with that shot, I'm gonna go ahead and take mine."

Justin floated toward the bald man leaving a trail of glowing red on the ground behind him.

Moorsblade got down on his knees and put his hands behind his back, smiling.

Justin extended his right hand, holding it about an inch from his opponent's forehead.

"Justin," Zoey called out, "Don't!"

"You want my best shot," growled Justin, "Take it to Hell with you."

Jess ducked and covered as Justin started his one-liner. Her eyes were shut tight and her ears were plugged by her fingers as he delivered his coup-de-grace. She could still hear and see the massive explosion but, when it was over, she was still mostly functional. Her black-haired counterpart in the jumpsuit had not been so lucky and now lay flat on her back, staring blankly at the ceiling, likely unconscious.

Light was streaming in through parts in the ceiling which had collapsed. The rails for the gantry crane and some of the scaffolding had simply crumbled from the vibrations in parts. The building would likely fall apart within the next few minutes.

The smoke emptied through the holes in the roof. The space where Moorsblade had been was now a crater as wide as the building itself. In the center of a crater, Justin levitated over a smoking black figure with a red hot large left shoulder pad. Justin looked down and laughed. Smoke and flames slipped out of his mouth as he did.

"See, now," said Moorsblade, still smoking, standing up, "I didn't think that was very funny."

The large bald man wiped his blackened face. The two barbells in his left eyebrow were as red as his shoulder pad and his jumpsuit was mostly intact. A few of his accessories, obviously made of less heat resistant parts, had melted away. He was still completely intact. Jess saw the color fading from Justin's face as Moorsblade hovered slowly from the ground to look his opponent in the eye.

"Yeah, not laughing now, are you, fat boy?" said Moorsblade.

The room seemed paused with the anticipation of what came next.

"My turn," Moorsblade said, smiling.

Before anyone realized what had happened, within a split second, Moorsblade had launched himself into Justin's chest at some ungodly speed, leading with his shoulder pad. It looked like a streak of smoke and fire as they shot diagonally upward and slammed into one of the gantry's main supports. Justin exploded into a cloud of smoke as the impact took him.

Jess, without thinking, called out telepathically:

258

"Zoey! Grab his feet and give me a boost!"

Without even knowing if Zoey was conscious enough to hear her request, Jess leapt into the air running. A platform of ice shot up from below her before she could fall. It snaked its way toward the confused Moorsblade who bashed at ice encasing his legs.

He stopped bashing as Jess approached and he launched into a coughing fit. She could see the smoke-form of Justin shoulder-deep into Moorsblade's mouth, clouding his lungs. Justin disappeared as Moorsblade gasped and managed to inhale the rest of him.

Jess leapt from the platform to Moorsblade's back, putting her hands on his soot-covered forehead. He was too busy clutching at his chest and throat as he choked and sputtered to worry about her presence. She closed her eyes and concentrated.

With the rush of being pulled through a tunnel the scene around her faded. Images of memories flew by her as she entered his mind. She had only done this once before while removing the skyscraper incident from Josh's head. Phalanx had called that practice.

She didn't know what she was looking for and she didn't really even know what she was doing. She was trying to get anything she could in the limited window between the Project psychic becoming conscious again and Moorsblade passing out from a lack of oxygen.

She relaxed and the memories started to flow through her. She could feel them copying into her head. She was seeing things from his perspective. She started to feel intimidated by the immensity of it all and wanted to find somewhere calm. She closed her eyes then opened them a moment later. She was on a long, narrow, wooden pier on a large lake, surrounded by trees. She could hear the wind and smell the water. She knew this was deep, she felt like she shouldn't be here.

A pain struck her in the temples and she fell, her knees hitting into the wood of the pier before she was pulled to her feet and into the air. The tunnel was moving in reverse. She felt the warm, wet streams of blood running from her nose and the fingers on her temple like hot knives jabbing into her mind. The other psychic was behind her, trying to dig her out of Moorsblade's head.

Something inside her mind snapped. More like a dam breaking.

Everything around Jess was thrown back violently by an invisible force. She didn't see Joey and Moorsblade push away from her and hit the ground. She didn't see the ice platform beneath her shatter like glass. She didn't see the way what was left of the roof exploded outward. She didn't see the gantry area explode into metal shards.

While she floated there, after everything broke down around her and started to collapse, she saw that pier at the lake. A child sat at the end, staring out into the water. She heard the splashes as he kicked his legs back and forth. She smelled the wild hyacinth and felt the dirt of the path before the dock beneath her feet.

She wiped at a tickling sensation below her nose and saw the blood. She could taste the copper in the back of her mouth. The lake faded and she now saw the destruction around her. Justin was regaining his form, having exited the unconscious Moorsblade, and now went unconscious himself. Zoey, the last one left standing, looked up at her as her vision faded and she collapsed out of the air. She didn't stay conscious long enough to find out if she ever hit the ground.

## XXVI

"I almost want to believe it," Justin said, pacing back and forth.

"You should," Phalanx said, watching him from his seat, "It's the truth."

They were back in their cave, assembled around the couch in front of LENNY. None of them had changed from their battle attire. They weren't convinced that they were safe enough at the moment.

"Not like there's any way we can actually tell," Mike said, "Our psychic is down and even she couldn't help us right now."

"It's called trust," Phalanx said, "I know it's in short supply right now, but spare some for me."

"You had nothing to do with any of that?" Zoey asked, "Nothing at all?"

"No," Phalanx said, "No matter what 'recordings' you may have heard."

"And you guys saw them take Kurt," Justin asked.

"Yeah," said Josh, "Mike, Budda, and I were outside the buildings. We watched the old guy and the kid with the giant arm nab him, the real him, from behind a control panel. We thought it was the holograms until the old guy saw us, said something, and Mike got kicked in the head by the girl in the black helmet."

Mike rubbed at the ice pack covering the deep purple bruise on his jaw in the shape of a sideways boot heel. It was starting to swell pretty bad.

"She stared at me for a second before she gave me a similar thing," he continued, pointing to the vertical bruise running from his temple to the bottom of his jaw, "Really awesome roundhouse, didn't have a chance to defend. I saw Budda run off, presumably to find you guys."

"I tried the communicator, but they weren't working," said Budda, looking more like the bust of a statue than his normally giant self, "I ran to warn you guys and I saw that big dude getting ready to pound on Justin, so I jumped in. Lot of good that did."

"Honestly," Phalanx said, "You fared better than many in that position before, trust me."

"How are you even alive?" Justin asked.

"I'm a rock," Budda shrugged with one shoulder, his half-torso propped up on the side of the couch, "I thought I should have been dead. I figured I might still have blood and guts somewhere down in me. Guess I was wrong. I'm as surprised as any of you that I'm still here."

"Did it hurt?" Zoey asked.

"I didn't feel anything," Budda said, "I never do."

"So, Kurt was taken," Mike said, "Jess is in some kind of coma, and Budda was torn apart. Not quite the ideal result for a training exercise."

"And it wasn't you," Justin asked, looking down at the seated Phalanx.

"I had absolutely nothing to do with it," he answered, "I will swear to whatever deific power you want. Either someone else sold you out or they set the trap themselves."

Justin continued pacing and stroking his goatee. Everyone was silent and contemplative.

"May I just say," Phalanx chimed, "You're all taking this extremely well. I'm honestly amazed I'm not bound and gagged right now. I'm impressed at your level of trust."

"You're in a forcefield," Mike said, "Everything but your head. You have room enough to breathe and move but you're not going anywhere. And, yeah, we know you've got other duplicates around but you're the one who was at the training site with us, so you would know the most about the treachery."

"I retract my previous statement," Phalanx said, "Still, a very smart move and good of you not to tell me."

"You know how they work," Justin said, "Any thoughts as to why they didn't chase us down once we ran for it?"

"A few ideas," Phalanx said, "Mainly, they got what they came for."

"What about your 'infallible inside source'?" Zoey asked, "What did they have to say?"

Phalanx sighed.

"They went dark," he said.

"Convenient," Justin said.

"Look, this all only happened a few hours ago," he said, "There's no way I could get any info that fast even if they were active. At this point, I have no real way to confirm or deny anything. Last I knew, we were still low priority. I even know that they know I'm around now and they're not making any moves to stop me. Last I heard, they even knew what I was doing here and didn't see it as a problem because they knew I wouldn't let you do anything that would jeopardize my perceived invisibility.

"The fact that two of you took down their heavy hitter might change the game a bit, but it seems likely that he'll be in every bit the coma as Jess after she did... well, whatever she did to him. Combine that with your nearly lethal choke-out, Justin, and you're likely to impress Williams more than anger him. It'll either further decrease his desire to mess with us or it'll make him want to bring you under his banner more than ever. That goes for everyone here."

"When can you find out?" Mike asked.

"Once my source lights back up," Phalanx said, "Who knows when that'll be. But, the fact that they haven't given chase just yet makes it likely that we're safe."

"We've got to go after Kurt," Budda said, "He'd do it for us."

"You'll never take them on their home turf," Phalanx said, "You're lucky you guys split up in the training. You made them divide their forces. If you run in after Kurt, you'll be facing an army."

"You could get us around that army, right?" Budda pled, "You could get us around the patrols and the surveillance and all that, right?"

"The layout of the place," Phalanx started with a sigh, "If it even is the same place, gets changed on an annual basis. It's been years since I've been there. There's no telling what they've got waiting if we try to get in there and my source, though infallible, won't have immediate knowledge of any of it. At this point, I would recommend spending some time in convalescence. You're going to need Jess if you're going to make it through and we need to figure something out to keep Budda as a viable asset. For now, we're safe and we should do everything we can to keep it that way."

"Say it again," Justin said, "Make me believe it."

"For now," Phalanx said, clearly, "We're safe."

"I'll be damned if this doesn't scream sequel," Justin said.

\*\*\*

As he approached the end of the dirt path, he saw a woman in a white dress with a wide-brimmed sun hat, dangling her feet into the lake at the end of the long, narrow dock.

The smell of hyacinth and honeysuckle lit up the air. Everything about this place was familiar and comforting to him except for the woman in white. He approached slowly, feeling the old worn wood under his feet creak as he walked.

She stared into the distance, her gaze locked on the other side of the lake. It seemed farther away than he remembered. The ripples from her gently kicking legs made small waves light up with the reflection of the sun as they disappeared into the deep, dark water away from shore. Her auburn hair yielded easily to the breeze.

She turned slowly toward him. He recognized her immediately as their eyes locked. She had the same look of confusion as he. She looked him over as he looked at himself, realizing he was dressed in a simple white t-shirt with blue jeans. He caught her squinting as her eyes touched on the metal barbells imbedded in his left eyebrow.

"What are you doing here?" he asked.

"Waiting for you," she said, "Where is this place?"

"Lake Eufaula, Georgia," he said, taking a deep breath and closing his eyes, "My Dad used to bring me here in the summer. We'd camp in the field over there and we'd swim and fish right off this dock. Those are some of the best days I can remember."

He opened his eyes and stared into the open water. It was calm. Quiet. Just before sunset with a slight chill in the air. All of the day-trippers had gone home. Only the campers and the hardcore fishermen remained after dusk. He could smell a faint campfire in the air.

"Why were you waiting for me?" he asked, still entranced with the lake.

"You don't have an accent," she said, "Every time I've seen you, you have that deep Georgian drawl. What happened to it?"

"I..." he said, thinking on it for a minute, realizing now that his last few statements had been in non-regional diction, "I don't know. Don't change the subject, though. What are you doing here?"

She shrugged.

"These are your memories," she said, "You tell me."

"Wait," he said, "You were there at the mill. You grabbed my head during the fight. You were trying to mess with my mind!"

He pulled his fist back and took a swing to crown her on the top of her head and likely punch her right through the dock. She looked up at him, complacent, and closed her eyes.

His fist slammed into her at full speed but she didn't budge. Her sunhat remained perched perfectly and she took no visible damage. The dock didn't so much as buckle. He stepped back in confusion, grimacing and grabbing his hand.

"That hurt!" he shouted, "What the hell was that? Some kind of forcefield or something?"

"I didn't do anything," she said, with a shrug, "I just didn't want you to hurt me."

"Well," he said, "I'm going to."

He leapt into the air, thinking he would fly up and hit her with all of his might on the way down. His jump fell short and he tumbled to the dock next to her.

"Now I can't fly," he said, his face down, "What did you do to me?"

"This place is beautiful," she said, paying no attention to his strife, "You say you used to come here as a kid?"

He rolled onto his back, his head at the edge of the dock. He was cradling his punching fist.

"You made me hurt," he said, "I haven't felt pain in forever."

"I know," she said, "I can't even think of a time you felt pain before."

"You don't know anything about me," he said.

"I know everything about you," she countered, "I copied all of your memories."

"Then why bother asking me questions?" he asked.

"Courtesy," she shrugged, "Besides, I'd rather hear it from you than extract the perspective."

"Why are we here?" he asked.

"This was your strongest calming memory," she said, "It was the first thing I saw in your mind when I was trying to suppress your more...

264

homicidal... tendencies. The dock, the smell of the flowers, even the temperature of the water. You remember this place better than you remember anything from your military career or your childhood. Even the most traumatic moments."

He quickly struck out his hand and tried to push her into the water. It was met with equal force and she remained where she sat. She looked down at his head and sighed.

"Stop being so childish," she said, "I wasn't here to kill you or anything. I was here for information."

"You won't get anything you need out of me," he said, defiantly, "I've been trained to resist..."

"Maybe you're not understanding this, big boy," she said, "But, I've already got it. You're a smart guy – maybe a little sadistic, maybe a little more psychotic – but you're smart. Use that."

"If you got what you wanted," he said, "Why are you still here?"

"Not sure," she said, frowning, "Your girl Joey was trying to mess with my head while I was messing with yours while you were suffocating. I'm kinda new at this psychic stuff, but I'm pretty sure that was a bad situation. Something effed up royally and I don't know what it was but I've got a feeling not even your girlfriend can help us out of this mess."

"She's not my girlfriend," he said, "She's my colleague. One of my team."

"You really think you can hide anything from me at this point, Johnny?" she asked, smirking.

"This is a turn," he said, "Most of the time I'm on the other side of the knowing everything about someone bit. We usually get dossiers on everyone we're going to interact with."

"Then your girlfriend psychically pumps them into your brain because you don't like to waste time reading." Jess finished.

"Knock it off, ok?" he pled, "I'm trying very hard to play nice right now and you're making it increasingly difficult. Can we start over? Civil this time?"

"You gonna try to hit me again?" she asked.

He sat up and put his feet in the warm water sitting next to her.

"I think we might be here a while," he said, "I suppose it would be better if calmer heads prevailed. Start over?"

"Start over," she confirmed, extending her hand, "Jess."

"John Moorsblade," he said, taking her hand, "Nice to meet you?"

"I guess it is," she said, smiling, "Now to the real problem: are we in my head or yours?"

The sun disappeared below the horizon before either of them could think of an answer to that question.

41168848R00151

Made in the USA
Charleston, SC
21 April 2015